St Mungo's Robin

Also by Pat McIntosh

The Harper's Quine
The Nicholas Feast
The Merchant's Mark

ST MUNGO'S ROBIN

Pat McIntosh

Constable • London

Constable & Robinson Ltd
3 The Lanchesters
162 Fulham Palace Road
London W6 9ER
www.constablerobinson.com

First published in the UK by Constable,
an imprint of Constable & Robinson Ltd 2007

A copy of the British Library Cataloguing in Publication
Data is available from the British Library.

ISBN 13: 978-1-84529-240-9
ISBN 10: 1-84529-240-5

Printed and bound in the EU

For Martin –

SEMPER

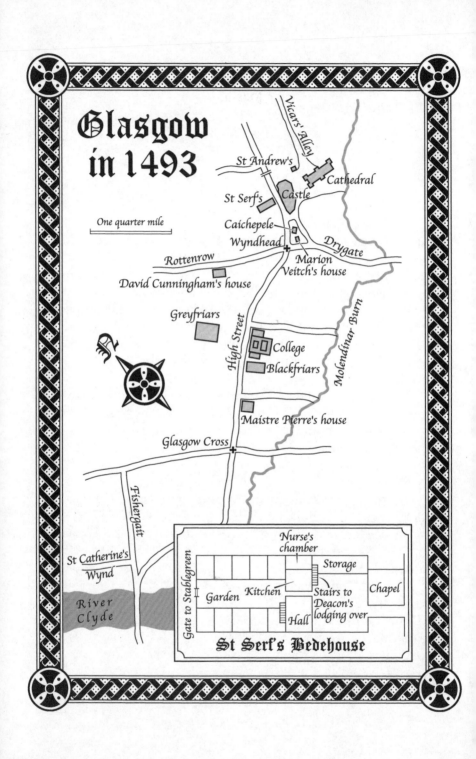

Glasgow in 1493

One quarter mile

Vicars' Alley

St Andrew's

Cathedral

St Serf's · Castle

Caichepele

Wyndhead

Drygate

Rottenrow

Marion
Veitch's house

David Cunningham's house

Greyfriars

High Street

College

Blackfriars

Molendinar Burn

Maistre Pierre's house

Glasgow Cross

Fishergait

St Catherine's
Wynd

River
Clyde

St Serf's Bedehouse

Nurse's
chamber

Storage

Gate to Stablegreen

Garden · Kitchen

Stairs to
Deacon's
lodging over

Chapel

Hall

Chapter One

Gil Cunningham worked out later that at the moment when the dead man was found in the almshouse garden, he himself was eating porridge, salted by a furious altercation with his youngest sister.

He had come down in the dark after Prime annoyed with himself for sleeping late, to find her in the hall of their uncle's house, bright in a fine scarlet gown, the neck and sleeves of her shift embroidered to match it. She had found a taper and was lighting all the stumps of last night's candles.

'Tib!' he exclaimed. 'I thought you were staying down the town with Kate.'

'Not another hour,' said Lady Isobel, setting the taper to the last wick on a pricket-stand, her vivid little face pettish in the blaze of light.

'How ever not?'

She shrugged. 'Kate spews if you so much as mention food, and you'd think nobody else ever went with child, the way Augie Morison behaves around her. And those brats of his, a body couldny stand to live with,' she added.

'The wee one was rude to you, was she?' said Gil shrewdly. She threw him a dark look and lit another candle. Gil lifted the snuffer and began to extinguish the guttering lights along the wall, saying, 'So you've come here instead. Does Maggie ken you're in the house?'

'I let her in at the kitchen door the now, Maister Gil.' Maggie Hamilton stepped into the hall from the turnpike

7

stair, a laden tray in her big red hands. 'And her kist is still in the yard in the rain where that Andy set it down. I wish he'd stayed till I saw him, I'd ha gied him a word for Lady Kate. Here's your porridge, the pair of ye, and just a wee bit butter to it, for it's to last. It's maybe only the two weeks to Advent, but the house'll be full of wedding guests by Monday night, and where you're to sleep, Lady Tib, I've no idea. And when did you last comb your hair, I'd like to ken?'

'Yestreen, most like,' said Tib in a vague tone which Gil decided was intended to be irritating.

'She could lie at the castle, with Dorothea,' he suggested.

'Dorothea? Is she coming? You've never invited her to your wedding!' said Tib scornfully. 'She'll cast a gloom over everything, with her long face and her veil.' She cast up her eyes and clasped her hands in brief mimicry, and the taper went dangerously near the tangled curls.

'You'll no speak that way about your eldest sister, Lady Tib,' ordered Maggie. 'Lady Dawtie was truly called before ever you were born, and none of this running wild like a wee Saracen the way you've been let. Comb your hair and eat your porridge, and then you can come down to my kitchen and gie me a hand, for I've baking and brewing to see to, and a new receipt for cannel-cakes that Jennet Clark gave me last night. I hope you've another gown in your kist,' she added, 'for you're not setting bread in that one. Is it no the one you're wearing to your brother's marriage? The idea, wearing it to go about Glasgow at this hour of the day!'

She set the tray down on a convenient stool, and turned and stumped out of the hall. Tib shrugged, blew out the taper, and slid a sideways glance at her brother.

'Eat your porridge,' he suggested. 'You'll be in a better mood.'

'So'll you,' she said pertly, but took the wooden dish and horn spoon from the tray. 'Where's the old man? And that dog of yours?'

'Socrates came down earlier,' said Gil, stirring the small

portion of butter into his porridge, 'likely Maggie let him out, and our uncle has a case to hear after Sext and –'

'Oh, he'll be over in St Mungo's tower by now,' agreed Tib, 'among all his dusty old papers. Does the dog sleep with you? Alys is going to love that. He'll want to make a threesome with you between the sheets. I hope she'll ken who's embracing her.'

Gil restrained himself with difficulty, and studied his sister. She was eight years his junior; he remembered her best from before he went away to school and university, when she had been a stout screaming toddler, furious with a world in which she was simply not old enough to do everything her siblings did. Fourth in line himself, he had sympathized with that, though not with the screaming. Now, at eighteen, she was a pretty young woman, but he thought again, looking at her, that she could almost be a changeling. In a family of tall, long-chinned, grey-eyed people, only Tib and the second brother Edward had inherited their paternal grandmother's small neat frame, heart-shaped face and hazel eyes. And Edward was dead at the battle of Stirling Field along with their father, their eldest brother, and James, third King of Scots of that name. In Tib's case her temper had also been part of the legacy, Gil reflected, eating porridge.

'When will Mother get here?' she asked now. 'And is Margaret coming? Kate never said, but I suppose if you've asked Dorothea you must want all your sisters at your marriage. We've not been all together,' she added thoughtfully, 'since Margaret was wed. Near six year.'

'They'll both be here the morn, by what Dorothea wrote to me.' Tib pulled a face, and Gil said mildly, 'What have you against Dorothea? What's she done to you?'

Before she could answer him, the door at the top of the kitchen stair was flung wide, to reveal only Socrates the young wolfhound. Spying his master, the dog sprang forward, singing with delight, so that the rebounding door missed his tail by some inches. Gil transferred his spoon to his bowl and held both high with one hand, the better to repel his pet's passionate greeting with the other. 'Good dog. Sit!' he said firmly. '*Sit!*' The dog sat down obligingly, still singing, his stringy tail thumping on the floorboards. 'I must teach you to shut doors,' he added.

Tib, watching, said as if she had not been interrupted, 'Just, you heard Maggie. Dorothea's a pattern of perfection, and I've to take her as my style-book. I was six when she left home, all I mind is her trying to teach me to say a rosary. Then she came back before she was clothed, and prayed over me, which was worse.'

'Tib, that was twelve years since,' said Gil. 'She was younger than you are now. So I suppose you'll not be a nun, then.'

'No, I will not!' she said explosively. 'Don't you start at that! Besides, what kind of a house would take me without a tocher of some sort?'

'What can you do, then?' he asked. 'Live with Mother until we can amass a tocher for you? It could take a while, Tib. Or will you go to Margaret or Kate? We need to settle you somewhere.'

'Spare me from either! Margaret can talk of nothing but the contents of her newest brat's tail-clouts, and Kate will be the same in another six months, no to mention Augie Morison's two wee jewels,' said Tib, with a brief simper in which he recognized, with some amusement, the older of his third sister's stepdaughters. 'Give your Alys her due, she doesny go on about that bairn her father's fostered.'

'Our Boyd cousins move with the court,' he suggested as Socrates, dignity recovered, paced over to push his nose under her hand. 'Maybe if Mother wrote to her kin, they might find a place for you.'

'Oh, aye,' she said, looking up from the dog, the acid in her voice again. 'I'll be waiting-woman to Marion Boyd, will I, and hope to catch the King's eye when he tires of her?'

'We need to do something with you,' Gil began again.

'I'm not in your tutelage, Gil!' she exclaimed. 'Nor I'll

not be sent about the countryside like a package because nobody will take a mind to me!'

'But you are,' he pointed out. 'I'm head of the family, Tib, like it or no, and I'll not have you wander about the countryside like a hen laying away, either. We'll need to find you a life you can tolerate –'

'Aye, like a package!' she said again. 'I'll no be subject to that, Gil Cunningham, and you canny make me! You've never found me a husband yet, and here I'm eighteen past and no tocher and no –' She blinked hard and turned away, rubbing at her eyes.

'Then what will you do?' She shrugged one shoulder, and addressed herself to her cooling porridge. Gil eyed her in exasperation. 'If you won't stay in Carluke with Mother, and I'd not blame you,' he admitted, 'we'll have to –'

'We!' she said furiously. 'Why *we*? Why must you always be meddling in my life? Just because you're settled down with a perfect French shrew of a housewife –'

'She's nothing of the sort!'

'I heard her yesterday, biting your head off for nothing,' said Tib triumphantly, 'and scolding at the servants when your back was turned. I wish you joy of her, Gil –'

'Alys is on edge about the marriage,' said Gil defensively, quelling the surge of anxiety her words set off, 'and she's organizing the feast herself. You try that and see what it does to your temper, madam!'

The incident she referred to had dismayed him badly. The clever, competent girl he admired and worshipped seemed to have vanished in the past weeks, to be replaced by a distracted snappish individual who drove the servants and herself unmercifully. The household, taking its tone from Alys's aged French duenna, kept its collective head down and smiled tolerantly behind her back. Gil himself had escaped the worst of her wrath, had in fact been able to soothe her, until the previous afternoon when a chance remark in support of one of the maidservants had brought the skies down on his head. He had backed off in dismay, and his sister Kate, also visiting the mason's house

11

in the High Street, had drawn Alys to her side, asking about music for the feast, but the disagreement had not been resolved.

'A perfect shrew,' Tib repeated now, 'so Kate and me and everyone else is to be boxed up and tidied away out of sight –'

'My marriage has nothing to do with it!' he began.

'Then why did we never hear a word of this till after it was arranged?'

'Why did I never hear a word of you not being content till now?'

'Nobody asked me!' she flashed. 'And you needny bother yourself, I'll see to my own future and no need for meddling from a lot of old women!'

She slammed her empty bowl down on the tray with such force that the wood split, and flounced off to the kitchen stairs. Gil finished his own porridge, rather grimly, set his bowl on the floor for the dog to lick and went up to put his boots on. Like their uncle the Official, Canon David Cunningham, senior judge of the diocese, he had documents of his own to see to over in the Consistory tower, but first he would go down to speak to Alys.

In his attic chamber, he kicked off the heel-less shoes he wore about the house and sat down on his narrow bed, aware of the strapping creaking under him. He lifted one boot from the kist at the bed-foot, but paused, staring at the small image before which he had said his prayers earlier. St Giles looked enigmatically back at him, his pet doe leaping at his side. Sweet St Giles, he thought, help me to mend this quarrel with Alys.

It had flared up very quickly. Alys had asked Kittock for a piece of paper with the menu for some part of the marriage feast on it, and scolded furiously when Kittock admitted it was mislaid. Gil had lost track of Alys's plans long since, but was dimly conscious that there were to be several instalments of the feast, over three or even four days, with different groups of friends and family invited.

12

He had said, half joking, 'Does it matter, sweetheart? Will anyone notice, if there's one meal the less?'

Kittock's expression had frozen, and Alys had turned on him, scarlet-faced, brown eyes sparking dangerously, and upbraided him in a torrent of wrathful French.

'Of course it matters! Your status and ours matter. I'm working all the hours there are so our marriage can be celebrated appropriately, at least you could be grateful, instead of trying to undermine me with my own household!'

'Alys!' he had said, astonished. 'Sweetheart, I am grateful, and I'm amazed at what you're doing, but I don't – I'm not trying to –'

'Then keep out of my business!' she said sharply. 'Let me manage things my own way.'

'It seems to me,' he began unwisely, and attempted to put his arms round her, 'as if you're doing too much. You'll be exhausted –'

'Just leave me alone,' she ordered, and stuck her elbows out so that one dug into his stomach. 'I've enough to do here without you getting in my way.'

Appalled, he had backed away, and found both Alys's duenna Catherine and his sister Kate trying to catch his eye with identical warning expressions. Kate had managed to change the subject to the music for the feast, and he had made his escape. Stout Kittock found him before he reached the house door.

'Never mind her, Maister Gil,' she had said comfortably. 'She's set herself far too much to oversee, but there's nothing even the maister can do to stop her when she gets like this, so never worry. She'll be fine once it's all over. Or once you're all over,' she added, nudging him and winking broadly. He had managed a smile, and got himself out of the house somehow.

Sweet St Giles, he thought again. Grant me wisdom to manage this girl. I love her, I admire her, I want only her happiness. Help us both to make a good marriage. Help us both to make it to the wedding.

The image seemed to stir, the painted face to flicker in a smile. At his side the candle flame leapt again in the draught from the window, where the grey light was growing. He bent to pull on the first boot, wondering why it was that when Tib shouted at him he shouted back, but when Alys snapped he was horrified.

Down the wet High Street, past lit windows and dripping eaves, he turned in at the tunnel-like pend which led to the courtyard of the mason's large stone house. Overhead, heavy feet tramped on the floorboards of the room above the entry, and a burst of raucous song and a smell of linseed oil told him that the painters were still at work. The courtyard itself was empty, though two paint-splashed ladders and a plank lay at the foot of the stair-tower in the near corner. Socrates bounded ahead across the shining flagstones to the main door, which opened as Gil climbed the fore-stair. The dog sprang in, tail waving.

'Gil,' said Alys. She acknowledged the dog's greeting, then drew his master in, helped him unwrap his wet plaid, and stepped into his embrace, slipping her arms round him under his furred gown. 'Gil, I am sorry,' she said into his collarbone. 'You are *a passynge good knyght and the best that euer I found* and I did wrong to shout at you.'

'I'm marrying a shrew,' he said teasingly, in the French they used when they were together. Then as she tensed in his grasp, 'I'm sorry too, that I angered you, sweetheart. What is it?' he asked, feeling her draw back slightly. She shook her head, not looking up at him. 'Alys, what is wrong?'

'I don't know.' She shook her head again, and freed one hand to rub at her eyes. 'But the painters say they need another week, and we still have to furnish our lodging, and the apothecary has no more rose petals or ginger, and we've run out of braid to trim my gown with, and everything's going wrong. Where has the dog gone?'

He held her away from him and looked at her, a slender

14

girl in a mended gown of blue woollen, her honey-coloured hair dragged back out of the way, her face pinched with distress so that the high thin bridge of her nose stood up like a razor.

'Likely down to the kitchen, to find Nancy and the bairn. Is he well?'

'John?' She blinked distractedly, and gave him a brief smile. 'Yes, he is well. He said my name this morning.'

'Good. Alys, rose petals and ginger you can manage without, a housekeeper like you,' he said firmly, 'and I can't advise you about the braid. Ask Kate, or use ribbons, or something. Whatever you wear, you'll be the loveliest woman in Glasgow. Come and sit down, sweetheart, and tell me about the painters.'

'You make it sound so trivial,' she said, following him into the hall. The household's breakfast was long over, and the great trestle table had been taken down and the board propped in its daytime place against the wall.

'It is trivial,' he said, pulling her down to sit beside him on the settle by the fire, 'compared with being married. My darling, how can feasts and dresses matter when we are to share the rest of our lives together?'

'But I want everything to be perfect!' she almost wailed, and rubbed at her eyes again.

'Alys, it will be perfect, because we'll exchange promises. And then,' he said ruefully, 'my sister Margaret's husband will drink too much at the feast, my godfather will tell jokes we'd rather not hear, the other burgesses will try to find out what was in the contract –' Her mouth twitched, and she slid a sideways, teary look at him. 'I've been to other weddings,' he said. 'All those things will happen, and you can't control them, so why worry about the rest?'

'And what will you wear? Are your new clothes ready? You told me you ordered them, but you've never said they've come home. And Maister Kennedy's?'

'The gowns will come home in good time,' he assured her. 'Blue brocade for me, red velvet for Nick, and I've a

15

new suit of clothes to go with it.' He took her hands in his free one. 'Tell me about the painters.'

Her face crumpled with anxiety. 'Maister Sproat says they need another week to finish the inner chamber, let alone the closet. The paint dries so slowly in this weather, even with the brazier up there. What if we have to set the bed up in the outer room, in case people get paint on their clothes when they – when we –'

'When they take us to bed?' he said, aware of the ache in his loins at the very words. 'I'd hoped we could avoid that,' he confessed. 'I've never liked the custom. All the jokes and the shouting and banging pots and throwing of sweetmeats and favours. It would shrivel anyone's pride.'

'You joined in when Kate was wed,' she said uncertainly.

'I did not,' he contradicted her, thinking of his sister, who went on two crutches because of a withered leg, and the shy merchant friend who was her new husband. 'I contrived to be in the way, so Augie could slip in the door alone and bar it from the inside. Those two of all people wouldn't want to be publicly put to bed. And nor do we.'

'I thought you would wish it,' she said. 'It's the custom, after all. You mean we might not have to?'

'If we're clever about it.' He bent his head to kiss her. She tilted her face so that their lips met, but drew back, shivering slightly, when he would have deepened the embrace. She seemed to react like this every time he kissed her now. Concealing his anxiety, he dropped a peck on the high thin bridge of her nose, and said, 'Sweetheart, shall we both go and talk to the painters?'

Up in the inner chamber of their apartment, under one of the eastward windows which looked on to the court-yard, they peered at the board of yellowish samples the laddie had prepared, while the laddie himself ground pigment on a slab of stone by the next window.

'Ye see,' said Maister Sproat, 'it doesny come out gold-coloured whatever I do. I think it's the ground we've used for the first coat, which is no a good white, owing to it no being Paris white, on account of Daidie could find none in Glasgow the now. And the linseed ile in the top coat wad take it more to a yellowy cast and all,' he added.

'It looks like earwax,' said Gil frankly. The laddie looked up grinning from his grinding-stone and Daidie, a spare fellow in a much-spattered canvas smock, snorted, but Maister Sproat nodded solemn assent.

'A good thought, maister,' he agreed, 'but no one that would appeal to my custom. No, no, "earwax-coloured" wouldny sell. What's more,' he added, 'the longer we spend trying to match yir gold colour, the later it is drying and the less time we'll have for the figures ye wanted by the hearth there. Saints, was it, or was it to be the Muses or the Virtues? I've a note o't somewhere.'

'The Virtues,' said Gil, 'since I'm getting a virtuous wife. *The best and fairest may That ever I saw.*' He looked down at Alys, and her elusive smile flickered in response. 'And maybe a saint on the other wall.'

'Aah,' said Daidie, ''at's bonnie, in't it no, maister?'

'It is an all,' agreed his master, 'and I mind now, we'd agreed the Cardinal Virtues. That's Prudence, Justice, Fortitude and Temperance,' he recited, and looked sternly at the laddie. 'Mind that, young Jos. But you'll no get your Virtues afore the wedding unless we can decide on a tint for these walls. If yir carpenters had shifted theirsels a bit putting in the panelling, we'd ha been in here sooner, and all would ha been done by now.'

'Does it have to be laid on in linseed?' Gil asked, ignoring this. 'Would some other sort of paint dry faster? And what would lay well on top of this ground colour? You're the colourman, Maister Sproat. Advise us.'

'Uncle Eck,' said the laddie softly. 'Maister,' he corrected himself as the older man looked round. 'There was that chamber we done for the Provost. You mind, we put milk-paint, two grounds and cover in that broken white, and then we glazed it red-coloured. It dried in no time, and it came out right well, you said it yersel.'

17

'It sounds well,' said Gil, turning to Alys again. 'Red? Or another colour?'

'Blue,' she said decidedly. 'Like the blue in the other chamber, but in milk-paint.'

'Aye, we can do that,' said Maister Sproat, with an approving nod at his nephew. 'Be done in two days, even working by lamplight, if we can get enough sour milk. And if I put a bit ox-gall to the last coat it'll wash down a treat every spring for years. And the same blue within in your closet, maister?'

'We've all the sour-milk curds you'd want, laid in brine at the yard, you ken that, maister,' said Daidie, and peered past Gil. 'Is that someone at your door?'

They all looked out across the courtyard to where a lanky figure bundled in a plaid was conferring on the doorstep with one of the maidservants. As they watched, she pointed, and the visitor nodded, came down the fore-stair and headed for the tower in the corner.

'It's Lowrie Livingstone from the college,' said Gil in some surprise, recognizing the young man. 'What's he doing here? In here, Lowrie,' he called, drawing Alys into the outer room as the messenger's feet sounded on the stair.

'Maister Cunningham,' said Lowrie. He stepped across the threshold on to the dustsheets, dragging his wet felt cap from his fair hair. 'And Mistress Mason. Good day to you both, and I'm sorry to break in on you this early. I've a word for you, maister, from Maister Kennedy.'

'From Nick Kennedy? Is there some trouble?'

'Aye, but it's no at the college,' said Lowrie. 'It's at the almshouse. St Serf's, up by the castle. Maister Kennedy sent me to fetch you,' he said, grimacing. 'They've found a dead man in the almshouse garden.'

The painters crowded into the doorway to listen, with exclamations.

'A dead man?' repeated Gil. 'Who is it? One of the bedesmen?'

'No the bedesmen, they're all present. We think it's the

18

Deacon,' Lowrie said cautiously. 'It wasny full day when I left to find you, and so far as we could tell in the dark he's been stabbed. So Auld – so Maister Kennedy said, since we're within the Chanonry and you're the Archbishop's questioner, we'd do better to fetch you first than last, so here I am.'

'What, the Deacon of St Serf's? Robert Naismith?' said Gil. 'And he's been stabbed?'

'Naismith? Is that him,' said Daidie with relish, 'that keeps Marion Veitch as his mistress? The bairn's three year old, and another on the way, poor soul. My cousin Bel works in her kitchen,' he explained, finding everyone looking at him.

'Can you come, maister?' said Lowrie. He indicated his muddy feet. 'It's raining hard. The old men were all for moving him at once, and I don't know how long Maister Kennedy can hold them off, though Mistress Mudie was offering them spiced ale for the shock to get them indoors.'

'You must go, Gil,' said Alys. 'But – will you come back later? There's still something.' She hesitated, seemed about to go on, then said only, 'You had better go.'

He nodded with reluctance. 'I suppose I must. As Lowrie says, it's within the Chanonry and I'm Blacader's man.' He gathered up the plaid which hung over his arm. 'I'll take the dog with me, and come down again as soon as I can.'

'Who was there?' said Lowrie, hunching his shoulders against the rain. 'Well. You ken Maister Kennedy's got the St Serf's chaplaincy? Seems it usually goes to someone from the college, and in the changes after Father Bernard was transferred, he was next in line. Worth quite a bit, I hear, so he takes the duties seriously. And as often as not he brings Miggle – er, Michael, and me to serve for him –'

'Michael Douglas? Your chamber-fellow?'

19

'The same. We'd come up as usual after Prime to say Mass for the old men, at least Miggle was here already, so they were all there too, and Mistress Mudie, and Maister Millar –'

'That's the sub-Deacon, isn't it? I don't think I've met him.'

'Aye. He's studying Theology.' Lowrie, nearly as tall as Gil, kept up with his long strides without effort, the skirts of his narrow blue gown flapping round his calves. 'Sometimes there's other folk to hear the Mass, but that's just in the chapel, they don't come within the almshouse itself.'

Gil whistled to Socrates and bore left-handed at the crossing called the Wyndhead, heading up the hill towards the Stablegreen Port.

'And what happened? When was he found?'

'After the Mass.' Lowrie looked away to their right through the drizzle, beyond the castle walls to where the towers of St Mungo's cathedral loomed grey against the sky. 'Is that Miggle coming there? We were still laving the vessels and putting them past, see, when one of the old men came tottering back into the chapel to say they'd found a dead man, could we come and see to it. We were just in time to stop them lifting everything into the hall where the light was. Then Maister Kennedy found the blood on him and sent Miggle over to St Mungo's, and I went to Rottenrow and they said you were likely down the town.' He paused at a narrow arched gateway, pushing open the heavy wooden yett. 'Here we are.'

Gil looked about him. He had never paid much attention to St Serf's almshouse, nor had it obtruded on his professional life, unlike the larger house of St Nicholas or the two pilgrim hostels. Its aged inmates were law-abiding and eschewed litigation, so it had not come to his uncle's attention as senior judge of the diocese, and its property and financial matters were handled by one of the other men of law about the Consistory Court.

The almshouse occupied one of the long narrow tofts which ran between Castle Street and the open land of the

Stablegreen. Beside the gate the east end of the chapel faced the street; there was no other break in the frontage, apart from the chapel's east windows which were now catching the grey light. By the same light, he made out lettering on the archway: YHE HOVS OF LEIRIT PVIRTITH. Yes, of course, he thought, appreciating the conceit. The House of Learned Poverty would be dedicated to St Mungo's teacher.

Beyond the archway, Socrates was already exploring a constringent passageway which ran between the boundary wall and the south face of the chapel, and seemed to open out into a wider space.

'Do they lock the yett?' he asked. 'Can anyone walk in?'

'Only in the daytime, and only so far as the chapel and the Deacon's house,' said Lowrie, answering the second question. 'There's a door each end of the passageway between the two yards, you'll see it in a moment, and there's the iron gate in the back wall of the garden. I think they lock them all at night.'

Gil followed his dog along the flagstones past the eaves-drips, Lowrie behind him, their boots ringing loud in the narrow way. At the far end, they came out at one corner of the outer courtyard and Gil stopped again to look round.

The small space was bounded on their left by the wall. Immediately on their right the door of the chapel stood open, shedding light on to the wet paving-stones. In front of them, opposite the chapel, was a substantial two-storey range, in whose stone-built lower portion were more lights, and argumentative voices. On the fourth side of the yard, next to a row of storehouses, a wooden fore-stair led to the timber-framed upper floor whose row of unlit dormer windows in the thatch gave it a top-heavy, important appearance.

'The Deacon's lodging?' Gil hazarded, nodding towards the stair.

'The same,' agreed Lowrie. 'This way. They're all in the hall.'

21

He strode confidently into the passage which led through the main range and in at the doorway of a long, low-ceilinged, sparsely furnished hall. At the far end a number of elderly men in black cloaks sat arguing round a table by a branch of candles.

'It's not right,' one of them was saying tremulously as Gil entered. 'He should be laid out like a Christian soul, no left lying under a tree wi his breast all bloody. Sissie could be doing that while we're waiting. And has he had any sort of absolution? We should be seeing to that and all.'

'What did he say?' demanded another voice.

'Far's Frankie gaed?' said a third, inexplicably.

'The man is here,' said another, in Latin. 'It's a great hoodie-crow,' it continued, in Scots, 'come to peck out our living een, for the robin willny rise up.'

'What did he say?'

One of the black-cloaked figures rose and advanced towards them, but was forestalled. A familiar voice said, 'Aye, Gil,' and Maister Nicholas Kennedy of the University of Glasgow emerged from the shadows behind the door, another man with him. 'We need a lymer here, no a sight-hound,' he added, catching sight of Socrates at Gil's heel.

'Aye, Nick,' Gil answered. 'What have you found, then?'

'Oh, it wasny me that found him,' said Maister Kennedy.

'It was Maister Duncan,' said the other man. He was taller than Maister Kennedy, with a lean face, a prominent Adam's apple, and a shock of light wiry hair which stuck out from under his floppy hat. He waved a bony hand to indicate the arguing, black-cloaked group, all seated again. 'One of our – one of our brothers. I'm Andro Millar,' he added, 'I'm the sub-Deacon here, I suppose I'm in charge if – if – if Maister Naismith's not able,' he finished with a slightly hysterical laugh. 'It's good of you to come so prompt, Maister Cunningham.'

'It's what Robert Blacader pays him for,' said Maister Kennedy, 'so he'd as well get on with it. He's out yonder by the gate, Gil. You took your time getting here, but at least it means there's near enough light to see by now.'

'So what's happened?' Gil asked.

'We – we – we found him, just after the Mass,' explained Millar. 'Out in the garden, by the back yett, I can't think how.'

Gil met Maister Kennedy's eye in the grey light from the near window.

'As near as I can make out,' supplied his friend gloomily, 'they all went out to their wee houses for ten minutes' contemplation afore their porridge was ready, and Maister Duncan saw something under the tree by the back gate and went to see what. And when he saw what, he raised the cry, and fetched Andro here, and then they came to fetch us.'

'And you were still laving the vessels by then?' Gil asked, raising one eyebrow. 'How long does it take you?'

'Aye, well, we've to wait till they're well out of sight afore we start,' said Nick, apparently feeling that this was adequate explanation. 'So when I found the blood, I sent the boys for you and Maister Mason –'

'That will save time, if Pierre is on his way already.'

'– and made them put a piece of sacking over the body.'

'Good.' Gil glanced at the gesticulating group round the table. 'I'll need to speak to Maister Duncan at the least, but we'll look at the body first, as soon as Pierre gets here. Are you sure of who it is?'

'Oh, yes, indeed,' said Millar, wringing his hands. 'It's Deacon Naismith, right enough. I ca – canny think what's come to him. He was well when I saw him last, and fine when he spoke to us all in the afternoon.'

Socrates rose, ears pricked, as feet sounded in the passageway. Gil looked over his shoulder.

'Ah, Pierre. Good day to you. And to you, Michael.'

'I have a *chantier* to run,' complained the master mason. He ducked under the lintel, a bulky shape wrapped in boiled wool, another shadowy figure at his back in a student's gown like Lowrie's. 'You forgive the delay, I hope, I had to give the men their instructions. I can expect no work from them next week after we celebrate your marriage, we should get on with cutting those pillars while we may, but – Yes, good dog, Socrates. So why are we summoned, Gilbert?' he demanded, switching to French. 'Who is dead in this House of Learned Poverty?'

The further courtyard was laid out as a little garden, with gravel walks through grass, tiny flowerbeds standing empty at this season, and several evergreens, overlooked by a row of small houses to either hand. Following Millar's stream of incoherent exclamations down the central path, Gil counted five chimneys each side in the grey daylight. Ten houses, he thought. There weren't as many as ten old men in the hall.

'I've seen Alys this morning,' he said quietly. Alys's father grimaced.

'She was wound up like a crossbow when we broke our fast,' he said. 'Did she say that a cart came in from Carluke with a bed on it.'

'A *bed*?'

'In pieces, with the hangings. And a word from your mother, saying she spent her wedding night in the same bed. It arrived yesterday, after you left the house,' Maistre Pierre said, with a sideways glance at Gil.

'Ah,' he said. That might explain things, he thought, if my mother is getting involved.

The garden ended in a high wall of rough-cut rubble, capped by a row of angular stones, a gate in its midst which must lead out on to the Stablegreen, with another green tree to either side of it. Millar stopped beside one of these and removed his hat, and beside him Maister Kennedy bent to draw back a length of sacking.

'There you are,' he said unnecessarily.

Chapter Two

'A terrible thing,' contributed Millar, his Adam's apple bobbing in his scrawny neck. He had flung on a great black cloak like those worn by the bedesmen, with a badge over the heart which Gil could not make out within the heavy folds. Replacing his hat he drew the mantle closer about him, and added, 'I canny think how it can have happened. He's no enemies, surely, nobody that would do this to him a purpose.'

Gil made no comment, but hunkered down by the sprawling figure beneath the tree. Socrates came to his side to sniff at the wet clothing, and Maistre Pierre crossed himself, his lips moving.

They were looking at the body of a short, rather plump man, lying partly on his left side facing the foot of the wall, right arm flung backwards almost into the lowest branches of the yew. The eyes were closed, but the mouth was wide open, giving the appearance of someone in the grip of a dream. A dream from which you'll not wake, Gil thought, looking the length of the corpse. It was wearing hose and long-sleeved jerkin of good tawny woollen with linen showing at the neck and wrists, darkened and reddened by a wide stain on the breast which Socrates was now inspecting closely, the coarse hair on his spine standing up. A long open gown of a darker brown was rucked up to waist level under the corpse's torso, its fur lining spiky with the rain. A belt of stamped leather, with brass buckle and fittings, supported a well-filled purse, a dagger and matching whinger, and a large bunch of keys. The smell of blood and stale urine mingled with the resiny scent of the yew-trees.

'What's he doing out here?' Gil wondered, pushing the dog's muzzle away from the sodden codpiece.

'Waiting for the Judgement,' said Maister Kennedy obtusely.

'Has he been moved at all since you found him?' asked Maistre Pierre. Gil looked up at him.

'I wondered that,' he agreed.

'No, no, Gil,' said Maister Kennedy. 'This is where he was lying. I think Duncan tried to lift him, but he's well set, and that was when they realized he was dead.'

'He is indeed,' agreed Maistre Pierre. He bent over the sprawled figure and tested the rigidity of the outflung right arm. 'Set, but not yet begun to soften. Dead sometime last night, I suppose. Well, it is Robert Naismith, Deacon of this place, on that we are agreed. And how has he died?'

'Last night?' said Lowrie. 'Not this morning?'

'Oh, certainly.' The mason was feeling carefully at the chubby face, and round the neck and the back of the head. 'He is like a stock. Gil, are his feet also hardened?'

'They are,' Gil agreed, attempting to flex one well-shod foot.

'Late afternoon or evening of yesterday, then.' Maistre Pierre turned his attention to the darkened breast of the jerkin. 'And this looks like what gave him his quittance. A knife wound, likely. There is a slit,' he poked cautiously, 'no, more than one, in the jerkin.'

'It's certainly blood,' said Maister Kennedy.

'We learn more when he is stripped.' One big hand explored under the corpse's flexed calves, then turned back a fold of the rumpled gown. 'No more than damp beneath him. *Oui, certainement*, it was dry last night, though it was raw cold. That fits.'

Gil stood up and looked about him. The grass was wet and trampled for some distance round the body.

'There was quite a crowd when he was found, then,' he said.

'Oh, aye,' agreed Nick Kennedy sourly. 'The whole house of them was here, and Sissie Mudie as well, all standing round arguing what to do next. And us and all,' he added.

Gil nodded, still looking at the garden. 'Pierre, how much can we learn if we examine him before he softens, do you think?'

'Likely we can see the wound,' the mason said, straightening his back carefully. 'There will be no stripping him before tomorrow, I should say, unless we cut the clothes from him, but we can look at his hands and such matters.'

'His – his hands?' echoed Millar. 'Why do you want to see his hands? They're clean enough. What can you learn from that?'

'Then I think we'd best get him in out of the rain. Maister Millar, is there a cart or something of the sort stowed away, that we could move him on, or should we try to lift him by his gown between us?'

'I – I –' began Millar.

'Sissie might have such a thing,' prompted Maister Kennedy.

'I'll go ask her,' volunteered Lowrie, and hurried off through the drizzle without waiting for a reply.

'You could get a closer look at him under cover, Pierre,' Gil prompted, 'and I'll cast about this place where he's lying before it gets any wetter. And then we'd best start asking questions.'

Maistre Pierre nodded morosely, and pushed the hood of his heavy cloak back a little so he could see the sky.

'Wetter it assuredly will be,' he said. Gil looked from his friend to the body.

'Where's his hat?' he said suddenly. 'He's bareheaded.'

'I was wondering that,' said Maister Kennedy. 'And how about a cloak and all?'

'He aye wears – wore a cloak,' said Millar. 'His bede-house cloak. Like – like mine, only with the Deacon's braid on. And a velvet hat wi a brim.'

'We need to find those,' said Gil. 'We'll need to make a search. Michael, could you – Michael? Where is he?'

'He came out behind me,' said Maistre Pierre. 'Has he slipped away?'

'I'll find him later,' said Gil. 'Maister Millar, I believe you should be present while the body is examined.' Millar grimaced, and clutched his cloak tighter round him, but nodded agreement. 'Nick, when must you and these fellows be back at the college? Have you time to spare?'

'I need to get down the road,' said Maister Kennedy. 'The joys of Peter of Spain are waiting for the bachelors at nine o'clock, though I dare say they'd not be sorry either if I missed their lecture. But Lowrie and Michael could stay and gie you a hand, Gil, if they're any use, for I ken they've no lectures till eleven this day.'

There was a rumbling and clattering in the passageway through the main range. Socrates growled warily, his hackles rising. 'Quiet,' Gil said to him, as a woman's voice joined the sounds. Lowrie appeared, pushing a small handcart and hindered by a stout woman bundled in a blue checked plaid over her black gown and white linen headdress, who trotted beside him exclaiming in annoyance all the way down the path.

'It's no right, he should be washed and made decent, what need have you to meddle wi the corp anyhow? Maister Millar, can you no put a stop to this? It's no right at all, my old men are fair owerset wi it, the souls, keeping him lying out here in the rain like this, and standing about staring at him –'

Millar turned to look at her, opening and closing his mouth like a carp in a pond, but failed to produce any sound. Maister Kennedy gave him a moment, then broke in:

'Deacon Naismith's been stabbed, Sissie, no dropped down with a seizure. We need to find who killed him.

28

Here's Maister Cunningham, that's Robert Blacader's man and responsible for finding out what we can. He needs a sight of the place where it happened, afore we can do anything at all wi the corp. And I'd say your old men wereny greatly harmed by the excitement,' he added, glancing at the windows of the hall, where a row of elderly faces peered avidly out at them.

'This is not where it happened,' said Maistre Pierre authoritatively. Gil nodded, but everyone else stared at him. Mistress Mudie recovered first.

'Well, if that's so, we can take him in-by, out this rain, and make him decent,' she proposed. 'At least somebody wi a sense o what's right has closed his een, but what prayers he's had I canny tell, what wi you heathens poking and prodding at him, no better than Saracens –'

With some difficulty, the body was hoisted on to the cart and wheeled away by Maistre Pierre and Andrew Millar, with Mistress Mudie hurrying behind them like a sheep-dog, talking unceasingly about the washhouse, the laying-out board and the bedehouse mort-cloth. Maister Kennedy watched them go, then glanced automatically at the unhelpful grey sky and said to Gil, 'I'd best lift my gear from the chapel and be away down the road. Come by the college and find me when you get a chance, and I'll tell you what I can.'

'I'll do that,' Gil agreed.

'Make it an hour when I'm no teaching,' Maister Kennedy added, 'and we'll try a jug of the new Malvoisie.'

'I'll bear it in mind,' Gil said, grinning. His friend nodded, and strode off, leaving Lowrie Livingstone standing by the gate to the Stablegreen.

'What are we looking for, maister?' he asked.

'Anything out of place,' Gil answered, noting the pronoun with interest. He hunkered down again and confirmed for himself Maistre Pierre's finding that the grass was no more than damp where the corpse had lain, then leaned forward to sniff at the flattened blades. Lowrie had stepped back along the wall, away from the gate, and was looking along its length, fair head on one side.

'You said,' he continued, elaborately casual, 'that is, Maister Mason said, he died yesternight. Or after sunset, anyhow. Is that sure?'

'He was well set.'

'Mm.' Lowrie walked cautiously round the yew-tree and looked at the scene from the other end. 'He couldny have set quicker for some reason? Does that happen?'

Gil sat back on his heels and looked at the younger man.

'Possible,' he admitted, 'but unlikely. How much quicker?'

'And you thought he might not have died here.'

'That's for certain,' Gil said. 'Even with all the trampling there's been, the traces are clear enough, or the lack of them. There's never a drop of blood on the grass, nor any trace of where he voided himself as he died, though his hose stank of it and his gown was up round his waist. And I can see no sign of either hat or cloak.'

'I see.' Lowrie looked about him. 'You think he was carried here? When?'

'That's what I have to work out.'

'None of these footprints is deep enough for someone carrying something.'

'That's what worries me.' Gil got to his feet and stepped across the Deacon's resting-place. 'He can hardly have flown here, before or after death, unless he was some kind of saint.'

'No,' said Lowrie, in positive tones. 'That he wasny.' He was surveying the gate now, peering closely at its inter-laced iron straps. 'This was locked. It still is.' Gil grunted. 'And that was sometime yesternight he was put here, you think?'

'All we can say the now,' said Gil, 'is that it was between whatever time he was killed and the time he was found.'

'But do we ken when he was killed?'

30

'Not yet.'

'How will you find who killed him, then?'

'By asking questions.' Gil stood up. 'Let's go in out of the rain. I wonder what Pierre has discovered from the corp?'

Socrates was sniffing intently at the door of one of the little houses, but when Gil whistled he came to join him with an amiable grin. Lowrie offered his hand for inspection, then followed Gil into the main range, slipping past him to open the heavy wooden door to the outer yard. As it swung open, the sound of raised voices met their ears.

'I canny believe it! Let me see my brother, he must –'

'– no the now, it's no suitable, they'll go to offer prayers for him in a –'

Andrew Millar was standing by the chapel door, in lively discussion with Mistress Mudie and a stocky man in legal dress whom Gil had often seen about the Consistory tower. Noticing him emerge from the main range, Millar said in relief, 'Here's Gil Cunningham, that's the man that's dealing wi it. Maister Cunningham, here's Humphrey's brother, Maister Thomas Agnew, wanting to know what's going on.'

'– and I canny have him talking to Humphrey the now, I'll not answer for it if his brother gets him worked up again, the soul –'

'I know you,' said Agnew. 'David Cunningham's nephew, aren't you no? Is it you that's to be married soon? What's been happening here?'

'The Deacon's dead,' said Gil baldly. 'Taken up dead in the garden this morning. It seems as if he's been stabbed.'

'Stabbed?' repeated Agnew in amazement. 'That's what Millar said and all, but I thought surely – who would do a thing like that? I hope no my brother,' he said anxiously.

'– and what kind of a brother would make a suggestion like that about a poor soul like Humphrey, I'd like to know –'

31

'Humphrey's been as vexed as any of them,' Millar reassured him. 'I canny think it was him, Maister Agnew. And it's no a good moment to speak to him, for they're about to go to Terce and Sext and then they'll say extra prayers for the Deacon, as Sissie says, and keeping the Office hours aye calms him.'

'Oh, aye, I suppose,' said Agnew reluctantly. 'And when did it happen? Naismith was wi me yestreen, but he left me after an hour. That's the last I spoke to him.'

'It must have been this morn,' said Millar before Gil could speak, 'or maybe in the night, for he was in his own lodgings when I came home about ten o'clock, and I canny think how it could have happened. Because,' he added to Gil, 'it's just come to me, the door here.' He waved at the door Gil had just stepped through. 'I locked it when I came in and went to my own bed, and it was locked just as usual this morn when we came through to say Matins. Deacon Naismith had a key on his ring, but –'

'Locked?' said Agnew. 'You mean this door's aye locked at night?'

'– in course it is, and the gate locked at the other end of the garden, some of these poor souls would be away down paddling in the Girth Burn if they wereny watched at night, your own brother's one of them, he'd a bad turn yestreen just after I'd got Anselm settled, he must have sung me out half the Apocalypse before I got the sleeping-draught down him –'

'That's a relief to hear, Mistress Mudie,' said Agnew warmly. 'D'you ken, I don't think Maister Naismith ever told me that. It's a great comfort to me, mistress, that you've such a close eye to my brother.'

Mistress Mudie smiled at that, and the light, catching one plump cheek, showed a dimple that came and went. She crossed her arms below her comfortable bosom, the movement shedding a waft of a strong herbal smell Gil could not place, and rattled on.

'– no more than my duty when all's said and done, but

32

I've a liking to your brother, maister, he's a poor creature just like the others –'

'So what's ado, Maister Cunningham?'Agnew asked. 'Millar tells me you're looking into this for Robert Blacader.'

Gil admitted this.

'I've not had time to learn much so far,' he added. 'The man was found stabbed this morn, and we know he was home last night –'

'Aye,' agreed Millar, nodding earnestly.

'– and that's about it. Might I come by and talk to you later?' he asked.

'To me?' Agnew's brows rose under his legal bonnet.

'You may have been the last to speak to him,' Gil pointed out. 'I hope you might be able to tell me something useful.'

'I don't see that,' said Agnew dubiously. 'If you ken he was here after he saw me –'

'– no doubt of that, his boots going up and down over my head, never troubled to put his house shoon on his feet, and when that man'll be done in the washhouse I canny tell, I haveny all day to wait to lay him out, and I've still to put his chamber straight, what wi seeing to that stramash and finding the barrow, and answering Frankie's kin that's home from sea, that was here looking for the Deacon as well, though I canny see how he didny tell the lad himself, the dinner will be late if I canny get on –'

'None the less,' persisted Gil, 'I'd be glad of a word. Will you be in your own chamber in the Consistory later today?'

The washhouse was one of the outhouses leaning against the north wall of the yard. Led to it by Mistress Mudie in full tongue, they found the Deacon laid on a board balanced across two of the great washtubs, his outstretched right arm pointing accusingly at the rafters. Maistre Pierre, a lantern in his hand, was carefully examining so much of the corpse as he could in its present rigid state, but looked up as they entered.

'Ah, Gilbert, there you are,' he said, and nodded to Lowrie. 'We have got the gown off him at least, which gives us a better look at the rest.'

'– never have tolerated such a thing for any of the bedesmen, why any Christian soul should have to put up with it for himself I canny tell –' said Mistress Mudie behind Gil.

'What have you found?' Gil asked.

'He had been drinking,' said Maistre Pierre. 'Not to excess, I am not suggesting he was drunk, but he had taken a refreshment. Also his supper, which one may clearly see was kale with lentils and meat of some sort.'

'Sweet St Giles,' said Gil. 'Can you tell me the vintage of the wine?'

'No,' said Maistre Pierre regretfully, 'though I think it was fortified. The smell is still in his mouth, very faint. Try for yourself.'

Gil bent, quelling his distaste, and sniffed at the open mouth. The cold lips and ginger-bristled jaw were still wet with rain and smelled of the man's stale breath, and a faint scent of the yew-tree under which the corpse had lain clung to the flesh, but there was also an intimation of alcohol, the treacly savour of a fortified wine. Malvoisie, perhaps, he thought, or sack or that stuff from Xerez. A lentil, fragments of dark green matter and a wisp of meat clung unpleasantly to the back teeth in the lantern-light.

'Yes,' said Gil. 'And his death?'

'Stabbed,' said Maistre Pierre, 'as I surmised. See.' He turned back the blood-stiffened folds of cloth fastidiously, exhibiting the wounds on the fleshy torso. 'This one, and this, have bled quite badly, but I think this is the one that reached the heart.'

'In the chest, no the back,' said Gil. "And the weapon? No a large one, I'd have said.'

'Well, for these, an ordinary small dagger, not much bigger than an eating-knife if that. But look at this.' He pointed carefully with one big forefinger. 'I checked the direction of the cuts. These two that bled are quite shallow, as if he was stabbed in anger by an opponent standing in front of him and using his left hand. The third is deeper, done with a bigger blade, and goes in direct, but also from in front, and has found the heart.'

'Two assailants? And one of them left-handed,' said Gil thoughtfully. 'Has his own dagger been used?'

'Quite clean,' reported Lowrie, investigating both weapons where they lay by the corpse's well-shod feet. 'And so's the whinger. And his boots are no worse than you'd expect if he was out in the burgh yestreen. Splashes of mud, no more.'

'Anything else? What's in his purse?'

'I have not yet examined the purse.'

'– the very idea, going through the poor man's things like this, and all before he's made respectable, lying there in all his dirt, the soul –'

'There is blood in the creases of his right hand, as if he put it to the wound, no more, but his fingernails are not damaged. And there is something else strange.' The mason ducked round Naismith's outstretched, accusatory arm to reach the head, and began to smooth the lank brown hair aside with a surprisingly delicate touch. 'Bring the light here, will you.'

Gil took up the lantern and obeyed. Lowrie followed him.

'– at least his eyes are closed, but can he no be left at peace under a decent length of good linen till he softens, with maybe a couple candles and one of my old men to –'

'There are these marks on his cheek, which I am not certain about, but also you must look at his other ear,' said Maistre Pierre. He took the light and held it carefully to shine across the left side of Naismith's face. 'See, this pattern in the skin.'

'Ridges and furrows,' said Lowrie, craning round Gil's

elbow. 'It's almost like the marks on ploughland that's been left to grazing for a year or two.'

'It's as if he's lain on something uneven,' said Gil. 'After death, do you suppose? While he set?'

'I thought so too,' agreed Maistre Pierre, 'though I cannot decide what. But there is also the ear. You see?' He moved the lantern, and pointed at the edge of the corpse's right ear.

'It's torn,' said Lowrie in astonishment. 'But there's no blood.' He looked from Maistre Pierre to Gil. 'I nicked Ninian's ear on the rim like that with a broken jug last year, and it bled all over him. Is it an old injury maybe?'

'There are little tags of skin,' said Maistre Pierre. 'It has not healed in any way, but nor has it bled.'

'So –?' Gil prompted, and recognized his uncle's teaching methods. Lowrie bent to look closer at the injury.

'So I suppose this must have happened after he died too. How? Is it related to the other marks? Are they both from some kind of rough treatment, maybe when he was moved to where we found him?'

'It fits,' agreed Maistre Pierre. 'Look at him.' He stood back, gesturing at the length of the body. 'Apart from that arm, he lies level from the feet to the shoulders, just as he was on the grass. But his head does not rest on this board, it did not rest on the grass, it lies as if on a cushion. A thin cushion,' he qualified.

'– as for sticking knives into him once he's dead, I never heard of such a thing, even if he is asking for a cushion for the poor soul's head now, and I don't have such a thing –'

'Do you mean, maister,' said Lowrie slowly, 'are you saying that he was already part stiffened when he was moved?'

Maistre Pierre grinned approvingly, his teeth showing white in his neat black beard.

'Indeed, I think so. Face, jaw and neck, perhaps, were already set. Then he was disturbed, and taken into the garden, a task I would not care for myself, and fell into the position in which we found him. In which we see him now,' he nodded at the unresponsive corpse. 'I suppose if the shoulders lay differently when he was set down, the head would not touch the ground.'

Gil studied the face, still locked in its dream.

'So he was stabbed in some other place,' he said slowly, 'and his eyes closed. Then he was kept there for some time, maybe an hour or two –'

'Perhaps as much as three, when the weather is so cold,' advised Maistre Pierre. Millar exclaimed inarticulately in the doorway.

'– maybe three, and then borne into the garden and left there. Why?' Gil lifted the fur-lined gown from the bench where Maistre Pierre had laid it, and began to turn it carefully, inspecting its heavy folds.

'– what a thing to be suggesting, that's no way to be treating a Christian corp –'

'He couldny stay where he was killed,' suggested Lowrie.

'Well, yes, but why? And why go to so much trouble? Why not simply leave him on the Stablegreen or out in the street? How was he got past the locked door here?'

'His own keys?' suggested Lowrie.

'But the keys are on his belt, so how did his bearer get out again?'

'Over the wall?'

'Mm,' said Gil doubtfully, and peered into the wide sleeve of the garment he held. 'What is this lodged in the fur?' He picked the pale scraps out of the soft hairs, and held them nearer the light. 'Grass, is it? Straw? Hay?'

Lowrie came to look, and lifted one of the flakes from Gil's palm.

'Straw, isn't it,' he agreed. 'Has he been kept in a hayloft or something?'

'– and anyway I heard him myself last night, he was certainly home by the time I had Humphrey settled, the poor soul, and in his bed no long after –'

'What was that, madame?' said Maistre Pierre, turning sharply.

Mistress Mudie, half his size, recoiled for a moment, recovered herself, and said again, 'I heard him last night wi my own ears, tramping about the boards over my head. He was in his own lodgings a couple hours afore midnight, maister, my word on it.'

'Tell us about it, mistress,' suggested Gil. Unnecessary, he thought, we'll hear more than we want to. 'Did you see him at all?'

'Oh, aye, of course I saw him,' she said, plump cheeks puffing out with importance. 'We had the accounts to see to in the afternoon, same as always, and then he had a word for the whole community, and then they all went to Vespers and Compline, and after it he went out of the almshouse in his good cloak and velvet hat.'

'It was dark by then?' said Gil, attempting to follow this headlong description.

'Compline's over by maybe half an hour after five o'clock,' supplied Millar.

Gil nodded acknowledgement, but Mistress Mudie rattled on. 'Oh, aye, full dark, but I seen him go out at the gate wi a lantern. And then,' pursued Mistress Mudie without apparently pausing for breath, 'I had supper for my old men to see to, and they talked a while by the fire, and then there's one or two I have to help to their beds, and Humphrey and all, and after I seen to that I was in my own lodging next the kitchen, and heard Deacon Naismith come in and walk about on the boards over my head, and eat the collation that I leave him in the court-cupboard to break his fast wi, and drink a beaker of wine, and then ready himself for his bed. And that,' she concluded triumphantly, 'was just afore you came in, Maister Millar, so you see there's no need of saying he was stabbed or anything, because it must have been someone in here if he was, and who'd do a thing like that to the Deacon I'd like to know?'

'So would I, indeed,' said Gil politely. 'Tell me, mistress, do you know where the Deacon went when he left yesternight?'

'Well, of course I do, though that's to say, he never said, but a body could tell,' she dimpled at Gil suddenly, 'ye can aye tell when a man's going to his mistress, the more so after what he tellt us all in the afternoon, will you be seeing yours when you've done asking questions here, maister?' I will indeed, thought Gil uneasily. 'He went out the gate in his good cloak and hat wi his Sunday gown under them, the same one he died in, look at him there, the soul, and his shoulders back, right pleased wi himself,' she demonstrated, causing a major upheaval under her decent black gown, 'he'd be going to his house by the Caichpele where the woman Veitch dwells, where he often goes for his supper –'

'So he was out of this place before six,' said Maistre Pierre, 'and returned – when?'

'I was back here about ten,' said Millar uneasily. 'And he was already home.'

'Returned before ten.' Maistre Pierre raised his eyebrows. 'A short evening with one's mistress.'

'How long does it take?' said Gil absently, and caught his breath. 'I mean –' He broke off, and felt his face burning.

'Longer than that, I hope, the first time,' said his betrothed's father unanswerably.

'– and he was later back than he's often been,' supplied Mistress Mudie, to Gil's relief, 'for it's quite usual he's in his lodging and walking up and down over my head before St Mungo's Vespers is ended, maybe eight o'clock –'

'I saw him go out,' said Millar. 'I was ju – just leaving, myself – a late lecture, six o'clock – I'm studying Theology,' he expanded, 'and he left ahead of me.'

'And you weren't back until ten?' Gil asked.

'– oh, aye, it was late, I'd to see Anselm and Duncan to their beds on my own, and Anselm was well worked up, the soul, I canny tell what about –'

'We sat a while discussing the lecture, and so forth. It must ha been ten o'clock I came up the road. I saw there was a light in the Deacon's lodgings, so I locked up and went to my own bed.' He turned in the doorway and pointed at the main range with its top-heavy dormer windows. 'That's my lodging at the end, you see, I reach it from the inner yard. The Deacon's bedchamber is just through the wall from me. I could hear him moving about and all.'

'And you're certain it was as late as ten?' Gil prompted.

Millar shook his head. 'I ken all was dark at St Mungo's and at St Nicholas when I came through the Wyndhead.'

'Ten o'clock,' said Maistre Pierre disapprovingly. 'I should have said earlier, but I suppose it is possible.'

'And this was all just as usual?' Gil asked.

'– usual enough, save they were all late back, for it's only the two nights in the week Maister Millar's no here to help me wi Anselm, and what he was on about I'd like to ken, his friend had tellt him all was well but he couldny see it and kept asking me –'

'Usual enough,' agreed Millar. 'The Deacon was often out in the evening, and back at a variable time, and as Mistress Mudie says I've two late lectures in the week, and I'm often gey late home after them. You can check that wi Patey Coventry,' he added anxiously, 'he's in the same class.'

'Oh, the Bachelor of Sacred Theology course?' Gil said in Latin. Millar nodded, looking relieved.

'– needing me much longer, I'd like to get the Deacon made decent, for I've the crocks to see to after their porridge and the lassie to send to the market, and then I've the dinner to get started, and the Deacon's lodging to redd up and the accounts to manage and I hope you'll oversee the accounts for today, Maister Millar, since Deacon Naismith's no able –'

'I have learned all I may from him just now,' said Maistre Pierre. 'What do we do now, Gilbert?'

'I'd like to see the Deacon's lodgings,' said Gil, 'you

should be present, Maister Millar, but I think we could let Mistress Mudie get on now.'

'– I tellt ye, I've no had a chance to get up there to redd up, I'd no like ye to think it aye looks the way it does first thing, but at least I can make sure Humphrey gets his draught –'

'I can let you in,' said Millar, 'but I need to take the old men to Terce. Maybe Cubby could lead the Office,' he said doubtfully, 'if Frankie's no back. He's got the best voice, they can all hear him. Then I could come back and help.'

'If you could. And you two,' Gil turned to Lowrie. 'If you can find Michael,' he amended, 'the pair of you could look for the Deacon's cloak and hat if you would. I'll send the dog with you, and you can tell me if he pays attention to any place in particular.'

'They mi – might be in his lodging,' said Millar. 'The cloak and hat.'

'True,' agreed Maistre Pierre, 'but having taken the time to put his boots on, why would he then go out bare-headed?'

'Michael's likely in the Douglas lodging,' said Lowrie. 'Socrates and I can go see.'

'And then,' said Gil reluctantly, 'I'll need to talk to the brothers. I've a notion one or two might have something useful to tell us.'

'– and that'll make a nice change for them, a civil learned young man to talk to, they aye like a new ear for their tales, the souls, and if that's you done here, maister, I'll see to covering him and a couple of candles the now till he softens and we can make all decent –'

Lowrie paused at the doorway, cast a sidelong, reluctant glance at the corpse in its pool of lamplight and crossed himself.

'It's an odd thing,' he confessed. 'I've been at the hunt, I've witnessed a many stags unmade and lesser game cut up, but this is no the same at all.'

'No,' agreed Gil. 'It's no the same at all. Say a word for

him when you get the chance,' he suggested, miming counting his beads. 'It helps.'

The young man nodded, and swallowed hard.

'I'll do that,' he said. 'Thanks, maister.'

Out in the yard, the rain was heavier. Lowrie ducked his head in a brief bow and hurried for the hall door, and Millar led the way to the fore-stair of the Deacon's lodging. Socrates, following Lowrie, checked at the threshold and emitted one staccato bark. Gil looked back from the stair and gestured, and the dog obediently padded off after the young man.

'Not locked,' said Maistre Pierre as the latch rattled.

'Oh, no,' agreed Millar, pushing the door open. 'We lock the outer gate by night, ye ken, and the hall door, and the back yett as Sissie said, but we've no locks to our own doors, save for the Douglas lodging, a course, and the boy has that the now.'

Naismith's apartment was both commodious and clean. The door admitted them to an outer room fashionably and expensively furnished with a handsome court-cupboard, four leather backstools and a table with carved legs. In one corner of the room stood a tall rack of shallow drawers, bundles of papers showing at their open fronts. Wall-hangings of verdure work made the place comfortable, and on an embroidered linen cloth on the table sat the remains of Mistress Mudie's collation: a wooden platter with the crumbs of an oatmeal bannock, the leaf wrap-pings of a green cheese, an apple-core. Windows facing on to either yard were stoutly shuttered, but a grey light fell through their glazed upper portions just under the thatch.

'And the bedchamber's yonder,' said Millar, nodding at the far end of the room. 'Now I'd best get down to see to the Office.'

'Mistress Mudie keeps house for the Deacon as well as for the brothers?' Gil asked. 'Alone?'

'Aye, and for me.' Millar grimaced. 'She's a good woman, and she loves caring for the old men, it's no just

42

a duty, and she's a good housewife, wi two-three kitchen hands under her, though you'd never think it the way she goes on about the cooking. Her talk doesny bother the brothers,' he added, with a wry grin, 'the most of them canny hear her.'

'I have no doubt she is a good woman, as you say, but her tongue would drive me raving wild in a day,' said Maistre Pierre.

'*Your semly voys that ye so smal out-twyne Maketh my thoght in joye and blis habounde,*' remarked Gil. Millar grinned again, then hastily rearranged his features in solemnity. 'So the Deacon left just before you did,' Gil continued, 'and came back late. How did he get up the stair last night? The moon's at the quarter, but it was full cloud. I'd need of a lantern myself, out in the street, even with the lights on the house corners, and in the yard here it would be like the inside of a barrel.'

'Oh, he'd a la – lantern,' said Millar, pausing on the doorsill. 'It's here. He's brought it home with him.'

'His own lantern? You can identify it?'

'Oh, aye.' Millar waved a hand at the object where it sat on the court-cupboard. 'Well, it belongs to the bedehouse. You can see, it's got the badge on the handle, and all.'

Gil went over and lifted the lantern. It was a well-made and well-worn specimen, of tooled brass set with pieces of mica. The shutter was fastened by a neat clasp whose pin was attached by a fine chain, and the handle was smoothly shaped and ornamented by a small shield with a heart on it.

'Douglas?' said Maistre Pierre. 'The Douglas arms? The same which you wear, maister?'

Gil looked attentively, for the first time, at the embroidered badge on Millar's cloak.

'The Douglas arms, with a difference. A heart on a shield,' he said, 'and an open book below it. Was it a Douglas founded the place?'

'The shield should be chained to the book,' said Millar, distracted, 'and LP on the pages of the book, to signify the

House of Leirit Puirtith, but the stitches aye wear away. It was James Douglas of Cauldhope was our founder, near sixty year since, as a house to support ten poor learned men. We pray daily for his soul and his wife's.'

'I never realized that,' said Gil. 'That must have been my godfather's sire – or his grandsire, indeed. Ten, is it? You don't have ten staying here now, do you?'

'No, no,' said Millar anxiously. 'There are si – six bedesmen. And I'd best leave you now, maisters, and go and lead them to Terce. I'll come back as soon as they've right started.'

'We must not delay the Office,' agreed Maistre Pierre, and Millar hurried off down the creaking fore-stair. Gil set the lantern back on the court-cupboard and prowled round the chamber, opening the shutters so that the damp air stirred and more light fell on the well-swept boards under their feet. Maistre Pierre laid the dead man's purse and belt on the table and looked about him.

'He did himself proudly,' he commented. He moved to the rack of papers and drew out a bundle. 'What are all these, I wonder? The accounts of the bedehouse, I suppose. I wonder where he wrote? I see no pen or ink. Perhaps in the inner room.'

'This does not add up,' Gil said. His companion nodded, peering at the papers he held. 'He was moving about up here two hours before midnight, with a locked door between him and the place where he was found dead this morning. He must have been killed almost immediately after he was heard here, but where did it happen?'

'His keys were on him. They could have been used to open the door.'

'But how did his killer get out again, through the locked door?'

'Perhaps it was one of the old men. Or Millar, or that talking woman. Who else has a key?'

'I hope the boys may find something to the purpose.' Gil turned his head as a sound of shuffling feet rose from the yard. 'And there is Naismith's bedchamber to search.'

44

Chapter Three

The inner chamber was half the size of the outer, most of the floor space taken up by a free-standing box bed positioned to avoid the worst of the draughts from the windows. It had a counterpane of the same verdure tapestry, and a matching curtain was drawn back on its one open side.

'Is that the kind of piece madame your mother has sent?' asked Maistre Pierre, following Gil into the room, 'or is it a tester-bed with pillars? The canvas was still over the cart when I left this morning.'

'It's this kind,' said Gil rather shortly. He was aware of his friend eyeing him sideways again, but concentrated on studying the rest of the chamber. There was a painted chest with a businesslike lock by the bedside, a rug made of two goatskins lay crumpled beside it, and a tall desk stood next to one of the windows, the inkhorn and pen-case Maistre Pierre had missed resting on a shelf beside the writing-slope.

'The bed has been slept in,' the mason said, 'this one I mean, I have no doubt of that.'

'Nor I,' said Gil.

Indeed, he thought, it could hardly be clearer. The sheets were creased, the counterpane rumpled, and the blankets had been flung back when its occupants – occupant rose before the dawn. He pulled back the bedding, and drew each layer up over the mattress until all was straight, then looked about him. A pair of slip-slop shoes sat neatly by the foot of the bed; a furred brocade bedgown hung on a nail in the bedpost above them.

Beyond the closed end of the bed another chest could be seen against the wall, with a pile of discarded clothing thrown on top of it. Gil went over to this and disentangled the garments. Black hose, rather stale, a mended doublet and jerkin, a short gown with a lining of black budge: the kind of garments a man wore about his own house, when not out to impress.

'He changed his garments before he left to go to supper,' he said. Maistre Pierre nodded. 'And then came in later and prepared himself for bed. He hasn't worn the bed-gown.'

'One does not always.'

'True.'

The pen-case on the desk was of tooled leather; Gil eased off the cover and looked inside. Several quills bound together in a scrap of paper, a penknife for trimming pens and scraping out blots, a bone rubber for smoothing paper or parchment after one had used the knife. Nothing unusual there.

He looked round. There was a candlestick with a burnt-down candle on the painted chest. He thought suddenly of Tib's intent face over the candles in the house on Rotten-row before dawn, and then of Alys sitting beside him in the firelight in her father's house.

'There is his purse,' said Maistre Pierre, breaking into that thought. 'I have it here.'

'True.' Gil took the item from him. Like most of Naismith's goods, it was large and well made, of red leather stamped with a pattern of small flowers. Undoing the strings, Gil tipped out the contents beside the candle-stick, the debris of the man's life rattling on the painted wood. Distantly aware of Mistress Mudie's raised voice, he sorted through the items. A smaller purse of coin, a set of tablets, two or three creased scraps of paper with writing on them, two pilgrim medals and a set of beads, a tiny

46

pot of ointment with a powerful smell, a small box of sweetmeats.

'What is the writing?'

'A receipt of some sort.' Gil unfolded one scrap. 'Herbs, quicksilver, fat from a cob swan, burnt feathers. Ointment, I suppose, but it doesn't say for what. This is another one, and this is a list of herbs. Hot milk or ale, honey – a soothing drink, I suppose.' He handed the slips to his companion. 'And in his tablets, notes of this and that, *Buy coal, Speak to Mungo Howie.*'

Maistre Pierre looked up from the little sheaf of papers in surprise. 'To Howie? I should have thought he could afford a better craftsman than that.'

Gil, aware of his friend's opinion of the several carpenters and joiners in the burgh, merely nodded and turned to the next leaf. The slats of wood were as long as his hand, the outer covers wrapped in red leather, stamped with the same pattern of flowers as the purse, and the wax filling the hollowed-out centres of the leaves had been stained red to match, rather than the more usual green. Here was a long list, incised in the careful script of a man who had come to writing late in life.

'This is a note of some property,' he said after a moment. 'Most of it in Glasgow. I wonder is it his own or the bedehouse's? And several names. A gold chain, the furnishings of this lodging.'

'Notes for a will, perhaps. Did that woman mention an announcement? Is that why he saw Agnew last night, to draw up some new document?'

'It's possible,' agreed Gil. He turned as footsteps crossed the outer room. 'Maister Millar. What did Deacon Naismith have to tell the bedehouse yesterday? Was he making great changes?'

'Not – not for the bedehouse,' said Millar earnestly from the doorway, 'no really.'

'Not really,' echoed Maistre Pierre. 'So what were his plans? Small changes?'

Millar fell back before them as they returned to the outer

47

room. 'Well, there were to be changes for the wardens, I agree. I was to have one of the wee houses, and Sissie another, and the Deacon was to occupy the whole of this main range.'

'What, as a house?' said Gil, startled. 'For himself alone?'

'Oh, no. He was to be married at Yule, he told us, so he wanted the extra space.'

'Married?' Maistre Pierre sat down and looked in amazement at Millar. 'He was not in Orders then?'

'Oh, no. At least, maybe in minor Orders. He was – I think he'd been a clerk somewhere, he kent the responses well and could sing the Office wi the old men, but he was no priest. To tell truth I never liked to ask him,' Millar confided.

'And he wanted to take over the main range. Even the hall?' said Maistre Pierre, lifting the bundle of papers he had left on the table. 'But where would the old men meet?'

'He never said.' Millar paused, looking thoughtful. 'Aye, you're right. I was so – I'm right comfortable in my lodging through the wall yonder,' he waved a hand, 'I was so took up wi wondering how the wee houses could be brought into order before Yule, I never thought about the hall.'

'Did he say who he was to wed?'

'He did not. I assumed it was his mistress,' Millar admitted. 'He's had her in keeping longer than I've been in post here, high time he did right by her. Frankie went away to break the morn's news to her, poor soul, and he's not back yet.'

'And how would that have left you?' Gil asked.

'No great change, I suppose,' said Millar blankly. 'I'd still be the sub-Deacon, I thought. There might ha been less for my income,' he added thoughtfully, 'for a married man would want more for himself, likely. And the same for Sissie, though a course he did say his wife would take over keeping the household.'

'Are things so tight, then?' said Maistre Pierre from the table. Gil and Millar both turned to look at him. He had the papers spread out before him on the polished surface and his tablets in his hand. 'The bedehouse is in poverty?' he asked.

'I think it isny well to do, for he's been making cuts lately. No more wine to their dinners, for instance. They wereny best pleased at that,' Millar confided.

'I can imagine.' Maistre Pierre was still surveying the papers before him. 'Are these all the papers, would you know?'

Millar shook his head. 'Maister Naismith saw to the accounts, though I kept them filed for him,' he said. 'He and Sissie dealt wi the day's expenditure every afternoon, which she'll want me to do now,' he added in dismay. 'And he saw to all the incomings and outgoings.'

'Oh, did he?'

'It should be all the papers, but there might be some elsewhere.' Millar drew out one tape-bound sheaf. 'This bundle is the – no, it isny. It's the dealings wi the burgh mills. This one,' he peered at the heading, 'is the tithes from Lenzie and those are from Elsrickle. And this – that's strange, these are all in disorder,' he said anxiously, pulling out one drawer after another. 'Deacon Naismith has – had his own way of working, like all of us, and these are no in the right shelves.'

'None of them?' Gil asked.

'Some of them are right,' said Millar, inspecting the contents of a package. Maistre Pierre twisted his neck to see the pages. 'They seem to be all complete, I think maybe it's just the packets have got rearranged, I canny think how.'

'Where did he work?' Gil asked. 'At his desk, or at the table here?'

'Mostly at the table,' Millar was still engrossed in the papers, 'but often in his chamber yonder. His writing-gear must be in there the now, for I don't see it. Oh, this is a strange thing, it's going to take all morning to sort it.'

Gil watched him pulling the bundles out and replacing them, and said casually, 'When the Deacon left here yesterday. Before six, I think you said.' Millar nodded. 'Did you see which way he went?'

'He went down the Drygate,' said Millar. 'Likely he'd be heading for the house by the Caichpele, as Sissie said. He's – he'd a quite kenspeckle way of walking, wi his shoulders back and his elbows out under the cloak, there was no mistaking him even by lantern-light.'

'And he was in the bedehouse when you got home.'

'Oh, aye,' agreed Millar. 'There was a light up here and he was moving about.' He stopped. 'I never got a sight of him,' he admitted, 'but I heard him clear enough, and who else would it be? I'd no need for a word wi him, I just gaed to my lodging and to my bed.'

'And you were talking with Patey Coventry and the rest of the class till the time you left the college?' Easily enough confirmed, if he was, Gil thought.

'Aye,' began Millar, and was interrupted by an outbreak of furious shouting below them in the inner yard. Socrates barked once, his deep warning tone. Gil, nearest the windows, stepped over to look through the glass, then hastily unfastened the shuttered lower portion.

'Look at this!' he said as Maistre Pierre reached him.

His friend stared down into the garden in some amusement. 'It seems the young men have angered the old ones. Should we defend them, Gil?'

The rain had eased slightly, and outside one of the little houses, Michael and Lowrie stood at bay, the dog in front of them. They were surrounded by an indignant gathering of elderly men, two of them waving sticks in a threatening manner, with Mistress Mudie clutching her plaid round her head and adding her voice to the chorus. The dog barked again. At the far end of the garden one or two passers-by were staring with interest over the wall from the Stablegreen.

'Merciful Christ,' said Millar at the next window, 'what have they done to set them off?'

'What's he say?' echoed someone from below. 'Tell me what's he say?'

'Sneaking around like thieves! And claiming you were ordered to search!'

'Fit war ye deein, loons?'

'– no way to behave in a decent bedehouse, as if any of my old men would do a thing like that –'

'Magpies! Pyots! And they were sent from that hoodie!' exclaimed a resonant voice, and continued in Latin; Gil had just time to recognize a phrase from the Apocalypse before Millar said again,

'Oh, merciful Christ. Sissie!' he shouted, leaning out at the open shutters. 'Sissie, get Humphrey out of there before he –'

'Maister Cunningham, is that you?' exclaimed Lowrie in relief, catching sight of Gil at the other window. 'They're no for letting us search their lodgings!'

Socrates gave out another deep bark.

'I never thought,' said Gil in dismay. 'I should have warned them no to try.' He leaned out like Millar and shouted 'Quiet!' at his dog. Socrates threw him a resentful look, but reduced his utterance to a threatening rumble, all his white teeth on display. There was something on the ground between his forepaws.

Mistress Mudie at the back of the group was tugging at the arm of one of the brothers, a man twenty years younger than his confrères by his bearing, the source of the sonorous Latin. She succeeded in dragging him away, still waving the other arm and declaiming, and they made for the door below the watchers' feet, Latin and Scots rising in a kind of motet.

'– *those who claim to be apostles but are not – we will throw you into prison, to put you to the test, for ten days you will suffer cruelly –*'

'– there now, Humphrey my poppet, calm yourself, they're no harm to you – come and sit down quiet and I'll make you a lovely cup of hot milk wi honey in it –'

'I'd best deal wi this,' said Millar, making for the door.

51

'They'll never digest their dinner if we don't get them calmed down.'

'He is garbling that text,' said Maistre Pierre critically. As Millar left he turned away from the window to the tall rack of papers, and extracted another bundle at random.

'I must go down too,' Gil said after a moment. 'Are you staying here?'

'Oh, for certain,' said Maistre Pierre, not looking up from a close scrutiny of the papers he held. 'Leave Naismith's keys with me if you are going. As I thought, Gil, none of this adds up. I would like Alys to see it,' he added thoughtfully, 'but not now.'

'Not now,' agreed Gil, flinching from the idea. He set the keys on the table by the dead man's purse and belt and crossed the room, listening carefully. Mistress Mudie's voice came up through the floorboards, babbling on like the mill-burn; Maister Humphrey replied, still in flowing Latin but less loudly. She seemed to be meeting with some success. Gil went out and down the fore-stair.

In the dripping garden, Millar had already drawn the bedesmen away from their siege, and the audience on the Stablegreen had drifted away. When the two students saw Gil they slipped round to meet him; Michael bent first, attempting to pick up whatever it was the dog had found, but Socrates put one hairy paw on top of it and bared his teeth a little further, then snatched the object up himself and came to be praised for defending the young men, waving his tail. Gil patted him, accepted his gift, and said in apology, 'I should have warned you no to try their lodgings, or at least to be careful how you went. Did they strike you?'

'Oh, it was no worse than my grandsire shouting at the servants,' said Lowrie easily. 'We've no found the cloak so far, maister.'

'Did the dog find anything? No signs of blood? What's this he's brought me?'

'No,' said Michael in his gruff voice before his friend could speak. He had grown in the six months since Gil had first encountered him at the University, but was still shorter than Lowrie, lightly built and mousy-haired, with a pointed chin and sharp cheekbones. 'No a thing. He checked the place where the corp was lying again, but he never went anywhere else after it.'

'This is a stocking,' Gil said in surprise, looking at the object his dog had given him. 'Where did he find it? I'd best return it.' He broke off, looking more closely. Still crumpled in the folds in which it had been slid off its wearer's leg, the item was wet from the grass and from Socrates' mouth, but otherwise relatively clean. He shook it out; it was finely knitted of linen thread, with clocks of fancy work on either side of the ankle, and it was barely longer than Gil's hand and forearm. The mark of the garter was clearly visible near the top.

'This was never an old man's garment. It's a lassie's stocking,' said Gil. 'What's that doing in the almshouse?'

The two young men glanced at one another.

'Er,' said Michael, the scarlet flooding up over his face. 'Er . . .'

'Michael has access to the Douglas lodging,' said Lowrie candidly, 'which is the last house yonder by the gate, and a key to the gate itself. Need we say more, maister?'

Michael threw him a grateful look. Gil glanced at the stocking again and knew a surge of envy. *Al nicht by the rose ich lay.* To be alone with one's sweetheart – abed with one's sweetheart, indeed – without all the tumult of feasts and invitations, wedding-clothes and linen lists –

'Well, well,' he said, mustering a grin from somewhere, and handed the stocking over. 'Don't make any promises your father won't approve, Michael. I hope you got her out well before it was light.'

Michael nodded, mumbling something indistinct, and hastily stowed the delicate object in the breast of his gown.

'We'd best be away, maister,' said Lowrie. 'We've a lecture at eleven o'clock.'

'So Nick said,' agreed Gil. 'Come in out the rain first, and tell me what you've found.'

'That's easy done,' said Lowrie, following him into the passageway through the main range. 'We've found neither cloak nor hat, and the dog showed no more interest in any of the places we've been.'

'And where was that?'

'No the chapel,' said Michael.

'No the chapel,' agreed Lowrie, 'since they were saying Terce, but we've looked in all the outhouses that were unlocked, save where the Deacon's laid out, and we looked in the kitchen. Mistress Mudie took the huff,' he confessed, 'and insisted we look in her own chamber off the kitchen and all, and in her kist. That was a bit – she'd that Maister Humphrey in the kitchen, the mad one, and the dog wasny very taken wi him. Anyway, we've been everywhere we could, except the Deacon's lodging and Maister Millar's. Oh, and we looked in here,' he added, waving a hand to encompass the shadowy hall.

'And the old men's lodgings?' Gil asked.

Lowrie made a face. 'We'd already looked in Michael's lodging – the Douglas house, the one at the far end on the right – and we'd got into all of them except the mad one's, which is when they cam tottering out wi their sticks displayed. So we never risked that one, maister, being wholly taken up wi defending ourselves,' he admitted. 'The dog wasny interested in any of their doors, except Michael's, and all he found in Michael's place was la – the lassie's stocking. So we've no been much help.'

'On the contrary,' said Gil. 'That's very useful. I wonder where the cloak is?'

'Why does it matter?' asked Michael.

'He went out in it,' said Lowrie, 'and now he's no wearing it.'

'He might have left it somewhere.'

'Miggle, you've seen him often enough.' In the thin light from the two doors Lowrie's lanky frame was briefly transformed to mimic a smaller, stouter, more self-important man. 'He'd never have left his bedehouse cloak, wi all that braid and the badge and all. Never mind it was a cold evening.'

'So now we ken it's no in the bedehouse,' said Gil, 'or at least if I can check Millar's lodging we'll ken. And thank you for searching.'

'There's another thing,' said Lowrie. 'I know about things setting after they're deid, maister, but how sure is the timing? It's a man we're talking about, after all, no a side of mutton.'

'Well, it can take longer,' said Gil, 'it can be slower, but it's no often quicker. Why?'

'Well, I wondered if the Deacon might ha been alive this morning.'

'This morning?' repeated Gil, startled. 'No, he'd never have set that quickly. Why?'

'Well, that's it,' said Lowrie. 'I thought I saw him in the chapel, when we came to say Mass, though he wasny in his usual place. So how could he have been dead last night, if he was at Mass this morning?'

'A good question,' agreed Gil. 'How certain are you that you saw him? Could it have been someone else?'

'No very,' admitted Lowrie. 'But I'd swear I saw an extra person within the quire, just the dark figure wi the badge on the breast like the others, and who else was it like to have been?'

Gil looked from one young man to the other. 'Did you see this, Michael?'

Michael shook his head. 'I'd the candle. You don't see much past that.'

'Come and show me where you saw him, Lowrie.'

They went out and across the outer courtyard to the chapel door, which was now closed. Within, the candles still burned on the altar of St Serf, on either side of a clumsy wooden crucifix.

Even with these, even with daylight seeping reluctantly through the narrow windows, the little box-shaped building was full of shadows. As a place intended for clerks to

55

worship in, it had no separate nave, but the stall seats faced inward, six on either hand, and their high backs and partial sides of Norway pine formed a sort of internal quire, with a painted screen and curtained doorway at its westward end to shut out the worst of the draughts. Socrates set off, claws clicking on the worn tiles, to explore the dim space between the pine uprights and the plastered outer walls where there was room for any lay folk who wished to hear the Office or the Mass.

'There's no vestry,' said Lowrie, 'so we robe in one corner or another. That corner, the day,' he waved a hand. 'We light the candle and the censer and go in, and Maister Kennedy begins the Mass.'

'And the bedesmen are there waiting for you?'

'I think they've said Prime by the time we get here.' Lowrie held the curtain aside, and he and Michael followed Gil into the quire. 'Maister Millar leads them in procession from the hall, so he was sitting up in his own place, I mind that. I'd the censer the day, no the candle, but it's still no that easy to see out into the dark, you understand, and the black cloaks don't show well, and the lugs of the stall sides hide all the faces. It can be quite strange,' he admitted, 'up here in the dark, wi all the voices round you and nobody to see. Just the same, their badges catch the light, and I thought I could see four each side, as if the Deacon was there and all. No in his own place opposite Maister Millar,' he gestured at the two more elaborate stalls nearest the altar, 'but down the west end next to Father Anselm. Maybe Mistress Mudie saw him,' he added, 'she was near the outer door when we came in, though she aye slips out after the Elevation to see to their porridge.'

Gil stopped at the altar step and turned, looking into the shadows.

'Go and sit where you thought you saw him,' he suggested. Lowrie obliged, spreading one hand across his chest to simulate the badge, and Gil nodded agreement. 'Aye, I see what you mean. Your face is hid by the side

56

where it curves out, but I can see your hand fine. Michael, what can you see?'

'The now?' said Michael nervously. 'I can see his hand, aye, if he'd a bedehouse cloak on you'd see the badge fine. And I'll swear the Deacon wasny in his own seat the morn,' he added.

'So was he here, then?' Lowrie asked. Socrates reared up, one paw on the book-rest, peering into his face, and he reached out and patted the dog.

'Aye, but he can't have been.' Gil paced down between the stalls, frowning. 'There's no doubt the man we lifted from the garden was dead by Compline last night.'

'Maister Forsyth's lecture,' said Michael.

'Aye, but before you go, Michael, I want a word wi you.'

The two students exchanged glances.

'I'll wait outside,' said Lowrie.

As the door closed behind him Michael seemed to brace himself as for execution. Gil eyed him with some sympathy, and said reassuringly, 'It's none of my duty to oversee your behaviour, Michael. I'm no asking who she is.'

'You're no?'

'No. Just watch you don't get entangled in something your father won't support.' Michael stared at him open-mouthed, and he went on, 'I want to know about your movements, yesternight and the morn – what time were you stirring about the bedehouse, and where. Even if you saw nothing, it helps.'

'Oh.' Michael swallowed. 'I never thought of that. We must have – Oh,' he said again, and put a hand on the nearest desk to steady himself.

'Did your lass come in by this gate?'

Michael swallowed again, and shook his head.

'Past Sissie Mudie?' he said. 'Not likely! I've got the keys,' he disclosed. 'I'd got permission to lie out of the college for the night, seeing as I was to ready the lodging for the old man – for my father. He's due in Glasgow the

morn for your marriage, maister.' Gil nodded. 'So I opened
the back gate for her. That would be about . . .' He paused,
reckoning. 'After Sissie was done trotting about getting
two of the old brothers to their beds. One of them has the
house opposite ours, and the other one's next the hall. It
would be near an hour after they finished their dinner,
I suppose, afore even she started. And then the mad one
began a great scene, and it took her long enough to settle
him. It felt like past midnight afore all was quiet, though
I suppose it wasny.'

'And you opened the back yett and let the lassie in,' said
Gil, 'and then what?'

'Well, she was a bit – with the waiting, you understand,'
Michael confessed hesitantly. 'Sissie took so much longer
than I'd expected, and it was gey dark out on the Stablegreen, even with a lantern, and my – she was a wee thing
upset, she said she kept hearing things. So I locked the gate
quick and we got within doors, and then . . .' He paused,
with the glimmerings of an embarrassed smile.

'That's all I need to know,' said Gil, suppressing his envy
again. 'So you locked the yett. You're quite certain?'

'Oh, aye. She wasny well pleased,' said Michael cautiously, 'that I took the time.'

'And you saw nothing untoward? Nobody moving
about or hiding behind trees?'

'I wasny looking,' said Michael.

'A light in the Deacon's lodging?'

'I wasny –' Michael stopped, and considered. 'No. I'd ha
noticed that. I saw no light up there.' He swallowed again.
'Maister, we'll be late for Tommy Forsyth's lecture. Could
I go, d'ye think?'

'And this morning?' said Gil, ignoring this. 'When did
you open the yett?'

'As soon as they all went away through to the chapel for
Prime. It was still full dark, and we never took the lantern
out wi us, we never noticed a thing, if that's what you're
asking. For all he must have been lying there by that time,'
he added tightly.

'And you locked the yett again after she left?'

'Aye.'

'Was either of you out at the yett at all between those two times?'

'No.' Michael licked his lips. 'We wereny across the threshold again till the morn. Nor looked out, even,' he added.

Gil considered the younger man, who looked back at him uncomfortably and then dropped his eyes.

'You'd best go to your lecture,' he said. 'No, wait! Gie me the key to the back yett. I'll leave it here for you, and I ken where to find you if I need you.'

'Aye,' said Michael unhappily. He opened his purse and drew out a pair of keys on a ring. 'I'll not separate them. Leave them on a nail in the lodging, if you will, sir.' He handed them over with reluctance, ducked one knee in a bow and left to join his friend.

Gil crossed the courtyard as the students' footsteps receded along the narrow passage to the outside world, and on an impulse tapped at the open kitchen door opposite the hall.

'Mistress Mudie?' he asked.

'Mistress,' called a muffled voice within. 'You're asked for, mistress.'

A door at the far side of the kitchen opened, and Mistress Mudie looked out.

'– never a moment in this place, who is it that wants me, oh it's yersel, maister, I canny think what you'd want to ask me that I haveny tellt you already, come away in but, just so long's ye don't disturb Humphrey here, he's feeling a bit better the now, aren't you my poppet?'

Gil crossed the kitchen, nodding to the young man laboriously hacking vegetables at the bench behind the door. Mistress Mudie drew him into a small snug apartment, furnished with a cushioned settle and a folding table, one or two stools, and a little prayer desk with a worn hassock by the door to an inner chamber. There was an overpowering herbal smell, whose source was not clear, and a definite note of almonds. *Betere is hire medycyn,* he thought, *Then eny mede or eny wyn; Hir erbès smulleth suete.* His eye took in a brazier burning on the hearth with a metal trivet over it where several small pots were heating.

The youngest brother was sitting in a chair beside this, clasping a cup in both hands and staring anxiously at the wall. His heavy black cloak was folded over the back of his chair, and he wore a long belted gown of grey wool. Hearing Gil's step he turned, and shrank back slightly.

'A hoodie,' he said, 'it's that hoodie again.'

'I'm no a hoodie,' said Gil reassuringly. Mistress Mudie nodded approval. 'I'm no here to attack anyone.' Feeling Socrates pressing against his knee he looked down, and saw with surprise that the the dog's head was lowered to glare at Maister Humphrey, the coarse grey hair standing up on his back and shoulders. Gil snapped his fingers and gestured, and the animal departed in something like relief.

'– aye, that's better, we're a bit feart for the big doggie even if we areny saying so, a course the mannie's no a hoodie, Humphrey my poppet, he's a good friend to the bedehouse, he's here to find out what's come to the Deacon –'

'The Deacon was a shrike,' said Maister Humphrey earnestly, staring at Gil. He was very like his brother, with a thin squarish face, round light-coloured eyes and light brown hair clipped very close, presumably by Mistress Mudie. The hands clasping the beaker were fine-boned and muscular, but the nails were bitten so short they had bled quite recently. 'He was a shrike, but now he's a robin. Because he died, you ken?'

'Why a robin?' Gil asked.

'He was making changes,' said Humphrey, 'a new nest for the bonnie yeldrin, another for the chaffinch,' he cast a quick, bright smile at Mistress Mudie, 'and the shrike himself to take a make and hae the meat frae our mouths.'

'That sounds bad,' said Gil, preserving his countenance.

'Oh, very bad,' agreed Humphrey, shaking his head. 'But he changed to a robin instead, and now he's dead. So it willny happen, will it?'

'No, it willny,' Gil reassured him.

Mistress Mudie gave him an approving look but said persuasively, '– no need to be upsetting ourselves wi talk like that, nor it wasny very nice to be calling the Deacon names, was it now, and what were you wanting to ask us anyway, till I get on wi my tasks here –'

'Last night, Mistress Mudie,' said Gil, dragging his mind back to the point at issue, 'you heard Maister Naismith come in late.'

'It was the birds woke me,' declared Humphrey, 'when they sang for joy at the shrike's passing. But I looked out after that, late, late, in the middle of the night, and there was a light in his lodging, so I wept sair, for they had leed to me.'

'– what I said already, I knew I'd tellt you all I could –'

'Was all quiet here by then?'

'– oh, aye, all asleep in their own wee houses they were, no a cheep out o them, even Humphrey was away wi the angels, weren't you no, my poppet?'

'How long had it been quiet?'

The continuous babble checked for a moment, as she stared at him.

'Half an hour,' she said. 'No as much as an hour, no I couldny say it was as much as an hour, we'd to warm the milk for you, didn't we no, Humphrey, and it was longer than I thought it would be, what wi the fire being low, and I heard the Deacon over our heads here no that long afore Maister Millar came in and all. And I heard him from here,' she added, 'our Andro, for he locked the door out there and went through to the garden, and I heard his boots on the stone and then on the gravel, and he went up to his own lodging which it's above the other end of the hall and the stair's in the garden by Anselm's door. And the Deacon was over my head all that time walking about in his boots too, never thought to put his house shoon on, and then sitting eating his piece for I heard the chair scrape at the table –'

As if on cue, footsteps could be heard on the boards above them. Pierre must still be studying the accounts, thought Gil.

Maister Humphrey looked up nervously. 'Is that him back?'

'– a course not, my poppet, the Deacon's dead, rest his soul, he's no walking about –'

Humphrey nodded, smiling. 'Now I mind. That's the other one,' he said. 'The other hoodie.'

'– now, now, fancy saying that about him –'

'He's searching for the deep secrets of Satan.'

'– we'll have none of that, my poppet –'

'Aye, and he gives *glory and honour and thanks to the one who lives for ever*,' said Gil quickly, switching to the scholarly tongue. The bedesman eyed him warily, then smiled again.

'*Praise and honour to the Lamb for ever and ever*,' he agreed, the Latin echoing off the creaking floorboards.

'Amen,' said Gil. Maister Humphrey relaxed, and drained off his cup and handed it to Sissie like a small child. The cuff of his grey gown was pulled and torn. Gil suddenly recalled his sister Margaret, whose clothes had always looked like that, because she chewed them. But she grew out of the habit before she was ten, he thought.

'Have you some milk for the hoodie, Sissie?' Humphrey asked, still smiling.

She set the cup aside and lifted a pipkin from the brazier, hand wrapped in a corner of her apron. '– saints be praised he's taken to you for it's no easy if he doesny take to a person, would you care for a drink of milk, maister, seeing it would make him happy? It's almond milk,' she qualified, 'seeing there's no milk to be had this time of year, but he likes it just as well and the herbs helps him.'

'A wee drop, then,' said Gil. 'Mistress Mudie, I've another thing to ask you.'

'– goodness me, as if I would have anything more to tell, I'm certain you've everything out of my head that's in it the questions you've asked us all this day already –'

'At the Mass this morning,' he continued. She was stirring a beaker, but stopped and paused again in her chatter to gaze at him, her plump face anxious in the light from the window. 'One of the lads thought he saw a seventh bedesman, like as if the Deacon was sitting down at the end of the stalls. Did you see anything?'

'Oh, I wouldny see him.' She shook her head so that the ends of her linen headdress swung. 'I never see him even when Anselm says he's been there. And to say truth at this time of the year it's that dark in the chapel there could be the choir of St Mungo's at the Mass and I wouldny notice them, let alone someone who –' She caught herself up, glanced quickly at Humphrey who was watching her and went on, 'someone who's Anselm's friend and no always in his own seat. No, I canny help you there, maister. Now here's this milk, a wee bit warmed ower just to take the chill off it and a spoonful honey in it –'

Chapter Four

Round the small blaze on the hearth at the far end of the hall, three of the bedehouse brothers were listening to a fourth who spoke in the loud, barking voice of someone who has been deaf for years. Three heads turned as Gil made his way down the room, Socrates behind him, but the speaker paid no attention.

'He'll have made his escape by the back way,' he was saying, 'I canny tell why the man's no looking at the back yett. That dog he brought would pick up the scent, quick as ye please, and take him to the ill-doer –'

'Barty,' said another brother tremulously, leaning over to face the other man. 'It's a sight-hound.'

'What did ye say? What did ye say, Cubby?'

'It's a sight-hound. Look at it. And here's the man to speak to us. Tell him what ye were just saying.'

'What's that? Playing? I wasny playing, Cubby.'

'He wasny slain here. It wasny on the bedehouse land,' said the frailest of the brothers, a scrawny man with a shock of white hair, his spectacles slipping sideways off his nose. 'He tellt me that.'

'Aye, Anselm,' said the one addressed as Cubby. 'I've no doubt, but the fellow has to report to Robert Blacader, he'll need more to give him than that.'

'He taught Robert Blacader,' said Anselm resentfully. 'He ought to listen to what he tells me.'

'Fit deein, mon?' demanded the brother opposite Anselm. He had removed his floppy velvet hat and hung it on the arm of his chair to dry; his head was completely

64

bald and gleamed in the firelight. As if to compensate, in addition to the luxuriant grey moustache he had large bushy eyebrows, and flourishing tufts of hair emerged from his nostrils and ears. They gave him rather the look of a Green Man in a church, Gil thought, perhaps one who had been pruned slightly.

'Forgive me, maisters,' said Gil, bowing politely to the gathering. 'I'm the Archbishop's Quaestor, Gil Cunningham. Might I get a word with you all?'

'It's you that's hunting for whoever slew the Deacon?' said the one with the trembling-ill. Gil nodded. 'Aye, well, we may no be much help, lad, but you can ask.' He indicated the intent faces one by one. 'Father Anselm, Maister Barty Lennox, Sir Duncan Fraser, and I'm Cubby Pringle.'

'What's he say?' said the deaf brother. Barty Lennox, thought Gil. 'Questions? Sit down and ask away, boy. What do you want of us?'

'I've two questions, maisters,' Gil said, drawing up a stool and collecting his wits. The dog sat down politely beside him, then lay down on his feet. 'I want to hear about how you found Maister Naismith's body, and I'd like to know when you all saw him last.'

The man with the trembling-ill, Cubby Pringle, spoke up first.

'It was Duncan found him. He dwells down that end of the close, opposite the Douglas lodging, and the two houses next him are empty, so he'd be the only one to go that far down the path.'

'Aye, aat's the richt o't,' agreed Sir Duncan incomprehensibly from under his moustache. 'The wee munsie wes juist liggin thaar pyntin intil the fir.' He demonstrated, flinging out his arm in imitation of the corpse's rigid gesture.

'Then he shouted, and we all cam running.'

'No running,' said Anselm, shaking his head. 'There's none of us can run.'

'What's he saying?'

'Hirpling, then. Andro came and all, and we agreed he was dead, and Frankie went for the laddie. What's his name?'

'Kennedy,' supplied Sir Duncan.

'Aye, young Kennedy. I wish Frankie was here, he'd tell you better. And Kennedy said he was stabbed, and we must send for you.'

'What?'

'He tellt me he was dead afore that,' said Anselm in argumentative tones. 'I kent it a'ready when we found him.'

'There was no sign of a weapon?' asked Gil.

'I tell you, he says it wasny on the bedehouse land,' reiterated Anselm. 'The weapon's no here either.'

'We'll need to find the weapon,' explained Gil, 'as well as his cloak.'

'What's he say?' demanded Maister Lennox. They explained to him, loud and slow, and he shook his head. 'No, there wasny a weapon. Was there, Duncan?'

'Na, na. A saa nae dirk, sauf the capernicious buckie's ain gully at's bellyban.'

'No,' translated Maister Pringle.

'Could he have been lying there already when you went to say Prime?' Gil asked. This time he faced Maister Lennox and spoke slowly.

'What d'ye say, time? Oh, Prime?' barked the old man, and shook his head. 'I wasny that end of the close afore Prime. Duncan, was he there afore Prime? Did ye see him?'

'It wis pick-mark, Barty. A'd no ha saa a cast-up whaul.' Sir Duncan mimed groping his way down the path in darkness. Gil nodded his understanding of this, smiling at him, and got a huge smile back, visible even under the sloping pent of the grey moustache.

'No way to tell, afore bird-peep,' agreed Maister Pringle.

'None of you heard anything in the night?' Gil asked,

facing Maister Lennox again. The old man shook his head with a sharp yip of laughter.

'No me, laddie!' he said.

'Nobody else?' Gil looked round the circle.

'A haard naither eechie nor ochie,' said Sir Duncan regretfully. 'Gin A had, A'd a gien him a han at the fellin, faae'er he wis.'

'Aye, well,' said Maister Pringle. 'I did wonder if I heard voices. Murmuring like a doocot it was. But it wasny Naismith I heard, for all I'm near the gate. Next the Douglas lodging, ye ken,' he explained to Gil.

'Likely it was youngsters on the Stablegreen, Cubby,' said Maister Lennox.

'In this weather?' retorted Maister Pringle.

'If they canny get the privacy at home, a tree'll do them,' said Maister Lennox with relish, apparently following this thread quite clearly. 'It wasny raining yestreen.'

'I heard,' said Anselm, clasping his hands on his stick. 'I heard him in the night, for he woke me to tell me the man was dead.'

'When was that?' Gil asked.

'Late, late. I was sleeping, and he woke me, so I rose and looked out, but it was a' dark, save for a star low in the west.'

On a cloudy night? thought Gil. Michael or his lassie? Michael did mention a lantern.

'And when did you last see Deacon Naismith?' he asked.

They looked at one another, and Cubby Pringle said in his trembling voice, 'Yestreen at Vespers, son. We've talked about that. He had a word for the whole house, and a strange word it was, and then we went to say Vespers and after it he gaed out.'

'When he went out, was he wearing his bedehouse cloak and hat, or another?'

'Aye, 's muckle bleck hap an's wellat bunnet wi the fedder intil't,' supplied Sir Duncan. His gestures depicted a cloak with a badge like his own and a plumed bonnet. Gil nodded his understanding.

'You didny see him return?' he asked.

'Na, na, we'd all gone to our rest,' said Barty.

'And what was the word he had for all of you?' he asked.

There was a pause, in which the old men looked at one another again.

'Changes,' said Cubby Pringle, as Humphrey had done. 'The meat of the matter,' he switched to a fluent old-fashioned Latin, 'was that we were to move out of our hall, our sub-Deacon and our housekeeper were to be put out as well before the Nativity and make use of two of the empty houses, though none of these are in good repair, and Cecilia our housekeeper was to be our nurse only and accept a lesser reward for it.'

'This was the first time you heard this?' Gil asked.

'It was. Cecilia asked who would be housekeeper and the Deacon replied, he was to be married and his wife would take all that into her hands.'

'Married?' repeated Gil. 'Did he say who he was to marry?'

'The Deacon did not tell us,' said Anselm in Latin.

'She'll be a disappointed woman the day,' commented Cubby in Scots, and Sir Duncan grinned uncharitably under his huge moustache.

'She'll be easit, mair belike,' he said. Anselm gave him a prim smile.

'And was that all he said?'

'Was it no enough?' demanded Barty Lennox in his barking voice. 'Aye, Cubby's gied you the sum o't.'

'And now he's dead,' said Anselm. He looked beyond Gil as the hall door opened. 'Is that Andro? Is it time to say Nones?'

It was still raining. Gil made his way down the garden with the dog at his heels, and paused to study the yett.

Drops of rusty water hung along the horizontals of the interlaced wrought-iron bands, and shook loose and fell to the threshold stone when he put the key in the lock. It turned readily, and the yett swung open silently on well-greased hinges. Michael again? he wondered. Socrates, recovering his spirits, leapt past him to attend to his own needs.

The gate led directly out on to the Stablegreen, an open expanse of ground dotted with clumps of bushes and hazel trees. Gil knew it reasonably well, since he often exercised the dog here, reaching it by way of the muddy vennel which led from Rottenrow nearly opposite his uncle's house. He stood still, considering what it would be like for Michael's sweetheart to stand here in the dark, alone, waiting for her lover to open the gate.

Socrates, having run *ventre à terre* in large circles for several minutes, returned to find his master inspecting the ground beside the wall. He joined in with enthusiasm, but nothing seemed to catch his attention at first. The earth here was firm, and had not taken clear prints, and the grasses were well trampled where many casual passers-by had come to stare over the wall. Pushing the dog aside, Gil worked his way along the boundary, and was finally rewarded by the discovery of two small square marks, sharp-edged, the length of a fingernail deep, with muddy water gathering in them. One was a handspan from the foot of the wall, the other perhaps three-fourths of an ell further out. He searched to either side along the wall, but found no more such imprints.

Standing up, he looked carefully at the wall which surrounded the bedehouse garden. The angular stones which made up its coping were at shoulder height, convenient to his eye. The rain was getting heavier, and was now running off the brim of his hat if he tipped his head forward, but the signs he was searching for showed up the more clearly.

He turned and scanned the surrounding area. The

trampled grass close by offered little information, but further away there were signs which interested him. Socrates, looking where Gil looked, put his nose down and set off on a trail just as Maistre Pierre stepped through the gate, clutching his heavy cloak round him.

'Well,' he said, 'what has the dog found?'

'I suppose the scent of whoever it was brought Naismith here,' said Gil. His friend raised his eyebrows. 'Come and look at this.'

The mason came obediently to stretch his neck and study the wet stonework. 'What am I looking at?'

'There.' Gil pointed cautiously. 'What do you see?'

'Scratches,' said Maistre Pierre after a moment. 'Two or three small scratches and a chip off the stone.' He cast Gil an interrogative look.

'I think,' said Gil, 'he was put over the wall.'

'Not through the gate?'

'Michael tells me the gate was locked. I wondered if that would make a difference, so I looked, and found this.'

'Go on.'

'I think these scratches were made by that great bunch of keys he bore, scraping on the stone as he went over.'

'Ah! And that was when his ear was torn,' said Maistre Pierre, nodding. 'It would work, though it does not explain the other marks on his face. But I would not care to lift such a burden so high myself. One person or more? Do we look for a strong man from a fair?'

'Perhaps,' Gil hedged. 'There are no footprints to show someone was carrying something heavy, but there are these.' Maistre Pierre looked where he indicated, tested the depth of the two small square impressions and frowned.

'A ladder?' he said. 'He climbed a ladder, with the corpse? In the dark?'

'Maybe,' said Gil. 'I can only find one set of marks. If it was a folding ladder, the other feet have left no trace.' He looked round. 'But if it was a ladder, we needn't look for a big man. No more than the middling size. Where is that dog?'

70

He whistled, and was answered by a peremptory bark from the nearest clump of hazel scrub.

'He has found something,' Maistre Pierre suggested.

'Surely not a squirrel, at this time of year,' said Gil. 'He was following a trail. I had better take a look. Do you see, someone has walked from here to those hazels.'

'Half the Upper Town has walked here since dawn,' complained Maistre Pierre.

Moving carefully to one side of the line of bruised grasses, they made their way towards the trees.

'Will you see Alys again today?' asked Maistre Pierre casually.

'If I can,' said Gil. His friend turned to look at him in the drizzle.

'She will be herself again once the festivities are over,' he said reassuringly. 'She has done this once before, though not so bad, a few years since when we had a feast for my fortieth name-day. At the feast itself she was the model of a good daughter, in her pearls and her best gown. All will be well.'

'Yes,' said Gil. 'It's not the feast that troubles me.'

'That will be well too,' said Maistre Pierre largely, and gave him a significant grin. 'She is sufficiently like her mother, God rest her soul, that she will make you a good wife in all ways. Do not worry, son-in-law.'

'Everyone keeps telling me that.'

'They are right.' The mason clapped him on the shoulder, and Gil grunted in response as they approached the thicket where Socrates' tail was visible waving under the branches. The dog threw them a brief look over his shoulder, but turned back to the object which had interested him among the hazel-roots, pawing at the ground round it. The coarse grey hair stood up in a ridge along his narrow back and his soft ears were pricked intently.

'Blood,' said Gil. 'He has found blood, or else a hedgehog. Good dog, leave!'

'But no,' said Maistre Pierre, 'it is something light-coloured. A piece of linen, I think.'

Socrates, recognizing that his master had taken charge of his find, sat back with his tongue hanging out, well pleased with himself. Gil bent over the object.

'Yes, linen,' he said. 'Very wet, but not particularly muddy. It has not been here long.' He straightened up to look round, and broke off a convenient twig to prod the cloth with. 'And yes, I think these are bloodstains. Good dog!'

'Is it a garment, or part of a garment? A napkin?'

'It's hemmed all round.' Gil turned another fold of the cloth. 'Neat stitches, too. It's not napery, it's a different weave, more like a towel, and far longer than it is wide. I think it's a neck-piece. A scarf.'

'Someone will miss it, in this weather,' said Maistre Pierre, tugging gloomily at his own where it was wrapped about inside the collar of his cloak to prevent the rain running down his neck. 'Whatever is such a thing doing here?'

'A good question. Don't move,' Gil requested. He lifted the wet cloth carefully on his twig and handed it to the other man, then cast about round the spot where the object had lain. 'The ground is much damper here than it is by the wall, and the dog was following a trail when he came here. Yes, indeed, there are footprints. A heel here, and there's a toe.' He bent again, pushing the wet stems of the dead grasses aside. 'Ah!'

'A complete print?' said his companion hopefully. 'Both of them?'

'Indeed, several, but I think only one person. Come and look.'

The marks were clearly visible, several footprints super-imposed as if a man had stood under the trees and shuffled nervously about while waiting for something. One print was distinct on top of the others, the clear outline of a well-shod foot.

'Smaller than mine,' said Gil, comparing his own foot with the print. 'A good sole, not much worn. Boot or shoe, I wonder? The sole is quite rigid, I suspect a boot.'

'Not helpful,' said Maistre Pierre.

'No.' Gil looked about him, and back at the gate of the bedehouse. 'This doesn't read.'

'Not read? You mean you cannot make out the prints? They seem clear to me.'

'Oh, those are easy enough. But what was he doing? He came from the gate, and stood here for a bit –'

'Dropped this.'

'– aye, possibly, and then I suppose went back to the gate. Why? These are recent prints, probably made last night. What was so important here that he would tramp about rough ground by lantern-light? Or even,' he added thoughtfully, 'in the dark.'

'Had he left something here?'

'No sign of that. And he wasn't carrying anything heavy. I wish the prints by the gate were clearer. Unless . . .'

'Unless?'

'I know someone stood by the gate for a time. And kept hearing things, so I'm told.'

'Aha! Our man came here to wait for him to leave, you mean?'

'She didn't leave, but went in through the gate, in fact,' Gil replied, sending Maistre Pierre's eyebrows up into the shadow of his hat. 'It seems Michael holds the keys to the gate and the Douglas lodging, and has taken advantage of it. I hope he can keep it quiet from his father.'

'Indeed,' said Maistre Pierre disapprovingly. 'And from her kin, whoever she is.'

'Or perhaps,' pursued Gil, 'our man found Michael's lass or someone else coming along the vennel behind him, and took refuge here until matters were quiet. But where was the corpse meantime?'

'Well, you may ask him when you find him. Now, this cloth. We take it somewhere to dry out? And dry out a little ourselves?'

'Yes, I think so.' Gil looked about him. 'Some of this makes sense, but not all. I need to think it through, and I need to know what you found in the accounts. Shall we put the keys back in the Douglas lodging and go round to Rottenrow?'

'We should speak to Millar first.'

The gate locked behind them, Gil followed the dog along the little gravel path to the door of the Douglas lodging. Looking along the row of neat houses in the rain, he saw that this end one was larger, with carving above the inscribed lintel, an upper floor, and a more elaborate outline to the windows. Socrates pawed at the door, and hurried in ahead of the two men when Gil opened it, sniffing round the floor with the air of one resuming an interrupted task.

'Not a bad lodging,' said Maistre Pierre, looking round with a professional eye. 'A snug building, indeed, if it is fifty years old. A good plan,' he added thoughtfully, 'to endow an almshouse and reserve a place for oneself.'

'The family uses it as a town lodging,' said Gil, hanging the keys on a nail on the back of the door as he had been asked and surveying the sparsely furnished outer chamber. 'It saves having to pay the burgh taxes on a townhouse, after all.'

'Yes,' said Maistre Pierre. 'That had occurred to me. What is that dog looking for?'

Socrates looked up, waved his tail, and continued on his patrol. Gil followed him, lifted the seat of the box-bench to peer into the storage space within, checked the fireside aumbry, felt carefully at the sack of meal on the overmantel, looked at the fire-irons where they stood in a box by the hearth. The dog threw him a withering glance and took his more acute senses into the inner chamber.

When, after a quarter-hour or so, Gil came down the precipitous stair with Socrates sliding behind him, Maistre Pierre was seated on the bench, his cloak thrown back and his tablets in his hand.

'The accounts are revealing,' he said, looking up. 'This is what I came out to tell you. Have you found anything?'

'Nothing of interest to us, though I had to drag the dog away from the bed in the inner chamber there,' Gil reported, smiling wryly. 'I hope the boy provided sheets for his leman. There are none there now, though there's the scraps of a love-feast.'

'Hah!' said Maistre Pierre in disapproval. 'Nothing else?'

'There's little above-stairs to see, let alone to search. I suppose Sir James will bring cushions and hangings with him to make the place habitable. Tell me about these accounts.'

'Here are the figures.' Maistre Pierre tilted the tablets so that Gil could read the columns inscribed on the green wax. 'You see, this is what comes in quarterly from one endowment and another, lands in Lanarkshire and some northwards by Kilsyth as well. That was donated ten years since by the grateful kin of one particular bedesman, it seems. The total is quite a significant sum.'

'And yet he has been making economies,' said Gil. 'Where was the money going?'

'Here,' said Maistre Pierre, turning a leaf of the tablets with a triumphant flourish. 'You see? Property by the Caichpele. Properties in Rottenrow. Properties in the Gallowgait. The records are all there, in the locked kist by his bed.'

'In whose name is this property?' enquired Gil levelly.

'In the name of Robert Naismith. And the conveyancing,' said Maistre Pierre, turning another leaf, 'was done by one Thomas Agnew.'

'Oh, indeed,' agreed Maister Millar. The community had said Nones and eaten its dinner, and the bedesmen were seated round the hall fire again, but Gil and Maistre Pierre had cornered the sub-Deacon in his own lodging. It was a single chamber, with a bed built into the panelling of one wall and a neat desk for a scholar opposite the hearth, five books on a shelf above it. There was no sign of a black cloak other than Millar's own, and no velvet hat visible. 'He's done the bedehouse's legal work ever since I've been here at any rate, I've no doubt he's – he was Deacon Naismith's man of law and all.'

'So Naismith was diverting the bedehouse's incomings to his own use,' said Gil.

Millar gave him a shocked look. 'Oh, I'm certain that canny be right. He'd no do such a thing. Would he?' he added dubiously, lowering his eyes to the figures on Maistre Pierre's tablets. 'I find this unbelievable, Maister Cunningham.'

'The figures do not lie,' said Maistre Pierre.

'You said something about a property out to the north,' Gil said.

'This one.' Maistre Pierre pointed with his thumb. 'A rich one, as you see.'

'Where is it? Who gave it?' Gil asked.

His friend shrugged. 'I was looking only at the figures. I think the donor's name was not in the papers I looked at, indeed. Do you know, Maister Millar?'

'I wouldny ken,' said Millar helplessly. 'It would be afore my time. I've never paid much mind to the bedehouse money, you understand. I take my part in the duties towards the brothers, and the Deacon's part as well half the time, and look to my studies between whiles, and he deals – dealt wi the money. Would Maister Agnew ken who was the donor, maybe?'

'I'll not ask him just yet.' Gil stared thoughtfully at the column of figures. 'Do we have the bedehouse outgoings there?'

'We do.' Maistre Pierre turned to another leaf. 'They seem to have been kept up daily, in great detail, which did not conceal that the outlays were very small for such a community. Perhaps only one-third of mine.'

'He oversaw the accounts daily,' agreed Millar. 'I tellt you that.'

Maistre Pierre nodded. 'The charitable receipts are noted and included, but even so Mistress Mudie must have worked wonders, to be feeding and physicking six

76

bedesmen and a household of six people from such an amount.'

'Oh, she does, she does. Which makes it the more vexing –' Millar stopped.

Gil eyed him for a moment, and then said, 'Talking of six bedesmen, Maister Millar, there's an odd thing. The boy Livingstone thought he saw a seventh this morning. Did you see anything?'

'When was this?' asked Maistre Pierre. Gil relayed Lowrie's account of the extra figure in the chapel, and found Millar shaking his head, an embarrassed grin on his face.

'No. No. We ken that one,' he said. 'We don't let on about it much, which I suppose is why the boy made the mistake. It's – well, to say truth, we believe it's one of the past brothers. I've seen him now and then myself, but he doesny attend every day, or even every week,' he added thoughtfully, 'whatever Anselm says.' He stopped, looking from one to the other of them. 'We get used to it,' he said.

'You are saying it is a spirit?' said Maistre Pierre with incredulity. 'A ghost?'

'Call it what you like, maister,' said Millar a little defiantly. 'I'm saying it's one of our past bedesmen, still coming to Mass where he worshipped for years, and no anything harmful.'

'But have you not called for someone to banish him?'

'Why? It's one thing the brethren and I were all agreed on. Whoever he is, he's another of our brothers, why would we do a thing like that to him? Besides, it would distress Anselm, who can see him, beyond bearing. We've prayed for his rest, maister, but it seems he still likes to hear the Mass, and there's no wrong in it, after all. Even the blessed angels rejoice at the Elevation, we're told.'

'*Ah, mon Dieu!*' said Maistre Pierre, staring at him.

'So it's possible Lowrie saw nobody,' said Gil.

'It's most likely,' said Millar earnestly. 'Nobody in this world.'

'And has anyone spoken to Agnew yet?' asked David Cunningham. 'Or indeed tellt the man's mistress, poor soul? I mind her father well, a decent man, it's a sore sicht to find the family brought down so far that she's to keep house for a clerk in this way.'

'Agnew was there this morning,' Gil reported. 'He was quite anxious for his brother. And I think one of the bedesmen had gone to tell Mistress Veitch, so we can likely assume she knows by now.'

'Maister Millar also said he would call on her,' said Maistre Pierre. He stretched his steaming legs closer to the hearth and took another swallow of spiced ale. Maggie approved of Alys, and by extension of her family, so the ale and the hearty plate of bannocks and cheese with it had appeared with only a passing reference to the time of the household meals.

'So it seems,' said the Official, clipping his spectacles on to his nose, 'as if the man Naismith has been farming the income of the bedehouse to his own benefit?'

'And considerable benefit at that,' agreed Gil. 'Enough to purchase several properties in the burgh. When would St Serf's last suffer an Archbishop's Visit, sir?'

'Who knows?' said his uncle, considering briefly. He rested his elbows on the arms of his great chair and steepled his fingers in front of his chin. 'No in my time, that's for certain. Robert Blacader has other matters on his mind than Visitations.'

'So the accounts have never been audited, and nobody but the old men could say him nay,' said Gil. 'Of the five I have met, only two are clear in their heads, and one of those is stone-deaf.'

'Do you think that was why he was killed?' asked the Official.

'I don't know yet,' said Gil.

'What have you found, then?'

Gil looked at Maistre Pierre, who raised his eyebrows but said nothing and reached for another bannock.

'Naismith left the almshouse last night, just before they said Vespers, which would be about half an hour after five by what Millar tells us. He went out wearing the same clothes he was found dead in, and the cloak and hat of his office over them. The almshouse people think he was going to see his mistress.'

'Who lives by the Caichpele,' supplied Maistre Pierre through a mouthful of bannock.

'Thomas Agnew says he was wi him later in his chamber in the tower, but left after an hour or so. He was heard in his lodging, well after nine o'clock,' Gil continued, nodding at the interruption. 'His bed had been slept in and the dole Sissie Mudie left had been eaten. This morning he may or may not have been seen at Mass, though if he was there he wasn't in his own seat. And then, not ten minutes after the Mass, he was found knifed in the bedehouse garden, between a locked gate and a locked door, stiff and cold as if he'd been dead near twelve hours.'

'Well!' said David Cunningham, but it was drowned by an urgent exclamation.

'Who? Who are you talking about?' Tib stood at the door to the kitchen stairs, white as the flour on the apron which covered her old grey gown. Socrates rose from his place at Gil's feet and padded forward to greet her. 'Is it someone dead at the bedehouse?'

'Aye, indeed,' said her uncle, turning his head. 'Seems the Deacon has been stabbed.'

'Stabbed?' she repeated blankly. 'The Deacon? Who's that? Who by?'

'That's what your brother has to find out.'

'But when did it happen?' Tib demanded. Socrates thrust his nose against her apron, tail waving, and she pushed him away.

'Last night sometime,' said Gil. 'Who do you know at the bedehouse?'

She gave a little gasp, and shook her head. Socrates sat down and grinned up at her face, then turned to look over his shoulder at Gil.

'No one,' Tib said earnestly, ignoring the dog. 'But it's so close. Just over the way and down the vennel.'

'Never fear, Lady Tib,' said Maistre Pierre in bracing tones. 'Your brother and uncle will keep you safe.'

'Yes,' she said, with a contrived smile. Her eyes slid away from Gil's, and she wound her fingers in the folds of her apron. He was about to speak when there was a knocking at the main door of the house.

'Tell Maggie I'll get that,' he said, rising.

'If it's another death, say you're from home,' recommended the mason.

What's worrying Tib? Gil wondered, making his way down the stair to the door, the dog at his heels. She seemed frightened for someone, rather than by something. It has certainly changed her tune from this morning, if she accepts that I might be of some use, he thought, lifting the latch and swinging the heavy door back.

'Well, Gil,' said the foremost of the three Cistercians on the doorstep. 'Let us in out the rain, and then I'll wish you happy.'

'Dorothea!' he said in delight.

By the time Sister Dorothea and her retinue of plump lay sister and small elderly confessor-cum-secretary had been drawn in, welcomed, and dried off, Maggie had appeared with more spiced ale and a large jug of wine, followed by Tib bearing a platter of new girdle-cakes.

'And I sent Tam to tell them at the court you'd be held up, maister,' Maggie added to the Official, and set down the tray to seize hold of Dorothea. 'Oh, my, Lady Dawtie, you're looking well. You've no changed a bit. Cellarer, is it, now, and keeping the accounts? You that used to hide from your lady mother when it was time to learn your numbers?'

'Sub-Cellarer,' Dorothea corrected her, emerging from the embrace with aplomb.

'We'll pray for your promotion,' said Maggie, and pushed her down on to a stool. 'Sit there, Lady Dawtie, my dearie, and hae a glass of wine. It's the good stuff.'

'I'd rather a wee cake,' said Dorothea. 'Herbert, Agnes, I commend Maggie's girdle-cakes. That's what I've come to Glasgow for, Maggie, no my brother's marriage.'

Tib, the apron discarded, helped to serve out the wine and cakes very properly, eyeing Dorothea under her lashes. Gil watched this with some amusement but could not blame her; he hardly recognized their sister himself. Had Dorothea really been this confident, this calm, at sixteen? It seemed unlikely, despite Maggie's assertion. He remembered a thin, hungry girl, impatient of the distractions of the world, always at her prayers. As he should have been himself at the time, given the plans their parents had nurtured for him, but at fourteen there were more exciting things to be doing.

'And I hear from Mother,' said Dorothea, passing her confessor the platter of cakes, 'that you've a benefice and a title now, Gil. Is that your doing, sir?'

'No, it's all your brother's own doing,' said Canon Cunningham. 'I reminded Robert Blacader of his existence, and so I believe did your mother, a number of times,' he added remotely, 'but it was Gil's own work made Robert that pleased wi him.'

'You put him to the blush,' said Maistre Pierre.

'But what work is that? Not this business of hunting down murderers, surely. Does Blacader think that worth a benefice?'

'He seems to,' said Gil.

'Oh, is that why they wanted you at St Serf's the day?' said Tib in tones of innocence. 'I thought it was just because you were at the college with that man Kennedy.'

'St Serf's?' said Dorothea. 'Is that the bedehouse? Is something wrong there?'

'Robert Naismith the Deacon was found stabbed this

81

morning,' said Gil baldly. She bowed her head and crossed herself, her lips moving.

'And has anyone tellt the lassie Veitch yet, that's what I'd like to know,' said Maggie from her position by the small cupboard. 'You mind Marion Veitch, don't you no, Lady Dawtie?'

'Marion? What's she – oh!' said Dorothea. Her face, narrowly visible within the folds of white coif and black veil, took on an expression of dismay. 'Oh, poor Marion. Where's she staying? I must visit her.'

'Veitch?' said Tib. 'You mean Marion that used to live at Kittymuir? I suppose that's why her brother was in Glasgow, if she lives here too. What's she to do with St Serf's?'

'Her brother?' said Gil. She threw him a look. 'Which brother? When did you meet him?'

'It was John, the one that went to sea, but I never met him,' she said lightly. 'Just I saw him in the street. Yesterday.'

'Sissie Mudie mentioned him today,' Gil recalled. 'I wonder what he's doing in Glasgow.'

'Visiting his sister,' suggested Canon Cunningham. 'Visiting their uncle. Did the uncle not teach you at the grammar school in Hamilton, Gilbert?'

'Frankie Veitch!' said Gil. 'I never fitted it together. Aye, he did, sir.'

'I must,' said Maistre Pierre with reluctance, 'go back to the *chantier* before dark. *Madame, j'suis enchanté de vous connaître.*' He bowed across the hearth to Dorothea, and she inclined her head in response. 'Perhaps your brother would bring you to supper with us tomorrow?'

'Indeed, aye, sir,' said Dorothea. 'Herbert and I are to spend the day with men of law, about the rents from our Glasgow properties. I'll be glad of something to look forward to at the end of it. Will I meet your daughter?'

'For certain.'

Dorothea smiled, her face lighting up in the way Gil recalled. 'I'm truly impatient to meet her, maister. A lassie who can wrench my brother from his destined career, and then convince Mother it was right, must be worth knowing. I hope he values her as high as she does him.'

Tib's face darkened. Gil was aware that his own expression changed, and also that Dorothea, as acute as their mother, had noticed both.

'How long can you stay?' he asked hastily. 'Have they found you somewhere to lie at the castle?'

Tib's expression soured still further, but she said nothing. Dorothea admitted to lodging at the castle, and began a lively account of a disastrous visit she had made to another Cistercian house which she forbore to name, and the moment passed.

But later, when she was bundled up in her travelling cloak again and striding down Rottenrow beside Gil, she said, 'What's eating at Tib?'

Gil shrugged. 'Who kens? She read me a fine rigmarole this morn when she arrived, about no being passed about like a parcel, and no wishing to stay wi Mother or Margaret or Kate. Likely it's to do wi first Kate marrying and now me, and she's left at home wi no tocher.'

'Kate was wedded wi no tocher,' said Dorothea thoughtfully.

'Augie Morison's doing well enough no to look for either coin or land wi her,' said Gil, smiling. 'The man's besotted on her, besides. Who we'd get to take a wild wee termagant like Tib I wouldny ken.'

They reached the end of Rottenrow and crossed the Wyndhead before Dorothea went on, 'Gil, did Mother no tell me this is a love match, you and Alys Mason?'

'It is,' said Gil.

She looked up at him through the drizzle. 'On both sides?'

He opened his mouth to say, *Yes, of course,* and closed it, recalling again the tension in Alys's slender body within his arms, the way she withdrew from his kiss. Dorothea fixed her gaze on the towers of St Mungo's, and after a moment remarked, 'I mind Marion Veitch well. It seems she was left with nothing.'

'I never heard,' said Gil. 'I knew John went to sea.'

It is a love match, he wanted to say. Alys feels as I do, I know she does. *I love my lady pure, And she loves me again.* But the words would not come to his mouth.

'I'd a word wi our uncle just now,' said Dorothea. 'The oldest brother died in the rebellion and they couldny pay the fines. John was at sea already, and the middle brother – William, was it? – had gone for a priest, and it seems as if Marion didny fancy keeping house for him and took this man Naismith's offer when it came to her.'

'William Veitch was a sleekit wee nyaff,' said Gil intemperately. 'I mind once he got me into a fight wi John with his lies, and got us both a beating. I'd not blame Marion if she didny want to share his rooftree.'

The directions Maggie had provided led them to a wynd off the Drygate. The houses along its muddy length were small, but seemed in good repair. Gossiping maidservants sheltered in the doorways, and the high wooden walls of the Caichpele were visible beyond the rooftops, though it seemed unlikely that tennis was being played in the steady rain.

The furthest house along the wynd was a two-storey structure of wood and lime-washed plaster, with a well-built chimney issuing from the centre of the thatched roof, and a tiny stone kitchen at the side of the house. They stopped before the door, and Gil rattled the wrought-iron ring up and down the twisted bar above the latch. Above them, a shutter opened, and a voice called, 'Who's that tirling at the pin?'

'I'm Dorothea Cunningham. Is the mistress home?' said Dorothea, stepping back to look up past the eaves-drips. 'We'd like a word.'

The maidservant looked back over her shoulder, then leaned out, nodding, and beckoned them in.

'Aye, come up, madam, come up, maister.' She withdrew and closed the shutter. By the time they had stepped inside and fastened the latch she was coming down the narrow stair at the back of the house, a pretty girl with her hair loose, clad in a grubby kirtle with the sleeves rolled well up and carrying a small child of indeterminate gender on her hip.

'Come away in, sir and madam,' she said. 'The mistress is up the stair. She's packing.'

Chapter Five

Marion Veitch was certainly packing.

They could hear her tramping back and forward across the boards as they crossed the hall and followed the maid-servant up the stair. Emerging into the warmth of the upper floor, Gil saw first a partly dismantled tester-bed, its red woollen hangings in disarray. Then a woman appeared from the shadows behind the bedhead, carrying an armful of folded linen and heading for an open kist by the window.

Gil had last seen Marion, he reckoned, at the dangerous age of twelve or thirteen when the parents of girls began to argue about how soon they should be married off. This girl's parents had waited too long, and she was now that awkward commodity, a pretty woman with no money of her own. Like Tib, he reflected, though a lot older. She had been a sweet, well-behaved child, and had grown into a beauty of the conventional type, with a pale, fair skin, golden hair visible under her linen coif, large blank blue eyes and a pink mouth made for kissing which just now was stretched in a doubtful smile as she stared at them. She had been weeping, he thought.

'Marion,' said Dorothea, and bent the knee in a curtsy, then went forward with her hands out. 'How are you?'

'Dorothea,' said Marion. 'Sister Dorothea Cunningham. A course, that's what Eppie said.' She put the linen down on the mattress, and took Dorothea's hands, then embraced her. 'I'm well, I thank you. How are you? Dorothea, my dearie, how long is it? I'd never ha known you. And you, Gil, it must be years. Will you stay to supper?'

'No, no,' said Dorothea reassuringly, 'we're expected back at my uncle's, but I had to see you when I heard of your trouble.'

Relief crossed Marion's face, but all she said was, 'Come to the fire, come and be seated, the both of you. Eppie, get Danny to bring us a refreshment, will you, lass.'

Eppie, who had set the child down, picked it up again and made for the stairs.

'He'll likely no bring it himself,' she warned, 'the strunt he's in the day, mistress.'

'It must be twelve years,' said Dorothea, sitting down on one of the pair of cushioned settles. 'We've all changed. I'm right sorry to see you again at a moment like this, Marion. I had to come by when I heard of it. But has none of your neighbours come in to sit with you?'

Marion shrugged. She was warmly but unbecomingly dressed in a dark brown high-necked gown, with a grey furred loose robe over it which hung open and lay in pools of marten-skin round her feet when she sat opposite her guests across the small brazier. A gold chain of strange work lay about her neck under the robe. Without the armful of linen to mask it her pregnancy was visible but not, Gil thought, very far advanced.

'They've been at the door, the most of them, but I sent them away, I'm too taigled. But it's no a bother to see you, after all this time,' she said, 'I was just packing. Gil, you're a man of law these days, are you no? Can you tell me how much of this I can lay claim to? I'd no like to go off wi something I've no right to take.'

Gil closed his mouth, swallowed, and said carefully, 'Your own clothes, your jewellery, items like your combs and spinning wheel and such like, are all paraphernal. That is,' he translated, seeing her anxious look, 'they're your own property and you can take them where you like. Also anything of the bairn's,' he added, 'clothes and toys and so forth.'

'But do you have to leave immediately?' asked Dorothea. 'Surely, whoever inherits the house, they'll give you time to find somewhere else.'

'Aye, likely,' said Marion. There was a short silence.

'I'm sorry about Maister Naismith's death,' said Dorothea, trying again. 'He'll be a sore miss to you, surely.'

'No, I wouldny say that,' pronounced Marion, gazing out of the open shutters at the lit windows of the house opposite. There was another silence. Gil slid a look at his sister, and found her eyeing him round her veil. He cleared his throat, and their hostess turned the wide blue gaze on him.

'Marion, how much did Andro Millar tell you?' he asked.

She considered briefly. 'My uncle Frankie came by wi the word first, and then my brother John, and Andro came later, but they never told me a lot. Just that the Deacon was dead. They found him in the bedehouse garden the morn. Is that right?'

'That's right,' agreed Gil. 'They never said how he had died?' She shook her head. 'He was stabbed, Marion.'

'*Stabbed?*' she repeated sharply.

Gil nodded. 'It was murder. I'm Blacader's Quaestor, and I'm pursuing the death to bring whoever did it to justice.'

'No need for that,' she said, the brief moment of animation over.

'Everyone deserves justice,' said Dorothea. Marion smiled kindly at her, but said nothing.

'When did you see him last?' Gil asked.

'Who, the Deacon? Yestreen, it would be. He was here at supper-time. He ate his supper wi the household.'

'What did you serve?' Gil asked.

'Stewed kale wi lentils, and a dish of roastit mutton,' she said promptly, 'and a plate of apple fritters to follow.'

'And Malvoisie to drink?'

'No,' she said blankly. 'Just ale. And my brother John was here. You'll mind John, a course. He's home from the sea, from Dumbarton, where his ship's in the now. Is that no good news?' she said, a smile crossing the empty façade. 'He fetched up at the door at noon yesterday, and I was that pleased to see him. Four year he's been away this time, him and – He brought me this chain,' she touched it vaguely, 'he says it's Moorish make.'

'It's a bonnie thing,' said Dorothea. 'You must have been thankful to see him. Was he here at supper too?'

'Aye.'

'How long did Maister Naismith stay?' asked Gil. 'Did you sit talking after supper?'

'No,' she said, the blank look returning. 'Naismith was to go out, so he said, about some business of his own, so he gaed off, and my brother was here a while longer talking over – talking over old times.' Was that a break in her voice? 'Then John went off and all, to his lodging down the High Street, and I went to my bed.'

'So you saw Naismith about six or seven o'clock?' Gil said.

'Aye, that would be it,' she agreed.

'What time would it be when he left?'

'Maybe half an hour after seven.' She sounded vague. 'Would that be right, Eppie?'

'Aye, I'd say so, mistress,' said Eppie, returning with the child on her hip. 'Can I leave the wean wi you a minute till I carry up this tray? Danny's still in a mood.'

The little one was passed over, smiling at its mother and, more shyly, at the visitors. It was an attractive child, dressed in a tunic of fine red wool protected by two layers of linen bib and apron. A mop of dark curls overhung a little pale-skinned face with huge blue eyes like its mother's. They could pose for an altarpiece, thought Gil.

'And who's this?' asked Dorothea, smiling back at the child.

'This is Frankie,' said Marion unhelpfully. 'We named her for my uncle,' she added, finally providing the detail Gil wanted. 'He's been right good to me. She's being a bit clingy the day, aren't you, my wee poppet? So Eppie's been minding her till I get this packing done. Make your obedience to the lady and gentleman, Frankie.'

After a little more coaxing Frankie slid off the settle, performed a wobbly curtsy, and hid her face in her mother's lap when it was praised. Marion and Dorothea exchanged indulgent glances.

'Where was Maister Naismith going when he left here?' Gil asked.

'He never said,' Marion declared. 'He was – he wasny given to discussing his business wi me,' she added firmly.

'But did it seem like something he was looking forward to, maybe an evening with friends,' persisted Gil, 'or was it a matter of business? How was he when he left?'

'Just ordinary,' said Marion. Eppie, reappearing on the stair with the tray in her hands, cast a sharp glance at her mistress but said nothing. 'Neither up nor down,' Marion elaborated. 'Will you have a cup of buttered ale?'

The refreshment was served out by Eppie, the ale steaming in the wooden beakers. It must, Gil reflected, have been already hot for the servants' mid-afternoon break, to have appeared so promptly. There was a plate of little cakes to hand round after it, at which Frankie emerged from her mother's skirts looking hopeful.

'You can have one cake,' said Marion, 'and then go down wi Eppie and have another one. You can come back to Mammy later.'

Gil watched as the two left, then began again.

'Marion, did Maister Millar tell you anything else?' She shook her head. 'There was someone in the Deacon's lodging by the time Millar got home last night, but we don't know where he was before that.'

'But I thought he was slain in the night,' said Marion, looking troubled, 'or maybe right early this morn. Was it no someone inside the bedehouse? Why does it matter where he was afore that?'

'It's quite possible it was someone inside,' agreed Gil non-committally, 'but if we know what his movements

90

were last night, who he met or spoke to, we might learn why he was killed.'

'Oh.' She stared at him with those wide blue eyes.

'You said he got here at supper-time. When would that be?'

'After they said Compline at the bedehouse? They're earlier than St Mungo's or St Nicholas, so Sissie can get the old men to bed and get her evening to herself. It was about his usual time,' she asserted.

'And he left about half an hour after seven. So he was here maybe an hour and a half, and had supper.' She nodded. 'What did you talk about? Was he glad to see your brother here at supper?'

'Aye, he was.' Was that a trace of reluctance? 'We spoke of this and that. My brother's prospects, the voyages he's made. The Deacon's rents. Your marriage,' she added, with a slight smile.

'His rents?' said Gil. 'Was there any sort of problem with his finances?'

'No that he mentioned. I think all was well there,' she said vaguely.

'And then he went out. He didny come back?'

'No. Why would he do that?'

'Could he have been going on to friends? Who were his friends?'

'He never said where he was going. Oh, he'd friends,' she added, a faint bitter note in her voice. 'All well-doing gentlemen of his own sort. Maister Agnew, Maister Walkinshaw, Maister – I canny mind. They've supped in this house, but I haveny met them.'

Gil frowned, aware of his sister looking at him in puzzlement, but decided to let that one pass meantime.

'So he left this house about half an hour after seven,' he said. She nodded.

'And that was the last you saw him,' said Dorothea. Marion nodded again, like a fairground toy. 'Marion, will I come wi you when you witness his shrouding? You'll want to say a farewell to him, will you no?'

'Oh, I'll no be there,' said Marion. 'I've nothing I want to say to Robert Naismith.'

Gil lost patience.

'Why not?' he demanded bluntly.

There was a pause, in which Eppie's voice could be heard downstairs; then Marion closed her eyes and put up her hand. It covered her face, but did not conceal the way her mouth twisted, or the tears which spilled from under her dark eyelashes. Dorothea set down her own beaker and crossed to sit beside her, taking her free hand in a comforting clasp. Marion put her head down on the creamy wool shoulder, golden hair tumbling loose to shine in the candlelight as her cap slipped sideways, and a great wail escaped her.

Dorothea caught Gil's eye and deliberately indicated the stair.

Following the voices, Gil found Eppie in the inner room downstairs, leaning against the frame of the kitchen door-way, her spindle in her hand. The child sat at her feet, crooning quietly to a wooden mommet. They both looked round as he crossed the room, but the voice grumbling in the kitchen continued.

'Who she thinks she is I'd like to ken, it's all ower the town she hasny a penny to call her own but what the man Naismith gave her, but there she goes, setting herself above honest working folk –'

'Danny,' said Eppie warningly. The voice was silenced, and its owner stepped into view, a small man with a belligerent expression and receding ginger hair. He was wrapped in an apron even more enveloping than the one which protected the child, but the sleeves of his jerkin were mottled with stains and white blotches and he clutched a wooden spoon in a menacing way in one broad hand. This was clearly the cook. Beyond him another young woman was rolling pastry at the big table.

Gil glanced quickly at the man's soft deerskin house shoes. The spreading folds of hide made it difficult to judge the size of the feet within, but they seemed to be large.

'You're Maister Cunningham that dwells in Rottenrow, aren't you?' said Eppie, and cast her spindle. 'It's you that's getting wedded next week, isn't it no?' she went on, drawing out the thread from the roll of carded wool in her other hand. 'No that many gets wed in the Upper Town.'

'That's so,' Gil admitted.

She nodded, watching the spindle twirl and swing. 'I thought that. We've the plans all laid for the rough music,' she assured him, and caught the spindle at the moment before it stopped turning.

Gil managed a smile, but Danny said, 'No wi my cooking pots you're no, Eppie Dunlop.'

The girl with the rolling pin giggled, and Eppie threw him a look.

'Oh, you,' she said. 'We'll use others, then, and you'll no get any of the sweetmeats when we're done.'

Another thing to remember, thought Gil in dismay. The night before the wedding at the groom's house, the wedding night at the bride's house: a serenade of bawdy songs accompanied by the beating of pots and pan-lids and any musical instruments whose players could be persuaded to join in, a piper, maybe, or one of the shawms from the burgh band, something good and loud like that. They would expect to be rewarded with sweetmeats and strong drink. Maybe Maggie would have that in hand.

'Were you all three here in the house yestreen?' he asked.

'Aye, we were,' said Eppie, winding-on her new thread, 'though Bel went home after her supper. Danny and I both live in,' she added, and cast the spindle again. 'I sleep up-by, wi the bairn, and my brother has his bed in the kitchen where it's warm.'

'Brother?' said Gil, startled, looking from one to the other.

'Oh, aye,' said Eppie, laughing. 'We're no like, are we?

93

He takes after our faither, the wee baldy man he was, and I'm the spit image of our mother when she was young. Or so my auntie tells us. Maister Naismith hired us thegither.'

'So will that be you all wi no place now?' Gil asked in sympathetic tones.

Bel shrugged, and Danny snarled something, and turned back to a pot on the charcoal stove. Eppie said more philosophically, 'Maybe, maybe no. She's no notion what was in the maister's will.'

'He won't have had the time to make one, surely,' said Gil.

'Oh, aye,' said Eppie. 'Did she no say? That's what they were talking about over their supper, her and the maister and her brother John Veitch.'

'Eppie,' said Danny in the same warning tone she had used.

'Well, we were all in here at the table thegither,' said Eppie. 'That's a bonnie man, her brother,' she added. 'I never saw him afore, but the moment I clapped my een on him, there on the doorsill, I kent who he must be.' She sighed, and the girl with the rolling-pin sighed in sympathy. 'And the bonnie things he's brought the mistress, too.'

'What did he have to say about the will?' Gil asked.

'Oh, aye. Well, the maister said,' she recounted, 'that he was wanting to make a new will, and he'd be going on to see his man of law after his supper to get it drawn up.'

'Draw?' said Frankie in a little piping voice at her feet. 'Frankie draw?'

'No the now, my poppet. Go and put Annabella to bed in Danny's shoe, see, over there. And John Veitch asked him,' she continued, the spindle idle in her hand, 'since the mistress said nothing, what he was looking to alter in it. Then he said he'd made other plans for the future, and he'd be wanting to leave his property elsewhere because of them. Then I think maybe the mistress kicked her brother under the board, for he fell silent, but after we drew the cloth and turned the board up, they went above stairs and there was a roaring tulzie, you could ha heard it in St Mungo's.'

'I certainly heard it down here,' said Danny sourly.

'What was it about?' Gil asked.

'All about the will, a course. He never said what the other plans were,' said Eppie in some regret, 'or no that I heard, but he was saying he'd leave this house and some other property to someone else, and if the bairn she's carrying should be a son he said he'd leave my mistress a house he owns down off the Gallowgait and if no then she was to be out of here when her forty days was up, and –'

'Making notes, were ye?' said Danny, peering into a saucepan. Bel, listening avidly, jumped and applied herself to the pastry again.

'Did he name the legatee?' Gil asked. 'The person he was leaving this house to,' he corrected himself.

'And what's that to you if he did?' demanded another voice behind Gil. He turned, and found himself looking at a large man in a furred gown, standing with booted feet planted well apart and glaring at him from the other doorway. Like Eppie, Gil was in no doubt about who this was. He had changed in ten years, but his fair hair and blue eyes creased at the corners would have identified him, even before Frankie abandoned her mommet, scrambled to her feet and scurried forward exclaiming,

'Unca John! Unca John!'

The scowl changed to a smile.

'Where's my best lassie?' said John Veitch. He bent and scooped the child up, tossing her high so that she squealed with laughter. 'Where's your mammy, wee lass?'

'Up,' said Frankie, pointing to the stairs. 'Up wi lady. I go up later.'

'And you're down here questioning Eppie,' said the seaman, glowering at Gil again.

'D'you no mind me, John? Gil Cunningham? I'm Robert Blacader's Quaestor now,' said Gil, wondering if he would ever get used to explaining this. 'I'm charged wi looking into any murders in Glasgow, or wherever he sends me.'

'What's it to do wi Robert Blacader?' demanded Veitch. 'Aye, I mind you. You're the youngest brother, aren't you no? And there were all those sisters you had and all.'

'That'll be one of them up above wi the mistress the now,' said Eppie. 'A white nun, she is. Maister Cunningham was asking about the supper, and I was telling him when the maister left.'

'Aye,' said Veitch rather grimly. 'Too busy to talk to me about my sister. Then I come up the hill the day to get a word wi him at the hour he appointed, face to face and man to man, and I hear at the gate that he's deid. But what's this about the supper? Surely he wasny poisoned? That canny be it, the rest o us have taken no hurt,' he added with a sardonic look as Danny's indignant snarl rose from the kitchen. 'And what's it to do wi Blacader?'

'This is Blacader's burgh, John,' Gil reminded him. 'No like where we grew up out in the Hamiltons' lands. If Naismith's killer can be taken, Blacader or his court will deal wi him first before he's sent to Edinburgh. And meantime, can you tell me when you left here last night?'

'Me?' The sailor contemplated the ceiling briefly, then smiled at the child whom he was still holding on his arm. 'I sang this wee one a song when she was in her cradle, didn't I, my flower?'

'Passy awa,' said Frankie triumphantly.

'That's right, a clever lassie. *Pasay l'agua, Julietta dama.* And then my sister and I had a long word. She was a wee thing distressed, as you'll understand if Eppie's tongue's been wagging already,' said Veitch disapprovingly. In the kitchen Danny clattered the saucepan on the stove and swore quietly. 'It would be, maybe, about nine o' the clock when I came away. Is that right, Eppie?' Eppie shrugged, and cast her spindle again. 'I went away down the High Street to where I'm lodged wi the Widow Napier, and sat a while talking wi her and all, her man's brother was a sailor and she likes to hear the tales, and then I gaed tae my beddie,' he concluded.

Frankie wriggled in his arms, and he bent to set her on the ground. She ran to her mommet, still fast asleep in a shoe much the size of Gil's, and began to sing to it. Veitch looked at her, then at Gil, and jerked his head towards the outer room. The clattering of Danny's pans followed as the two men moved out of earshot of the child.

'Where are you lodged?' Gil asked, sitting down on the tapestry-covered stool Veitch indicated.

'I tellt you. The Widow Napier.'

'Aye, but where's that? Where does she dwell?'

'Oh, I see. Away down the Fishergate. St Catherine's Wynd. It's right handy for the shore.'

'Why not here, with your sister?'

'I wasny certain how she was placed.' That sardonic look again. 'As it turned out, I was right to be wary. The deceased was away less happy to clap his een on me than Marion herself was, poor lass.'

'Was he, now?' said Gil. 'So he'd not have wished you to stay here?'

Veitch laughed shortly.

'No,' he said.

'And you never saw Naismith again after he left here,' said Gil.

'No,' said Veitch again. 'He was long away and talking wi his man of law by the time I went out. Or so I suppose.'

'Do you know who that is?'

The seaman reflected briefly, staring unfocused at the well-swept floorboards. Gil took the opportunity to inspect his feet, which were encased in a pair of heavy boots, well-worn and tarry but well-cared-for and rather larger than Gil's own.

'Arnot? Andrews? Something like that.' The man glanced at Gil, his mouth twisting. 'I was more concerned wi my sister, you can believe it.'

'I do. Did he name the alternative legatee?'

97

'No,' said Veitch, 'but it shouldny be hard to find out who she is, if you can find the man of law.'

'She?'

'Aye. Did Marion no tell you? That's what really couped her ower. Three and a half year she's kept this house and warmed his bed for him, she's carrying his bairn, and he picked that moment, over the supper-table wi the household listening, to tell her he was to be wed. And no to her. So can you wonder that I spent the morn hunting for a man of law that would take on her case?'

'She told me little more than that,' said Dorothea. 'But what she did tell me agrees in substance.'

It had stopped raining, but neither of them wished to loiter in the raw cold, and they had taken refuge in the chapel of the bigger almshouse of St Nicholas, right by the Wyndhead. Seated on the stone bench which ran round the box-like nave, Gil had summarized what he had learned from the servants and from John Veitch.

'What more did you get from her?' he asked. She folded her hands in her lap and considered them for a moment in the attenuated light from the south windows. Suddenly, irrelevantly, he recognized the biggest change in her. The hunger he recalled had been fed, but there was also, under the poise and the air of command, that stillness at the centre that he had seen in one or two other great religious he had known.

'The oldest brother, who held Kittymuir, died at Stirling Field,' she said now, 'the same as Father and our brothers. As Uncle David said. It's a strange thing,' she digressed, 'that so few were slain on the King's side, the late King's side, and yet we seem to know the most of them.'

'No,' objected Gil, 'none so strange surely, it tells where the fighting was thickest. So they were left without money, were they?'

'From what she says,' said Dorothea, recalled to her account, 'John was at sea, which must be right, and the sleekit William was a priest by then, somewhere over in Ayrshire, and their mother died of grief that same summer. So when they couldny pay the fine in the autumn, Marion was put out of the land, and took refuge with William in the first place. Then William found she was carrying Frankie, which can't,' she said thoughtfully, counting on her fingers, 'have been before Yule of that year, of '88, or even the next spring, and he put her out of his house and all. And John still being at sea, she accepted Naismith's offer of shelter and she's kept that house for him ever since. I suspect it may have been William who got Naismith the post here in Glasgow as part of the bargain.'

They looked at each other in the failing light.

'There are gaps,' said Gil. She nodded. 'But I suppose she has held the house rent-free more than three years. Well, hardly rent-free,' he admitted, 'but the law doesny allow for that form of service. She has had only custom on her side to prevent him putting her out of it when he pleased. Had he any other requirements of her?'

'He had her dine him and his friends every few weeks,' said Dorothea, 'provide the dinner from the money he gave her, but hide herself and the bairn out of sight. She did some fine sewing for St Mungo's, hoping to turn a penny or two of her own that way, and he took the money she got by it.'

'Ah!' said Gil. 'That would have counted for her if it had come to law. It could be considered as rent, even without a contract.'

'Aye, but it hasny come to law.' Dorothea looked down at her hands again. 'And finally he announced in front of the household that he planned to be married to someone else, who would get her house.'

'He's humbled her,' said Gil. 'I suppose she wouldny wish to show that to me.'

Dorothea turned to give him an approving look.

'You're right,' she said. 'She never loved him, but she's done her duty according to their original agreement, and he served her like that.'

'He's no been a man I'd care to have either as friend or client,' said Gil roundly.

Dorothea laughed.

'There's my brother,' she said. He raised his eyebrows. 'It was strange to watch you the now, acting like a man of law, questioning Marion so clearly, acting just the way I would myself with one of our pupils in trouble.'

'Why not? A man of law's what I am.'

'No doubt of that. None the less, Gil, last time I saw you you were fourteen and your voice was just changing. But there the now you sounded like the brother I mind.'

'You've changed and all, but no as much as I have, then, for I'd have known you anywhere,' said Gil. 'Are you happy, Dawtie? What's it like, being the bride of Christ? It's what you aye wanted, but is it what you expected?'

Her face lit up, visible even in the dimness.

'Gil, you can have no idea. This is what I was made for, in particular since I've been sub-Cellarer. To have charge of so much, to be responsible for my share of the House's dispositions, and wi all that, to be – no just allowed, but required to take all the time I could wish to my prayers – there was once a sister, one of ours, a German, wrote that she felt *like a crumb of bread dipped in a jar of honey*. That's it exact.'

'And the obedience to your superiors?'

Her long mouth quirked. 'Oh, well. It's the price one pays. If I'd stayed in the world I'd be obedient to Mother, or a husband, or someone.'

'Or to me,' he said. The quirk became a wry smile.

'Or to you,' she agreed. 'Just as well I'm no, you've enough to deal wi, what wi Tib and Alys. What is it between you and Alys, Gil? I thought, from what Mother wrote, the lass chose you herself, but I don't see all well wi you just now.'

'No – no, it's fine,' he said, aware of his face stiffening.

'Is she changing her mind, or something?'

'I . . .' he began. 'A course not, but . . .'

'But?' She watched him for a moment, then said, 'Is

100

she maybe a wee thing less loving than she seemed a while since?'

'How did you ken that?' he asked helplessly.

'I've seen one or two brides in the weeks afore their marriage. And it happens to novices, indeed we worry if it doesny. They start to wonder, to have doubts, to question the decision.'

'I – that's what I'm afraid of.'

'You're in no doubt yoursel, Gil?'

'No! No, *My love will not refreyd be, nor afound*. But . . .' he halted, unable to bring out the words. She eyed him with sympathy, and finally supplied:

'If she had changed her mind, you wouldny hold her to it.' He nodded dumbly. 'So of course you darena ask what's wrong for fear it might be that.'

It was almost a relief to have it spoken. He drew a deep breath, and nodded again. She put a hand over his, and they sat in silence for a while.

'Dawtie, I'll need to go out after supper,' said Gil after a time. 'I'm sorry for it, when you've just got here.'

'Mm?' said Dorothea, as if from a great distance. She turned to look at him again. 'Never apologize. I can go down to see Kate. What do you have to do?'

He sighed. 'I ought to go back to the bedehouse. And I need to see Agnew.'

'Who is that? Oh, Naismith's man of law, is it? And brother of one of the bedesmen, you said.'

'Aye. He has a chamber in the Consistory tower, I can likely find him there.'

'What will you ask him?'

'About the will. About whether Naismith met him yestreen. Whether he kens who Naismith was planning to marry, since nobody else seems to.' He got to his feet, and stretched his back. 'He'll not have the answer to the other question I have just now.'

'And what is that?'

'Who was Frankie's father? Naismith was a well-set-up fellow, going bald, but brown-haired. Marion's hair is gold, and her brother's near as fair. The wee one has Marion's eyes, but she never got a head of curls that colour from Naismith. Her father must be dark, and probably curly-headed.'

'And light-eyed,' said Dorothea. 'Brown eyes carry strong, remember.'

'Aye,' said Gil. So Alys's children will have brown eyes, he thought. That's if – that's assuming –

'All will be well, Gil,' said his sister, watching him in the shadows. She patted his elbow then cocked her head at the darkening windows and continued, 'I must go up to the castle and say Vespers. Have you time to get over to the Consistory before Maggie has the supper on the table?'

Asking one of the clerks of the Consistory tower at the west end of St Mungo's got Gil directions to a chamber on an upper floor, above the courtrooms by a different stair from the one he himself used. Climbing up the spiral he was aware of the smell of success at this end of the tower; traces of sandalwood and cedarwood from furs which had to be guarded from the moth mingled with beeswax (furniture worth polishing and servants to polish it, he thought) and the distinctive scent of the heavy straw matting, all shot through with the familiar musty intimation of paper, parchment and ink. On the landing he had been referred to, the smell of matting was even stronger, and fragments of straw lay underfoot as if someone had recently swept out the chambers. He recalled the flakes of straw in the sleeve of Naismith's fur gown. This must be where they had come from.

He tapped on Agnew's door and called the man's name, but there was no response. After a moment the door to the next chamber opened and a head popped out, level with his elbow.

'Tammas is away down to St Serf's,' it announced. 'Oh,

it's you. David Cunningham's nephew, are you no? Blacader's Quaestor, now, they tell me.'

Gil admitted this, and the other man stepped on to the landing and tipped his head back to look at him, holding his legal bonnet on with one hand. He was more than a foot shorter than Gil, dressed in a belted gown of rusty black whose fur lining showed worn at collar and sleeves. A name swam upwards in Gil's mind: Maister Robert Kerr, one of the forespeakers of the Consistory court. David Cunningham spoke of him with respect.

'A bad business, this at the bedehouse,' Kerr said. 'Was it one of the brothers killed him right enough? Tammas is beside himself for fear it should be shown his own brother did it, poor soul.'

'There's no saying yet,' Gil answered. 'We've more questions to ask. I was hoping Maister Agnew could help me himself. Is he long gone?'

'A half-hour or so,' Kerr offered. 'Aye, he was telling me he had spoken wi Naismith yestreen. Indeed, I knew that from my own observing, for I was still at my desk when the man came up the stair, and I heard Tammas welcome him by name.'

'What time would that be, maister?' Gil asked.

'Late,' Kerr said, and grimaced. 'The clerk that brought Naismith up here lingered to ask how long they would be, since Compline was long over, and they'd be wanting to lock the doors and go. I never realized how late it was myself till then. I rose and left my papers immediate. My steward wasny well pleased wi me,' he admitted, grinning ruefully and showing chipped teeth, 'for my supper was spoiled.'

'So you've no idea how long Naismith was here? Or what they talked about?'

'No to the first,' said Kerr with legal precision, 'and as to the second, I could hardly tell you if I did hear what they discussed, seeing it would be private between Tammas and his client.'

'True,' agreed Gil. 'So it was a legal matter, then? No a social visit for a glass of Malvoisie or the like.'

'I assume so, since Naismith came here and no to Tammas's own lodging. As to the wine,' he added, 'I've never heard Tammas offer it to a client. A mistake, that. It brings in good custom, young Cunningham.'

'I'll bear it in mind, sir,' said Gil, nodding. 'Do you know where that might be? Maister Agnew's lodging, I mean.'

'Vicars' Alley,' said Kerr after a moment's thought. 'This end, right by St Andrew's chapel. Likely you'd get him there nearer supper-time. Unless he lingers over his papers,' he added, with another rag-toothed grin, and vanished back into his own chamber.

All three Cistercians were in the hall when Gil got back to the house in Rottenrow. Climbing the stairs from the front door he heard Dorothea's voice, and as he stepped into the hall he had just time to see that his uncle was showing the elderly priest one of his books by the light of a branch of candles, while the two women helped Tib to set up the table. Then he was struck in the chest by Socrates' forepaws. Tib paused in her distribution of wooden trenchers to watch the dog leaping round him, simmering with delight at his master's safe return from the dangers of the burgh, and said caustically,

'Mother said that beast thought he was a lapdog, and I see he's not learned any different yet.'

'He's not a year old, Tib. He'll be calm in a moment.' Gil snapped his fingers at his pet. 'Down! That's better. Am I late?'

'No to say late,' said his uncle, breaking off his discussion, 'since Maggie kept the supper for you. Likely we can eat as soon as she hears you're in the house.'

'Forgive me, sir,' said Gil, bending his knee in a bow. 'I went out again to look for Maister Agnew. Just as well I missed him, or I'd ha been later still.'

'Have you found out who did it yet?' asked Tib, setting the salt on the board.

'No,' said Gil, 'though we've cast all about and asked a great many questions.' He turned to the pottery cistern which hung by the door, and ran water to wash his hands.

'Who have you questioned?' Tib asked.

'Marion Veitch and her brother,' supplied Dorothea.

Tib flicked her a glance but said nothing. The lay-sister dragged one of the benches to the table, and Gil said, 'Most of the almshouse, Nick Kennedy's two servers, but not yet Naismith's man of law.' He lifted the linen towel to dry his hands, and Socrates stood up, one paw against the wall, and lapped at the soapy dregs in the brightly glazed basin. 'I might go over and see if he's home after we've had supper,' he said, looking at Dorothea, and she nodded.

'Not bad for one day,' commented Canon Cunningham, coming forward. 'Tib, shout down to Maggie that your brother is home, then perhaps we may eat.'

Once the household was seated at the long board, and all were served, Tib returned to the subject, demanding, 'What happened at the bedehouse, anyway? All you said before was that the man had been found stabbed. When did it happen? Why do they not know who did it?'

'You put yourself forward too much, Isobel,' said her uncle severely.

She went scarlet, and stared at him in indignation, but Dorothea said, 'No, uncle, I think she does right to ask. It was almost within earshot of the house here, any of us wants to know what's being done to find the guilty.'

'A true word, Lady Dawtie,' said Maggie roundly. Gil, with resignation, helped himself to another portion of baked salmon and summarized a select few of the facts he had gathered so far. Well aware that anything he said in front of his uncle's household would soon be common property in the Chanonry, he restricted himself to the finding of the corpse, Mistress Mudie's evidence, Agnew's statement that he had last seen the Deacon about Compline, and the traces at the Stablegreen gate of the almshouse.

'Over the *wall*?' repeated Tib, white-faced. This time her uncle did not rebuke her, but Dorothea put a hand over hers. 'Do you mean the back wall? The one by the Stablegreen? When? When was this?'

'I do,' agreed Gil. 'I think by means of a ladder, or so the traces tell me, at any road. It isny there any more,' he said reassuringly, seeing that she was still very pale. 'The body's in the washhouse waiting while it softens, and I've no idea where the ladder can be. As to when . . .' He paused, considering what he knew. 'That depends on who moved the corpse and how many people were involved,' he said finally. 'Maybe between nine and ten, maybe later.'

She shivered, and cast a grateful glance at Dorothea, though she drew her hand out of her sister's clasp.

'It just – it just doesny seem right,' she said lamely. 'Leaving him lying like that.'

'If a miscreant is so lost to all sense of sin as to kill another man deliberately,' said the elderly priest in his soft voice, 'we canny expect him to treat the dead wi respect.'

'Well said, Herbert,' said Dorothea.

'And yet,' observed Gil, 'Naismith's eyes had been shut.'

'Likely somebody couldny abide him staring,' said Maggie cheerfully.

Tib bit her lip and looked down at her supper, then said abruptly, 'Uncle, will you forgive me? I'm no feeling very well.' Not waiting for his consent, she rose, and pushed her trencher across the table at Gil. 'Here, gie that to your lapdog. I'll see you all later.'

As her feet hurried up the stair toward the solar, Dorothea closed her eyes and crossed herself, her lips moving.

'You need to find that ladder, Gilbert,' said David

Cunningham, ignoring this episode. 'And the Deacon's cloak and hat. That should take you forward.'

'There's a many ladders in the Chanonry,' contributed Tam the stable-hand from further down the table. 'Near every household must have such a thing.' He began to count them off on his fingers, mumbling to himself, and Gil said resignedly,

'That's for the morn. I can see my day mapped out already.'

Chapter Six

'You were lucky to catch me at home,' said Maister Agnew in legal Latin. 'Aye, Hob,' he added as his servant brought in a tray, 'just leave the jug there.'

'Aye, but you'll no be spilling this one?' said Hob bluntly. He was a wizened man with a scrubby beard; his livery jerkin and hose, closely examined, were quite new but he wore them as if they were out at the elbows and knees.

Agnew gave him a black look, and flapped a dismissive hand, saying, 'You'll take a glass of Malvoisie, Maister Cunningham? I believe you're about to be wed, so we'll drink to that.'

'And keep it off the matting,' said Hob as he reached the doorway. 'Once in a week's enough.'

'Hob! Get away hame!' said Agnew. His man snorted, and ducked out of the door. 'You'll ha to excuse him, Maister Cunningham. He's been too long wi me. Some wine, then?'

The wine was golden in the glass but belied its promise. Gil kept his face straight, and said reassuringly in Latin, 'I won't keep you, if you're promised somewhere. But there are a few things I hope you might shed light on, regarding Deacon Naismith's death.'

'You said that before,' said Agnew. He was remarkably like his brother, but his hair was fashionably longer, his face was fatter, and the lines at mouth and forehead signalled his presence in the day-to-day world of the Consistory. 'He was with me about this time last evening, after supper, for an hour or so, but I never saw him again after that.'

'Was that here?' asked Gil innocently, looking round the hall where they sat. He had friends among the cathedral songmen, who made up most of the inhabitants of the two rows of identical houses of Vicars' Alley, so the size and shape of the room were familiar to him. This one was brightly painted with false panelling in black and red, with vases of stiff improbable flowers depicted on the red squares. The beams which supported the floorboards overhead were also decorated, with vines wriggling along their length, and the shutters at the window had more flowers, startlingly unlike the ones which would be visible in the little yard outside in summer. 'Is it new painted?'

'Handsome work, isn't it?' agreed Agnew in Scots. 'You'd not believe what George Bowster cost me, first and last, but it was well worth it. It's Eck Sproat your gude-father's got in, I hear? I hope he's as good,' he said dubiously, and returned to Latin for the business of the evening. 'No, I saw Deacon Naismith in my chamber in the Consistory tower. The clerk that brought him up to me asked how long we would be, since it was time they were away, so I am certain it was late. The Deacon stayed while we dealt with the matter that brought him.'

'And what was that?' Gil asked.

'He was planning great changes in his life,' said Agnew easily. 'Some more of this Malvoisie?'

'No, thank you. I've another call to make. Changes, you said? So naturally he would turn to you, since you conveyed so much of his other property.'

'Naturally,' agreed Agnew, smiling slightly.

'He must have come to you in the first place as the bedehouse's man of law.' Agnew nodded. 'Perhaps you can tell me about the financial arrangements there. Is the Deacon in complete control, or is there other supervision?'

'The Deacon is in control,' said Agnew, pursing his lips and nodding. 'I dare say the founder's family have the final direction of their own donations, but the other properties are at the Deacon's disposal entirely, those that are outright gifts.'

Improvident, if true, thought Gil.

'So he made the most of the opportunity,' he said aloud.

'Naturally. The very most, indeed.' Gil raised his eyebrows and Agnew confided, 'I have sometimes wondered if he was altering the terms of some of the dispositions.'

'Dear me,' said Gil. 'Without your concurrence, I assume.'

'Oh, I assure you! I would certainly have advised against it if he had consulted me.'

'How long have you acted for the house?'

'Ten or twelve years, I suppose.'

'And how long had Maister Naismith been in place? How did he come by the post?'

'Four years at Candlemas next,' said Agnew promptly. 'As to how he came by it, I can claim no knowledge, but I recall him saying that he had been master of a smaller house at Irvine before he came to Glasgow. He has – had friends in Lanarkshire, perhaps they knew the founder's family.'

'I can check that,' said Gil, 'if it becomes relevant. And you said he was planning changes. Are you able to say what they were?'

'Well, it can do no harm to tell you, I suppose, since it cannot come to pass now. He was hoping to be married, and had great intentions for the bedehouse, and for his property round the burgh of Glasgow and elsewhere.' Agnew felt in his sleeve, then looked about him. 'No, of course, they're in the tower. I have the notes for the new will I was to draw up for him in my other tablets.'

'Had you drawn up the previous will? Did the principal legatee remain the same?' Gil asked neutrally.

Agnew took another sip of his execrable wine, and considered his answer.

'No,' he said at length. 'The principal legatee was not the

same. It was originally – I expect you can guess who it was, I hear you've already questioned her. The new will would have left most of his property, including the house by the Caichpele, to his wife. Contingent on the marriage taking place, of course.'

'Of course.' There was a pause. 'And who was that?' Gil prompted.

Another sip of the Malvoisie.

'It was to have been a kinswoman of mine. Widowed, you understand, with a nice little settlement in coin and land. The marriage was in my hands.'

'Very provident,' said Gil, wondering how the widow felt. 'So the Deacon was planning to be married, and wished to rearrange the disposition of his properties,' he summarized. 'I'm sure you'd have wanted to drink a toast to that. Did you discuss anything else? Did it affect the almshouse, or any other individual? Was he making provision for Mistress Veitch?'

'Very little, in my view,' said Agnew, assuming an air of disapproval. 'And that conditional on the child she's carrying being a son. No, there was nothing to be writ down that affected the almshouse.'

'I see.' Gil set his glass on the fine rush matting. 'So this took you an hour or so.'

'We had to disentangle his ideas somewhat. You know what it can be like.'

Gil nodded. 'And then?'

'He left, without saying where he was going. And then I left.'

'Not together?'

'No, he was ahead of me, by – oh, not by as much as a quarter-hour. I had papers to straighten, notes to make for this morning. I never saw him alive again.' Agnew bent his head and crossed himself.

'Did it seem as if he was going home, or to meet someone else?'

Agnew looked up in surprise. 'I never thought of that.' He considered briefly, gazing at the wriggling vines

111

along the roof-beams. 'No, I would not say he was going home, though who he was going to meet I could not speculate.'

'Did he seem in any way worried? As if there was anything wrong?'

'No, no,' Agnew assured him. 'He was considerably annoyed, for I think –' He broke off, but then shook his head. 'It can do him no harm now to divulge these matters, and may do some good. I got the impression that the former principal legatee, or perhaps her family, had raised objections to his change of plans which the Deacon felt were not justified. He said that it was his business, and none of theirs.'

Gil nodded, appreciating this version of what Eppie had called a roaring tulzie.

'Did he feel he had got the better of them in argument?' he asked. 'Did he anticipate any kind of retaliation?'

'Some legal action, you mean?' said the other man of law. Gil held his peace. 'None was mentioned, nor any threat of violence. Yes, the Deacon seemed to feel he had got the best of the discussion. Do you imply that this had some bearing on his death?'

'I imply nothing,' Gil said mendaciously. 'I must ask about everything, because somewhere in his last hours lies the answer.'

'Ah. Yes, of course.' Agnew crossed himself again, and took another sip of wine. Gil cleared his throat, and changed the subject slightly.

'After the Deacon left, you also went out, you said.' Agnew nodded. 'Where did you go yourself?' The other man began to assemble an offended look. 'I must ask everyone who saw him,' Gil pointed out.

'Oh.' The expression changed, and Gil realized he knew what was coming next. 'Well. To tell truth, Maister Cunningham, I was with – I was with a lady.'

'A lady? Would she be willing to confirm that, if it came to it?' The expression changed again. No, she would not,

Gil deduced. 'Not publicly, of course,' he added. 'We can be discreet about it.'

'Aye. Very possibly,' said Agnew, licking his lips. Who on earth was he seeing, Gil wondered.

'Does that mean,' he pursued as tactfully as he could, 'that you wereny home all last night?' And was the whole of Glasgow lying with a lover, he thought sourly, or just everyone connected with this death except me?

'It does,' agreed Agnew, and licked his lips again, rather anxiously.

'It must be a worry for you,' Gil said, to get away from the subject, 'all this happening at the almshouse. Is your brother secure there?'

'Not as secure as I would like,' said Agnew, interpreting the word differently from Gil's intention. 'I hope it may not prove to be his doing that the Deacon is dead, though whether the poor fellow is responsible for his actions is arguable at the least. His mind is *a fugitive and a wanderer upon the earth*, a sad case.'

'It seems unlikely that it was your brother who killed him,' said Gil. 'The signs tell me a different story.'

'It's kind of you to reassure me,' said Agnew, and drained his glass. 'Now, can I tell you anything else?'

All six of the bedesmen were seated in the pool of candle-light round the fire in the hall, discussing the morning with Maister Millar. Gil stood at the open door for a few minutes, studying them.

Despite the livery they were far from identical. (But why should they be identical? he thought.) Of the two who used sticks Anselm was frail and scrawny, with his spectacles still sliding off his nose; Duncan was big and bald and wore that flourishing moustache. There was the stooped Cubby with the trembling-ill, his hand shaking badly as he listened to Millar explaining why they needed to find the Deacon's cloak, and Barty with his head cocked anxiously to catch the words. There was Humphrey, with his blank smile. The sixth was another lean white-haired fellow, taller than the others, who was sitting slightly aloof from the circle and looking on with sour amusement. As Gil watched, this man glanced round, met his eye, and rose and moved stiffly to meet him.

'*Salve, magister,*' Gil said, pulling off his hat and bending one knee like a schoolboy.

'*Salve, puer,*' returned Maister Veitch.

'I'm sorry to see you here in this place, maister.'

'No need, Gibbie, no need. I've been well cared for till now, and the danger we were in's been averted.'

'What danger, maister?' said Gil. 'What can you tell me?' He looked about him. 'Is there somewhere we can talk, sir, and I'll see if Mistress Mudie can give us –'

'Sissie has her hands full,' interrupted Maister Veitch, lifting one of the row of lanterns from the shelf by the door, 'and I'd as soon no drink anything the now, for reasons you'll well understand when you come to be my age, Gibbie. No,' he went on, opening the lantern, and set light to the candle within from the one set ready on the shelf, 'come to my lodging out this rain, and you'll listen to me. You'll be looking for Naismith's enemies, I assume? There may be more than you bargained for. Millar's a good man, but he's too much faith in other folk's goodness.'

'Is that right, sir?' said Gil. He followed his old teacher out into the dripping garden. 'So who would you suggest might have killed him?'

'Anyone inside these gates, for a start,' said the old man bluntly, opening his door.

The little house was a commodious place for one person, smaller than the Douglas lodging but significantly bigger than Millar's chamber above the hall. The outer room contained a chair, a settle and two stools round an empty hearth, and a small desk for a scholar stood against the opposite wall, with five books on the shelf above it, and an inkstand and a stack of paper lying ready. The door to the inner chamber stood ajar in the fourth wall.

'I've begun work on that study I always wanted to

make,' said Maister Veitch, and cracked his cloak like a blanket to shake the rain off it, so that the candle flames danced wildly. Hanging the heavy swathes of cloth on a peg behind the door he bared his head, revealing a thick white thatch receding at the temples, and flourished his velvet bonnet at the settle before hanging it on another peg. 'Hae a seat, Gibbie.'

'The Early Fathers?' recalled Gil, and got an approving nod.

Seated in his own great chair, marking off his points on gnarled fingers with the same gestures he had used when expounding the mysteries of Latin declensions in the dusty schoolroom in Hamilton, Maister Veitch set out his view of the situation in the almshouse.

'He'd set each of us against him,' he said in the scholarly tongue, 'all six of the brothers, for different reasons, long before yesterday's announcement. Sissie, whatever she says, had no reason to love or respect him. Millar, a good man and a good scholar, had a very different vision for the bedehouse from the one Naismith followed. And I regret to say the fellow's dealings with my kinswoman Marion have been far from honest.' He paused, one forefinger on the other, then moved on to the thumb. 'Which I suppose,' he added in Scots, 'wad gie me the mair cause to dislike him, though I know I didny kill him.'

'But what had he done to them all?' asked Gil.

Maister Veitch began his count on the other hand.

'As to Duncan Fraser, I've no idea,' he admitted. 'He's forgotten all his Latin beyond *Paternoster* and *Ave*, you've likely noticed, speaks only the Scots tongue he spoke as a boy, somewhere beyond Aberdeen or Tain. The rest of us canny make out a word he says, poor fellow. But if you mention Naismith's name, he turns purple, so we'll assume there's ill feeling there.' He paused, considering. 'Cubby Pringle with the trembling-ill – he leaves down crumbs for the birds, which was always worth a laugh from the Deacon, but there's worse. Cubby was put out of his parish after he spilled the Blood of Christ over the

115

Bishop's Easter cope. He's done more penance than he needs for it already, but Naismith cast it up at him as a joke every time Cubby spoke to him.'

'They'd never wash the wine out of a cope,' said Gil thoughtfully. 'I take it the thing had to be destroyed? And that was attached to Maister Pringle's name?'

'Precisely.' Maister Veitch paused again. 'He made a mock of Anselm in the same way, about a matter Anselm takes seriously.'

'The ghostly brother at the Mass?'

'Oh, you've heard about it, have you? Aye, Anselm's aye on about it. He claims to see him far more often than the rest of us, claims he actually talks to him – I've no seen him at all, myself – and he lets us all know. He's childish, poor fellow. And Barty and I both had a serious difference wi Naismith about the way he uses the bedehouse's income.'

'Ah,' said Gil.

'It's only since I was here,' said Maister Veitch, 'maybe a year, that we've tried to discuss it wi him. Till then I suppose he assumed none would notice.' He smiled a thin teacher's smile in the half-light. 'Anselm's beyond matters like that, we'd no ken if Duncan did notice, and Cubby's too good a man to be aware of it, like Andro. Barty says he'd had his suspicions, and once I began asking about this and that we uncovered more and more.'

'Per exemplum?' Gil prompted, and got another approving glance.

'There was a silver crucifix when I came here,' his teacher said. 'There was still plate in the hall two year since, Barty says. The meals we're served are wholesome enough, Sissie sees to that, the good soul,' he grimaced, 'but we get meat less often and it's cheaper meat these days.' He spat at the empty grate in the small hearth. 'And that's another of his penny-pinching decisions – we've no to get a fire in our own lodgings now. He said it was for safety, and I suppose in Anselm's case or Humphrey's that might be true, but we all kenned what he was at.'

'Where is the money going?' Gil asked.

'Into his pocket, we assumed,' said Maister Veitch. 'And only yesterday he called us all thegither and announced, among other things, that he would be taking back – those were his words – all our books, since old men ha no need of books, in order to sell them for the bedehouse funds.' The indignation quivered in his voice. 'Those books by the desk are mine, dear-bought over a lifetime, and Barty's two are his. There's a many missed meals behind each one of them.'

'Your books? What did you say to him?' asked Gil in dismay.

'We tellt him they were ours,' said Maister Veitch bitterly, 'but he reminded us that the brothers hold their property in common. I kent that, but I wouldny ha accepted the place if I'd no been assured that books was a different matter. I've had time, this past year, to make a start on the Early Fathers, I'll no see it snatched away.'

Gil eyed his teacher with sympathy. After a moment he said, 'And yet the man was a clerk – he could read, I think.'

'A stickit clerk,' said Maister Veitch in contemptuous Scots, then, reverting to Latin, 'He was parish clerk to my nephew William in Irvine at one time. It seems he wished to be a priest himself, but there was neither money nor patronage to support him to his ordination. This gave him a dislike of priests and learning, and even William found him difficult and snatched the opportunity to get him another post, first in Irvine and then in Glasgow out of his way. Had I known him better, I would have waited for a place in Hamilton, rather than come here myself.'

'An unpleasant character,' Gil said thoughtfully. 'And had he given the bedehouse folk any other cause to dislike him?'

'Oh, he had. As well as bullying Sissie about the accounts –'

'Bullying her?'

'Oh, it was all done very civilly, but I've heard him. He

117

aye forgot,' said Maister Veitch with another thin smile, 'that my ears are near as sharp as they ever were. He went over the household outgoings wi Sissie every day after the noon bite, and he'd aye a suggestion about how it could ha been less. She was near weeping the last time I heard them,' he said thoughtfully, 'for he'd said we wereny to have wine any more, even on feast days, but only ale. But then he went on to press her about some receipt he'd promised Andrew Slack the 'pothecary. She was reluctant to give it over, since it was her granny's and no to be handed on to just anybody, but he pressed her to it, and if she was to expect any reward for it, my name's no Frankie Veitch. Much more like that Naismith and Slack would split the profits to be made.'

'We found two or three receipts in his purse,' said Gil. 'And what about these changes he was to make? His marriage, and the use of the hall, and so on.'

'Aye,' said Maister Veitch. 'Aye, he called us all into the hall, after he'd done bullying Sissie, and told us he was planning changes. Andro was to give up his lodging and take one of the empty houses. Sissie was to have another, I think, and she was to leave off the housekeeping, be our nurse only, and be paid less for it. But none of the empty houses is fit to live in. The thatch leaks, the shutters willny fasten. One of the hearths is fallen in.'

'Was this the first you'd heard of these changes?'

'It was. Sissie asked who would oversee the house-keeping and the kitchen, and Naismith said she had no need to worry about that, for he was to be married, and his wife would take all into her own hands. And afore he left the hall,' said Maister Veitch slowly, 'I said, to him alone, did my niece know of this, and he answered that it was nothing to do wi her. Which I took to mean that he was proposing to marry some other woman.'

'You don't know who?'

'I do not.'

Gil was silent for a space. At length he said, 'And the sixth brother?'

'Eh? What did ye say?'

'You've told me about five of the bedesmen,' Gil prompted. 'The sixth is Maister Humphrey that quotes the Apocalypse. What quarrel did he have wi Naismith?'

'Ah.' Maister Veitch turned to stare into the empty grate. Gil waited. After a pause, the old man said, 'Do you ken the tale, Gibbie?'

'No, sir,' said Gil blankly.

'Ah. Maybe it was before you left me and came to the school here in Glasgow. Aye, it would be fifteen year or more since. Humphrey Agnew was studying Theology at the college here, wi an altar to mind out at St Thomas beyond the Stablegreen Port.' Gil nodded. He was acquainted with the crumbling little chapel of St Thomas Becket, which like most churches of its dedication in Scotland was the best part of three hundred years old and looked it. 'He and a fellow student went fishing one day, no in the Clyde but further afield, up to the Kelvin.'

'Ah,' said Gil. 'Fishing. They used the irresistible bait?'

'A consecrated Host.' Maister Veitch pursed his lips, nodding. 'Which Humphrey stole. Bad enough, though there's aye a few does it. But the other fellow put his foot in a pothole in the riverbed, and lost his footing and was swept away and drowned. A judgement, I suppose you might say.'

'A severe judgement,' said Gil, 'for a crime which could be said to injure only himself. And Humphrey? What happened to him? Did he escape the judgement?'

'He went mad,' said Maister Veitch baldly.

'Mad? He's known to be mad, then? I wondered, from something his brother said. So what's he doing here? Surely there's some better place for him – one of the big hospitals, Soutra, St Leonard's?'

'He didny run mad immediately,' qualified his teacher. 'He was ill wi grief for a while, and then it seemed he was back to himself, and he finished his studies. Then he began to see people as birds – I've heard him call Naismith a cuckoo and a shrike, which didny best please the man.

119

And then it seems, bit by bit he began to abhor water. First it was rivers, as ye'd understand, and then wells and buckets, and got so he couldny lave the vessels after the Mass, and then couldny witness others at the same task.'

'Ah, that's what Nick meant.'

'Very likely. It's a problem every morn at the end of the Mass,' confirmed Maister Veitch. 'Now he gets difficult if he's out in the rain, as well as if he's angered at something. He starts by quoting the Revelation, and then he gets violent. I've seen him try to throttle his brother Thomas.' He sighed. 'Sissie can control him for now, but he should really be a place he can be shut away, poor fellow, for if he gets any worse we'll have the whole of Glasgow coming in to bait him like a bear.'

'I'd a word wi his brother before I came round here, but not about this. I never knew before that he'd such a problem in his life,' said Gil. 'Poor devil.'

'So I'd no recommend you question Maister Humphrey direct,' said Maister Veitch drily, 'without a guard. Your father-in-law would be a good candidate.'

'I'll maybe no disturb Maister Humphrey at all, then,' said Gil, 'but I could do with a word with Anselm if I may.'

'I wish you luck,' said Maister Veitch in the same dry tone. He leaned forward to see out of the low window. 'No, your luck's out, Gibbie. There's a light in his lodging. Sissie'll be helping him to his bed. Try the morn.'

Out in the street, Gil considered the sky. It was too cloudy to be helpful, but he thought the time could not be much past eight o'clock. The taste of Maister Agnew's Malvoisie was still in his mouth. Nick Kennedy won't be teaching, he thought, and set out towards the college.

The taverns of the Upper Town were brightly lit and noisy, but the streets were quiet. At the Wyndhead he became aware of another lantern bobbing towards him from the Drygate on hurrying feet, its patch of light catching a drab skirt, an apron, the ends of a checked plaid. He paused politely to let the woman go past him, and raised his own light to show his face. The other lantern checked, and then came forward hesitantly.

'Is that you, sir?' The voice was young. 'You that was at my mistress's house the day,' she qualified. 'Talking to Eppie and Danny and all.'

'Aye, that was me. You must be Bel,' Gil hazarded. Reassured, she came forward into the light of his lantern, smiling shyly. 'Is that you away home now? It's a long day for you.'

'It's no so bad,' she said. 'It's no a bad place at all. Danny's a cross thing, but Eppie and me has a good laugh, whiles, and the mistress is easy enough.'

'Are you bound down the High Street? Can I see you to your door, lass?'

Bel giggled, and bobbed a curtsy by way of assent. Gil turned, offering his arm as if she was a lady, which extracted another giggle and a nervous clutch at his sleeve, and they made their way on down the hill by the light of the two lanterns.

'That must have given you all a turn, Maister Naismith's death,' Gil suggested. 'How's your mistress now? She seemed in a great shock this afternoon.'

'She was awfy quiet over supper, even wi her brother there,' admitted Bel. 'My, he's the bonnie man,' she digressed, like Eppie. 'The big handsome fellow he is, it's no surprise wee Frankie's that taken wi him. She was at him again the night, *Sing to Frankie, Unca John, sing*. Same as last night. He'd even to sing the same song. Some foreign song he learned while he was away at sea.'

'Was Frankie upset by the shouting last night?' Gil asked.

'I missed the worst o't,' confessed Bel with regret, 'for I was early away, but Eppie said she was. She said it was as good as a play, save that the wee one was screaming, for my mistress was weeping, and the maister was shouting that he'd leave his property where he wished and she'd no

121

claim on him whatever she said, and her brother was roaring like the devil on a cart, raging up and down wi his gown swinging, trying to say the maister owed her for her maidenhead, and he said –' She stopped. Gil made an interrogative noise. 'Forget what I was saying,' she said unconvincingly.

'He said?' Gil prompted.

'I forget!' she said again.

'And at supper,' said Gil after a moment, steering them both past a sagging midden. 'What was it he said at supper? You were there, were you no?'

'Oh, that was about altering his will,' she said in some relief, 'like Eppie tellt you, sir. And he'd other plans. He never said what they were,' she added regretfully, 'but I suppose they'll all come to naught now.'

'Aye, likely,' agreed Gil.

She came to a halt under a lantern at the mouth of a vennel and let go his arm. 'This is me here, maister. And thank you kindly for your company, sir.' She bobbed to him. 'I've been right glad of it, sir, for there was someone watching the house when I came out.'

'Watching the house?' Gil repeated. 'Mistress Veitch's house? How do you know?'

'I seen him when I came out,' she assured him. 'He was standing in the corner atween the two houses across the vennel, but I got just a glimp when I put my own light up to be sure I'd shut the kitchen door right.'

'What, just standing there?'

She nodded, her plaid falling back from her face in the light from the lantern overhead.

'Standing watching the house, looking up at the lighted windows above. A big wicked-looking man wi a great black beard. I'll be keeping an eye out when I go to work the morn, you can believe it, sir.'

'Nobody you knew? Had he a weapon?'

She shook her head.

'Never seen him afore in my life,' she asserted. 'I never saw a sword or nothing, but likely it was hid under his cloak. So I was right glad of your company the now, sir. My thanks on it.' She bobbed again, and turned away into the narrow space between the houses. Gil waited until her lantern vanished into the shadows, and went on down the street, frowning.

'Your sister's to lie at the castle?' said Nick Kennedy, pouring wine. 'Oh, aye, the guest-hall they keep for visiting religious. Well, it saves your uncle having to fit her and her folk in at Rottenrow. And what like is Agnew's lodging?'

'Very comfortable,' said Gil. He accepted a glass of sweet golden Malvoisie and said thoughtfully, 'What can you tell me about the man Naismith, Nick?'

Maister Kennedy fitted his feet beside Gil's on the box of smouldering charcoal on the hearth.

'No a lot, you know,' he said, and paused to consider the wine in his own glass. 'Patey was right, this is no bad. I must tell John Shaw that. The last barrel he got for us wasny fit to drink. Sharp as verjuice, and I'd swear there'd been a cat at it.'

'I think I had some of the same shipment from Agnew the now,' said Gil.

His friend grinned, and went on, 'No, I've no much information about Naismith. He'd been in Irvine, so he said once, but he came from, let me see, somewhere out into Stirlingshire, away up the Kelvin. Lenzie or somewhere like that,' said Maister Kennedy, an Ayrshire man.

'Did you see him wi the old men? The brothers? How was he wi them?'

'Ah.' Nick peered into his glass of Malvoisie again, but found no inspiration in it. After a moment he said, 'I'll tell you this, Gil. For all Sissie Mudie talks like a cut throat, she's a good nurse to those old men, and she kens herbs like no other, and to see her wi poor Humphrey Agnew would lesson anyone in charity. But even wi her in the

123

place, I'd not have cared to put any kin of mine there under Naismith's governance.'

'Is that right?' said Gil.

Nick shot him a glance, and said, 'What do you know, then? I've seen that expression afore.'

'I'd a word wi old Frankie Veitch. He taught me my letters in Hamilton, before I came here to the grammar school.'

'You know everyone.'

'No quite. I didny know this man Naismith,' Gil said, 'and I don't much like what I hear of him. *An orgulous knight*, as Malory says.' He related Maister Veitch's assessment of the inhabitants of the bedehouse, and Nick nodded.

'I've heard the Deacon, making a game of one or another of them. None of that surprises me. But I wouldny say . . .' he paused, 'I wouldny say any of the old men had the strength to stab a man three times, nor to drag him out where we found him, even old Veitch. Sissie might,' he added dispassionately, 'and Andro's a different matter, but you've seen what a nervish, loup-at-shadows creature he is.'

'Aye.' Gil held out his glass. 'Is there any more of that Malvoisie? We wouldny want it to spoil. Tell me, was Naismith a man of habit? Was he at Mass every morning?'

Maister Kennedy paused with the jug in his hand. 'Most mornings, I'd say, but not every morning.'

'And in his own stall?'

'When he was there? Oh, aye. Well, usually. Odd times he was late, he'd slip in at the tail and sit near the choir door.'

'Oh.' Gil accepted the returned glass. 'Next to Anselm?'

'Oh, you've heard about that, have you,' said Nick, as Maister Veitch had done. 'No, he wouldny sit next to Anselm. I'm told it can be gey cold in the stall next to Anselm.'

'Lowrie thought he saw him in that stall this morning,

but Millar said it was more likely this other –' He stopped, shaking his head.

'Mm,' said Nick. 'No this morning.'

'You're very sure.'

'Sure enough.' He gave Gil a doubtful look. 'You're no priested, this may not make sense to you.'

'Try me.'

'Aye, well. I don't see Anselm's friend myself but – Look, when you say a Mass, it's no always the same. Sometimes your words come right back at you as if you were standing next a wall, and sometimes they vanish as if you were speaking down a well,' said Nick hesitantly, 'but sometimes – sometimes it's as if something – some*one* else you canny see joins in wi you, and the whole thing takes a life of its own. You ken?'

'Like prayer,' said Gil simply.

Nick nodded in relief. 'Aye, exactly. Well, in St Serf's, when it's one of the good Masses, the better Masses I mean, then when we go to get a sup of porridge wi the old men, Anselm will be yapping on about his friend being there. It aye happens. And once or twice, when Naismith was making a joke of it at Anselm, trying to make out he'd seen the extra brother himself that day, I could tell what Anselm was going to say for it hadny been one of the uplifted Masses.'

'And?'

'It wasny one this morn. What was Anselm saying?'

'Anselm agreed wi you. So far as he was making sense at all,' Gil qualified.

Nick's dark-browed face split in a grin, then became serious. 'So who did Lowrie see? The boy's sharp-eyed and sensible, I'd believe he saw something, so who was it?'

'That's one of the things I need to find out.' Gil took another sip of wine. 'You mentioned Humphrey Agnew, Nick. How was Naismith with him?'

'No bad, for all his faults, and for all the names Humphrey called him. Better than the poor soul's brother, at all events. I've seen Naismith help Sissie to get Humphrey out the way and calmed down when his brother's got him rampaging.'

'The brothers Agnew don't get on?'

Nick shrugged. 'Tammas never humours Humphrey. He starts reciting the Apocalypse and Tammas says, *No need for that now*, or *Calm down, Humphrey.* Humphrey tells you the Deacon's a shrike and Tammas tells him no to be ridiculous. A quarter-hour of that and Humphrey goes for his throat, tries to throttle him. Nearly got him a couple of times that I've seen,' he asserted, 'but the Deacon dragged him away and Sissie got Humphrey out the room. The poor man ought to be somewhere he can be locked up, but he's happy at St Serf's.'

'Why a shrike?' Gil wondered. 'He says he's a robin now, because he's dead. Oh, and Pierre and I are hoodies.'

'All in black as you are, wi a grey plaid, I can see how he'd think you were a hoodie,' said Nick, 'but a robin? Maybe like the one in the bairns' rhyme? *Who killed cock-robin?*'

'*I, said the sparrow, wi my bow and arrow,*' recalled Gil. 'But it was a dagger killed Naismith, no an arrow. I wonder who he's cast as the sparrow? And do you tell me you have to wait till he's out of sight after the Mass before you can lave the vessels?'

'Oh, aye. Or he starts on the Apocalypse again and then gets violent, it seems. I've never taken the chance. Let's talk of something more cheerful. How's the wedding plans going? Got the bed set up yet?'

'The painters are still at work.'

'It's to be hoped they finish afore the great day,' said Nick, 'or we'll all be covered in paint when we put you to bed. Oh, aye, my new gown came home.' He got to his feet, setting down his glass, and went to the kist at the foot of his own bed. 'Wat Paton's man brought it round this afternoon. Now is that no braw?' He shook the garment out and held it up, a long gown of dark red velvet with a heavy fur lining. 'Mind, I still think we should ha been both of us in our Master's robes, but I'll do you proud as your groomsman in this, will I no?'

'We'd be more symmetrical in academic dress,' Gil agreed, 'but I'll tell you, we'll be warmer in these. Mine's much the same, but cut in blue brocade. We'll make a good turnout.'

'And I'll get years of wear out of this,' said Nick, in satisfaction. 'Provided the moth doesny get into it.' He stroked the fur again, and folded the rich material with care. 'I'd ha stood up for you anyway, Gil, you'd no need to bribe me like this. And have you got the rings ready?'

Gil thought briefly of the two circles of gold in their little silk pouch, stowed in his uncle's strongbox for safety. His was quite plain, set with a single dome-cut garnet; Alys's was the most delicate work he could commission in Glasgow, ornamented with linked hearts and the single word, *SEMPER*. Always. He found he was rubbing his ring finger, and stopped.

'Aye, the rings are ready,' he said.

By the time Gil left the college, after a quick word with Patrick Coventry the second regent, depute to the gentle Principal Doby, it was late. The rain had stayed off, but the cold wind whipping dark clouds across the stars was not an improvement. He paused outside the great wooden yett, hitching his plaid up higher, and considered what to do next. Of the options which presented, going home to the house in Rottenrow was the more sensible and less attractive.

He turned downhill, towards his lodestone.

Chapter Seven

There were still lighted windows in the mason's sprawling house, and lute music floated faintly on the wind. Gil picked his way across the courtyard, avoiding the bare plant-tubs; as he set foot on the fore-stair the door opened and more light fell across the damp flagstones.

'Gilbert,' said Maistre Pierre with pleasure. 'Alys thought she heard your footstep. Come in, come in, and take some wine. We have been sitting above stairs. Did you learn anything from the Deacon's mistress? Is that where you have been? Perhaps,' he said, and grinned, white teeth catching the candlelight as he lit the two of them up the stair, 'I should object, if you come to your betrothed from calling on another man's mistress.'

'I was well protected,' Gil assured him, following him into the little painted closet. 'I took Dorothea with me.' Alys had set her lute in its case, and turned to greet him, her honey-coloured locks gleaming in the candlelight. He gathered her close and kissed her, then released his clasp as he felt her draw back slightly.

'How is she, poor creature?' she asked. 'The man's mistress, I mean. And your sister? Is she tired from the journey?' Her hand slid into his like a little bird into its nest. *To see her fingers that be so small! In my conceit she passeth all That ever I saw.* But she won't let me kiss her, he thought.

'My sister is well,' he answered her, and sat down with her on the cushioned bench. 'She's looking forward to meeting you tomorrow. She and I went to see Marion Veitch after you left us, Pierre, before supper.'

'And?' Maistre Pierre was pouring wine, not Malvoisie but the red Bordeaux wine he favoured. Gil took the glass in his free hand and described the visit to the house by the Caichpele.

'That poor woman,' said Alys again as he finished. 'She has been very badly treated. I hope Sister Dorothea was able to comfort her.'

'It's a sorry tale,' Gil agreed. 'But as matters stand, she won't lose by the man's death. His existing will was much more generous to her and to the little girl as well, Agnew tells me.'

'Oh, you have seen the lawyer?'

'After supper. And also Maistre Veitch at the bede-house.'

'Who else benefits from the old will?' asked Alys.

Gil looked down at her where she leaned against his shoulder, and smiled. 'There are one or two bequests of named property to his kin, by what Agnew says, and something for the bedehouse, something for the child by name, and the residue goes to Marion Veitch. I would say he's purchased several plots of land since it was drawn up. She'll be a wealthier woman than he intended.'

'Oh,' said Alys thoughtfully. 'So the man's death comes very convenient for her.'

'It does.'

'And for who else?' asked Maistre Pierre. 'Did he have enemies, have you discovered?'

Gil grimaced. 'According to Maistre Veitch anyone in the bedehouse, not only the six brothers but Millar and Mistress Mudie as well, had cause to dislike him. Marion's brother John was very angry with him last night. I don't yet know who his friends were, other than Agnew and one of the Walkinshaws, and I must find out. I should have asked Agnew just now.'

Maistre Pierre grunted, and sipped his wine, pausing to savour it respectfully.

'What else do we know about the Deacon?' he said. 'Consider how did he die. That is the first thing'

'Did you say he was killed somewhere else?' said Alys.

Gil nodded. 'He was stabbed, by two opponents, one of them left-handed. After he was dead his eyes were closed, and he lay for a while in one position, perhaps as long as three hours, and then he was moved to the bedehouse garden, where he fell into another position.'

'Do not forget the marks on his face,' prompted Maistre Pierre, 'and the straw in his garments.'

'Straw?'

'Flakes of straw,' agreed Gil. 'Those may have come from Agnew's chamber in the Consistory tower. Someone has been sweeping the chambers, I think, and his stair is covered in fragments.'

'So that confirms Agnew's story.' Maistre Pierre took one of the little cakes from the half-empty plate on the tray, and bit it thoughtfully.

'So far,' agreed Alys. 'What else, Gil?'

'His keys were on his belt,' continued Gil, 'and gate and door were locked as usual. It seems most likely that he was moved somehow to the Stablegreen and put over the wall into the garden, rather than being taken in by the door.'

'And then he was heard walking about,' said Alys.

'Someone was heard. There was a light and movement in his lodging about ten o'clock, witnessed by Mistress Mudie and by Millar separately.'

'You make it very clear,' said Maistre Pierre. Alys reached for the plate of cakes and offered it to Gil.

'You think it was not the man himself who was heard in his lodging,' she said. 'So who was it? And why?'

'One of those who killed him, one assumes,' said her father.

'But who?' she persisted. 'Who is most likely?'

'A good question,' agreed Maistre Pierre. 'Gilbert, of those we know, who had the means to kill him?'

'Virtually all.'

'We need only one. Take the woman first, the mistress. Could she have killed her lover? She has reason, God knows it.'

'Naismith broke his news, and there was an argument, but he left the house after it,' said Gil thoughtfully, 'we have witnesses to that.'

The mason waved his empty glass in one large hand. 'Perhaps she went out later and waited for him to leave the Consistory tower.'

'You saw her, Gil. Could she have done that?' asked Alys. 'Waiting alone in the dark for the right person to come along, so that she could stab him?' She shivered.

'She's a timid soul,' Gil said, and thought of Michael's leman, waiting in the dark for a different reason. He put his arm round Alys's waist. She clasped his hand, fingers moving in a quick, private caress, and shifted it to her shoulder. What did that mean, he wondered, tightening his grasp obediently.

'Her brother!' suggested Maistre Pierre. 'He could have knifed the man, whether in St Mungo's Yard or in the street.'

'Or they both did, together – you said there were two opponents.'

'That's possible,' agreed Gil. 'And then they hid the body as we thought happened, and put him over the wall later. And a man like John Veitch could have carried the Deacon without trouble, alone or with –'

'Ah! And while he did that, she went into the bedehouse in her lover's cloak –'

'Why?' said Alys. 'What is the benefit?'

'To cover up the time or the place where he was killed. To make it seem he was killed inside the bedehouse instead of outside.'

'I would certainly prefer it,' said Maistre Pierre plaintively, leaning forward with the jug of wine to refill Gil's glass, 'if it were not Naismith who came home to the bedehouse last night. Experience tells me he was dead long before the footsteps were heard.'

Alys nodded.

'It can't have been Naismith,' Gil agreed. He pulled a face. 'There are tales – McIan the harper could tell you some – of people who were seen and heard after they were dead, but I think Our Lord was the only one who appeared after he was dead and consumed a meal.'

'And we are not told that He slept in His bed,' said Alys.

'If that is what happened – the body over the wall, someone else in the Deacon's lodging – it didn't only disguise the time and place of death. It also got the impostor time with the accounts,' Gil said thoughtfully, 'which had certainly been searched, by what Millar says. I wonder what he – or she – was looking for? And of course once Millar had come in, the outer gate was locked as well as the door between the courtyards, so the impostor was trapped, even if he had originally intended to leave.'

'Whoever it was took a risk,' observed Alys. 'The body might have been found before he could get away.'

'He would have heard the outcry, and had time to hide somewhere about the place. The chapel, for instance. I suspect he did not remove his boots, whoever he was. Anyway, John Veitch claims he slept in his own bed last night. I've still to go down and find this Widow Napier he's lodging with,' Gil admitted. 'And his boots are bigger than the prints we found in the clump of trees.'

Alys turned her head to look at Gil from within the circle of his arm.

'And the man of law,' she said. 'He thinks it was his brother who killed the man.'

'He's worrying about very little, I should say. The brother is certainly mad, and it seems he can be violent, *so vexis him the thoghtful maladie*, but if Millar is to be believed, the door was locked between the Deacon's lodging and the bedesmen's houses. And Mistress Mudie corroborates that,' Gil added. 'Mind you, she would certainly lie to protect Humphrey.'

'It is possible,' said Alys, 'surely, even if she was not lying? If it was indeed Deacon Naismith in his lodging when the light was seen, he might have come down into the garden later, locking the door behind him. You said his keys were with him.'

'His keys,' agreed Gil, 'but no lantern. It was cloudy last night, the moon would give no light –'

'Perhaps he had one, but whoever killed him took it,' suggested Alys.

'That would mean,' he said glumly, 'that anyone in the bedehouse could have killed him. Even Mistress Mudie had good reason. Those receipts in Naismith's purse were hers, Pierre, family remedies that the Deacon forced her to reveal, and it's clear enough from what Maister Veitch tells me that any of the brothers might have had a reason, as well.'

'But Naismith did not die where he was found,' Maistre Pierre reminded him. 'We thought it was not in the garden.'

'We don't know where he died. We don't know for certain that he was put over the wall,' Gil admitted. 'The marks we found are circumstantial, no more. The dog found nothing to interest him in the little houses, but he's no lymer, he doesn't hunt by scent. It would help if we could find the Deacon's cloak and hat.'

'Hmm,' said the mason. 'We keep coming back to it – both Mistress Mudie and Millar maintain there was someone in Naismith's lodging by ten o'clock last night. She heard footsteps, he saw a light.'

'If she was lying,' said Gil, 'he might simply agree with her, for whatever reason – being sure she was right, or some such thing. Or perhaps she had gone up herself and lit the candle and eaten the dole, so that Millar did see a light.'

'And rearranged the accounts?' said Alys. 'Can she read? Oh, yes,' she recollected, 'you said the receipts were hers.'

'Or did Millar himself go up there?' suggested Maistre

133

Pierre. 'Is it the woman who is agreeing because she is sure he is right? I am not convinced she is capable of lying, her tongue runs too freely.'

'If Millar had rearranged the accounts,' said Gil thoughtfully, 'he had no need to tell us they were in disorder. We would never have known it. I'm inclined to think he was telling the truth – that he went straight to his own chamber when he came into the bedehouse.'

'What about the kitchen hands?' said Alys. 'Do they live in? Have you spoken to them?'

'Ah!' said Gil. 'Another thing to do tomorrow.'

'Meantime,' said Maistre Pierre, nodding agreement, 'if we accept this evidence, we have someone in the Deacon's lodging last night. We also have an extra figure at the morning Mass.' He cocked an eyebrow at Gil. 'Was it real, or was it spectral?'

'Oh, aye, if it was real, easiest by far to assume those are the same person. But if we do, we must assume neither was the Deacon, because he was certainly dead long before Prime, and possibly dead before Mistress Mudie first heard footsteps overhead.'

'I should have said ten to fourteen hours before I saw him, though I cannot be certain.'

'That would be, I suppose between seven and eleven last night,' Gil reckoned. 'We know he was alive about half an hour after seven, when he left the house by the Caichpele, and if it was not Naismith that Sissie heard we can probably assume he was dead by ten. That fits.'

'How accurate do you think her sense of time is?' asked Alys.

'I don't know about that, but she did say she heard someone moving about over her head after Millar had come in,' Gil supplied. 'Millar's story is clear enough – and Patey Coventry confirmed it for me just now.'

'Ah,' said Maistre Pierre in disappointment. 'That certainly discounts my next idea.'

'What, that one of the brothers leapt up that stair and stabbed him before the door was locked, then carried him

134

down into the garden without Sissie noticing? I thought of that too, but there was no sign of a fight, let alone a death, in Naismith's lodging. In any case it wouldny account for the extra figure at Mass, and nor would the idea that he was killed in the garden or in one of the wee houses. We would have to accept that what Lowrie saw was – not real. No, the only way it works is for the man last night to be the same as the man this morning.'

'Man or woman,' Alys put in.

'As we said,' Gil agreed. 'Marion Veitch is as tall as Dorothea. Hidden in a great cloak and a hat, she could be taken for a man.'

'While her brother dealt with the body, as we surmised,' said Maistre Pierre.

'Aye, that would work, but who minded the bairn if she was out of the house overnight? I'm not convinced Eppie could lie for her mistress, she talks too much, like Sissie Mudie, and the man Danny certainly wouldn't.'

'I could get a word with the painter's man,' suggested Alys. 'He will have spoken to his cousin this evening. Along with the whole town,' she added, her quick smile flickering.

'I've spoken to her already,' said Gil. 'I encountered her on her way home, and convoyed her down the road.'

'Oho!' said Maistre Pierre, grinning again. 'Yet another lady! And only – how many days is it to the wedding?'

'What did she say?' asked Alys. Gil bent his head to rub his cheek on her hair, and she nestled in against him.

'She confirmed some of Marion's story,' he admitted, 'if only by hearsay, for she says she was earlier leaving the house last night than tonight. But she said something odd.'

'What was that?' Alys prompted him after a moment.

'She seemed quite certain the house was being watched this evening.'

'Watched? You mean someone standing out in the cold,' Alys began, and faltered as she saw the parallel.

135

'Waiting alone in the dark for the right person to come along,' agreed Gil.

'Did she see the watcher?' demanded Maistre Pierre.

'A big man with a black beard. But you're here, so she must have been imagining it,' said Gil, at which his friend grinned absently and stroked the beard, considering.

'There are not so many black beards in Glasgow,' he commented. 'Most Scotsmen go shaven like you.'

'Save the Earl of Douglas, and he is fair,' amended Alys absently. 'I wonder if she really saw anyone. You know what servant lassies are like, if anything goes wrong in the household.'

'They see bogles behind every bush,' agreed Gil. 'This one seems less silly than most.' He paused, as something else came back to him. 'Now, I wonder what that was?' Alys looked up at him questioningly. 'She repeated Eppie's account of the quarrel last night, with a little more. It seems John Veitch claimed Naismith owed his sister for her maidenhead, and Naismith made some sort of reply which Bel refused to tell me. Claimed she had forgotten.'

'Something to her mistress's discredit? Does she like her place there?' asked Alys shrewdly.

'I'd say so. I wonder if it concerned Frankie's parentage.'

'I'll talk to the painter's man,' she said decisively.

'The jug is empty,' said Maistre Pierre, peering into it. 'I think we must send you home, Gilbert. There is much to do in the morning.'

Eating her porridge in the candlelight before dawn, Tib seemed much more inclined to be friendly. She had greeted Gil civilly with an account of how Maggie's share of the kitchen work for the feasting had progressed. Unused to lively conversation at this hour, he responded with encouraging monosyllables while he ate.

'Are you still chasing after the man at the bedehouse?' she asked at length.

'I'll chase after him till I find who killed him,' said Gil, and put his empty bowl down for the dog.

'So you'll be there again all day? What must you do there?'

'This morning, for certain,' he agreed with caution. What had changed her tune, he wondered.

As if she had heard his thought, she said lightly, 'I'd like to know about it. It's what you do for your office, after all, and there's no other office like it that I ever heard of.'

'I'll ask questions,' he supplied, 'as I did most of yesterday. I'll get another look at the dead man, since he's likely softened and been stripped by now, and set someone to hunt for ladders in the Chanonry, fruitless though that's like to be. As Tam said, near every house must have one at least. And I'll go over the accounts.'

'Oh, accounts.' She pulled a face. 'Why?'

'I think the reason he was killed may be hid in there.'

'Oh,' she said again, and then, 'How? Accounts are just accounts, surely?'

'They tell where the money is,' said Gil, 'and where it came from.'

'I suppose so,' she said, scraping her own bowl. 'Who have you to ask questions of?'

'The kitchen hands, for a start.'

'Can I come too? I could do that for you.'

He looked at her, startled. 'Can Maggie not do with your help here?'

She opened her mouth on a sharp answer and visibly thought better of it.

'I'd like to help you,' she offered winningly. 'You'll want to get this out the way before your wedding.'

His objection crystallized, and he realized it was unworthy. It should be Alys who helped him, as she had done before, not this vixen of a sister.

'What do you want to ask the kitchen folk? Who is there? Any good-looking laddies?' she asked, with irony.

'Just the one, and he reminds me of wee William here.'

137

She pulled a face. 'Tib, if you're serious, it would be a help. Just be sure Maggie doesn't need you.'

'I can make shift without her,' said Maggie, stumping into the hall as he spoke. 'Are ye done with they bowls yet? Aye, I see you,' she added to Socrates, who had come to wag his tail at her.

'Maggie, have you a moment?' said Gil quickly, as something leapt into his mind. 'You ken all there is about the doings of the Chanonry, you're the likeliest to tell me. Does Maister Thomas Agnew have a mistress anywhere?'

'Agnew?' She paused, a wooden porringer in each hand, to consider this. 'No that I've heard. His man would be more like to tell you, that's Hob Watson that dwells on the Drygate.' She frowned, and set one dish inside the other to carry them out. 'I'll ask the men. Tam might ken something.'

'Thanks, Maggie,' said Gil.

'Now get out my sight, the pair of you. And be sure and come back for your noon bite the day. Your sister's to be here, for one thing, and she's a busy woman.'

I am surrounded by busy women, Gil thought. Even Alys, who usually has time to talk, is too busy to help me. He found himself thinking of the brief embrace they had shared last night at the door. She had leaned against him, a warm armful, smelling faintly of rosemary hairwash and lavender linen, but when he had tried to kiss her mouth she had tensed within his grasp. Is she too busy to kiss me? he wondered, and laughed at himself. But the doubt remained.

When they reached the bedehouse Maister Kennedy was just leaving, and met them in the yard with his vestments in a bundle under his arm.

'Aye, Gil,' he said. 'Where are you at wi this business?'

'No a lot further,' Gil admitted, and paused to introduce his sister. 'Tib's to help me question the household. How are they the day?'

138

'Much as usual,' said Maister Kennedy offhandedly, changing his bundle to the other arm in order to raise his round felt hat to Tib. 'I wouldny say they're grieved for the Deacon. You'll find them in the hall.'

Humphrey appeared in the doorway behind him, staring anxiously at the three figures in the yard. Beyond him, Mistress Mudie's head popped watchfully out of the kitchen. Socrates retreated, equally watchful, to the door of the chapel.

'It's a bonnie lassie,' said Humphrey after a moment, and came out to join them. Tib bobbed another curtsy and gave Gil a doubtful look. 'She's here wi the hoodie, but she's no his make.'

'Not my make,' Gil agreed, 'but my sister.'

'I see that,' said Humphrey. 'But she's no a hoodie like you. She's a wood-pigeon, aren't you no, lassie?'

'If you say so, sir,' said Tib politely.

Humphrey considered her carefully for a moment, and nodded. 'Aye, a wood-pigeon, crying always for its sweetheart.' Tib gave Gil another doubtful look, bright colour washing down over her face. 'Pray for me, lassie,' Humphrey went on, 'as I will for you, for we need one another's prayers.'

'I will, sir,' said Tib, more at home with this reasonably conventional request.

'Aye, and your sins shall be white as snow, though they were red as blood,' said Humphrey earnestly.

Tib bent her head and crossed herself, still blushing, and Maister Kennedy said, 'Humphrey, get away in and stop worrying the lassie. She's no worse than the rest of us, she's no need of your lectures.'

'I was just going to my prayers,' said Humphrey, ignoring this, 'in my own lodging. So you'll ken I'm asking forgiveness for you.'

He nodded to all three of them and turned to go back into the building. Maister Kennedy watched him going, clicking his tongue impatiently.

'Poor soul,' he said. 'He should be locked away.'

139

'*Cloudy hath bene the favour That shoon on him ful bright in times past.* He does no harm,' said Gil. 'Get away down the road, Nick. You've a lecture to deliver, if I mind right.'

Mistress Mudie, having seen her favourite out of sight, hurried across the yard with an armful of linen and a basin, pausing to curtsy but not speaking directly, and vanished into the washhouse. A fragment of her chatter floated past them.

'– all to do in this place, the dinner to see to and the Deacon to be made decent –'

Leaving Tib to insinuate herself into the bedehouse kitchen in her own way, Gil stepped into the hall and paused, looking at the brothers where they sat, as he had seen them before, round the brazier at the far end. Neither Millar nor Humphrey was present; of the others, Maister Veitch, Cubby and Barty had their heads together in loud and animated discussion, Duncan was listening and nodding, and Anselm was sitting with his eyes closed and his hands folded on his breast. Gil went forward to bend over him and touch the hands.

'Father Anselm? Might I have a word?'

'I wasny asleep,' said Anselm, blinking up at him past his crooked spectacles.

'I never thought it, sir,' said Gil, and pulled up a stool.

'You had a dog wi you yesterday,' said Anselm, peering around for Socrates.

'I left him out in the yard the day,' Gil said clearly.

'Pity. It's a good hound,' said the old man. 'Was that no a terrible thing yesterday? And those laddies trying to search our lodgings and all. Terrible, terrible. The world goes from bad to worse.'

'It's a sorry business,' Gil agreed diplomatically. 'Father Anselm, might I ask you a thing?'

'You can ask me,' said Anselm, blinking. 'I might no ken. I forget, you understand.'

'Yesterday morn,' Gil prompted. 'Can you tell me what you all did? You went to say Matins just as usual?'

140

Anselm nodded, and clutched at his spectacles as they slid on his nose.

'Just as usual,' he confirmed.

'So how did that go? Did you meet here?'

'Aye, here in the hall,' Anselm concurred, 'and Andro had the keys and unlocked the door to the Deacon's yard. I don't like it being locked,' he confided, 'what if there was a fire or a great flood or the like? I could never get ower that wall if there was a great flood.'

'That's a good thought,' agreed Gil. 'Maybe it should be considered. So Maister Millar unlocked the door. Then what?'

'We went in a procession, just as we aye do. It was raining,' he added. 'So we went across the yard in a procession and Andro unlocked the chapel as he aye does, and we gaed in and said Matins and Prime.'

'Were you all six there?'

'Seven,' agreed Anselm.

'Six,' said Maister Veitch, turning his head.

'What did ye say?' demanded Barty.

'The lad that was thurifer at the Mass thought he saw seven,' said Gil.

'Seven,' said Anselm flatly. 'He wasny there yesterday morn. He spoke to me in the night, but he'd to be elsewhere in the morning.'

'Where?' asked Gil, wondering if he would regret the answer.

Anselm pointed a wavering hand at the murky windows on the garden side of the hall, and smiled toothlessly. 'Out yonder, a course. He'd to say the Intercession for the Deacon.'

'Anselm, there was only the six of us,' said Maister Veitch.

'What are ye saying?' demanded Barty.

'There was seven, Frankie,' said Anselm again. 'Humphrey and you and me on the one side, Cubby, Barty and Duncan on the tither, and Andro as well. Makes seven.' He counted the names off. Gil nodded.

141

'So who was sitting beside you?' he asked.

'Frankie here.'

'I sit beside him,'said Maister Veitch at the same moment.

'And on your other side?'

The old man thought, nodding slowly, and then gave him a look through the lopsided spectacles which Gil could only describe as crafty.

'He came in late. It wasny him, you ken that, don't you no?'

'It wasny who, Anselm?' asked Maister Veitch. 'Your friend? Was it your friend? Or was it the Deacon?'

'There was naebody on the end,' asserted Barty.

'No on your side. He wasny your side,' said Anselm. 'He was my side.'

'But who was it?' asked Gil. 'Father Anselm?'

'It wasny him,' said Anselm, and champed his jaws at them. 'That's all I'm telling you. It wasny him.'

No persuasion could extract any more lucid statement from the old priest. Gil gave up when he judged that Anselm was becoming distressed, and left quietly to find Millar. He met the sub-Deacon in the narrow passageway, on his way to summon the brothers to Terce.

'His keys?' Millar said distractedly. 'I can give you those after the Office, Maister Cunningham, if you wouldny mind waiting. Aye, Sissie's laying him out the now, she was wi him when I came across the close.'

'That's fine,' said Gil, aware of animated discussion from the kitchen beside them. His sister's voice was raised among the rest, apparently trying to correct someone. 'I'll not hold up the Office,' he went on, 'I'll get a word wi you after, if you don't mind.'

'Aye, gladly,' agreed Millar. 'The sooner this is cleared up the better I'll like it.' The young man Gil had seen before popped out of the kitchen doorway like a rabbit pursued by a ferret, looked at them in alarm and set off for the outer yard, head down, cooking-knife still in his hand. 'The brethren are all overexcited, maister, and Humphrey

142

was neither to hold nor to bind yestreen at supper, what wi the rain and his brother and everything else, though Sissie got him calmed down after it –'

As if on cue, Mistress Mudie hurried back into the building from the yard, the young man behind her, and dived into the kitchen. Socrates followed them, but came to push his nose under his master's hand. As Mistress Mudie passed, Gil caught a wave of marjoram and a shred of her perpetual chatter: '– turn my back an instant, interfering wi my kitchen, I'll sort this –' He felt the old, familiar sinking sensation in his stomach. Millar, with great presence of mind, nodded to him and moved in dignified haste into the hall to summon the community to prayer. Gil, gathering his courage, stayed where he was.

His misgivings were justified. Mistress Mudie's voice rose sharply over the argument, which had almost ceased at her entrance.

'– and what has it to do wi you, lassie, whoever you are, coming into my kitchen and working the three of them up about witchcraft or the Deil Hisself in the close, no need of saying you was sent here, putting the blame on that man of law indeed, I never heard of such impudence and you gently-bred and all, you'll get out of my kitchen afore I –'

'I never mentioned witchcraft,' said Tib indignantly. 'It was them. I was trying to say it couldny be witchcraft, it was cold iron stabbed the man –'

Gil moved to the doorway. His sister was giving ground before Mistress Mudie, who was puffed up like an angry partridge and chattering on, red-faced,

'– no excuses, encouraging them to talk when they should ha been getting the dinner on, asking questions about matters better left alone –'

'Mistress Mudie,' said Gil, and she stopped briefly, staring open-mouthed at him. In the background a girl and an older woman he had not seen before had become ostentatiously busy over a basket of vegetables. 'I'm sorry if we've inconvenienced you,' he offered, 'coming by at a bad moment. Maybe we can find another time when you're less busy in here.'

'– don't know why you're asking more questions, Maister Cunningham, indeed I don't, you must have heard all there is to know about what happened, and as for this malapert lassie telling me sic nonsense, it's no your own lassie, is it? I've heard better things o your bride –'

'It was the truth!' exploded Tib. Gil put a hand on her shoulder and she ducked away and fell silent, looking warily sideways at him. Socrates growled in warning. The younger of the two maidservants shrieked dramatically, but Gil gestured with his other hand, and the dog retreated to the hallway.

'My sister was here at my bidding,' he said firmly. 'I'm truly sorry, mistress, if we've inconvenienced you. I can see now this is no a good time to be in your way.'

'– you should ken better by your age, though I suppose men never ken when a house is at its most taigled, but a well-reared lassie ought to ha more sense and all, and as for you, Nannie, I'll no hear another word from you the day –'

The older maidservant scowled at her. Tib seemed about to speak, but Gil tightened his grip on her shoulder, drawing her towards the doorway.

'We'll get away out your road now,' he said. 'I'll see you later, Mistress Mudie, for I still have questions for you.'

'Questions!' She flung her hands above her head. 'Aye questions! You'll be lucky if I've an answer left. Aye, you can take that malapert lassie out o my sight, and if I never set een on her again it's too soon. And good riddance to the pair of ye!'

They retreated in some disorder. Socrates nudged at his master in relief, but Gil pushed him away and drew Tib out into the yard.

'Are you going to let her talk to you like that?' she demanded in a whisper, trying to free her wrist as he towed her up the stair to Naismith's lodging. 'I never said

144

any of those things, except that you'd sent me, and that was true –'

'I know that,' he said, closing the door behind the dog. 'Keep your voice down, we're above the kitchen here.'

'I know *that*!' she said pettishly. 'It's not my fault if she keeps a pair of stupid women like that to work under her. As soon as I mentioned last night they started on about intruders, and worked each other up talking about it. The older one says it was witchcraft, the young one says it was the Deil in the garden made away wi the man. They're fixed in their minds about it. And the laddie was just feart for what that woman would say when she heard them.' She giggled. 'He kept saying to them, *What if the mistress hears you? I'll tell her on you!* And finally he did.'

'It was a good try,' said Gil. And how do I question them now? he wondered. Sissie will never let me near them after that. 'My thanks, Tib,' he added, exerting all his charity.

'Oh, well.' She shrugged one shoulder. 'I'm sorry I never got what you wanted to know. But what an old harridan, scolding at me like that and never believing a word I said. And the way she spoke to you, and all!'

'She's anxious for her position here, since the Deacon's death,' Gil pointed out. 'A new man will likely make changes.'

Tib snorted, but said only, 'What will you do now?'

'These accounts.' He turned to the rack of little drawers and pulled out the topmost bundle of papers. 'And when I get the keys from Millar I must go through the papers in the man's kist through there. Get another look at the body, look for the ladder –'

'Ladder? Oh, at the back gate,' she said, and shivered, but went on sharply, 'What, hunting all round the out-houses in the rain? I fancied you'd ha been seated some-where in comfort, asking questions, and a clerk to write down the answers.'

'No,' Gil said, as the recollection of previous investiga-tions rose in his mind, of pursuing and being pursued through moonlit scaffolding by a whispering killer, of playing cards with his enemy in a cushionless hall. 'You're thinking of the old man,' he added. 'Time enough for that when I'm his age. But if you still want to help, and you want to be seated in comfort, I can give you some of these documents to sort.'

She looked doubtful, but once he had explained what he wanted and lent her his own tablets in which to make notes, she settled by a window and began extracting the names of the various parcels of land for him. Gil took another bundle of papers from the rack and tried to concentrate on the same task, but his sister kept up an irregular flow of comments on the names of places and persons in the documents, with remarks about the weather and about Maggie's activities the day before, and he found himself thinking more of how he could get her off his hands again, and where. Could I induce her to go back to the house in Rottenrow, he wondered, or would she go down to see Kate?

'What a name!' she said, for the fifth or sixth time. 'Some folk have no thought for their bairns, the names they saddle them with. Imagine being called Wenifreda. And this is another Douglas donation,' she added. 'Four – seven – eight of them witnessing this paper.'

'The bedehouse is a Douglas foundation.'

'Oh, is *that* why –' she began, and broke off. After a moment she went on diffidently, 'Gil, do you think it was the Devil in the garden that night?'

'Seems unlikely,' said Gil. 'What reason would he have to come for Naismith rather than anyone else in Glasgow?'

'Maybe he was – well, carrying on wi black Masses, or witchcraft as those silly women said, or the like.'

'We've found nothing to suggest it.'

Tib seemed about to answer him, but was forestalled by a sudden mixed shouting from the garden. As she turned to stare out of the window, the separate voices became identifiable, and running feet sounded in the passage below the chamber where they sat.

'Humphrey, calm yoursel! Help! Help me!'

146

And Humphrey's resounding Latin: *'Trust them not, for all their fine words! Day and night they accuse him before our God –'*

'Humphrey, be still. Let go, man!'

Tib looked in horror at Gil, who was already making for the door.

'What's happening?' she demanded. 'Gil, stop them!'

'Stay here, Tib,' he ordered. 'Socrates, stay! Guard!'

In the narrow passage through the building there was a complicated struggle going on, with many exclamations and choking noises, and two dangerously waving sticks. As Gil arrived, Mistress Mudie burst out of the kitchen and dived under an elderly elbow, babbling in two very distinct tones of voice.

'– whatever's happening, who's upset you my poppet? It's no that brother of yours is it, now, now, Humphrey, that's no way to treat your brother whatever he's been saying, if that's Maister Agnew he deserves what's come to him, such things as he's been trying to –'

'The accuser shall be overthrown –'

'Sissie, get him off!' That was Millar's voice. 'He's about throttled Maister Agnew!'

Gil pushed past a bony shoulder, deflected Anselm's stick from Cubby's head, and assisted Mistress Mudie in attempting to prise Humphrey's fingers from about his brother's throat. The Latin flowed over the whole scene.

'Trust them not, for all the fine words they give you!' That isn't the Apocalypse, thought Gil, trying to dislodge a thumb. *'How long must it be before we are vindicated, before our blood is avenged? It calls out to the mountains and the crags –'*

'– saying such things about his own brother, trying to make out he would take a knife to anyone, let alone the Deacon that's been so good to him, no wonder the poor soul's owerset wi it, hearing the like from his own kin –'

'I hold the keys of Death and of Death's domain – I have the power to make men slaughter one another, for God's word and for the testimony they shall bear!'

'Brothers, please, I b-beg of you, calm yoursels!'

'Humphrey, my poppet, let go, come and sit nice and have a wee drink –'

Agnew was going black in the face and the choking sounds were diminishing; the grip about his throat was amazingly strong. Gil, with hindrance from Mistress Mudie, managed to get hold of one of Humphrey's little fingers and tugged backwards. The old trick worked. Agnew himself managed to break the grip of his brother's other hand and fell back into Millar's arms, drawing a crowing breath. Cubby and Maister Veitch got between Humphrey and his quarry, and Gil and Mistress Mudie drew the struggling bedesman towards the kitchen door, the Apocalypse rising above the general uproar.

'The beast shall be taken prisoner, and cast into the lake of fire, and all the birds shall gorge themselves on its flesh!'

I hope they like roast meat, thought Gil.

'– lovely milk for you, wi soothing herbs in it, and a wee bit honey, all for you, my poppet, and I hope the man of law didny hurt you tugging at your fingers, if you'll just come and have a nice sit-down and drink your milk –'

'We will conquer him by the testimony which we will utter –'

'St Mungo send he doesny turn into a cheese,' said Maister Veitch's dry tones.

Humphrey was steered struggling through the kitchen, where the three servants stood quickly out of the way as if they were used to this happening, and into Mistress Mudie's chamber. She thrust him down in the chair by her hearth.

'– there now, my poppet, your milk won't be a moment, and how can I thank you, maister, it's a charitable act you've just done, best you get away the now, he'll be right enough once I get his draught down him –'

'Are you sure?' Gil asked, trying to get his breath.

'The accuser of our brothers shall be overthrown,' declaimed Humphrey, *'for Michael and his angels shall wage war upon*

him, though he be allowed to mouth bombast and blasphemy!'
Then, in Scots, 'The white eaglet, the goggie, will fling his brother from the nest, and snatch his share of the carrion!'

'– all's well, Humphrey, sit nice now, oh, aye, maister, he's better already and Simmie's there if I was needing any help, there now, and some honey to go wi the milk –'

Gil retreated to the hall, where the rest of the embroilment had taken refuge. Agnew was seated in one of the chairs by the hearth, sipping water in small painful swallows, his breath whistling in his throat. The brethren were ranged about him arguing, and Millar stood by making anxious noises and asking questions.

'But how did it happen?'

'The nane o us saw it.'

'Andro, the man must be keepit out o here! Humphrey's never so bad as when he's been round him.'

'He's never gaed for any o us afore this.'

This was probably no time to question Agnew himself. Extracted from the hall with a request for Naismith's keys, Millar added little to what Gil had already guessed.

'Humphrey wasny at Terce, but neither Sissie nor I knew his brother was in the place,' he said, wringing his hands in distress. 'He must have come in quietly afore the Office when Humphrey was resting in his own lodging, and stayed talking wi him far longer than I'd ha thought advisable. The first we heard was the shouting, and then Maister Agnew came running in from the garden, and Humphrey after him trying to get him by the throat.'

'What had he said to provoke him?'

'He's aye been able to anger him,' said Millar, 'but I think from what Humphrey said, afore he went off into the Apocalypse, as ye heard, and then tried to strike Duncan wi his own staff, that Maister Agnew was wanting him to confess to having slain the Deacon.'

'That's what his texts suggested,' Gil agreed.

Millar nodded, still wringing his hands. 'Agnew's took it into his head it was his brother, though I've tried to tell him it wasny possible because of the way the locks are, and that, and he must have tried –' He turned his head as the argument in the hall grew louder again. 'Maister Cunningham, I'll have to leave you till I deal wi this.'

Chapter Eight

Tib was still sitting at the window, the dog at her feet, staring anxiously at the door, when he returned to the upper chamber.

'What was it?' she asked.

He sat down, sighing. 'The mad bedesman tried to kill his brother.'

'Mad? I didn't know one of them was mad!'

'I've mentioned it before,' he said mildly. 'He's shut in with Mistress Mudie now. She'll dose him with something to calm him, and the others are no harm to anyone. Except Maister Veitch,' he added, 'who beat me black and blue to get the Latin into me.'

She sat in subdued silence for some time, then said, 'Gil.'

'Mm?' He set down the paper he was studying.

'This is a deal more work than I imagined you did.'

'It's all in the detail.'

'And in mad people trying to kill each other.'

'That doesny happen often,' he said reassuringly.

'I hope no,' she said. Then, turning her head, 'My, is that sunshine?' She stretched her back. 'Gil, would it be safe now if I go down into the garden for a wee while? I've not seen the sun for days.'

'Humphrey won't go for you even if he sets eyes on you. Don't annoy Mistress Mudie,' he said. She snorted. 'And for God's sake, Tib, if any of the old men speaks to you, be civil.'

'What d'you take me for?' She shook out her skirts and

pushed her hair back from her brow, arranging the curling locks with a gesture Gil realized he had seen in all his sisters except Dorothea. 'Can I no question them for you?' she added with an air of innocence. 'Old men like me. They try to pinch my chin.'

He grinned, and waved her towards the door.

'Get away out and walk in the garden,' he said. 'I'll see you in a wee while.'

Is it simply because she is my sister, he wondered, as her footsteps receded down the creaking stair, or are our natures incompatible? With Alys beside me I get more done than when I'm alone, but with Tib in the room I can't concentrate.

Socrates lay down on his feet. He sighed, and bent his head to the documents again. Somewhere in this dusty pile was the reason for Naismith's death, he was certain.

He had turned over only another two pages when more steps on the stair heralded Maistre Pierre, a neat hank of linen tape in his hand.

'I have measured the distance between those feet,' he said without preamble, 'and sent the men out, since they are doing nothing useful today. Wattie has the joint-ill and cannot hold a mallet, and the journeymen were celebrating something last night and will not be fit to work safely before noon. If Robert Blacader ever wishes to see his aisle finished, he had best pray for a miracle. So they may as well search the Upper Town for our ladder.'

'Oh, the ladder!' repeated Gil, in some relief. 'I was thinking of the wrong kind of feet. That would be valuable, Pierre.'

The mason checked a moment, staring at him, then guffawed.

'Feet? What kind of feet had you in mind?' he demanded. Gil shook his head, aware that his colour was rising, hardly recognizing why. 'No, I only measured the ladder. Feet!'

'Is my sister in the garden?'

'Yes, she was out there, talking to those two students.

152

I would say she was well entertained. Certainly she hardly noticed me at the gate.' Maistre Pierre set a familiar bunch of keys on the table. 'And it seems the talking woman has finished laying out the corpse. Do you wish to come down and inspect it?'

Gil rose and crossed the room to the window where Tib had been sitting. Out in the garden was a tableau: the three young people stood conversing by the door of the Douglas lodging, Tib with her hands demurely folded at her waist, Michael leaning casually against the house wall, Lowrie tossing up his felt cap and catching it again. Seeing movement at the window he looked up, clapped the hat on his fair head in order to take it off again, and called, 'Good day, Maister Cunningham. What more have you found?'

Tib turned sharply.

'See who's here, Gil!' she exclaimed with a bright smile. 'You mind Michael, don't you?'

Gil, with a sneaking feeling of shame, recognized rescue.

'I mind Michael well,' he agreed from the window, 'and Lowrie. Good day, the both of you. Were you going down the road any time soon? Could you see Lady Tib to where she wants to be next?'

Robert Naismith was laid out on the board in the wash-house, with linen under him, and the length waiting to complete the embrace piled in creamy folds at his feet. His mouth was already closed and bound, sealing in the lentils and the scent of wine. Gil thought of Thomas Agnew's vile Malvoisie, and wondered where the dead man had drunk his last draught. There were candles at the head of the board, and Sir Duncan Fraser with a fearsome set of beads at its foot, shining head bent over his fingers while the prayers slid out from under the luxuriant moustache. The dog padded in past Gil to check the space, raising his long nose to sniff at the hanging edge of the linen shroud.

'Sir Duncan,' Gil said softly. The old man looked up, still

153

murmuring. 'Did you hear anything, the night Deacon Naismith died?'

The prayers halted, and Sir Duncan peered at him with watery blue eyes. After a moment he shook his head, absently stroking Socrates. 'Naither eechie nor ochie. A tauld 'e.'

'Nor see anything, out in the garden?' Gil asked hopefully. 'Lights, maybe, or movement?'

The old man considered, his bushy eyebrows meeting in a frown. 'A seed wir boanie Andro come hame, wi's lantron. Gaed up his steps, juist as ayeways.'

'What time was that?' Gil asked, following this with difficulty.

'Late. Lang efter Sissie was dune wi Humphra, peer saal.'

Gil nodded, and patted Sir Duncan's bony elbow.

'Thank you, sir,' he said. 'I'll not keep you from your prayers.'

'Ye're a lang-heidit laddie,' said Sir Duncan approvingly. 'Collogue wi Frankie, at's my rede.'

'I'll do that,' said Gil. He was still holding his hat, out of respect for the corpse, but he bent knee and head in salute to the old man, and turned to Maistre Pierre as the lumpy black beads in the gnarled fingers slipped round and the soft ripple of prayers began again. Socrates, having completed his survey, paced out into the yard.

Maistre Pierre was peering at the back of the Deacon's head. 'I can find no other injury than the knife wounds,' he reported. 'There is only this, which still puzzles me.' He laid the head down and turned it so that the light fell on the undamaged ear. 'It begins to fade as he softens, but it can still be seen, this pattern on his ear and jaw.'

Gil shielded his eyes from the candles and examined the marks again. Ridges and hollows marked the skin, showing up in certain angles of the light. He touched the cold flesh, but could make no sense of the impressions.

'I wonder, should we draw it?' he suggested, 'since it will fade, as you say.'

154

'A good idea,' agreed Maistre Pierre with enthusiasm, extracting his tablets from his sleeve. 'I do that, while you inspect his clothes yonder. I hope that excellent woman has not brushed and shaken them already,' he added in guarded tones.

Gil lifted the pile of tawny woollen and stained linen and took it to the daylight, where he turned the garments cautiously one by one. The furred gown offered no new information, other than a few pulled threads in the dark brown stuff of one sleeve which fitted well enough with the idea that the body had been put over the wall. He shook out the stinking hose and scrutinized them, holding them fastidiously by the points still threaded in the eyelets at the waist, and was rewarded by two more pulled threads and another scrap of straw caught in the weave. Agnew's chamber in the tower had left its trace.

The jerkin and shirt, stiffened with blood across the breast, were slashed where the knife had gone through them. Was this why Humphrey said the Deacon was a robin, he wondered, seeing the extent of the dark stain. He was examining the cuts in the linen when Socrates, ranging about the yard, pricked his ears and bounded towards the entryway, tail waving. Gil heard the light footsteps in the same moment. The whole day brightened round him, and he set down the armful of fouled garments as Alys appeared round the corner of the chapel, plaid over her head against the chilly breeze. Socrates leapt round her, pushing his long nose under her hand, and she paused to greet him, then crossed the yard to meet Gil.

'*Nou skrinketh rose and lylie flour.* My hands stink,' he said, 'I won't touch you,' and bent to kiss her as she tilted her face. She put up her own hand to touch his jaw, and smiled up at him.

'I have spoken to the painter's man,' she said, 'and I thought I would come out and tell you what I learned from him. Gil, what has happened? You look as if something is awry.'

155

'Ah – Alys,' said Maistre Pierre from inside the wash-house before Gil could answer. 'We are inspecting the body. Come tell me what you think of this.'

Comparing her father's competent rendering with the original impression on Naismith's softening flesh, Alys said after a moment, 'It reminds me of something. He has lain on something after he died, I suppose.' Maistre Pierre nodded. 'But what? Not rope, but could it be string, set close together? Something with cord wrapped round it?' She demonstrated with her hands. 'Where was he?'

'I wish we knew,' said Gil. He turned to set the pile of clothes back where he had found it. 'He certainly went to see Agnew, and brought the proof away with him in these scraps of straw, but after that – Pierre, is the man's purse still in his lodging?'

'It is.' The mason stepped away from the corpse, bowed to it and crossed himself. 'I think the dead has no more to tell us. Now you are here, come up and help us with these accounts, *ma mie*. I am certain there is more to be learned from them. Gilbert, you may wash your hands at the kitchen drain if they trouble you.'

Gil, making his way obediently towards the kitchen, found Alys at his elbow.

'I met with your sister on the road,' she began quietly.

'Which sister?' he asked, pausing by the door into the building.

'Lady Tib.' He noted the formal reference, where Kate was always *Your sister Kate* or simply *Kate*. 'She was with Michael Douglas and the other young man, you called him Lowrie.' Gil nodded. 'We stopped to pass the time of day, and she told me of the incident earlier, and also made some reference to *madame* here at the almshouse. I wondered,' she went on diffidently, 'whether anything required to be smoothed over.'

They were speaking in French, but he still dropped his voice.

'Oh, Alys. Yes, indeed.' He moved away from the door and from the range of outhouses, and explained rapidly.

'She wanted to help me, so I set her to question the kitchen hands, and somehow it didn't work. There are two women there, who began talking about witchcraft, and the kitchen-boy took fright and summoned his mistress, who was incensed.'

She nodded, her elusive smile flickering, and turned towards the buildings.

'I'll see what I can learn,' she promised.

He could not work out how she did it. As they reached the kitchen door Mistress Mudie appeared from her own chamber, and cast them a glance of weary belligerence.

'— it's that man of law again, I hope wi no more questions, kind as he is, for my head's as empty as a pint pot by now, and another lass wi him, is it your bride this time, maister? That's right kind of you to bring her to see us, and such a bonnie lass and all, but I'm no certain it's the time of day for visitors —'

'You must be Mistress Mudie,' said Alys. 'I'm Alys Mason. I'm told you are herb-wise, and I wished for your advice, *madame*.'

Mistress Mudie's expression altered. '— depends what you were wanting, there's matters I'll no deal wi —'

'Of course there are,' agreed Alys. She stepped into the kitchen and bobbed a neat curtsy. The two women exchanged formal kisses, and though Mistress Mudie's conversation did not seem to halt as she bustled in and out of her own chamber, by the time Gil had rinsed the uncompromising smell of stale urine off his hands at the stone sink in the corner she and Alys were seated at the long table discussing a small pot of ointment, while Socrates watched alertly from the doorway and the young man hacking vegetables worked on at the other end of the board. A coin was exchanged, Alys murmuring something about a donation, and Mistress Mudie's dimple appeared as she smiled.

'— oh, that's kind, I canny take payment in course but this'll buy a wee treat for my old men, this should sort your lassie's hands in a day or so, dearie, Mallie there has

157

the same trouble and I aye give her some of this to put on when it's bad –' The two kitchenmaids looked round at this, then returned hastily to their work as Mistress Mudie glared at them and chattered on, now apparently to Gil, '– that good of you to come out to help us when you're as taigled, but the idea that someone made away wi the Deacon I canny get used to, it's surely a mistake of some sort, it's made Humphrey sore distressed, the poor soul, you saw him the now, he'd like a wee word, if you'd be so good, he's still here in my chamber where his brother canny find him if he comes by again wi no warning –'

'Maister Humphrey?' said Gil, picking this thread out of the tangle. 'How is he now?'

'– oh, he's as jumpy as a flea, and no wonder, wi his own kin making such accusations against him, so if the two of you could indulge him, lassie, Maister Cunningham, I'd take it as a real deed of charity –'

'I'll speak to him, of course,' said Gil, wondering how it was that he was still *Maister Cunningham* but Alys was *lassie* as soon as she stepped into the kitchen. 'Alys?'

'And I,' she said, a little reluctantly.

Humphrey was sitting by the brazier in Mistress Mudie's chamber, biting at his cuffs and staring anxiously at the wall. Hoccleve again, *Noon abood, noon areest, but al brain-seke*, thought Gil. When they entered he looked round sharply, shrinking back, but recovered when he recognized a familiar face.

'It's you that's asking the questions,' he said through Mistress Mudie's tumbling speech. 'I saw you this morn. And this one's your bonnie make.' Alys, tense beside Gil, nodded in acknowledgement. 'And I see it now, maister, you're no a hoodie. I took you for a hoodie, but I can tell now you're a heron.'

'A heron?' said Gil involuntarily. 'Why ever a heron?'

Humphrey gave him his blank smile.

'Oh, it's quite clear to me. A heron that goes stepping about in all the mud,' he demonstrated the deliberate gait with his hands, 'watching his feet, and then *stabs!* wi his beak.' Gil felt Alys flinch beside him as Humphrey stabbed with his beakless head. 'And this is your make, maister. A heron like yoursel, she is.'

'This is Mistress Mason,' said Gil formally. A heron? he thought. In her blue woollen gown, the grey plaid over her shoulders, her plumage was the right colour, but that was all.

'– no a very nice thing to call a bonnie lassie –' agreed Mistress Mudie.

'Maister Humphrey,' said Gil, on a venture. Humphrey turned his blank smile on him again. 'You mind you told me that Deacon Naismith is a robin, now that he's dead?'

'Aye, that's right, he's a robin,' agreed Humphrey.

'So who's the sparrow?' Gil asked hopefully.

Humphrey shook his head. 'No, no. There's no sparrow here. Frankie's a kestrel, see, and Anselm's a coal-tit, and Cubby's a yaffle,' he counted on his fingers, 'and Barty's a barn-owl, and Duncan's a jay, you can tell, but there's no sparrow in the place.'

'And Maister Millar?'

'Andro's another owl,' Humphrey said confidently.

'Now that's enough, my poppet, you and your games, calling folk all sorts –' said Mistress Mudie reprovingly.

Humphrey ignored her, and looked from Gil to Alys again. 'And you're to be wed soon, wi kirk and Mass, Sissie tells us.'

'That's right.'

With unnerving suddenness, Humphrey's eyes focused, and his expression changed to one of professional pastoral concern. He raised his right hand with its bleeding nails, and pronounced a blessing on their coming marriage in rolling Latin phrases. Gil found his throat stopped, but Alys's tongue was loosed. Bending her head she crossed herself and said gently, 'Thank you indeed, Maister Humphrey. I hope you'll pray for us.'

'And you for me, my lassie, if you will, for Our Lord

159

kens I need it,' said Humphrey. Then, abandoning sense, 'Sissie, have you a bit fish for these two herons?'

'They'll eat in their own place, my poppet,' said Mistress Mudie, wiping her eyes on her sleeve. 'And maybe you'd best go now, for he's no been good the day, it was all too much for us yesterday what wi one thing and then another –'

'The poor man,' said Alys as they stepped into the yard.

'Much sorwe I walke with For beste of boon and blood,' Gil quoted. 'It seems he is mad for grief and guilt.'

She nodded, then looked around, and drew Gil to the chapel. The little building was full of shadows leaping from the two candles on the altar; nothing else moved, although it felt almost as if someone had left as they entered. Through the roof? Gil wondered, amused at himself. There's only the one door.

'The two women sleep out,' Alys was saying quietly, 'as I suspected when you said they were talking about witchcraft. No wonder the laddie was frightened. And he sleeps under the table or on the hearth, and saw and heard nothing moving, not even the Devil.'

'Alys, that's marvellous,' he said, drawing her into his arms.

'I do wonder,' she went on, 'now I have seen the boy, whether he would think to mention it if Mistress Mudie had left her chamber later. He must be used to her going in and out at all hours if she's needed.'

'Difficult to find out.' Gil tightened his clasp. 'What did you learn from the painter's man?'

'Oh, yes.' She paused, ordering her thoughts. 'He spoke to his cousin last night, indeed she must have told the half of Glasgow about it all. The only new thing I learned is that Naismith may have known the little girl was not his. You said the dates didn't add up, didn't you?'

'Mm,' he said, and kissed the top of her ear.

'I wondered if her brother thought it was Naismith's.'

'What would that do?' he said.

'I don't know. It gives him the more reason to dislike the man, if Naismith was repudiating his mistress and his child as well.'

'Did Daidie know who is the child's father?'

'He said not.'

'If this was a verse romance, it would turn out to be the mysterious watcher.'

'Oh, Daidie mentioned him too. By today he'd become a giant with a black beard and a bloody sword.' She looked up at him, her quick smile flickering. 'The Watch won't venture along the Drygate this night, I imagine.'

'I wonder what Bel really saw? I'm not inclined to believe in her watcher, giant or not.'

She nodded, and laid her head briefly on his shoulder, then drew away slightly. Reluctantly, he let her go, and she bent the knee to the altar and crossed herself.

'What is my father doing with the accounts?' she speculated. Heart heavy, he followed her out across the yard and up the sounding stair.

Maistre Pierre had all the bundles of paper arranged on the polished surface of the table, and was peering at one sheet held at a distance, his tablets in his other hand.

'The man wrote appalling small,' he complained as they entered. 'This is that very profitable estate, you recall, Gil, out by Kilsyth. The total is considerable.'

'May I see?' Alys took the paper he held, and ran a finger down the returns. 'Where was it all going? This alone would keep the bedehouse in comfort, I should have thought. Whose gift was it?'

'Now that's interesting,' said Gil, scrutinizing the opened packet on the table. 'It was gifted by the parents of Humphrey Agnew, specifically for his keep.'

'Surely that isn't the original?' asked Alys, looking round his shoulder.

'No, an extract only.' He was still studying the abbreviated phrases. 'The parchment must be filed safe elsewhere.

161

See, here it merely says, *ad domusdei S Servi, de Thomasi Agnew et Anna Paterson ux suis, pro bono Umfridi fil eis.*'

'I would have expected better Latin,' she said critically.

'Not necessarily.' He turned the leaf and skimmed over the other side. 'This lists the boundaries of the land, and the buildings and tenants. It seems to include an entire ferm-toun. Nothing here about the terms of the gift. The parchment will have the detail – what prayers are expected, and how much care Humphrey gets in return for the income.'

'He must need a deal of care, poor man,' said Alys. 'Gil, what is all this about birds?'

'He seems to see the folk around him as birds,' Gil agreed. 'Maister Cubby as a woodpecker, Millar as an owl. And the Deacon was a shrike and then a robin.'

'Why a robin?'

'*Because he's dead*,' Gil quoted. 'Whether he means the one in the bairns' rhyme – *I said the sparrow with my bow and arrow* – or the one St Mungo brought back to life, I've no notion.'

'St Mungo's robin? But the saint will not bring the Deacon back to life.'

'It seems unlikely.'

'Naismith was making a good profit from the situation,' said Maistre Pierre. He had gone on to another sheaf of paper. 'Now this is a Douglas gift. If the family uses the place as a townhouse, I imagine the Deacon would have less freedom to divert these funds.'

'And you said the man's own papers are in his kist,' Alys prompted.

'It is locked,' said her father without looking up. 'The keys are yonder.'

Following her after a short time, Gil found her on her knees before the painted kist, its lid open. She was going methodically through the packets of paper and parchment from one of the inner compartments, but as he knelt beside her she inspected the last one and gathered them up to put them back in the kist, their dangling seals clicking together.

'I wondered if the bedehouse papers were here,' she said, 'but these are the documents for the man's own possessions. What about this? Ah!' She scooped another handful from a different compartment and gave half to Gil. He contrived to touch her fingers as he took them, and she looked round, smiled as their eyes met, looked quickly away. What is the matter, he wondered, trying not to look at the bed beyond her. Mistress Mudie had obviously been up to clean the lodging, for the mattress was stripped, the bare pillows piled at its head and the tapestry counterpane folded neatly at the foot.

'Here is the Kilsyth gift,' said Alys. She handed him the crackling document. 'Is this the complete disposition?'

'It is,' he agreed, running his eye down the lines of careful script. 'Drawn up by Thomas Agnew the younger, it says –'

'Is that the same man?'

'It must be. It doesn't add much to what we know already,' he admitted. 'The property seems to be dedicated to Humphrey's keep, and to revert to the bedehouse absolutely after his death.'

'Unwise,' she said, pulling a face. 'What if he became worse and had to be sent somewhere he could be shut away? How would he be supported then?'

'I suppose the parents felt the bedehouse would pay for that out of this gift.'

'Perhaps the previous Deacon was less acquisitive.'

He nodded, and folded the parchment carefully back into its creases. 'I'll ask Millar if I may take all these documents for safe keeping just now. Then we can go through them at more leisure.'

'A good plan. And what is this?' Alys lifted a piece of paper from the floor. She turned it over, looking at the writing, and unfolded it. 'It's a map, with notes. Did it fall out when I unfolded that disposition? There are names on it – is that Auchenreoch? Queenzie?'

'It must have,' said Gil, answering her second question. 'Those are names from the Kilsyth property.'

'Someone has planned great things.' She turned the sheet of paper to read more of the notes. 'A vast house, by the look of it. *How* many cartloads of stone? Do you know the writing?'

'It's Naismith's.' Gil grinned. 'The bedehouse properties are at the Deacon's disposition, and he has certainly made the most of the situation, as your father said. Ambitious!'

'Did you say,' she recalled thoughtfully, 'that the man of law suggested he might have been altering the terms of the dispositions?'

'I did.' Gil unfolded the parchment again and spread it out on the swept boards between them. 'I wonder. What do you think? I see nothing irregular here.'

'No,' she said after a moment. 'It's all in the one hand, isn't it.'

He looked down at the neat paragraphs, and then at her face beside his, leaned forward and kissed her. She moved at the last moment, so that it landed on her cheek rather than her mouth, but she turned her head slightly and returned the salute, a single, clinging kiss. Then, with a little shiver, she drew away and scrambled to her feet.

'I must go down the hill,' she said. 'There are things I must see to.'

'We'll show this to Pierre,' said Gil, 'and get these papers packed up, and then I'll come with you. I have to find John Veitch's lodging and speak to the widow.'

Leaving Maistre Pierre planning to go out and find his men, they set out to walk down the High Street, arm in arm, the dog at their heels. The wind was still chilly, with spatters of rain in it.

'I hope it will be dry next week,' said Alys doubtfully, pulling her plaid up with her free hand. 'The brocades will be spoiled if it's wet.'

'We should have made it a double wedding with Kate and Augie Morison, in September, as they suggested. They had a fine day.'

'I wish we had, now.' She looked up at him, and quickly away. 'It would all be . . .'

'All be what?' Gil drew her aside to avoid a ranging pig outside one of the small cottages on the steep slope called the Bell o' the Brae. 'All be over by now? Is that how it seems to you, Alys?' He stopped, turning to look down at her. 'Something to be got over?'

'No!' she protested, going scarlet. 'Gil, no!' She glanced about them, moved closer and put her hand on his chest. 'I want to be married, more than anything, I swear it. We'll be together, we'll be partners, man and wife. It's just . . .'

'Just what?'

She looked away, biting her lips.

'I can't explain. I don't know.'

'Alys.' He gathered both her hands in his. 'Something's troubling you. Tell me.'

'I can't explain,' she repeated, shaking her head. Resolutely she pulled away, took his arm and set off down the street again. 'Gil, can you tell me anything about this – this bed your mother has sent?'

'Bed,' he repeated. 'Oh, Pierre mentioned it.'

'Sh-she says it was her marriage bed.'

'If it's the one I think,' he said cautiously, 'it's a box bed like the one in Naismith's lodging, much the same size but with a lot of carving about it. Saints and Green Men and so forth. The hangings were red cloth, if I mind right.'

'Red,' she said doubtfully. 'They are still in the canvas. Lucky we decided on blue for the walls, then. It ought to fit in the chamber if it's a box bed. I was afraid it might be a tester-bed,' she admitted, 'built for a higher room.'

'Do you mind?'

'It's generous of her.'

'That doesn't answer me.' She was silent. 'Did we have a bed other than this one?'

165

She shook her head. 'I hadn't – I was going to – there are several beds in the house that would be suitable.'

'Your mother's bed?'

She crossed herself at the mention of her dead mother. 'My father sleeps in that.' She sighed. 'Red hangings will be very smart, and I expect the men can set it up easily once the painters are done. Perhaps we should get the hangings out of their canvas now and air them.'

Gil whistled to the dog as they reached the pend which gave entry to the mason's sprawling house.

'I'll leave you here, sweetheart,' he said, handing her the packet of the bedehouse documents. 'We need to talk, but I must get this matter out of the way as soon as I can.'

'I know that,' she said. 'Do you want to leave Socrates with me? He can play with John in the kitchen till you come back.'

The children running in St Catherine's Wynd broke off their chase and nodded when he asked for Veitch's landlady, grinning and pointing at the building beside them, and one boy who seemed to be their leader shouted up at the windows, 'Haw, Widow Napier! Mistress Napier! Ye're socht!'

'Who seeks me?' returned a shrill voice. A shutter two floors up was flung wide, and a white-coifed head peered out. 'And you bairns should be away hame for your noon bite by this, the lot of ye!'

'We're to get one last game, Mistress Napier,' called the ringleader. 'You're het, Davie Wilson.'

Gil identified himself as the children scattered again, and the widow peered suspiciously down into the wynd.

'You'd best come up, sir,' she said after a moment. 'It's yon stair there, two up and at your left.'

The building was a timber-framed structure with a skin of boards, and a peeling figure of some saint painted near the stair door might have been St Nicholas, patron of children, students and sailors. As he picked his way cautiously round the turns of the stair Gil reflected that not only the presence of the patron saint of sailors might make John Veitch feel at home here; the building creaked like a carvel in a gale.

'And what's your business wi me, maister?' demanded the widow in her doorway.

'I think you've a man John Veitch lodging wi you,' said Gil, halting a couple of steps below her landing so that his head was level with hers. She was a skinny little woman, clad in decent homespun with a clean white linen headdress. One hand clutched her beads for protection.

'Is John a friend of yours?'

'I knew him when we were boys,' said Gil. 'I blacked his eye a couple times.'

She relaxed a little at that.

'Aye, well, he's no here the now,' she said in her shrill voice. 'He's at his sister's, where they've no their troubles to seek for, you'll maybe have heard.'

'Is that right?' said Gil, hastily revising his approach to this witness. 'No, I've not heard. I'm sorry if he's got troubles in the family. I only came by to ask his pardon for no meeting him last night – no, the night before that it would be now.'

'Night afore last, maister?' she said, staring at him. 'I wouldny ken about that.'

'Oh,' said Gil. 'I'd trysted wi him for the Compline hour at a tavern up the High Street, and I never got there till near an hour after it. Likely he went on somewhere else,' he suggested.

'Oh, very likely,' she agreed, nodding hard. 'He's no here the now. Are you a writing man, maister?' she speculated, eyeing the pen-case hung at his belt. 'You could leave him a scrape o your pen if you wanted.'

'That would be kind, if you'd pass it on.'

'Oh, no trouble. And while you've your pen and ink out, maybe you'd scrieve a wee thing for me and all?' she said hopefully. 'Come away in, then, maister, and get a seat.'

167

The widow's message was for her sister in Dumbarton, a list of disjointed statements about members of their kindred. Perched on the stock at the edge of yet another bed, its curtain draped over his back, bent nearly double to lean on the stool she had offered him as a writing-surface, Gil made notes in his tablets, then selected a piece of paper from the small store he carried in his pen-case, flattened it out, weighed it down with the beaker of ale she had insisted on pouring for him, and began compressing the string of facts into the smallest space he could manage while she assured him that her sister's neighbour's son would be able to read it for her, or if not, then the priest would likely oblige. 'Though I don't know,' she said doubtfully, 'she said Sir Alan read her the last one, a year ago, and when I saw her at Yule she hadny heard the half of what I sent by it.'

'I'll write as clear as I can,' he said. Behind his heels, under the creaking frame, lay a low truckle-bed, covered in a worn checked plaid, along with a bundle of unidentified timbers fully as long as the bed. Presumably the widow let out one bed and slept in the other, he speculated, copying his note about her sister Christian's son Will's new apprentice. 'Did John say where he went the other night when I missed him?' he asked.

'No, no, maister, he never said, but I'm thinking it was some kind of mischief,' she said tolerantly, 'for the pair of them came in here after daylight, having hid in a pend from the Watch, so they tellt me, and John had his boots wet as wet, it was a mercy he had his seaboots wi him and could put those on when he went out again and his friend got a bit sleep. There's his good ones still hung up filled wi moss and rags, but he wasny that worried. Sailors gets used to wet feet, he tellt me.'

She pointed at the window, where a pair of sturdy leather boots hung in the opening.

'Good boots,' said Gil, eyeing them. 'They're never local make, though.'

'No, he said he got them in some foreign place. Spain, or

Portingal, or the like. They've both got all kinds of foreign stuff about them.'

'They?' said Gil. 'Has he a friend lodging wi him? He never said.'

'Oh, aye.' Relaxing further, she confided, 'I'm right glad he brought him here. It brings me in a bit more coin, for I never like to ask strangers to be bedfellows.'

'I'm sure that's wise,' said Gil solemnly. 'I wonder, is it anyone I know? His brother William, maybe?'

'Oh, no, it's no his brother, he's no like him at all. Dark-headed, and a great black beard. It's a fellow called Rankin Elder. Off the same ship, they tell me.'

'Is that right? Well, likely I'll meet him if I catch up with John. And does John have my cloak, would you know?'

'Your cloak, maister? What like is it?' she said, peering at him.

'A black one, with a collar, and braid on it.' He finished the letter. 'What name shall I put at the foot, mistress?'

'Sybilla Thomson,' she said promptly, 'relic of John Napier. A black cloak wi braid and a collar, sir? No, John's got nothing like that. He's got his boat-cloak, but that's brown, just the brown fleece.' She reached past him to draw aside the curtain, revealing the interior of the bed. Striped blankets were neatly folded back and a greyish sheet was stretched over the bolster at the head. Two scrips lay at the foot, neither one big enough to hold the bulky folds of material which made up a bedehouse cloak. 'He must be wearing his cloak, a cold day like this, and the other fellow the same. There's all they brought with them from Dumbarton, maister.'

Down in the street, he put the widow's small coin in his purse, making a mental note to give it to St Nicholas at the first opportunity, and walked on to the end of the wynd. It petered out into a narrow track between a diminutive chapel and two leaning sheds, and suddenly debouched on to the riverside. He looked up and down the banks, and at the gold-brown water of the Clyde, the same colour as

Alys's eyes, chattering over the sandy shallows in mid-stream. The biting wind whipped at its surface, raising silvery ruffles. Under the bank, where the water was deeper, one or two small boats were tied up, their oars presumably gone home with their owners, and several larger craft had been dragged out on to the opposite shore. There was a cormorant drying its wings on the sternpost of one. On this shore, a well-trampled path led downriver along the bank.

He turned to walk back through the wynd. The little alley was quiet, the children presumably called home for their midday meal. Which was where he should be, he realized in dismay.

'I told you this morn,' said Maggie grimly. 'Lady Dawtie was here and away again, and got a bite wi your uncle and the household. And where's Lady Tib, I'd like to know? I've kept you two-three bannocks and cheese, and that'll ha to do you, Maister Gil, for I've more to do than run about cooking twice for them that canny come home at the right time.'

'It's more than I deserve, Maggie,' he agreed, sitting down on the settle by the kitchen fire. The kitchen-boy gaped at him, and moved anxiously to the other end of the spit. 'Give me that in my hand and get on with your work, and I'll be away out from under your feet as soon as I've eaten it.'

She snorted, but seemed to be mollified.

'I've a word for you, too,' she said, pounding heavily at something in the big stone mortar. 'I asked Matt about the man Agnew, and he says, Aye, he has a mistress.'

'Oh?' he said hopefully, and took a bite of a bannock. William the kitchen-boy suddenly got to his feet and scurried out into the scullery.

'He's no sure where she dwells,' she added. 'He says he thinks she might be a Chisholm or some surname from that part.' William returned, walking carefully and bearing

170

a brimming cup of ale. 'Oh, a clever laddie!' Maggie exclaimed. The boy glanced at her, moon-face beaming, and ale splashed on the flagstones at his feet. Gil hastily took the beaker and thanked him, and William grinned again, ducked his head in embarrassment and went back to his post at the spit. 'Anyway, he says he'll ask about and see what he can learn. Did you no find Agnew's man Hob? Tam said he'd ken the woman's lodging.'

'Not yet.' Gil took a pull at the ale. 'I've one or two things to see to in the Chanonry, I'll likely come across the man while I'm about them. You mind I'll be out for supper tonight? I'm to take Dorothea down to meet Alys.'

'Lady Dawtie let me know.' Maggie sifted the fragments in the mortar through her fingers, and applied the pestle again. 'I tellt her she'd relish her supper. Your lassie keeps a good kitchen.' She looked sharply at him. 'Is all well wi you, Maister Gil? Have you and her had a falling-out?'

'No,' he said hastily. 'No such thing.'

'She's likely doing too much. She'll be fine by the morning after you're bedded,' said Maggie cheerfully.

Chapter Nine

'My maister?' said Hob, standing in the doorway of the house in Vicars' Alley. 'Maister Agnew? What's that to do wi you, might I ask, maister?'

'He told me himself,' improvised Gil, 'but I never made a note of it, and now I've forgotten what hour he said he got home. Were you here that evening or had you gone away early?'

'No to say early,' retorted Hob, his scrubby beard twitching. 'No to say early,' he repeated, 'but I still canny see what's it to do wi you.'

'I'm hunting whoever it was killed Deacon Naismith,' Gil said soothingly, 'and Maister Agnew was the last person we ken saw him.'

Hob snorted.

'That daft pair o women Sissie Mudie's got in her kitchen,' he said. 'They're saying it's the Deil cam for the Deacon. No, it wasny my maister. He was elsewhere that night.'

'Was he, now?' said Gil. 'D'you mean he never came home? How d'you know that?'

'When you've been wi the one maister as long's I have,' said Hob, 'you can tell these things.' He leaned against the doorpost, looking challengingly at Gil. 'Was there anything else you were wanting, maister?'

'So where was he?' Gil began to play in a meaningful way with the strings of his purse. Hob glanced down and curled his lip. 'Tell me what you know.'

'No a lot,' said Hob dismissively.

Gil opened the purse and took a coin from it. 'It would help if I knew where everyone was,' he suggested, making the coin appear and disappear between his fingers.

'Aye, I suppose,' said Hob, and stood upright away from the doorpost. 'You'd best come in for a bit. It's cold standing here. But I've the supper to see to,' he warned.

Following the man into the painted hall, Gil paused and added a second coin to the one in his hand.

'You were away before Maister Agnew came back in the evening,' he prompted. Hob nodded, his eye on Gil's fingers. 'What time would that be?'

'Soon as I'd syned out the supper-dishes. He gaed out when he'd eaten, took his tablets and a bundle of papers wi him, so I took it he'd some business to attend to. I seen to the crocks and gaed out mysel.' He leered slightly. 'I'd company to see.'

'And you're saying your maister was from home that night. Had he been back and gone out again, do you suppose?'

'Oh, aye. He'd been at the Malvoisie, sticky glasses all ower the hall. It'll no last, the way he's going through it.'

'Glasses? Brought someone home, had he?'

Hob shrugged, and hitched his jerkin back up one shoulder.

'Maybe. Maybe no. There was one rolled away in a corner past where he'd spilled the stuff, it's as like him no to bother lifting it, just fetch himsel a clean one off the cupboard.'

'If it was dark, he might not see it,' said Gil thoughtfully. Hob grunted, in a tone which clearly conveyed scepticism. 'And then he went out again. Where would he be going, would you think?'

'I'm no paid to watch him like a wet-nurse, ye ken,' Hob retorted.

'Just the same, I'll lay money you've a good notion where he slept that night,' Gil hazarded, making the two coins slide about in his fingers so that one appeared, then the other. 'I take it he was from home the rest of the night?'

Hob wagged his head from side to side, the moth-eaten beard twitching as he pursed up his mouth.

'Likely he'd trysted wi his – er – wi someone for midnight, or some such daft hour.'

'Why would he do that?' wondered Gil.

Hob shrugged again, watching the travelling coins. 'How would I ken? But he came home afore it was light, and he'd no come far, for he wasny wet, and he was –' The man gave Gil another sideways leer. 'He'd wrestled a match or two in the night, I'd say. He was about done. No best pleased to see me, either,' he added. 'It's a poor thing, when a man gets cursed for coming out early to his work.'

'It seems unfair,' agreed Gil. 'She lives near here, then?'

'Aye.' Gil raised his eyebrows and waited, but Hob gave him a disagreeable look. 'The maister'll tell you hissel if he wants you to ken.'

Gil tossed one coin up, then the other, and caught them in his other hand.

'And his cloak was dry?'

'He wasny wearing a cloak.'

'No?' Gil groped on the rush matting for the coin he had dropped, and straightened up. 'No cloak? And his hat?'

'No hat neither.'

The coins made their way into Hob's palm, and Gil turned to leave.

'It's quite a chamber this,' he commented. 'What wi the paint and the matting. Is it easy to keep? We've a lodging to furnish out the now.'

'Aye, so I've heard.' Hob leered again. 'Easy enough, when the maister doesny spill things on it. He'd a full glass of Malvoisie overturned on the strip yonder the other day, so he tellt me. So he turned it, to save getting our feet sticky. So he tellt me,' he repeated, and opened the door for Gil. 'But Tammas Hogg two doors up tellt me a good way

174

to sort that, so we'll try it the morn's morn. And now I'll say good day, maister, for I've his supper to get started.'

Leaving Vicars' Alley in the dying light, Gil strode along with his head down, thinking hard. He passed the little chapel of St Andrew, aware of the sounds of the Office from within, and made his way round the western towers of St Mungo's. Here the most senior of the men of law who inhabited the Consistory tower were already leaving, early lanterns lit, discreet murmurs of conversation dropping as he came past. He slowed his pace and raised his hat to one or two, but went on to the Wyndhead and turned left into the Drygate.

Marion Veitch's house was lit and busy. His nose told him they were to have mutton stew with broad beans for supper; Eppie's expression when she opened the door told him the moment was not convenient.

'I'll not keep your mistress long,' he said reassuringly. 'It's another thing I want to ask her. Or you might know the answer,' he added.

'Well,' she said with reluctance. 'Come in out the cold and I'll ask her. What was it you were wanting to ken?'

'Something about the Upper Town.'

Her eyebrows went up, but she left him by the light of two candles and went up the narrow stair to report to her mistress. He heard the conversation as a series of hissing whispers, over the little girl's quiet singing. Then feet moved on the boards, and Marion came down, the fur lining of her dark brown gown sweeping the stairs, the candles glinting on the gold chain on her bosom. She seemed more alive than she had yesterday, her movements brisker, but her face was not encouraging.

'It's ower late for calling, Gil,' she said. 'Unless you were able to stay for your supper? It's mutton.'

'And beans,' he agreed. 'No, Marion, I thank you, I'm bidden to the Masons' the night with my sister. How are you the day?'

Over their heads the child laughed, and began her song

175

again. It seemed to be nonsense: *'Vendy may vendy may, esty sack o kay-o.'* Or was it French?

'I'm managing,' said Marion, a trifle impatiently. 'What was it you wanted to ask?'

'Do you know if Thomas Agnew,' he began, saw how maladroit the question was, and carried on perforce, 'has a mistress?'

'Do *I* ken?' she repeated. 'No.' She began to turn away.

'Do you know of a woman by the name of Chisholm, or something like that,' he hazarded, 'somewhere in the Upper Town? No far from Vicars' Alley. Or would any of the household know?'

'No,' she said again. 'Gil, I canny stand here and talk, I've as much to see to. Come back a time when I'm less taigled and we'll talk all you please.'

He got himself out of the house with civility, and paused out in the wynd. Above him, the child was still singing.

'Kate and for ailos, kate and for ailos,' went the little voice. A man laughed, and answered her. Gil stared up at the window, but someone slammed the shutters shut, without looking out. Along the house-wall the kitchen door opened. As he looked round a head popped out, and was followed by the rest of the maidservant Bel. She beckoned sharply, and he moved towards her.

'It's no Chisholm, maister, it's Dodd,' she said rapidly. 'Ellen Dodd, and she dwells in the next wynd but two down the Drygate on the other side. I've a cousin in the same wynd.'

'And Agnew calls there?' The girl nodded, glancing over her shoulder. 'Bel, many thanks. Is all well in the house here?'

'Oh, aye,' she said, and broke into a huge smile. 'Better than well. I'll need to go, maister.'

She slipped back in out of the rain, and he was left looking at the shining silvery planks of the oak door.

'Well, well,' he said aloud, and turned to make his way back to the street.

176

The next wynd but two on the other side of the Drygate was another pocket of small houses, all lit and bustling as the supper was prepared. Gil stopped at the first house, asked for Mistress Dodd, and was directed further along.

'Another man calling on her, is it?' said the maidservant who had answered the door, peering at Gil in the light from behind her. 'Well, that's no surprise.'

She withdrew and shut the door before Gil could defend himself, and he heard the bar thudding into place.

Mistress Dodd's house proved to be a modest structure with sagging thatch and crooked shutters. When Gil rattled the latch one of these was flung back and a head popped out, white kerchief-ends swinging.

'Who's that at this hour?'

'Does Mistress Ellen Dodd dwell here?' he asked.

'What if she does?'

'I'd like a word with her, if I may.'

'And who's asking? What's it about?'

'I'm a man of law,' he said reassuringly. 'My name's Gil Cunningham. I've a couple questions for the mistress. It won't take long.'

The woman snorted, and withdrew. He heard female voices within, and after a moment the door was unbarred.

'You'd better no be long,' said the maidservant sourly. 'Her supper's about ready.'

She lit him across the outer room and into a small chamber, clearly painted by the same hand as Agnew's hall in lozenges of red and green, with pots of blue flowers in them. At its centre, standing to greet him, was a lady who somehow matched the chamber well.

'I'm Ellen Dodd,' she said, assessing his sober dress with one swift look. 'Are you from the Consistory Court? There's no harm come to – to my friend, is there?'

'No, no,' he said, and introduced himself and his position. 'I'm looking into this matter of Deacon Naismith's death.'

She crossed herself at the mention, and waved him to a

stool, sitting down opposite. She was a well-rounded woman, dressed in a kirtle of blue wool with a loose gown of black velvet over it, and gave the impression that either garment, firmly fastened though they were, could slide off at any moment. Curls of tawny-coloured hair escaped from her French hood.

'I'm no particular friend of Deacon Naismith,' she said. 'I've heard o the man, for certain, but I've never met him that I ken, I've no information for you there.'

'I never thought it,' said Gil. 'What I have heard . . .' He paused, looking for the words, and she leaned forward as if eager to hear them. '. . . is that you may be able to confirm what another person told me.'

'Me?' She sat upright, spreading one small plump hand on her black velvet bosom and displaying two valuable rings. 'Oh, if I can help you, maister, I surely will. Who was it? What did he tell you?'

He, thought Gil.

'The last I know of Naismith's movements,' he said cautiously, 'he was with Maister Thomas Agnew in the Consistory tower, for maybe an hour, after supper that evening.'

'Oh,' she said faintly, making big round eyes.

'Maister Agnew,' he pursued, 'tells me he left him, and a little later he went out himself to call on someone, and spent the rest of the night there. I believe you might know something of that?'

She looked down modestly at the rush matting under their feet.

'I –' she began. Was she blushing? Gil thought not, though the candlelight made it hard to tell. 'Well, indeed, maister. I confess that's the case indeed. Maister Agnew spent that night wi me in this house.'

The face remained downturned, the hand spread on her bosom, but she was looking sideways at Gil under her lashes, and the corner of her mouth quirked, inviting Gil to consider how Agnew had spent the night. *Som can flater and some can lie*, he thought, *and some can sett the mouth awrie*. No accounting for tastes.

'Thank you indeed, mistress,' he said obtusely. 'When did he arrive? Can you recall?'

'Perhaps the middle of the evening?' she suggested. 'More than an hour after I'd eaten my supper, if I mind right.'

That fits, he thought. 'And when did he leave? Late, I imagine,' he said, giving her the oblique compliment she seemed to expect. She looked gratified, but shook her head.

'No, no, it was early. Before it was light,' she assured him.

'You mean he was here the whole night? Most of the hours of darkness?'

'Aye, that would be it,' she said complacently. *Al nicht by the rose ich lay*. But this one's flower was long since borne away, he guessed.

'And had he a cloak with him? Do you recall which one it was?'

'A cloak?' she repeated. 'Er – I think he did.' Again the inviting glance, the quirk at the corner of the mouth. 'I never saw him to the door,' she admitted. 'I wasny dressed for it.'

Gil made his way back up to the Wyndhead in the rain, deep in thought. It was full dark now. The more public-spirited burgesses had already lit the lanterns or torches which they were required to hang out at their house corners, and the deep shadows between these were broken by more lanterns, borne by people hurrying homewards as their working day ended. As he passed the end of Marion Veitch's wynd, he nearly collided with her brother, cloak pulled up about his nose and head down against the rain.

'You again,' said Veitch, recoiling. 'Seems to me I keep meeting you round here. Here or the bedehouse – Frankie was just saying you're never away from the place.'

'I'm still trying to find who killed the Deacon,' said Gil

mildly. 'Your sister will be the better for knowing the answer.'

'I doubt that,' Veitch flung at him, tramping past towards the house. Gil watched him to the door, then plodded on up the busy street.

Reaching the crossing, he was unsurprised to see Maistre Pierre's bulky form appear out of the darkness, illuminated by his own lantern.

'Not a productive day,' said his friend. 'What have you discovered?'

'One or two things,' said Gil. 'I've spoken to the Widow Napier, and I've just had a word with Agnew's mistress. I was going round to the bedehouse to see how Humphrey is.'

'I join you.' Maistre Pierre turned to stroll with Gil, lantern held low to light their steps. 'The men have found a many ladders,' he reported, 'but none of them the right size. If the uprights were the right distance apart, the feet were too big to have made those prints. I have a list of those places they were found, so we do not repeat the work tomorrow.'

'Good work, just the same.'

'They did not think so. I had a full account of which households were friendly and which took exception to being asked such a thing. Luke seems to have met with most success.'

'Luke's a good laddie.' Gil checked as he recognized an approaching figure. 'Good e'en to ye, Maister Agnew.'

'E'en,' said the other man of law hoarsely, and paused. His face appeared drawn and strained in the pool of light from their combined lanterns, and he had a soft cloth wrapped about his throat.

'Have you been calling at the bedehouse again? How is your brother, poor fellow?'

'Aye,' agreed Agnew, speaking with difficulty. 'Better. At's prayers.' He bent his head and crossed himself to indicate his meaning.

'That must be some relief to you,' said Gil. Agnew

180

nodded, smiling, and put his free hand to his well-wrapped throat.

'Forgive,' he said. 'Home.'

'I hope your man can give you something to soothe that,' said Maistre Pierre. 'Red wine with syrup of cherries in it would be good, or a little poppy syrup perhaps.'

Agnew nodded and smiled again, raised his round felt hat and walked on. Gil looked after him, frowning.

'I'm surprised he got access to his brother,' he said quietly as they continued up the street. 'Sissie would be watching him like a hen with one duckling after this morning's scene.'

'Perhaps she was busy with the supper,' suggested Maistre Pierre.

It was a bad moment to call at the bedehouse too. The old men were gathered round the fire in the hall, discussing the morning's events, while the kitchen-boy and one of the women set up their table and spread a mended linen cloth. The brethren greeted them as familiars, but Cubby said straightly, 'The half of Glasgow's been here the day. Frankie's nephew's just left us. You'll no be wanting to stay while we get our supper, will you?'

'No, no,' Gil assured him. 'We're expected at home soon.'

'The meals are the highlights of our day,' Maister Veitch said. 'When Humphrey doesny outshine them.'

'Where is that poor man?' asked Maistre Pierre. 'We met his brother on the way.'

'His brother?' Maister Veitch looked from him to his neighbours in some concern, and craned to see out of the window. 'There's been no shouting,' he said, 'and there's no light at his window. I hope he's no ill.'

'Shall I go and see?' Gil suggested.

'Better to let Sissie ken, and she'll see to him. He's been as jumpy as a squirrel all day, and no wonder.'

Gil went out obediently and found Mistress Mudie just

overseeing the dishing up of the supper. She greeted him with disfavour, but when he explained his presence she snatched up a lantern, lit it and set off indignantly into the garden.

'– never kent that man was here again, if he's done my poppet any harm I'll see him in the Bad Place for it, what a way for anyone to treat his brother –'

Gil, standing in the doorway of the main range, watched her trotting down the path to the door of Humphrey's darkened lodging. She rattled at the latch, and opened it, her loving words floating through the rain, and stepped in.

She cried out, and dropped the lantern. It fell with a crash, and went out, and in the sudden dark she screamed and screamed.

'Pierre, bring lights!' Gil shouted, hurrying down the garden. 'Bring lanterns!'

Inside the little house he bumped first into Mistress Mudie, her familiar herbal smell overlaid with sharp terror, and then into Humphrey. It had to be Humphrey, he smelled of damp wool and almond milk like Humphrey, but he was taller than Gil, and moved oddly as he recoiled from the encounter. Mistress Mudie was still screaming, huge ragged sounds that tore at the ears. Humphrey bumped into him again, and Gil realized what was wrong just before Maistre Pierre appeared at the doorway with a lantern.

'Mon Dieu!' he said. 'He has hanged himself!'

'We must cut him down!' said Gil. 'Set the light there and hold him for me!'

He dragged a stool from the hearth and stood on it, drawing his dagger to saw at the rope as the mason raised the black-faced body on his shoulder. Several of the bedesmen arrived at the door, exclaiming and asking questions to which there was no answer. Maister Veitch and the deaf Barty failed to make Mistress Mudie sit down, but did succeed in halting her dreadful screams, and Millar pushed his way into the house as Maistre Pierre set

182

Humphrey's body carefully on the ground. Mistress Mudie flung off Barty's restraining grip and threw herself to her knees beside her darling, fumbling with the rope at his throat. She got it free and flung it aside, then fell to patting and rubbing at the limp and bloody hands, all the while making a thin wailing sound which made Gil's hair stand up.

'What's happened?' Millar demanded unnecessarily. 'Humphrey! What's he done? Christ and His saints, is he dead?'

'I would say so,' pronounced Maistre Pierre, who had been feeling for a heartbeat. 'He must have been hanging for a quarter-hour at least, maybe longer.'

'The candle is cold,' said Gil, feeling it and setting it back on the mantel-shelf. Millar looked at him blankly, and back at Mistress Mudie sobbing over Humphrey's body.

'But why?'

'His brother was here again,' said Maister Veitch. 'So Gibbie says.'

'Aye, he was, but –'

'We met him on the road,' Gil expanded. 'He said he'd left Humphrey at his prayers.'

'I doubt he's persuaded the poor soul it was him killed the Deacon,' speculated Cubby from the doorway. 'And he's hanged himsel for remorse.'

'We canny tell it was remorse,' said Maister Veitch argumentatively. 'He's no left a note or anything, has he?'

'Why other would he do sic a thing?'

'Maybe he realized he was mad.'

'He knew he was mad,' Gil said. 'Just today he asked Mistress Mason to pray for him because he needed it, he said.' And her prayers would be doubly important now, he reflected.

'What a thi – what a thing to happen!' exclaimed Millar. 'St Serf protect us! Oh, this is a dreadful time! And I'll ha to send to le – to let Agnew ken. He was here just the now, asking me about the Deacon's papers. And the Deacon laid out in the washhouse already, and now another grave to be ordered –'

'We cannot leave him here on the floor,' said Maistre Pierre. 'Where can we lay him?'

'On his bed,' suggested Gil.

Mistress Mudie was prised away from the body with difficulty, and it was borne through and laid on the narrow bed in the inner chamber. Gil drew the checked blankets back to the foot of the bed, and laid the sheet over the engorged face, but Mistress Mudie snatched the linen away and tucked the blankets round Humphrey as if he was asleep, then dropped to her knees beside the bed, hands over her face, and rocked helplessly back and forward, sobbing thinly.

'*Who can not wepe com lerne of me,*' said Gil quietly. Maister Veitch glanced at him and nodded.

'Far's wir supper?' demanded Duncan from the garden. 'It mun be spiled by noo.'

'Sissie,' said Millar, bending over her. 'Sissie, will you see to the supper?'

She shook her head, still rocking over the body.

'Leave her,' recommended Maistre Pierre. 'Surely the kitchen can serve it out by themselves? The old men must eat.'

'Eat? Surely not! I don't think I could,' said Millar.

'When you get to be our age, Andro,' said Maister Veitch in the house doorway, 'you see these things different. We'll hae our supper, and I'll say Grace if you've no mind to.'

'Aye, do that, Frankie,' said Millar gratefully, and turned to speak to Gil just as heavy footsteps sounded in the passageway in the main building. Millar swung back, wearing the expression of a man who has reached the end of his endurance, and two muddy men in jacks and steel helmets tramped across the garden carrying lanterns. The badge painted on their worn leathers was clearly visible, the Douglas heart on a white ground.

'Christ and his saints preserve us, I thought Sir James was to be here the morn's morn,' said Millar faintly.

184

'He set out early, a cause of the weather,' said the first man-at-arms. 'He'll be at the door in a quarter hour or so. Is the lodging open, maister? We've a couple pack-loads of hangings and such out in the street.'

'I feel guilty,' said Gil with some compunction, 'leaving Millar in such a hideous case, but I do not feel I can face my godfather just now.'

'Difficult, is he?' said Maistre Pierre.

They were in a tavern at the top of the Drygate, where they had taken brief refuge from the cold wind after stopping at the chapel of St Nicholas' bedehouse. The house was packed with other people who had the same idea, but they had managed to get two seats, and a harassed girl had brought them a jug of ale and two beakers. Gil poured for both of them, and said in French, above the noise of the place,

'Quite apart from what's just happened at St Serf's, he'll be full of questions about the marriage and doubtful jokes. Did you hear the one about the bridegroom and the turnip, that kind of thing. I was at his daughter Janet's wedding. Neither bride nor groom knew where to look at one point.'

'We all have kin like that. Mine are in France, I thank God. What do you make of what has just happened at St Serf's?'

'A sorry thing. What do you?'

Maistre Pierre shook his head. 'It might have been suicide.'

'No note, as old Veitch said.'

'The man was deranged. He might not have seen the need for a note.'

'He was priested, and what's more, he recalled it this morning.'

'I have known priests take their own life before now. Lives,' the mason corrected carefully.

185

'There was no stool near where he was hanging, that he might have stepped off.'

'That is a stronger argument. And his fingers had bled.'

'He bit his nails badly,' Gil observed. 'They had bled before.'

Maistre Pierre finished his ale, and reached for the jug. 'So the only sign is the absence of a stool.'

'Perhaps Sissie kicked it out of the way when she went into the house.'

'I saw none closer than the hearth.'

'We can hardly expect to get sense out of Sissie tonight.'

'True. Let us leave the question for now. What else have you found today?'

Gil leaned forward, to avoid having to shout, and described his afternoon: Marion Veitch's demeanour, his encounter with Hob, and what he had learned from Mistress Dodd and the Widow Napier. Maistre Pierre listened, frowning, and tapping his beaker on his knee.

'So Veitch lied,' he said. 'I wonder what he was doing. Do you think he was hiding from the Watch, or was he here in the Chanonry stabbing the man Naismith?'

'One or the other,' said Gil, 'though if he was truly hiding from the Watch I do not know why he lied to me. When I saw him, he had not the look of a man who had spent the evening drinking.'

'Sailors are hard-headed.'

'True.'

'Could he have done it?'

'I would have said so. Moreover, there is a path along the riverbank which would bring him home without going through the burgh. Provided he knew the ground,' Gil qualified.

'Leaving his sister to be the extra worshipper at Mass in the morning.'

'Aye.' Gil pulled a face, peered into the jug, found it empty, and put his beaker down beside it. 'We had best go home. I need to wash before I bring Dorothea down to supper.'

'Before we go,' said Maistre Pierre, 'what is the one about the bridegroom and the turnip?'

'And he gave us his blessing, only this morning,' said Alys. 'That was a grace, that he remembered his calling before he died.'

Dorothea nodded and crossed herself, murmuring *Amen*, and Maistre Pierre did likewise.

The supper was long since cleared away; the household had retired to the kitchen to exchange new tales with Agnes the lay sister, and family and guests were seated round the brazier in the hall of the mason's big stone house. The three women were together on the high-backed settle, Alys's honey-coloured locks gleaming in the candle-light between Dorothea's black veil and Catherine's black flowerpot cap and embroidered gauze. In the shadows at the edge of the group, Herbert the secretary murmured softly over his beads.

Gil moved his feet from under Socrates, and said, 'I wish I was certain of what had happened.'

'You think,' said his sister, 'that it might not have been his own action?'

'It was one or the other,' said Gil. 'Either he hanged himself, from grief or remorse or the realization that he was mad, or someone did it for him.'

'How easy would that be?' speculated Alys. 'I thought you said Humphrey nearly had the better of it this morning. Could one of the old men have the strength? If it was his brother –'

'Has anyone else a reason to kill him?' asked Dorothea.

'Not that I can see, and I can't see why his brother would kill him either,' admitted Gil. 'He's been – he was well supported and well cared for there in the bedehouse, no need to worry about him.'

'– then surely,' Alys persisted, 'after this morning's fight, his brother would find it the more difficult to get the better of him and hang him. His hands were not bound, were they?'

'What, like an execution? No, and his fingers had bled recently, though that's no proof.'

'Was the rope marked with his blood?'

'What rope was it?' asked Dorothea. 'Where did it come from?'

'I asked,' said Maistre Pierre. 'It was the length they use to keep the yett open when needful. It hangs on the back of the yett mostly. It was wet with the rain,' he added, 'there were no marks to see on it.'

'On the back of the yett,' repeated Alys. 'Out at the street? How did Humphrey come by that? Mistress Mudie would never have let him go out across the yard.'

'He might have slipped out without her seeing,' said Gil. 'After all, Agnew got in without her seeing him twice today.'

'So either,' said Alys, 'Maister Agnew went in, with the rope, and got the better of a man who nearly killed him this morning –'

'– who left him still badly shaken when Pierre and I met him this evening,' Gil added. She nodded acknowledgement.

'– or some mysterious other got in very quickly and did the same between Agnew leaving the bedehouse and Mistress Mudie finding him and then left unseen, or else Humphrey went out to the gate after his brother left and got the rope, and – and –' She covered her mouth with her hand. 'Oh, the poor man. And poor Mistress Mudie.'

Catherine nodded and reached for her beads. Dorothea put her hand over Alys's other one and said, 'None of these seems very likely, and none of them has a reason. Do you suppose it's connected to the death of the Deacon, Gil?'

'More logical to assume it is,' he said.

She nodded. 'And how far have you got with that?'

'Not very. Oh, Maggie handed me back this.' He dug in

his purse and drew out the length of linen they had found in the trees. Was it really only the previous day? 'Cluttering up her kitchen long enough, she said.' He spread it out across his knee. Maistre Pierre reached out and drew the stand of candles closer, and they all peered at the strip of cloth. Stiff from drying above the kitchen fire, it was creased and marked, but the quality of the cloth was obvious.

'And the stitching,' said Alys, leaning forward to touch the hemming. 'This is fine work. And see, a little ornament at either end, done in the same thread.'

'Are you sure it's a neck-kerchief and not a household towel or such?' said Dorothea.

'No,' said Gil. 'All I know is where we found it and what the dog thought of these.' He traced the dark stains on the cloth. 'Hard to be sure in this light, but by daylight it certainly looked like blood.' Catherine crossed herself again and renewed her efforts with her beads. 'I'd say someone had wiped his blade here, but this bigger stain is more as if he had staunched a wound.'

'Or wiped up a splash of – of whatever it was,' said Alys. 'May I see?'

Gil handed it over. Their eyes met, but she took the piece without any attempt to touch his fingers. She and Dorothea scrutinized it carefully, paying close attention to the embroidered ends. After a moment Dorothea said, 'Look here, Alys. Is it an initial? A mark of some sort?'

'You are right,' said Alys, tilting her head. 'What is it? Could it be N?'

'It could,' said Dorothea doubtfully, 'or it could be two letters. What about I V?'

'For John Veitch?' said Gil with reluctance.

'Marion does fine sewing,' said Dorothea. Brother and sister looked at one another.

'John had cause to kill the man, for certain, though I don't know yet what Marion inherits under Naismith's original will, and he lied to me about where he was that night.'

189

'Could he have done it?' asked Alys.

Gil nodded, sighing. 'Not only could he have done it, I don't know who else might, since the last person to see Naismith has someone to swear to his whereabouts later.'

'We have two deaths to consider now,' said Alys. Gil looked up at the *We* and she smiled faintly at him. 'If the Deacon was killed outside the bedehouse it could have been almost anyone, I suppose –'

'Except that whoever it was, he knew a lot about the customs of the house,' said Dorothea.

Alys nodded. 'John Veitch had good reason to kill him, as you say, Gil, and he has lied about where he was that night, and here is this scarf which may be his, found in the Stablegreen, but would he have known all the things the killer evidently knew?'

'His uncle could tell him those,' said Gil.

'Or the woman helped him,' said Maistre Pierre.

'Surely, if it was his uncle who helped, John had no need to carry the body round to the Stablegreen,' objected Dorothea. 'The old man could have told him enough to put it in the Deacon's lodging, where it would never have been found till the morning.'

'Maister Veitch would have known Sissie was listening,' said Gil. 'All would have to sound as usual.'

'And why would John find it needful to kill Humphrey?' said Alys.

'We know he was at the bedehouse this evening,' said Gil. 'I met him on the Drygate, Pierre, just before I met you. Oh, and there was a man above in Marion's house when I called, teaching the child another song. I wonder if it was this fellow Elder.'

'Why might John Veitch kill Humphrey?' asked Maistre Pierre rhetorically. 'Had Humphrey perhaps seen or heard something to his disadvantage?'

'Humphrey said nothing that made any sense about the night the Deacon died,' said Gil, 'except something about seeing a light in the Deacon's lodging, but that only confirmed Sissie's account.'

'Perhaps he had said something to the other bedesmen,' offered Dorothea.

'I need to ask,' agreed Gil. 'I must question them about this afternoon, but it was hardly the moment when we were there, what with Duncan demanding his supper and my godfather arriving at the door.'

'It doesn't work, does it?' said Alys. 'What about Humphrey's brother? He was the last man to see the Deacon, so far as we know. Could it have been him?'

'I haven't yet found a reason, and I doubt now if he had time,' said Gil. 'His mistress says he was with her that night, from an hour after supper – he must have gone straight there after Naismith left him.'

'But he could have killed his brother,' said Alys thoughtfully.

'Why?'

'You don't need a sensible reason to want to kill a brother,' said Dorothea. Gil looked at her in astonishment. 'Or a sister,' she qualified the statement, and smiled at him. 'Not a sensible reason, just a strong one.'

'He had the opportunity,' persisted Alys, 'if he was in the bedehouse just before Humphrey was found, and he might have managed to get the better of him and –' She pulled a face, and Dorothea nodded.

'Or what of the bedesmen?' said Maistre Pierre. 'I should say the only one with the strength is your teacher, Gil.'

'He had a strong arm when I was a boy,' agreed Gil, 'but he's past sixty now, could he have carried Naismith any distance, or lifted Humphrey to get him suspended the way we found him? I admit he'd enough reason to kill Naismith, and living with Humphrey would drive anyone to murder I would think, poor soul.'

'Still questions to ask,' said Maistre Pierre.

'Many questions,' said Gil. 'Tomorrow I'd like to find

this mysterious friend of John's, who might tell us something to the purpose, and locating the weapon and the place Naismith was killed would be good.'

'And the ladder,' supplied Maistre Pierre.

'Look for an unclaimed lantern and a patch of blood somewhere about the old men's houses. Question the old men themselves about Humphrey. And there is probably more. But chiefly, what I would like to find would be a clear reason for someone to kill either man. I still think Naismith's death may lie in the accounts.'

'Yes,' said Alys. 'It hangs on that. Too many had the opportunity.'

Dorothea nodded agreement.

'I wish you were free to help me,' Gil said, looking at Alys. She met his eye and nodded seriously.

'There is all to supervise here,' said Catherine in French, breaking off her prayers.

Gil studied the row of faces opposite him. He was certain that Catherine approved of Dorothea, and that Dorothea liked Alys; he no longer trusted his ability to read Alys's response to his sister. He tried to tell himself it hardly mattered, that Dorothea would return to Haddington and he might not see her face to face again in this life, but it was still important.

'I have been thinking,' announced Maistre Pierre, 'that a likely place to find two sailors is in a tavern, no? Suppose after we escort Sister Dorothea back to the castle, you and I were to go drinking?'

Chapter Ten

There was a thunderous sound, somehow entangled with a dream about Paris. He knew it must be a dream, because he had not had a drinking head like this since he left France. The thunder went on, and on. So did the dream, which became more vivid. Not only a headache as if an axe was buried in his brow, but a tongue too big for his mouth which tasted like an ashpit. Socrates barked near at hand, once, then again, and a voice exclaimed,

'Maister Cunningham! Maister Cunningham, can you waken!'

'Likely no. He was ower late home last night, and a skinfu' wi it.' That was Maggie. Not a dream, then. 'Out the way, son. I'll sort him.'

Light, and footsteps. He was aware of a distant shouting, and the dog's paws scrabbled as he left. Then cold water stung his face and neck. He surfaced, spluttering and wincing, to find Maggie staring down at him by the light of a candle. Someone stood behind her in the shadows.

'Are ye awake, Maister Gil, or do ye want the rest of the jug?' demanded Maggie. Gil struggled on to one elbow and shielded his eyes from the candle. There was more distant shouting, and the dog barked, equally distant now.

'Awake,' he managed. 'What' you do that for?'

'Aye, well, there's trouble below stairs,' she informed him grimly. 'Here's Sir James Douglas round from the bedehouse and raging like Herod in the hall, and your uncle from home, as he might ha kent at this hour. Will you get up, man, and deal wi him?'

'Bedehouse.' Gil sat up shivering and wringing water from his hair and his shirt. This did not seem to make sense. What bedehouse?

'St Serf's,' persisted Maggie. 'Aye, I thought you were well away when you got home last night. Get you away down to my kitchen, young Lowrie,' she said over her shoulder, 'and if you'd be so good as to put another stoup of ale next the fire in the blue-glazed pint pot, it would speed matters. As for you, Maister Gil,' she turned back to Gil as footsteps clattered away through the attic, 'let's have you out of there.'

Bemused, he allowed himself to be dragged out of bed, his shirt pulled over his head, a cold wet cloth scrubbed across his shrinking flesh. When she began to rub him dry with energetic strokes of the discarded shirt, he stuttered a protest.

'Maggie, what's this about? No, I'm awake, I'm awake!'

'Then you can drink this, and wash the rest yoursel.' She thrust a beaker at him. The contents fizzed darkly, and a familiar mysterious, pungent smell hit his nose: Maggie's poison, his brothers had called it. Her cure for a night's drinking. He swallowed it like medicine, and she turned her back to let him strip, pronouncing, 'I've no idea what's ado, Maister Gil. All I ken is, your godfather's down there calling for you or your uncle, abusing his Michael that's your mother's godson, and like to take an apoplexy with fury. And two of his men cluttering up my kitchen, I could do without.'

This hardly made sense either. He groped his way into clean linen, hose and doublet, tied his points with difficulty, found a jerkin and a budge gown in the kist at the bed-foot, took a moment to salute St Giles and his white doe and promise them a more formal obeisance later. As soon as he was covered Maggie dragged the window-hangings back, the rings rattling on the pole, and the room was flooded with unpleasantly bright light.

194

'When did I get home, Maggie?'

'How would I know? Long after the curfew it was, Our Lady alone kens how you wereny taken up by the Watch, the way you came stotting up the road.'

Memory surfaced. There had been singing. He and Pierre had gone from one tavern to another looking for, what was the fellow's name, Veitch, and the other one. Had they found him?

'Was I on my own when I came in?'

'Maister Mason saw you to the kitchen door.' She lifted the cooling candle to follow him down the stairs. 'I'll have a word to say to him when I see him, and all,' she added grimly.

That was something, anyway. More memories rose up. Some of the singing had been sea songs. Yes, they had found John Veitch, and the man Elder – that was his name. They had had a long conversation somewhere, the four of them. He recalled writing something down in his tablets, and felt in his sleeve. No, not this gown. Purse? His purse was at his belt. He patted it to make sure the tablets were in it, and crossed the solar to go down to the shouting in the hall.

His godfather, lightly built and balding, was standing in front of the hearth, arms akimbo so that his short furred gown spread round him like the wings of an angry hawk. The steel-blue of gown and jerkin added to the effect, but his expression was more like a wildcat's than a hawk's as he roared at his youngest son.

'You'll no preach *family* in my lug! What right have you to use the word in my hearing, you ill-faring half-lins custril? A pick-thank attercap I've raised to be my Benjamin!'

Socrates barked again, and pain stabbed through Gil's temples. Seeking his dog, he discovered him at the other side of the room, head down and hackles up, standing protectively in front of Tib who was seated white-faced in their uncle's great chair. Sir James, seeing him enter the hall, jerked an arm in an imperious gesture.

'Come here, godson, and tell me how much of this you're responsible for.'

'How much of what?' Gil asked, crossing the room. The answer struck him just before Sir James spoke, so that he heard his own words through a rising, roaring anger. He stopped in the middle of the floor to wait for it to ebb, staring at his godfather.

'This pair of masterless blichans, these sliddery dyke-lowpers,' said Sir James, not mincing words, 'have beddit one another. As to whose notion it was, I've my own ideas, but what are you going to do about it, Gilbert, tell me that?'

'Tib,' said Gil grimly, turning to look at his sister. She got to her feet, her eye sliding from his, swallowed hard and nodded. 'And Michael,' he went on. Michael looked sideways at him round his own shoulder, with a faint grimace of apology. As well you might, thought Gil. No wonder you were afraid of me, that morning in the bedehouse chapel.

'Well?' demanded Sir James. 'Is that all you've to say, sir?'

'It's all I can say, till I ken the facts, sir,' responded Gil.

'Oh, the facts! The facts are easy enough to be discernit. Our tottie litchour here, having the keys o the lodging in his hand, made use of them to slip his leman into the place, the which I spied as soon as I was within the door yestreen.' Gil recalled the sudden, early arrival of the Douglas outriders, and with it the rest of the events of his visit there. 'And while I mind o't, what's going on in the place? All this about the Deacon found dead, locked in the garden, and one of the brothers dead by his own hand and all? What's ado? Did he slay the Deacon and then himsel? Have ye found that out yet, or has that passed by your attention and all?'

'I'm working on it, sir,' responded Gil automatically.

'Hah!' said Sir James witheringly. 'If it wasny him that's slain himsel it'll be some enemy of the man's from Stirlingshire. I kent I should never have appointed a Kilsyth man,

196

whatever the Veitches said. That's if it's no Frankie Veitch, who I never trusted, no since he tried to tell me Michael's cousin Gavin wrote verse. And this ill-doer here has taken advantage of all the stramash, bringing a woman into the almshouse my grandsire built. But it wasny till I set eyes on him this morn,' he snarled, 'and persuaded the truth from him wi a belt's end, that I kent just how bad.'

Tib came forward past Gil, the dog pacing watchfully beside her, and stopped beside Michael. Gil could see how their hands touched and twisted together, hidden from Sir James by the folds of her grey gown.

'Aye, sir,' she said clearly. 'We've beddit. We're promised, each to ither.'

'By all the saints, you're no!' he roared at her. The hands tightened on one another. 'You shameless racer, what makes you think you've a claim on my lad? I've better things in mind for him than marriage wi a wee trollop that parts her legs as soon as her hair!'

'You'll no say that about my mother's daughter, if you please, sir,' said Gil politely.

'I'll say what I like if your mother canny control her daughter, godson,' snarled Sir James.

'That comes well from a Douglas,' remarked Gil. 'Do you suppose your kinsman William Elphinstone would have a post about him for Michael, sir? Something in Aberdeen, maybe?'

There was a difficult silence. Then Sir James, nephew of that Douglas lady whose bastard son was now Bishop of Aberdeen, swore savagely at Gil, flung away across the room and sat down in the great chair Tib had vacated. The two young people turned to face him, Michael putting his arm round Tib, at which his father glowered.

'How often?' he demanded. 'How many times has this happened? How long –'

'A month or more since we met,' said Michael, his deep voice very shaky. 'But that was the first time we –'

'Our Lady be praised!' said Douglas. 'Wi any luck she'll

197

no howd from the one service, there'll be nothing you'll need to gie your name to.'

'But we want to –'

'Michael,' said Gil quietly. All three looked at him. 'You can't be wedded. There is an impediment.'

'What impediment?' said Tib in alarm.

'I'd have thought you'd be ware of it. Quite apart from the question of Michael's future and your lack of a tocher, there's the mutual spiritual relationship. Michael is our mother's godson, you're my sister and I'm godson to Michael's father. Holy Kirk won't –'

'But Gil, a dispensation, surely? It's no as if it was real –'

'At a cost of £10 of Flemish money,' said Gil, 'which is near £25 Scots the now. Four or five years' excess rents for a wealthy household, Tib, and we're no wealthy.'

She stared at him, then turned her head to look at Michael.

'No need of marriage, then,' she said bravely. 'I'll be your mistress. There's plenty clerks have a lady in keeping. Look at –'

'You deserve better,' said Michael, going scarlet.

'Better! A trollop like her! And I'll not help you to ruin by buying you a dispensation, either,' declared Douglas. 'You're bound for the Kirk, my lad, and service to the Crown. I'll not have my plans set aside to satisfy a pair of radgie pillie-wantouns!'

'Father,' said Michael, his voice stronger, 'I've no need to be a priest, surely, to serve the Crown? I've no notion to the priesthood, I canny –'

'What's that to do wi it? You'll do as you're bid, Michael, or I'll beat the daylights out of you. I'll see you established on the ladder to fortune afore I dee, if it's the last thing I do.'

Gil bit his lip, but neither of the young people noticed the infelicity.

'Sir,' said Tib from within her lover's arm, 'our families

are old friends. I – I ken you were at school wi my own faither. Will you no be a faither to me, now he's gone?'

Good, but ill-timed, Gil thought, flinching from the noise as Sir James boiled over at her in a torrent of indistinct rebuttals. If only his head was clearer. He was aware of little more than his own smouldering rage at the utter stupidity and self-indulgence of such behaviour.

'I think we're agreed, sir,' he said firmly, cutting across his godfather's tirade, 'that this should never have happened and it should go no further.'

'Gil!'

'Aye, very likely,' said Sir James, 'but what do we do now, eh? That's what I want to know of you, Gilbert. Or where's your uncle? What's David got to say about it?'

'But we love each other!'

'Father, I –'

'Be silent!' roared Sir James, 'or by the Deil's bollocks I'll have your tongue out!'

Gil suddenly recalled his father saying in exasperation, *Trouble wi James is he's more talk than thumbscrews, till you put a blade in his hand.*

'What we do now –' he began.

'What we do now,' broke in another voice, 'is sit down quiet wi a drink and a bite.'

Dorothea came forward from the kitchen stair, Maggie behind her with a steaming jug and a platter of little cakes.

'Good day to you, sir,' she said, and bent her knee in a curtsy to the gaping Douglas. 'It's good to see you so little changed, after all these years. I'm right glad Maggie sent to tell me you were here in my uncle's house.'

'Dorothea,' he said, recovering himself. 'Sister Dorothea. Aye, well, it's good to see you and all, lass. Are you well? No need to ask if you're happy.'

'I am indeed, sir.' Gil set a stool for her, and she smiled quickly at him. 'Shall we all be seated, and these two miscreants may serve us?'

Maggie set jug and platter down on the low cupboard at

the end of the hall, and assisted Tib in finding the pewter beakers and pouring spiced ale for Michael to distribute. Then she stationed herself by the cupboard, obviously hoping to be unobserved. There was quiet movement on the kitchen stair, which Gil took to be Lowrie waiting to learn his friend's fate. So that really was him with Maggie, he thought, when she came to wake me.

'What's done,' said Dorothea, cutting across Sir James's continued complaints, 'is no to be undone, though I dare say many lassies wish it might be.'

'I don't!' said Tib defiantly from where she stood with the platter of little cakes. 'I don't regret a thing.'

Michael slid her a glance under his eyebrows, and they exchanged a complicit smile. Gil found himself grappling with another surge of combined anger and envy.

'Aye, but what do we do next?' demanded Sir James. 'Michael, come over here to my side, away from that wee trollop.'

'Wait,' said Dorothea. 'We wait, sir.'

'Oh, we do?' he said. 'And what use of waiting? Michael's future is determined, madam, he'll no step aside from it whatever comes to one ill-schooled lassie.'

'You forget, sir,' said Dorothea, rigidly sweet as a sugar-plate saint on a banquet table, 'that Michael is my mother's godson.'

'Aye, and what Gelis Muirhead will say about this I canny think!'

'I can,' said Gil quietly.

Michael shivered, and Tib put her chin up, but Dorothea cast him a repressive glance and pursued, 'Aye, sir. My mother is a Muirhead. Kin to Dean Muirhead of this chapter, kin to the Boyds whose daughter Marion goes with child to the King, kin to your cousin Angus's lady.'

'No need to involve Mother!' said Tib sharply. 'Or any of you! We'll sort our own future. We love each other, we don't need more than that.'

'Aye, and how will you do that?' Gil demanded over Douglas's indignant spluttering. 'What will you live on?

Where? You can't be married, what will you do? You need your kin to find Michael a place and some sort of income.'

'We'll think of something,' said Michael. 'I'll determine in September next, we've got till then.'

'Determine?' repeated his father. 'Determine? What makes you think I'll pay for you to finish your studies, let alone take your degree? Do you ken what I laid out for your brother Robert at the end of his four years, in fees and graces to one regent or another? Why should I put out the same for a thankless loun such as you've proved to be? I'd sooner take you home wi me this day and put you down the bottle-hole.'

Gil, watching, thought this was perhaps the first time either Michael or Tib had realized that matters really might not fall out as they wanted. Horrified, they drew closer together; Michael transferred the jug to his other hand and put his arm about Tib again, and she shrank in against him. Dorothea said gently, 'If you do that you'll prevent him following the path you've set out for him, as well as any other path, sir.'

'Aye, I will that,' said Douglas fiercely.

'Our mother might have a word to say about that, too,' Gil commented.

'It seems to me, Sir James,' said Dorothea. Everyone looked at her. 'It seems to me that there are several problems.'

'Just the two,' said Douglas.

'There is Michael's future,' said Dorothea, ignoring this, 'there is Tib's future whatever it is, and if in some way these should be together there is the question of what Holy Kirk will say about it.' Gil nodded. 'None of them is simple, and all of them involve waiting a longer or shorter time.'

'Oh, no,' said Sir James. 'Michael will do as I've planned for him. There's a post for him wi the Treasury at Stirling next autumn, and he –'

201

'No!' said Michael urgently. 'Father, no! I'd sooner teach in the grammar school!'

'Mother could do better for him than that,' said Dorothea dispassionately.

'And Tib –' Gil began.

'I've said my last word on it,' said Sir James. He got to his feet. 'Michael, let go your wee trollop and say fareweel. And if I find you've set your een on her again I'll burn them out.'

Jug and platter fell unheeded. The jug shattered, the pewter dish spun briefly then grounded on one of its cakes. Michael, his arms wrapped tightly round Tib, said over her head, 'Sir, I've committed no crime –'

'You have, in fact,' said Gil, 'against me.' Everyone turned towards him. If only his head would stop aching, he thought. 'There's the question of filial disobedience,' he acknowledged to his godfather, 'but Tib's been robbed of her maidenhead, that was a part of her marriage portion, and as her lawful tutor I will require some recompense to her.'

'*You* will?' shrieked Tib, wrenching herself from her lover's arms. 'It's nothing to do wi you! It's *my* life, it's *my* –'

'Tib!' said Dorothea warningly.

'Recompense!' repeated Sir James in incredulity. 'It's well seen you're a man of law!'

'I am,' Gil agreed. 'So what will you do about it, sir? I'll agree Tib should ha been better schooled, but the same could be said of Michael, who's taken a girl of good family to his bed without consulting his seniors or hers. There's blame on both sides, but only the one's been wronged, and it's no Michael.'

'He didny –' Tib began.

Dorothea rose and went to her. Maggie stepped forward to join their colloquy, and Gil said politely to his god-father, 'So I'll ask you again, sir. What recompense will you make her?'

There was a pause, in which the women whispered

202

together, urgent and sibilant. Sir James said sourly, 'What are ye after? Coin, is it? You want paid for her pearl?'

'At its crudest,' said Gil, 'yes. I'd sooner see it as a way to dower her, since Michael's robbed her of what was near her only asset. And should misfortune follow –'

'Oh, aye. If it should, how would we ken it for Michael's?'

'By the heart birthmark,' suggested Gil before he could stop himself. Dorothea looked round with a brief, quelling glare.

'She was a maiden when she came to my bed,' said Michael, renewing his grip of Tib's hand and lifting his pointed chin at his father. 'I'll not hear that said of her, sir.'

'You can be silent, you wanton,' snarled his father. 'Aye, well, godson, if that's the attitude you're taking, we'll discuss this when it's more convenient. And if I can agree wi you, we'll hear no more of this, will we?'

'Oh, I haveny offered that, sir,' said Gil.

'I'll not be bought off like a side of mutton!' said Tib furiously past the creamy wool of Dorothea's shoulder.

'What's more,' Gil added, 'if Michael's to attend you to my marriage, he'll have to encounter Tib. He canny fail to set eyes on her.'

'Then he'll no attend me,' said Sir James roundly. 'I'll have him gated in the college till next harvest, anyway.'

'If they will each promise,' said Dorothea, 'swear before my uncle's altar yonder, no to be alone with the other in the next month, would that satisfy you the now, sir? And meantime we may discuss it at more leisure, as you say.'

There was a pause. Maggie nodded. Tib bit her lip and looked uneasily at her lover, who gave her a reassuring smile.

'Aye, it will have to do,' said Douglas at length. 'And St Bride send we've sorted it out by Yule.'

It was quiet in the Deacon's lodging in the bedehouse.

Once Sir James had departed, still breathing fire and dragging his son by the arm, Maggie had begun a flood of recriminations about Tib's behaviour which Gil could not staunch. She had eventually been persuaded down to the kitchen by the extraordinarily useful Lowrie, while Dorothea dealt with the furious weeping her words had provoked in Tib. It seemed likely that the noon bite would be late, or inedible, or both, and Gil had taken himself out of the house in the hope of finding distraction, the dog at his heels.

He should, he acknowledged, have gone down the hill to tell Alys this latest bitter crumb of family news, or to inform Kate, who would be tormented by guilt when she heard it, but instead he had found himself heading round to St Serf's with the thought of a soothing time with the accounts. Sir James did not appear to be there, for which he was thankful, but before he could reach the upper chamber he had encountered Millar in the courtyard, in helpless discussion with Thomas Agnew.

'Maister Cunningham!' the man had said, in some relief. 'It was y – it was you found poor Humphrey. Will you tell Maister Agnew –'

'What happened?' asked Agnew hoarsely. 'He was well enough when I left yestreen, just afore I met you in the way, Maister Cunningham. He seemed calm and resigned, just kneeling to his prayers. He'd asked my forgiveness for attacking me yesterday morn,' he added, and turned his face away, wiping something from his eye. Millar made a sympathetic sound.

'I trust for your sake he had it, maister,' said Gil, and Agnew sighed and nodded and crossed himself. 'I know little more than Maister Millar here. Sissie went to his lodging, and found him hanging in the dark. I ran to help, but she had dropped the lantern, so I could see nothing. When we got him down we found he'd used the rope from the gate here –'

'From the gate?' repeated Agnew. 'How did he get that?'

'I ca – canny tell,' said Millar, wringing his hands again.

'He never got out here to the yard, Si – Sissie kept that good an eye on him.'

'He got hold of it somehow,' said Gil, 'and he'd used that to hang himself from one of the beams of his lodging. I would say, if he was at his prayers when you left, he was hanging for no more than a quarter-hour, but it was long enough.'

'Oh, my poor brother,' said Agnew, crossing himself again. Gil and Millar did likewise.

'So you're saying he was calm and seemed as usual,' prompted Gil. Agnew gave him a sharp look.

'He wasny usually calm,' he observed. 'I'm saying I'd had a reasonable conversation wi him, the first in a good while, and he seemed quiet enough, resigned in his mood, just about to kneel.'

'Had he a light?'

'Why, no. We'd been sitting in the light of my lantern. I offered to set his candle for him, but he'd have none of it. I suppose he'd no need of it for what he intended. No wonder he seemed resigned,' he added, with a painful smile, and added in Latin, '*I am in great terror, in terror such as has not been*. My poor brother.'

'Resigned to what?' Gil asked. The Psalter, he thought. Better than the Apocalypse, at all events. Agnew shook his head, and put a hand to his bruised throat.

'His madness? The knowledge of what he could do in the wild fits? He never said.' He turned to Millar. 'Where is he? Can I see him?'

'Oh – aye!' said Millar. 'Though I'd maybe best get Sissie away first if I can, she'll no want to face you –'

'St Peter's bones, why no?'

'She's took it into her head you've something to do wi his death,' said Maister Veitch, approaching from the door to the main range. 'Andro, will I draw her away for you?'

'If you would, Frankie,' said Millar gratefully. 'And we'll ne – need to talk of his burial, Maister Agnew. It'll be a difficulty. He'll go in our own place, never fear that, but

I canny tell when. He's still not stiffened, but Sissie willny let us wash him yet, for all that.'

'Aye,' agreed Agnew. 'I can see it'll be an inconvenience.'

Gil watched them go off along the passage through the main building, and in a moment Maister Veitch returned, supporting Mistress Mudie. She clung to his arm, her head bowed, her linen headdress unpinned and its folds pulled across her face, and the two figures reminded Gil of the supporters at the foot of a Crucifixion. They vanished into the kitchen; he waited, obedient to the significant look his teacher had given him, and after a while the old man emerged into the passage again and jerked his head.

'Anselm has a word for you,' he said. 'Did you catch all the man said?'

Gil nodded.

'He never left straight away,' said Maister Veitch, 'whatever he lets on.'

'Oh?'

'I'll let Anselm tell you.'

The remaining brethren were by the brazier in the hall as usual. Gil, looking round the group, saw that this second death had shaken most of them far more than the first. Cubby's tremor was preventing him from speech, Duncan and Barty sat staring distantly into the charcoal glow mouthing at nothing, Maister Veitch himself looked more like a death's-head than ever. Anselm, on the other hand, was livelier than Gil had yet seen him.

'There you are, laddie. I've to tell you this,' he said without preamble. 'He says so. He says you'll ken what to make of it.'

'What have you to tell me?'

'I'm telling you, am I no?' The old man reached out to pat Socrates' head, and the dog licked his wrist. 'See last night, laddie. That man was here, aye? Puir Humphrey's brither. I kent he was here, though nobody else did, for I saw him.'

'Where did you see him, sir?' asked Gil, since this seemed to be the expected question.

'In the chapel,' said Anselm, nodding triumphantly. 'I was in there mysel, having a wee word. Times my own prayer-desk's the right place, you see, and times the chapel's right.' He grinned toothlessly as Gil showed his understanding of this. 'Agnew came in, and knelt at the altar steps. He seemed gey owerwrought, muttering away, asking forgiveness for something. He never noticed me,' he asserted, 'for I wasny in my stall, I was outside the choir in a wee corner of my own I like to sit in. Then at the last he rose and went out.'

'How long was he there?' Gil asked. 'When was this?'

'It was just afore you came in,' said Anselm firmly, 'for I rose after him and went to see if the supper was ready, and I'd just sat down when you and your friend came in. And he'd been there a good time. Maybe the quarter of an hour, maybe as much as half an hour. And I'll tell ye, I saw his face as he went, and I canny think he got what he asked.'

'Thank you, sir,' said Gil. 'It's good of you to take the trouble.'

'Oh, I wouldny ha bothered,' declared Anselm, 'but he said it was a thing you should hear of.'

Gil withdrew, and cast a glance in at the door of the kitchen where Mistress Mudie sat lost in her terrifying silence while the three servants stood watching her; then he climbed up to the Deacon's lodging, where at last there was the peace he craved.

He arranged the bundles of tape-bound accounts on the polished wood of the table, but he sat for some time with his hands folded on top of the nearest, staring unseeing at the bare trees of the Stablegreen visible in the thin sunshine beyond the end of the garden, with the dog lying on his feet.

He knew he should be considering how best to amerce his sister's appalling misdemeanour, and how to break the news to his uncle, or else dealing with the almshouse and its problems – and what should he make of Anselm's tale? Instead he found himself still resonant with that anger which had struck him in the hall in Rottenrow when he realized what his godfather was implying, combined with – yes, it was envy, he admitted. It had been Tib who trysted with Michael, Tib who waited in the dark outside the gate which he could just see, for her lover to bring the key and let her in. He shied away from imagining the embraces in privacy, the sweet surrender – but he saw again, clearly, the way she had swayed into Michael's arms in the hall. The way Alys used to lean on me, he thought. St Giles assist me, I must deal justly with Tib, though I don't know what justice might mean in the case. And there's the bede-house to consider too, though my head feels like a rotten turnip.

He rose and began pacing about, trying to marshal his thoughts about the bedehouse. The Deacon had almost certainly been killed elsewhere and put over the back wall an hour or two later, and left to stiffen under the trees. Meanwhile his killer, or another, had spent the night in this lodging, slept in the Deacon's bed however briefly, attended Mass in his cloak and hat and then left the premises.

Why? he asked himself. The accounts, yes, but why the accounts? Why not the other papers? They were locked in the kist and the key was on the Deacon's belt in the garden, of course. He paused a moment to think of the killer's reaction at that point, and looked at the bundled accounts ranged across the table. We probably have all we're going to get from these, he thought. The documents I took back to Rottenrow are the next step.

And Humphrey's death last night, how did that fit? How much of Anselm's story, which his invisible friend thought so important, should he take into account? Had Agnew talked his brother into a state where he would hang himself, and if so was it done deliberately? Had he done more than that? Or had John Veitch called for more reason than to see his uncle? Why would John need to dispose of Humphrey? Why would anyone, indeed, he wondered.

There were familiar footsteps on the stair up from the courtyard. Socrates raised his head and beat his tail on the floor as the door opened, then rose to greet the new-comer.

'I went round by the house. Sister Dorothea thought I should find you here,' said Maistre Pierre, patting the dog. He pulled another of the leather backstools up to the table and sat down. 'She bade me tell you she would speak to Lady Kate. A bad business, Gil.'

'Yes,' said Gil baldly.

'What will you do?'

Gil shrugged. 'Wait. Think it over.' He pulled himself together. 'Did you manage to avoid Maggie? She was threatening a word with you.'

'She got it, but she seemed subdued.'

'St Giles be thanked. She should be grateful to you for seeing me home. As I am.'

'How do you feel this morning?'

'Evil,' he admitted.

'I am not surprised. I tell you, it's the last time I suggest an evening's drinking. I had no idea men of law could hold so much and still stay upright.'

'Cunninghams are hard-headed.'

'Like sailors.' His friend eyed him carefully for a moment, then drew a bundle of papers towards him. 'These are the tithes from Elsrickle,' he said, mangling the name. 'Where is that?'

'The Upper Ward,' said Gil, turning his head cautiously to read the superscription. 'Beyond Biggar. It's wool coun-try, the takings should be good. Aye, maybe we need to go over these again. I'm certain there's something in the papers I need to know.'

'Perhaps also in the notes for the man's new will.'

'Well, those are in Agnew's hands.'

'But no. You have them.'

'I do?' Gil stared at him. 'No, they'll be in his chamber in the Consistory.'

'They were,' agreed Maistre Pierre, 'but they are now in your possession. Do you not recall?'

'Recall what?' said Gil, in growing dismay. 'When? What are you saying?'

'Last night.'

'Pierre, what are you talking about? What did we do?'

Maistre Pierre looked hard at him across the table.

'We met the men we sought,' he said, 'in the fourth or fifth tavern.'

'I recall that,' Gil admitted, searching his memory. Details began to surface. The conversation with John Veitch had been difficult at first. It had taken a while to persuade the two sailors that he and Pierre were friendly, but they had succeeded eventually. It seemed the pair had not identified Gil with the man who had called at their lodging. Then what had happened? There were mariners' tales in his head, one about a great worm that ate ships, another about fish which flew like birds. No certain information. 'They told us little, I think,' he prompted hopefully.

'Oh, very little. They insisted they were on their ship the night we were asking about, which is patently not true, and I recall they told us a tale about how Dumbarton Rock fell from a giant's apron. I think they said his apron.'

'Oh, aye,' said Gil vaguely.

'Then the Watch came by and cleared the tavern, and you set off up the street.' There was a gleam of humour in Maistre Pierre's eye. 'I thought I had best come too, and followed you, whereat you decided that we two must go and look at Agnew's chamber.'

Gil shook his head. 'I didn't. Surely I didn't.'

'Oh, but you did. We had two lanterns, after all, and the tower was empty and you had your key to the great door.' He grinned as Gil's expression turned to horror. 'All you lifted were the tablets.'

'Then where are they now?'

'You put them in your purse.'

'No, these are mine –' He opened the purse and reached in, and froze as his fingers encountered, not the soft leather pouch in which his own set lived, but folds of brocade and a loop of braid. 'Sweet St Giles protect me!' he said. He set the alien object on the table and stared at it in deep dismay. 'If these are Agnew's, where are mine, Pierre?'

'I have them. You put them down, possibly as an exchange, which I felt to be a bad idea.' Maistre Pierre felt in a sleeve and produced Gil's own set in its pouch. Gil looked from one to the other and buried his aching head in his hands.

'This is theft,' he said. 'What was I thinking of? He could have me taken up by the Serjeant, or fined by the Sheriff.'

'He need not know you took them,' said Maistre Pierre reassuringly. 'I am hardly like to tell him, since I was there, I am complicit in the theft.'

'Did anyone see us in the tower?'

'I do not think it. I saw no lights, at all events.'

'St Giles be praised, I had no recollection of this when I saw the man here this morning. Is he still on the premises?' Maistre Pierre shrugged. Gil stared at the brocade bag. 'Perhaps I can put them back. Or maybe I could leave them in St Mungo's, or the like.'

'Without reading the notes?'

'They may not help. Most of us use some private shorthand of broken words and odd letters, we may not be able to read his.'

'I too,' agreed the mason. 'We can try.'

'We could, I suppose.'

Almost of their own volition, Gil's hands went out to the brocade bag and drew out the tablets it held. Maister Agnew had selected a set with covers of carved bone; the image on the front was a Crucifixion attended by a pair of gigantic robed figures, bowed in grief like Maister Veitch and Mistress Mudie.

'Clumsy work,' said Maistre Pierre disparagingly. 'You

211

cannot tell Our Lady from the Evangelist. Local, do you think?'

'Not a Glasgow workshop.' Gil reluctantly unwound the strip of braid which held the covers shut, and turned back the Crucifixion to reveal the first leaf, its hollowed surface filled with greenish wax and marked by neat lines of quickly incised notes. 'Well, it makes sense of a sort, though his writing is not easy.' He turned the leaf to study the other side. 'These are notes from a few days ago. St Giles be thanked, he has dated them.'

'What do they deal with?'

'Not bedehouse business. A couple of dispositions. I mind my uncle mentioning this one, it's been discussed in Chapter.' He turned the next slat, and the next. 'Aha! This one is headed *Robt Nasmyth*. Yes, this is it.'

'And what does it say?' asked Maistre Pierre after a moment. Gil tilted the leaf towards him. 'No, I can make little of this. Scots I can read, but abbreviated Scots is another matter.'

'I'd need the existing will to compare it,' said Gil, 'but it seems to be a fresh document rather than a codicil. He's listing his possessions. As you said, properties in several parts of Glasgow. The furnishings here. A gold chain and some other jewels. The chain to Andro Millar if he is still sub-Deacon, the furnishings to a kinsman in Kirkintilloch, a property in the Gallowgait to Mistress Marion Veitch on condition, and the bulk of the rest to a Mistress Elizabeth Torrance, relict of one Andrew Agnew of Kilsyth.'

'Brutal,' commented Maistre Pierre.

'Yes,' said Gil. 'Interesting. The notes simply stop there. No sign of the residual legacy being conditional on the marriage.' He lifted his own tablets and slid them from their purse. 'These must go back, somehow, but first I'll copy the dispositions. And then – I wish I could think clearly. I don't understand what has happened here at all.'

'If we go on asking questions, we may find out,' said Maistre Pierre comfortably. 'I have set the men to continue the search for the ladder.'

'That's good, though I suppose even if we do find it we may not learn much from it.' Gil finished the copy and fastened the strip of brocade round the misappropriated tablets. 'St Giles aid me, I must get these back without being caught.' He lifted the brocade bag to push the tablets back in, and checked as something crackled inside it. 'What's this?'

'Yet another document,' said Maistre Pierre as Gil drew out a folded parchment. 'Has he been working on it, to have left it with his tablets?'

'I don't know.' Gil looked at the superscription. 'It's a copy of the Kilsyth disposition. It must be the family copy – he would have it, of course, if the parents are dead.' He refolded the parchment carefully, tucked it back into the bag with the tablets, and put the whole thing into his purse. 'We must confront Marion and possibly her brother as well with the scarf, I must try to recall what we learned from the sailors last night. There's all to do here. And I suppose I have to speak to Tib. But first I must return these.'

'Have you a pretext for calling on the man? Condolence, questions, information?'

'Aye, that would be the best way. I'll think of an excuse on the way round there.' He rubbed at his eyes. 'I'm too old for drinking sessions like that.'

'I'm glad to hear it,' said his future father-in-law.

Chapter Eleven

In the event, there was no need of a pretext for calling at Agnew's house. As they rounded the corner of the little chapel at the near end of Vicars' Alley, a clamour broke out ahead of them, with shouting and indignant exclamations. Socrates growled warily, his hackles rising.

'*Mon Dieu, que passe?*' demanded Maistre Pierre. Gil made no answer but quickened his pace as a number of people emerged from the house next to the chapel and trampled noisily across its small garden, a powerful voice roaring at the centre of the group.

'Ye willny take me! It wasny me killed him! Get yir hands off me!'

Doors opened along the street, heads popped out into the grey light, as servants and a few of the clerical residents responded to the noise. Socrates barked, other dogs joined in. Thomas Agnew appeared in his doorway, hat askew, shouting hoarsely over the tumult in his yard:

'Take him if ye can, send for the Serjeant! Send to the Sheriff!'

'What's ado?' Gil demanded of the nearest figure, just as the man tripped over a flying foot and went down full length. Helping him up, Gil found he knew him. 'Habbie Sim, what are you at, brawling like this in the midst of the street?'

'Agnew's man's dead,' responded Maister Sim, brushing damp earth from his grey chequered hose, 'and this fellow was found redhand wi the corp. But he's no for being held.' He settled his red velvet hat straight on his tonsure and turned back towards the action.

'Hob dead?' repeated Gil in astonishment.

'I never touched him! I found him like that –' The man at the centre of the swaying, struggling group was on the ground too, pinned down among the winter kale with a captor kneeling on each limb. Gil craned round a liveried back and the prisoner saw him. 'Gil Cunningham! You'll speak for me – I'd no cause to kill this fellow, I never seen him afore in my life. Make them let me up!'

'John Veitch,' said Gil. 'If they let you up, will you stand and answer?'

'I will. I swear it.' The big seaman wrenched at one arm, nearly unseating the fellow holding it. 'I swear by St Nicholas' pickle-tub. Only let me up off this kale!'

'No – no – he's slain Hob,' cried Agnew wildly. 'He's lying in there in all his blood, the puir chiel, and this fellow standing ower him –'

'He's sworn he'll stand and answer,' Gil said. 'We can accept that, maister. I know John Veitch well.' But well enough? he wondered. The five or six men who had taken the big seaman prisoner were reluctantly persuaded to let him stand up, and surrounded him watchfully as he lifted his plaid from the mud, then pulled his furred gown straight, replaced his lop-eared bonnet, and braced himself to face the crowd around him. Agnew was still demanding the presence of Serjeant or Sheriff and lamenting his servant. Gil cast a quick look round the gathering and turned to the other man of law.

'Maister Agnew, wait a space,' he said. 'Here are ten of us in your yard, and five at least are householders. We can make a start on the matter, even if we still need to send to the Sheriff when we're done.'

'Aye, certainly,' said Maister Sim eagerly at his elbow, 'and find out what's been going on here.'

'Bloody death has been going on,' pronounced Maistre Pierre, appearing on the doorsill behind Agnew. He met Gil's eye over the heads of the crowd. 'As has been said, a

215

man lies within, dead in his blood and cooling fast.
I would say he is dead at least an hour, perhaps two.'

'An hour!' repeated Agnew, turning to look at him.

'An hour ago I was wi my uncle at the bedehouse,'
protested Veitch. 'Send and ask him, he'll tell you!'

'Aye, nae doubt he will,' said the man grasping his
elbow, and there was some laughter. 'But where were you
in truth?'

'We'll begin at the beginning,' said Gil. 'Who accuses
this man?'

'Maister Agnew,' said several voices. Agnew pulled himself together, smoothed down the breast of his dark red
gown, and shooed away Socrates who was sniffing with
interest at its furred hem. Gil snapped his fingers, and the
dog came obediently to sit beside him.

'I accuse him,' Agnew said. 'I am Maister Thomas
Agnew, as you ken well, Maister Cunningham, and I'm a
man of law practising here in the burgh.' Heads were
nodded round him in agreement. This was proper
procedure.

'And who is the man accused?'

'John Veitch, as you ken well, Maister Cunningham,'
said the accused with a resilient gleam of humour.
'Maister's mate and one-third partner in the *Rose of Irvine*
now lying at Dumbarton.'

'He's accusit,' pursued Agnew without waiting for his
cue, 'that he slew my servant Hob, who lies in there dead,
which I ken he did for I found him standing ower the corp
when I came back to the house the now.'

Some of the group nodded again, but Gil's friend Habbie
Sim objected.

'Tammas, if the man's been dead an hour or more, that
canny be right. It's no as much as an hour since you came
running out shouting. It canny be a half-hour, indeed.'

'Aye, very true,' agreed the man next to him.

'An hour, half an hour, what matter?' exclaimed Agnew.
'I saw him, I tell you, neighbours, standing above the
corp.'

216

'John Veitch,' said Gil formally, 'what do you say?'

'I slew nobody this day,' said Veitch. A strange turn of phrase, thought Gil. 'I came to the house to seek a word wi Maister Agnew here, and found the door standing unlatched. So I stepped in to wait, and found the servant lying in the hall,' he nodded at the hall window, 'and afore I could decide whether to call for help or if he was past aid, in comes Agnew and begins shouting Murder for the Serjeant.'

'As well I might, seeing him standing there wi his hands all bloody!'

Veitch turned up his palms and looked at them.

'One hand,' he corrected. 'Just the fingers, where I touched him.' He held out both hands to Gil; as he said, the fingers of the right were sticky with blood, but neither the thumb nor the palm was marked. Gil pointed this out to the bystanders.

'Aye, but it's the man's blood, sure enough,' argued the man at Veitch's other elbow, a stout fellow in St Mungo's livery.

'We canny tell that,' said Gil mildly. 'I see no other source of blood hereabouts, I agree, but it canny be proved that it is or it is not Hob's blood. Now somebody has to view the body.' He looked round the gathering again. More people had joined them, including some of the few women who dwelt in this street of clerics and songmen, but the original group would supply an assize. Selecting four of the likeliest including Maister Sim, he led them into the house. Agnew followed, gobbling indignantly.

'Can we no get this over wi, send for the Serjeant and get the man taken away, so I can treat my poor servant decent and get his blood washed off him?'

'It'll no take long, Tammas,' said Maister Sim, closing the door firmly in the faces of the interested bystanders.

The scene they encountered would give some of them ill dreams for months, Gil estimated. The hall stank of blood, and at its further end, on a crumpled heap of the fine rush matting, the man Hob was sprawled on his belly. Beside

217

him, incongruously, lay a bundle of yellow-green kale leaves. The mats under him were soaked dark red, and his face was turned towards them, fixed in a grimace of astonishment. Socrates, head down and hackles up, stared warily back.

'Aye, poor Hob,' said one of the assize, and crossed himself. 'He was a surly bugger, but he never deserved this. St Andrew call him from Purgatory.'

There was a general murmur of *Amen* and flurry of signings.

'I have touched nothing save his cheek, to gauge how far he had cooled,' said Maistre Pierre at Gil's shoulder, 'but so far as I can see it was several wounds to chest and belly that have bled like this'

'Like Naismith,' said Gil.

'Aye, but all by the same hand by the look of it. None was like to be his death instantly, I would say he bled to death and it may have taken the length of a *Te Deum*.'

'A good quarter o an hour,' said Maister Sim the songman. 'Wi all the trimmings.'

'So it wasny a quick stab and Hob dropped deid,' proposed the man who had spoken first.

'Aye, you're right, Willie,' agreed another.

'No, it was a savage attack on an innocent man!' said Agnew.

'Do you mean,' said Maister Sim, shocked, 'that Veitch stabbed him and then stood and watched him dee?'

'We cannot tell that,' said Maistre Pierre. 'Certain he died unsuccoured, you have only to look, but there is nothing to say that he was watched.'

'Now we've seen how he lies,' said Gil, 'we can look at the wounds. Pierre, give me a hand to turn him.'

They rolled Hob's limp form over and laid him straight, staring now at the wall beyond the crumpled mats. Maister Sim, biting his lip, stepped closer but like the mason touched only the cheek of the reeking corpse, gathering his green brocade gown away from harm with the other hand.

218

'I should say any of these wounds would have killed him eventually,' said Maistre Pierre, turning back the slit and saturated jerkin. 'You see them, maister?'

'Aye, I see them,' said Maister Sim, peering at the clotted hairy flesh. 'Three to his chest at least, and a couple more in his wame.' He retreated with some relief and looked at Gil thoughtfully. 'You're the Quaestor, man, and the huntmaster and all. What do you read here?'

'There's no sign he fought back,' said Gil.

'What about these mats,' objected the fourth member of the assize, a minor cleric whose name Gil could not recall. 'They're turned up just where he lies, you see that.'

'They're none so easy rucked up,' said the man called Willie, scuffing at the mat he stood on. 'And there's no other sign o a rammy. Nothing owerset, and that fine pricket-stand still by the wall. Now me,' he expanded, 'if someone cam at me wi a knife, I'd ha seized that for a weapon. It'd take the feet from under anyone, that would.'

'Aye, you're right, Willie,' agreed his friend. 'So that's a puzzle, that is.'

'Was he maybe in the act of turning the mats?' suggested Maister Sim, prodding the braided rushes with one red shoe. 'These squares are stitched together, are they, six or eight at a time.' He gestured to outline a mat. 'So he was just turning a couple of them when he was surprised.'

'Cut down in the midst of his day's darg!' exclaimed Agnew bitterly. *How long shall the wicked exult?*

'Aye, but how was he no stabbed in the back?' said Willie's friend. 'If he was bending to his work?'

'He would stand to greet whoever came in,' said the cleric.

'He'd a gone to the door, surely,' said Willie.

'No if it was someone he knew,' objected his friend. 'Maybe the fellow just opened the door and shouted, the way you do when my maister's no at home, and stepped within.'

'The man Veitch claims no to have set eyes on Hob till he

found him dead,' said the cleric thoughtfully. 'Maister Agnew, had Veitch ever been at your house afore this?'

'No,' said Agnew with reluctance, 'no that I can say. But who's to say he wasny here at some time when I was out the house?'

'What was the weapon?' Gil asked. 'Is there any sign of it?'

'He'd put it up afore I found him!' expostulated Agnew. 'Of course it's no here, it's at his belt!'

'Dagger,' said Maistre Pierre briefly, bending to inspect the cuts more closely. 'Much like any in this hall,' he added, casting an eye round the group.

'So what do you read, Gil?' prompted Maister Sim again. Gil looked the length of the hall and then down at the corpse.

'He was taken by surprise,' he said slowly. 'He was in the midst of his day's work, as Maister Agnew said, suspecting nothing. If he did answer the door to whoever slew him, he went back to his work when the man came in, so he'd no mistrust of him.'

'Now that's no like Hob,' said Willie, and his friend nodded agreement.

'And then what?' asked the cleric. 'Do you say they quarrelled?'

'Nothing to show that,' said Gil. 'But Hob wasn't expecting violence. His own blade's still at his belt. He's never touched it.'

'That fits wi what we can see,' said Maister Sim, and the other men nodded.

'Should we have the man in that's accusit,' proposed Willie, 'and get a look at his dagger?'

'Aye, and make him touch the corp,' agreed his friend. 'That'll show us whether he's guilty, that's for certain.'

'And then we can send to the castle,' said Agnew, 'and get him taken away.'

'We can take him round there ourselves, if he's guilty,' said the cleric.

The superstition had been useful before, Gil reflected,

220

turning to the door to summon Veitch and his self-appointed guards. The widespread belief that if a man's killer touched his corpse it would accuse him in some way meant that making someone touch a body could provide a good measure of how much guilt he felt, unless, like Gil, he was not impressed by the idea.

Veitch stepped into the room, rubbing at his arms where his keepers had gripped them. As many people as would fit into the doorway craned after him, with excited comments about the blood and the body.

'Look at his dagger!' exclaimed Agnew. 'It's the right size. Has it been used? Has he cleaned it maybe?'

'Let me see your dagger, John,' said Gil, holding out his hand. Veitch looked at him, then at the corpse, took a moment to cross himself at the sight then unfastened the weapon from his belt and passed it to Gil.

'It's clean and oiled,' he said. 'I saw to it on Sunday after Mass, as it's my habit to do. The only other blade I've on me's my wee eating-knife, and who in his right mind uses his eating-knife for murder?'

'No if he wants to eat wi it again,' agreed Willie's friend. Gil drew the dagger from its sturdy leather sheath and turned it towards the window. As Veitch said, it was clean and well-kept, sharpened and gleaming dully in the thin light.

'This has not been used since last it was cleaned,' he said, showing it to the assize. 'And there's been no time to clean it since Murder was cried. It was not this weapon killed Hob.'

'Then he used another,' said Agnew. 'Maybe Hob's own dagger! I tell you, I found him standing red-hand ower the corp, he must be guilty!'

'Tammas, that doesny follow,' said the cleric. 'I've stood ower a many men, aye and women and bairns, that I never slew.'

'Aye, but that's your calling,' protested Agnew. 'No, maisters, it's plain enough, this is the fellow that slew my servant and we should have the Sheriff here, no some daft laddie placed by Robert Blacader to please his family.'

Gil made no comment, but handed Veitch's weapon back to him, at which Agnew howled indignantly. Ignoring him, Gil said, 'John, will you touch the corp for us?'

'Gladly, aye,' said Veitch, bracing his shoulders. 'Mind, I've already touched him.' He displayed his marked fingers, and stepped forward.

'And do it wi some respect,' challenged Agnew.

Veitch moved along the room to where Maistre Pierre still stood by the corpse with his beads in his hand. Agnew hurried jealously at his elbow and the four men of the assize followed closely. Gil outpaced them and stepped beyond the corpse to a position where he could watch them all, avoiding the blood-soaked matting, Socrates keeping position by his knee.

Veitch nodded to him, then went down on one knee by the body, crossed himself and reached out to touch the averted face. Like a striking adder, Agnew's hand shot out and closed on his.

'Make sure you touch him,' he said savagely. 'We'll ha no pretence, man!' He jerked at Veitch's arm, slapping his open palm heavily down on Hob's bloody breast.

Everyone present heard the faint groan which escaped the dead man under the blow. Gil felt the hair on his neck stand up.

'Christ and Our Lady protect us!' said Willie, stepping back and crossing himself.

'Look! Look!' crowed Agnew, white-faced. 'I said – I said he slew Hob, and Hob himsel has tellt us it's the truth!'

Veitch stared where he pointed, and then looked up at Gil, horrified. From the pallid lips of the corpse a thread of fresh blood was trickling.

'It was the force of the blow caused him to groan,' said Maistre Pierre. 'As I told the Sheriff. The last breath was still in the man's lungs, and the blow forced it out.'

Gil nodded, aware of a level of relief at the explanation quite ridiculous in a rational man. 'As if I punched you in the breastbone.'

'Precisely. And if there was still liquid blood from where he bled inwardly, it might have gathered when you and I moved him, and that also was released by the blow. But I suppose,' the mason continued gloomily, stepping over the puddle at the castle gatehouse, 'there is no use in telling it to the witnesses.' He looked back over his shoulder at the tower where John Veitch was now imprisoned, still vehemently protesting his innocence. 'How long have we got?'

'The morn's morn, Sir Thomas said,' Gil quoted in Scots. 'Properly the law should be done on him within this sun, wi no more ado.'

'If we ever see the sun,' commented his friend in French.

'Indeed. But since he won't confess to guilt, and you've cast some doubt on it, there must be a more formal quest, and it might as well follow on from the quest on Deacon Naismith. I wish Sir Thomas had let me question John just now, but he was within his rights to refuse it. What worries me is that with three deaths in the Upper Town within three days, John may simply hang for the lot and the investigation will be closed whether I like it or no.'

'Can the Sheriff do that? Surely your commission is direct from the Archbishop.'

'Aye, and as Archbishop not as overlord,' Gil agreed, 'but ultimately, in Blacader's absence, Sir Thomas represents the law in the burgh.' They reached the Wyndhead, and he paused, looking down the Drygate. 'Look at this. Someone must have taken the news to her.'

Marion Veitch was hurrying towards them, skirts gathered up, the ends of her plaid flying, the kitchenmaid Bel at her side. Seeing them she changed direction and halted in front of them, panting.

'Gil Cunningham, what's this they tell me about my

brother?' she demanded. 'He never slew a man in Vicars' Alley! I'll no believe it!'

'I don't believe it either, but he was found standing above the body,' said Gil, and she clapped both hands over her open mouth. 'I tried to act for him, Marion, but the bystanders insisted he touch the dead and the corp bled. He's in the castle now, and there's to be a quest on it the morn's morn.'

She swayed, and Bel jumped forward to support her.

'There, mistress, hold up!' she said. 'Come and sit down yonder.'

Maistre Pierre took her other arm, and they helped her to the foot of the Girth Cross where she sat limply on the steps, staring at Gil.

'He never,' she said. 'He never.'

'Why did he go to Agnew's house?' Gil asked. She shook her head. Socrates sat down beside her, and she patted him mechanically.

'To ask about the will. Is it Agnew that's slain? What happened, Gil? Why's John been taken?'

'Agnew came back to his house, so he says,' Gil related precisely, 'and found his man Hob stabbed and bled to death, and John standing above the corp.'

'When did your brother leave you?' Maistre Pierre asked. She rubbed a hand across her brow, pushing her linen cap askew.

'Kind o late in the morning. After Sext, maybe?' She shivered, pulling her plaid closer about her, and Bel bent to put an arm round her.

'Come back to the house, mistress,' she urged. 'There's nothing you can do the now.'

'No – no, I want to see John. He'll be –'

'They'll no let you in, mistress. Come back and get warm,' Bel coaxed.

'Indeed I think it wiser,' offered Maistre Pierre. 'Come, we will walk with you.'

After a little more argument she got to her feet and set off weakly down the Drygate, her maid supporting her protectively. The street was busy, with people returning from the market further down the High Street, but she made her way among the passers-by without apparently seeing them.

'I'll no believe it,' she said again. 'He'd no call to. He'd not been to the man's house afore, he'd likely have to ask the way. Why should he kill someone he never saw afore?'

'Ah!' said Gil. 'Now if we can find whoever he asked –'

'Would you?' She turned her blue eyes on him. 'Would you ask about, Gil?'

'I will,' he said, 'if you'll answer a few things for me.'

'Aye,' she said after a moment. 'I suppose. Fair's fair.'

Back at the house she seemed to have recovered a little from the shock of John's arrest, and dismissed Bel with affectionate thanks, though the girl would have stayed with her. Seated in the hall, upright and formal in the great chair which must have been Naismith's, her visitors on the tapestry-upholstered stools, she said, 'Did you find that woman you were asking for?'

'I did,' said Gil. 'I'm sorry to have bothered you at a bad moment yestreen. This is no a lot better.'

'Oh, I'm no much occupied right now,' she said, with faint irony. 'What are these questions you've got?'

Gil looked at Maistre Pierre, but found his friend's attention on the ceiling, beyond which Frankie was talking to someone. Occasional sounds of sweeping suggested it was Eppie.

'One or two things,' Gil said, and hesitated. 'Marion, you said John went to ask about the will. Do you ken what the Deacon's original will was like?'

'No,' she said.

'He never showed you it?'

'No,' she said again. Under the crooked cap her oval face was pale and pinched. Above them the child began singing again, the same tune as last night. Socrates cocked his ears to listen, but did not move from his position at Gil's feet.

'I know what the new one was to have been,' Gil persisted, and checked as he realized that Agnew's tablets were still in his sleeve. Well, it had been no moment to return them. 'I wondered how much you were to lose by it,' he went on.

'He said he'd see me right,' she said indifferently. 'I aye trusted him.'

'But the trust was misplaced,' said Maistre Pierre. She flicked a quick glance at him – was she startled? Gil wondered.

'Yes,' she said, and shivered.

'He never settled any property on you?' Gil asked. She shook her head. 'Or got you to witness any of his papers?' Another shake of the head. 'Did you sign anything for him?'

'He kept all his business separate,' she said at last. 'I kent nothing about the bedehouse, nor his transactions in the burgh. Thomas Agnew tells me they're considerable, but I never heard of any of them.'

'Agnew's spoken to you?' said Gil, startled. 'What was that about?'

'Oh, aye. This morning.'

'This *morning*?' repeated Gil. 'Before or after John went to see him?'

'Oh, long afore. That's why he went, see,' she explained. 'The man was here and spoke to me about the Deacon's business, explained that all he left uncompleted would be void now, but he never said aught about the will. So John gaed to ask him when he came back fro the bedehouse.'

Gil waited, but no more was forthcoming. After a moment he changed the subject.

'Marion, when did your brother come to Glasgow?'

Another quick glance.

'Two days since,' she said. 'No, it's the day afore that now, isn't it? The day Naismith dined here and then –' She stopped, apparently unwilling to finish the sentence, her expression quite blank. 'John turned up at my door afore noon that day,' she resumed, 'and I was fair glad to see

226

him, for he'd been away almost four year. He'd never set een on my wee girl.'

'He was on his own?'

'On his own.'

'Was it a good venture?' asked Maistre Pierre with professional interest. 'Where had he been?'

'He's pleased enough,' she said. 'I don't know all where he's been. Spain and the Middle Sea and Araby, maybe.'

'*As far as cercled is the mappemounde,*' offered Gil.

Marion glanced briefly at him, but merely went on, 'He's come home a wealthy man.' She put up a hand to cover her mouth. 'And what good it'll do him –'

'Has he been to Portingal?' suggested Maistre Pierre. The smile vanished.

'No, that was –' She bit off the words. 'That was one place he never said,' she finished carefully. Maistre Pierre looked at her oddly, but did not comment.

Gil felt in his sleeve and drew out the stained scarf.

'Do you ken this piece of linen, Marion?' he asked, unfolding it. She looked at it, and her gaze sharpened.

'No,' she said. 'What is it? Where did you get it?'

'It has an initial on it,' he said, turning the end of the strip towards her. She made no attempt to reach for it. 'Or perhaps two. It might be *N*, it might be *I V.*'

'It might be a number,' she suggested. 'What's the stains on it? Where did you get it?' she asked again.

'I think it was dropped by whoever put Deacon Naismith into the bedehouse garden,' said Gil, watching her carefully. Her eyes widened slightly.

'You mean it was in the garden?' she said, still staring at the thing.

'Not in the garden,' said Maistre Pierre. 'Maister Cunningham's dog found it.'

Again the quick glance at him. Then her eyes went back to the scarf, studying the fine white stitchery on the end Gil was holding up.

'I've never seen it afore,' she said.

'What is it?' Gil asked. 'We thought it might be a towel,

227

or else a neck-scarf, but women ken more about such things.'

She shook her head. 'It could be either.' Gil held it out to her, and she shrank away from it. 'Where did you say you found it?'

'Where would you think such a thing might be found?' asked Maistre Pierre.

'How would I ken?' she asked, her voice rising slightly. 'I – I don't – I've never seen it afore,' she reiterated.

The house door opened. She looked up, and something like relief crossed her face. Socrates scrambled to his feet and Gil turned, as a man's voice demanded, 'Marion, have you seen John this day?'

A big voice, not shouting but pitched to carry in a gale. Maistre Pierre looked at Gil, his eyebrows rising, and round the open door appeared a man to match the voice, big and broad, booted feet planted firmly on the wide boards, his short dark curls level with the carved lintel. Rankin Elder, drinking companion of John Veitch, who had told them the tales of flying fishes in a tavern on the High Street.

'You!' he said, staring at them, and put his seaman's bonnet back on his head. 'What are you doing here?'

'Rankin – John's been taken up by the constables!' said Marion. 'They're saying he's killed a man in Vicars' Alley.'

Elder pursed his lips in a silent whistle, and came forward to Marion's side, putting one hand on the back of her chair and looking down at her in concern, his manner subtly possessive.

'And did he?'

'We do not think so,' said Maistre Pierre.

'Is there any need for you to be here?' demanded Elder, turning his head to look at them again. 'Mistress Veitch is grieving for her friend,' he added formally, 'and she doesny need to be pestered wi questions.'

'I'm trying to find out who killed her friend,' said Gil, putting a little emphasis on the term. And why did he assume we're questioning her, he wondered. 'That's why I'm asking questions. Have you seen this before?'

He held up the strip of linen. Elder cast it a cursory glance and said, 'Looks like John's neckie. He'd lost it. Where did you – Is that blood on it? When did that happen? He was well enough the morn when he left the lodging.'

'When did he lose it?'

'Och, it was days ago.' The man relaxed. 'Was it the night he fetched me from Dumbarton that he missed it?' Marion was staring up at him, frozen with dismay. Belatedly, he met her eyes, and backtracked. 'I don't recall. Might ha been sooner than that.'

'When was that?' asked Gil.

'Three nights since, if it's any of your mind.'

'Three nights? The night Naismith died? When did he set out to fetch you?'

'I've no idea about that,' said Elder. 'He reached me some time the third watch. And that's certainly none of your mind.'

'And you're sure the scarf is John Veitch's property?'

'No,' said Elder. He looked at Marion again. 'And now you'll leave, gentlemen, while we think what's to do about John. And whatever we do, we'll do it without your help.'

The noon bite in the house in Rottenrow was much as Gil had feared. However since his uncle was not present and Alys was, he could have eaten dry stockfish and not noticed.

She was in the hall, helping Maggie and Sister Agnes set up the board for the meal when they came in. Socrates hurried forward to speak to her, nudging her with his long nose. Her face lit up, and as soon as the cloth was straight she left the task and came to kiss Gil.

'Dorothea has told me,' she said quickly in French.

'About Tib, I mean. I came up – I've been with her – Gil, you won't be severe with her, will you?'

He had no chance to answer before her father claimed her, embracing her as if he had not seen her a few hours previously. Maggie eyed Maistre Pierre and said, through the clatter of the wooden trenchers she was distributing, 'There's just the one hot dish for the table, since we're all owerset the day, but there's plenty bread and half a kebbock o cheese. We'll no go hungry.'

'Where is Tib?' Gil asked. Maggie grunted.

'Shut in her chamber and willny speak to me,' she announced. 'Says she'll no eat. Lady Dawtie's wi her the now, but . . .' Her voice trailed off, and she continued setting the table. Alys returned to help her, and Gil gestured for Maistre Pierre to wash his hands at the bright majolica cistern by the door.

'Have you been at the bedehouse?' said Alys in Scots. 'How are they this morning?'

'The old men are all very shaken, and Mistress Mudie hasn't spoken since last night, I think.'

'Ah, the poor woman. She has suffered a great loss – that man was the centre of her life.' Alys inspected the table. 'Is that it, Maggie? Shall I tell Dorothea we are ready?'

When the household was seated, without Tib, and Dorothea's secretary had said Grace for them, Alys returned to the same subject. Gil appreciated her restraint; he had no wish to discuss Tib's misbehaviour in the hearing of the stable-hands. It was surprising how much French the men understood, particularly at times like this when they probably knew more than he did about the subject already.

'Did you learn any more, Gil? Is there anything new since last night?'

'Not at the bedehouse,' said Gil. 'Anselm had an odd tale about Agnew, but that was all.'

'No,' said her father gloomily, 'all is happening elsewhere today.'

'Why, what's happening?' asked Dorothea.

'John Veitch is taken up for killing Agnew's servant,' supplied Gil.

'I heard that!' exclaimed Tam from further down the table. 'Is that right the corp sat up and accusit him?'

'That Hob wouldny tell you the time o day,' objected the other stable-hand, Patey. 'I canny see him telling tales like that after he's deid.'

Beside him Matt nodded agreement, but did not speak.

'Does Marion know?' asked Dorothea.

'She does.' Gil described their meeting with Marion and the encounter with Rankin Elder at the house.

'A sailor?' said Maggie. 'That would explain it, wouldn't it no? If he's been at sea all this time.'

'It would explain much,' agreed Maistre Pierre, accepting the dish of bannocks from Gil. Dorothea cocked her head enquiringly, and he set the bannocks down and began to enumerate on his fingers. '*Item*. She said she had never seen Naismith's original will, did not know what was in it, but she was seated in the master's great chair as if she is now owner of the house.'

'Yes, of course,' said Alys. She captured the bannocks and sent them down the table. 'She is about to become a respectable wife.' She glanced quickly at Gil and away again, blushing.

'*Item*. She has spoken to the man of law this morning but it seems they spoke only about Naismith's transactions in the burgh. *Item*. Her brother returned the day the man was killed, apparently alone, from a successful venture to Spain and the Middle Sea, but not to Portugal though the child was singing a Portuguese song.'

'Oh, is that what it was?' said Gil, understanding.

The mason nodded. 'And then the linen cloth,' he went on.

'She knew it well,' Gil said. 'I would say she knew every stitch.'

'When she realized it was connected with Naismith's death, she was frightened,' agreed Maistre Pierre. 'She pretended not to know what the stains were.' Dorothea

231

snorted inelegantly, and Alys coloured. 'That was when our drinking-companion of last night appeared.'

'I heard about last night,' said Dorothea, with an amused look at Gil. 'Maggie seems to feel there's no ale left in Glasgow today. How's your head?'

'Don't ask.' Gil took up the thread. 'Anyway, Rankin Elder recognized the piece of linen as John's property, which he had lost –'

'Ah!' said Dorothea.

'Exactly,' agreed Maistre Pierre.

'Which he said John had already lost when he fetched Elder from Dumbarton three nights since.'

'Three nights?' queried Alys. 'What did he mean by that? Before or after the Deacon died?'

'He was not in the mood to answer more questions,' said Maistre Pierre.

'It doesn't work,' said Gil, rubbing his forehead. 'There isn't time.'

'Time?' asked Maistre Pierre.

'For John to have gone to Dumbarton the same night the Deacon died,' supplied Dorothea, 'whether this other man helped him at the bedehouse or not.'

'And yet the widow said John wasn't in his bed that night, but turned up in the morning along with Elder, as if the two of them had made a night of it.'

'With their feet wet, you said,' the mason recalled.

'Elder's boots are too big,' said Gil, 'but John's that were drying – the ones that had got wet – are a good size to have made the prints we found.'

'He'd a temper,' said Matt from further down the table. Gil looked at him. 'Veitch.'

'He's right, you ken,' said Maggie doubtfully. 'I mind you and him fighting, Maister Gil. I've no knowledge o this man Elder – did I hear he was an Ayrshire man, from whatever port John sails out of?'

'That would be the accent,' Gil agreed.

'They're saying he's her sweetheart home from sea,' contributed Tam from opposite Matt. 'And he's driven off this giant wi the bloody sword that was haunting the wynd where she dwells.'

'Certainly,' said Gil, 'I'd believe he was wee Frankie's father.' He looked at Alys. 'Just like that romance we thought of. She's even named the child for him, if Rankin is a by-name for Francis the way it usually is.'

'Is that right!' said Maggie. 'I aye thought it wasny the Deacon.'

'Maister Gil,' said Matt. 'The woman Chisholm.'

'I found her,' said Gil, 'but she's no a Chisholm, she's a Dodd.'

'Oh, her,' said Patey. 'My sister Jessie and her waiting-woman is gossips. Thinks gey well o herself, she does.'

'Chisholm, Dodd. One of they names,' said Matt, spooning yesterday's kale.

'A Dodd? Is that Ellen Dodd?' said Maggie sharply. 'Dwells off the Drygate?' Gil nodded. 'Well, well. Thomas Agnew's mistress, is she? No wonder she puts on airs. Her and her jewels.' She spread one large red hand and looked at it. 'If I'd gone that road, nae doubt I'd have jewels and all.'

'You have treasure in Heaven, Maggie,' said Dorothea softly.

Maggie sniffed. 'Aye, very like. But I'll have a word to say to Jennet Clark, so I will, letting her sit in at her hearth talking as if she's a married woman.'

When the meal was ended, the table cleared, the men retired to the kitchen with Maggie, and the family gathered round the hearth, Dorothea and Alys looked at one another. Dorothea nodded slightly, and Alys turned to Gil.

'Gil,' she said formally, 'Tib has something to say to you. Will you hear her?'

Assuming the well-worn phrase meant an apology of some kind, Gil grimaced, but nodded, and she slipped from the hall.

'Did you tell Kate?' Gil asked Dorothea.

'I did, and stayed with her a while,' agreed his sister. 'She's fair grieved to think Tib met the laddie under her roof, but I think that can't be right.'

'Surely not,' said Maistre Pierre. 'Perhaps in the market, or about the burgh?'

'She's known him most of her life,' Gil pointed out, 'and so has Kate. None of us could ha guessed they'd –' He stopped, biting off the words.

'Bed one another,' supplied Dorothea bluntly, just as Alys returned hand-in-hand with Tib. There seemed to be a new understanding between the two girls; Gil glanced at Dorothea, who smiled encouragingly. Maistre Pierre strolled casually to the far side of the room, and fell into contemplation of the little altarpiece in David Cunningham's small oratory where master secretary Herbert was already engrossed in copying out a document. Tib let go of Alys and came forward to where Gil stood by the hearth. Stiff-necked, she went down on one knee and whispered uncomfortably,

'My brother, I acknowledge that I have behaved badly, and I ask your pardon.'

Embarrassed and astonished, he stared at her. Although she had obviously spent the morning weeping, behind the puffiness her eyes were hot with anger. The formal apology was costing her dear. Nor, it occurred to him, had she expressed any sort of contrition. She had said just enough to allow him to answer her without loss of dignity as nominal head of the family, a consideration which meant nothing to him but a great deal to Alys.

Across the hearth Dorothea cleared her throat meaningfully, and he realized that he was still staring at Tib, who was beginning to look apprehensive.

'Oh, get up, Tib,' he said, putting his hand out to her. 'That was well done. Do it again for the old man and we may dig you out of the pit yet.'

She scrambled to her feet, acknowledging his comment with a wry look, accepted his kiss and said, 'Aye, but there's more, Gil.' Alys came forward to stand beside her, and she looked along her shoulder at the other girl. 'Alys thinks I might have something useful to tell you.'

There was a muffled exclamation, and Maistre Pierre swung round from his study of the little Annunciation scene. Gil stared at his sister in dismay, and after a moment she looked down, fidgeting with one foot.

'I never thought, till the day,' she admitted. 'And how could I ha told you if I had?'

'I suppose that's true,' said Gil fairly. 'Go on.'

'When I was – when I –' She swallowed, straightened up, and began again in the middle of the tale. 'I went to the back gate of the bedehouse and waited for M-Michael to let me in.' Gil nodded. 'I had a light, but I held it low. There was somebody else moving about the Stablegreen, wi no light, or maybe a shut-lantern. I saw nothing, but I could hear movement.'

'Could it have been an animal?' Gil asked. 'A goat, maybe? A pig?'

She shook her head.

'It was bigger than that. It could ha been Finn mac Cool,' she said, with a sort of inverted bravado. 'I was that feart, and Michael took for ever to come to the gate, and someone had left a great cart by the wall that I walked into and bruised my hip. I tell you, Gil, by the time I got through the gate and into the light I was near screaming.'

'A cart,' he said. Alys nodded; beyond the hearth Dorothea turned and moved to the settle. 'What kind of cart, Tib?'

'One of those handcarts. Two wheels and two handles.'

'And two legs at one end to hold it steady when it's not being pushed along,' he said, and met Maistre Pierre's eyes across the room. 'What like was it, Tib? Did you see what colour it was?'

'Colour? By lantern-light? It was dark-coloured,' she said rather sharply, 'that's all I can tell you, and there was a fancy pattern on the end bit between the handles, done in light paint.'

'But no name or sign of who it belonged to?' She shook her head. 'Could you draw me the pattern?'

'Likely.'

'Tib, was the cart empty?'

She swallowed hard. 'No, it wasny. There was a kind of big dark bundle tied on it wi a rope. Was – was that the dead man, Gil?'

'You tell me,' he said. 'Was it big enough to be a body?'

'It could have been,' she said, and swallowed again. 'If he was maybe curled up.' She bent her head and whispered something he did not catch.

'Oh, no, Our Lady be praised you did not look closer!' said Alys, putting an arm round her. 'Who knows what might have happened?'

'Amen to that,' said Gil.

There was a pause, and then Tib looked up in consternation. 'You're saying it was whoever killed him that I heard moving about out on the Stablegreen? So I was right to be feart?'

'Likely it was,' agreed Gil. Across the room Maistre Pierre met his gaze again, and reached for his cloak. As his friend's footsteps diminished down the stair to the front door, Gil continued, 'Tib, thank you for telling me this. I'd ha thought of asking you sooner or later, I've no doubt, but you've saved us some time.'

'Aye, well. You haveny gone into the speech about *See what happens when a lassie misbehaves*,' she said. 'I'm grateful for that, Gil.'

'Can you add anything else?' he asked.

She shook her head. 'I've thought and thought, but I don't recall any more.'

'The gate was locked, was it? And you left it locked again?'

'Oh, the gate. Aye, it was locked fast, and M-Michael took the time to secure it again, though I was trying to pull him away to come into the light. And in the morning . . .'

236

She paused, thinking it through. 'Aye, it was still locked in the morning.'

'What about lights in the bedehouse? Movement?'

'I wasny attending,' she said, with one of her wry looks, and suddenly blushed scarlet. Then, just as suddenly and to her own obvious embarrassment, she began to cry. 'Oh, Michael! Oh, Alys, when will I see him again?'

Alys exclaimed in sympathy and drew her to the settle, but Dorothea took her hand and said more astringently, 'Come on, come on, Tib. Greeting's no help. Far better to be at your prayers in your own chamber.'

'What, for forgiveness?' said Tib sharply through her tears.

'Contrition has to come first,' said Dorothea. 'More use to ask Our Lady for a solution to your difficulties.'

'That is true. You might get an answer,' said Alys, patting her other hand.

'Oh, she'll get an answer. And it might not be *No*.'

Chapter Twelve

'Your sister is very wise,' said Alys.

'I hope you mean Dorothea?'

Her quick smile flickered. 'Too many people forget,' she persisted, 'that the saints can say No as well as Yes.'

'True.' And is that what St Giles is saying? he wondered. That I won't get help to deal with my marriage? Then something in her voice alerted him. 'What have you petitioned for, sweetheart?'

She went scarlet, and turned her head away. He sat down beside her on the cushioned settle and put his arm round her.

'Is it anything I can give you?' She shook her head. 'Would it help to tell me?' Another shake of the head. 'Alys, if there's something you lack, something you need, in mind or body or spirit, you should bring your need to me. I may not be able to supply it,' he admitted, 'but if I'm to be your husband I should know of it.'

She shook her head again, with a wry little laugh.

'Has St Giles helped you in all you've asked for?' she countered. Her face was still turned away from him. 'Because if you lack anything, your wife should supply it if she is able.'

'Perhaps we should ask together,' he said. 'Alys, look at me.' She did not turn her head. 'What is it you lack, sweetheart? Tell me.'

He tightened his clasp of her shoulders, trying to draw her closer, and she stiffened. Socrates sat down at their feet, looking from one to the other, and whined anxiously.

'Tell me what you lack, Gil,' Alys whispered.

'What a pair of fools you are,' said Dorothea crisply from the door to the stairs. 'I know love is blind itself, but Heaven preserve me from blind lovers.'

Gil gaped at her, and she came forward to sit in their uncle's great chair, shaking her head at them. The dog went over, waving his tail.

'Are folk no daft, Socrates,' she said, patting him. 'There's Tib up there got herself into a right pickle, all for love, and here's your maister and lady down here, neither able to see what's worrying the other.' She looked up at them, and Alys moved imperceptibly closer to Gil, staring back at her. 'It isn't for me to expound it,' Dorothea pronounced, to Gil's great relief, 'but the sooner you each confess to the other what's eating at you, the better it'll be. Look at the symmetry in what you were both saying the now. Can you not see it?'

'Symmetry?' said Gil.

'Think about it,' she said.

'Of course he sees,' asserted Alys. 'Dorothea, you need not worry. We'll dispute it between us.'

Dorothea smiled, then rose and swooped on her, kissing her on both cheeks.

'You will now,' she agreed. 'Welcome to the family, Alys. Gil,' she went on, 'Tib said to me the now, Did I think all these deaths were linked. She seems right troubled by it all, I suppose since she realizes she came near seeing whoever that was on the Stablegreen in the dark. Where have you got to with it?'

'Little further than last night,' admitted Gil.

'Then why don't you,' she said, as if proposing a treat to a child, 'take Alys out and show her where it all happened? A fresh eye to the ground might be a good thing.'

Gil looked at Alys, his heart leaping at the suggestion despite his sister's tone of voice, and saw the same response in her eyes. She turned to Dorothea and said, 'But what about you, Sister? Would you not wish to see it as well?'

Dorothea shook her head. 'I'll stay here. Someone ought to be with Tib, and someone must tell our uncle when he comes home.'

'Dawtie, that's heroism,' said Gil frankly.

She gave him an affectionate smile. 'You've enough before you the now, Gil. Go on, the pair of you. Away and get some fresh air.'

Before Gil could answer, there was an urgent knocking at the street door. They looked at one another, and the knocking continued, along with a muffled shouting.

'Tell Maggie I'll get that,' Gil said, making for the stairs. As he descended the shouting became recognizable as his name:

'Maister Cunningham, Maister Cunningham! Come quick!'

He opened the door, and a young man almost fell into the house, saving himself by catching hold of the doorpost. As Gil identified the kitchen-laddie from St Serf's the youth stared at him, gulped and exclaimed, 'Can you come quick, maister? You're wanted at the bedehouse. There's been a miracle.'

'A miracle?' repeated Gil in astonishment. A double echo floated down the stairs from the hall; the women must be listening.

'Aye, maister, a true miracle. It's Humphrey,' said the boy. 'He's risen again. And he's cured of his madness and all.'

Striding up Castle Street in the rain, with Alys hurrying beside him and the boy at their heels, Gil realized he could hear shouting and exclamations from the bedehouse yard. He could not make out what was being said, but it sounded more excited than angry.

'They've all come to witness the miracle,' said the boy. What did Mistress Mudie call him? Simmie, that was it.

'Nannie ran out in the street shouting about it. I kenned it wasny right,' he said earnestly, 'but I couldny stop her. So then all the folk cam in to see what was going on, and Maister Millar tellt me to fetch you.'

The wooden yett was standing open, and the yard beyond the end of the chapel appeared to be full. As Gil picked his way along the narrow passage, someone's voice lifted from the courtyard, high and confident in the alto line. It sounded like Millar: '*Te Deum laudamus* . . . We praise thee, O God, we acknowledge thee to be the Lord.' The Church's great, ancient hymn of thanksgiving and praise. Well, if Simmie was right, the house had something to give thanks for, he thought, as the other voices joined in, one quavering voice to a part.

They rounded the corner of the chapel in time to see Anselm, at the tail of the tiny procession, totter through the door, and the crowd in the yard close in behind him like the waters of the Red Sea. Using his height and his elbows, Gil achieved a place for himself and Alys by the arched doorway, and peered in under the clumsily carved tympanum. Behind them in the yard, exclamations and questions flew.

'Was that him? Was that the one that's rose up?'

'No, it was the young one, she said. They ones were all full old.'

'What was it, anyway? What did he dee of?'

'What about the other one that's deid? Is he risen and all?'

'Oh, he'll no rise up. You've only to put your head in at the washhouse door to tell that. Quest on him's the morn's morn.'

The five old men, with Millar at their head, moved singing into the little choir, settled themselves and finished the *Te Deum*, following it with a *Gloria*. Gil, standing by the door, waited until Millar began to recite, and recognized familiar words from the Gospel.

'*Iesus dixit* . . . Jesus said, Our friend Lazarus has fallen asleep, but I shall go and wake him.'

241

'The raising of Lazarus,' said Alys softly. 'Is it true, then?'

A very proper choice, if so, thought Gil. He turned as Simmie began to tug at his sleeve.

'Can you come into the house, maister?'

They made their way through the crowded courtyard, avoiding more questions, and through the door which opened as Simmie reached it. The younger maidservant, bright-eyed with excitement, barred it behind them and said, 'They'll not be long, they're just offering thanks the now. Is that no lucky they'd no ordered his grave dug yet?'

'When did this happen?' Gil asked.

'Why, just the now. No an hour since. The Douglas's men's gone out to find him, but I'm glad Simmie got you first, sir, for Maister Millar was wanting you. Come in and sit a wee bit till they're done singing.'

'Did you see it?' said Alys as they followed her into the empty kitchen. The fire was burning and the charcoal in the range was lit; behind them Simmie picked up his chopping-knife and resumed his endless task of chopping roots for the stew.

'Is Humphrey really alive?' Gil asked.

'Oh, maister! Oh, it was the most . . .' She paused, lost for words. 'My mistress knelt wi him all last night,' she explained. 'She was praying and mourning him the whole night. Then she came into the kitchen for a bit the morn, and sat as if her tongue was locked.'

'I saw her then,' Gil agreed.

The girl nodded. 'We got her to eat and drink a little, Nannie and me, while his brother was wi him, and she sat a bit longer after that. Then she suddenly rose up about an hour ago and said, *He needs me*, and went out to the garden. And Nannie and me followed her,' she continued, her narrative gaining pace, 'and saw her go into Maister Humphrey's lodging, and then she screamed out, and came to the door, and called us ower, and said, *He's breathing*. And we couldny credit it, but we went in, and there he

242

was. He'd got colour in his face, and his breath going regular, and his hands warm, just as natural as could be. My mistress is wi him now, feeding him a wee bit bread and milk.'

'*Dieu soît bénit!*' said Alys, and crossed herself. Gil stared at the maidservant, as unable as she had been to credit the tale.

'Has he woken?' he asked.

'Oh, aye. He's no said much, but he kens us all, he's named us, even Simmie and me. But maister,' she continued, 'the rarest thing of all, he's cured of his madness. He's as clear in his head as you or me, maister.'

'I recall nothing,' said Humphrey.

Denial of injury, Gil thought, is the price of forgiveness.

The first, immediate service of thanksgiving was over, and Humphrey himself was washed and fed and seated in invalid state by the hearth in the bedehouse hall, the brothers round him, Gil and Alys standing by the window. Mistress Mudie, unable to let go of her chick, stood by his side fussing with his rug or his garments.

'Nothing?' said Millar. 'Have you no notion what happened?'

'I have no notion,' said Humphrey earnestly, 'save that my dear Sissie here tells me I was found hanging in my own lodging. The last I recall was going to my rest after dinner. I suppose that was yesterday.'

'His speech is greatly altered,' said Alys to Gil, who nodded. The whole man was so altered he was hardly recognizable, his bearing and expression confident and pleasant. There was something more, Gil thought, which he could not place.

'And the day?' said Cubby. 'What happened the now, laddie?'

'I woke,' he said simply. 'I woke from the most beautiful dream I have ever had.'

'So is Mistress Mudie's,' added Alys in the same under-tone. Gil realized that this was true; the little stout woman had not uttered a word for at least a quarter-hour.

'Well, and what hast thou dreamt?' asked Maister Veitch, with a sardonic lift of one eyebrow. Gil recognized a line from the Skinners' Play, but Humphrey's face lit up.

'Oh, my brothers, such a dream,' he said. 'I dreamed I was lying in my own bed, in the darkest night that ever was, so dark that I was afraid. Then a single beam of light shone, and I rose and followed it, and looked out of my lodging into the garden, as we've all done many times.' Elderly heads nodded. Mistress Mudie bent and pulled the rug higher across his knees, a glow in her eyes. 'I saw the garden full of flowers, and filled with a great light, and three beautiful young men dancing in the midst of it.'

'Young men?' said Anselm doubtfully. 'He never said there was young men here.'

'Wheesht,' said Duncan.

'They were dancing in a reel-of-three,' Humphrey con-tinued, 'naked and shining as newborn babes, and each of them had the face of my friend Andrew Stevenson, who was drowned when he and I went fishing. Then I wept for my guilt in Andrew's death, but one of the three came forward and drew me out into the light, and kissed me on the brow and the cheek and the mouth. And I woke, and kent that I was forgiven.'

That was it, thought Gil. That same inner calm that he had seen in Dorothea radiated from Humphrey's thin square face.

'Now I understand,' said Anselm, and pushed his spec-tacles straight.

'But who were the young men?' said Barty, who seemed to have heard this without difficulty.

Anselm retorted, with unaccustomed vigour, 'Don't be a fool, Barty. Who else would it be but the Blessed Trinity? He tellt me that,' he added.

'You have received a most particular grace, Humphrey,' pronounced Duncan in Latin.

'Have I not!' agreed Humphrey.

'No just forgiven,' said Maister Veitch, 'but cured. You ken you've been mad these ten year and more, laddie?'

'Is it a miracle?' asked Alys.

They had escaped from the bedehouse, where the brothers were settling down to discuss the event in full theological detail, while Millar composed a letter to the Archbishop. Sir James had returned just as they left, but Gil had managed to avoid him; he had no wish to analyse the situation for his godfather's benefit. They had returned to Rottenrow, collected the dog, and were now out on the Stablegreen as Dorothea had first suggested.

'I've heard of it happening,' said Gil, 'that a hanged felon survives, though it's rare. But the dream, or vision, or whatever it was, is outside my knowledge. That does seem like something beyond the ordinary frame of things.'

'It seems like a singular grace,' Alys said. 'The man is so altered. And not only Humphrey himself, Gil, did you notice how much Mistress Mudie is changed too? I suppose if it was her prayers brought it about, she must feel . . .' Her voice trailed off.

They wandered along the path from Rottenrow, hand in hand in silence for a little. The short November day was nearly over. It had stopped raining for now, but the grasses were dripping and the wet bare branches of the hazel-scrub gleamed in the low light. Socrates galloped ahead, hunting for interesting scents. Gil was simply enjoying being in Alys's company with no other intrusions, and when she finally spoke again she echoed this:

'How long since we had time like this, Gil? Just the two of us?'

'Days,' he said.

'A mistake,' she admitted. 'I'm sorry.'

'Why should it be your fault?'

'I've been too busy,' she said. 'I see it now. I left the house today when Dorothea brought me the news, and . . .'

She paused, considering her words. 'Your sister's concerns – Tib's, I mean – are a more important matter than the feast. I am sure my household can manage without me. And if they can manage without me for this, they can manage for other reasons, and I should have left them before.'

'Is that what Dorothea meant, just before Simmie came for me?'

'No,' she said quietly after a moment, then halted, looking round. 'Is that the back of the bedehouse? Where was the cart that Tib saw?'

'Here,' he said, accepting the change of subject, and stepped off the path into the long wet grass to look for the marks of the handcart's legs. She picked up her skirts and followed him, peering at the two little indentations, and then looked up and down along the wall.

'And the linen scarf?' she asked.

'That was yonder.' He nodded at the clump of hazels. 'I suppose he heard Tib following him, saw her lantern perhaps, and drew away from the gate, and saw the trees as a place to hide. He must have been nearly as alarmed as she was, when she simply stood here waiting for Michael to open the gate. I could wring her neck,' he added. 'She was always the spoilt one, but this is outside of enough.'

'She is very much in love,' said Alys. 'That affects one's judgement.'

'Not mine.'

She smiled quickly, hitched her skirts higher and set off towards the hazel stand, picking her way carefully through the rough grasses. He paused a moment to admire her ankles, then followed her, catching up in time to point out the footprints still visible among the tree-roots, and the place where the piece of linen had lain.

'These are good boots,' she agreed, studying the prints, 'but there's nothing distinctive about them, is there? Did you say John Veitch's boots were the right size?'

'Short of measuring them,' said Gil cautiously, 'I'd say so. But so would Millar's be, or Humphrey's indeed.'

'Yes,' she said, and looked about. 'And while he stood here, whoever he was, he dropped the scarf. Do you still have it with you?' He produced it from his sleeve and she took it, turning it over carefully. 'Marion Veitch knew it, you thought.'

'She studied it as if every stitch was familiar,' he confirmed. 'And the man Elder recognized it as John's neckie, though he tried to deny it afterwards.'

She turned the end with the initials over.

'I wonder how else it might have got here,' she said thoughtfully. 'I suppose if it isn't John Veitch's then it has no connection with the death.'

'It could be quite unconnected,' Gil agreed. 'But the initials are his.'

'Yes, if it is *I V*,' she admitted. She folded the strip of linen and handed it back to him. 'And the cart. I wonder how the cart got here – what path it took to the bedehouse gate. There are these prints here, so could the tracks of the wheels still be there?'

'They could,' agreed Gil. He looked about. 'There are three ways it could get on to the Stablegreen, assuming it didn't come out of the bedehouse. The way we came in just now,' he pointed, 'or the vennel off Castle Street, or the path that comes in from the Port.'

'Which is most likely?'

'The Castle Street vennel is nearest.'

Socrates came loping back with a satisfied grin just as they found a single wheeltrack, in a patch of damp earth near the Rottenrow end of the path. He inspected the place they were studying, and turned towards the open ground again, nose down, apparently following a trail.

'For a sight-hound,' said Alys, 'he seems to have a good nose. What has he found?'

'I can't believe the scent is still there,' said Gil. 'I wonder if he remembers finding the trail before, when I first brought him out here after the death?'

They followed the dog back out on to the green, hand in hand again.

'So what did my sister mean?' asked Gil as they approached the bedehouse wall. 'What is it we've to dispute between us?'

'Oh.' Her fingers tightened nervously on his. 'Well, it's – I think it's –'

'Symmetry,' he said, into the pause. 'We'd been saying, just before she came down, that we both lacked something. Was that it?'

'Yes, but – I think she saw something more than that,' said Alys doubtfully. 'I think she wished to say that there is a symmetry in what we lack. That you and I have been praying for the same thing, or for something which matches. But it hardly seems –' She stopped again, face downturned, the bright colour washing over her cheek. Gil studied her for a moment.

'Do you feel she's meddling?'

'No, no!' exclaimed Alys, turning to face him. 'No, she spoke out of concern for us, that was clear. I just can't –'

'Can't what?' he coaxed.

She shook her head. 'Doesn't matter.'

'What do you lack, Alys?'

She shook her head again, and muttered something he did not catch. Before he could ask her to repeat it, there was a shout from the vennel behind them. They both turned, to see Maistre Pierre making his way towards them in the fading light, waving.

'We have found a handcart!' he announced as he came closer. 'Well, we have found more than one,' he added, 'but this one is dark and has a pattern on the spar between the handles. I am certain it is the right one.'

'Already?' said Gil. 'That's good news. Where is it? Where did you find it?'

'Ah. That is the strange thing,' said Maistre Pierre. 'It was in the chapel in Vicars' Alley. What is it, St Andrew's?'

'In the chapel? Does it belong there?'

248

'So it seems. Luke tells me that the man who informed him that it was there also told him they use it to collect for the leper-house.'

'Of course they do,' said Gil. 'I've seen someone at the kitchen door from time to time, begging bread or meal or the like. I never thought of that – though of course we were looking for a ladder earlier.'

'Exactly. I have left Luke negotiating with the priest to borrow the cart, since I suppose we shall have need of it.'

'If Tib sees it,' suggested Alys, 'she can tell us if she remembers the pattern.'

'Very likely,' agreed her father, with a note of disapproval. 'What are you two finding out here? I thought we had gone over this ground to extinction. And what is this about the bedehouse? They seem to be talking of little else at the Wyndhead.'

'Father, a miracle,' said Alys, her eyes shining. 'The brother who was dead, Humphrey, is risen and cured of his madness. The boy came for Gil, and we've been in and seen it all and spoken to him.'

'Risen?' her father repeated, staring at her. 'But he was certainly dead. I found no heartbeat.'

'There have been one or two half-hangit men in legal history,' said Gil, using the Scots phrase. 'And I suppose the shock might cure him of his madness,' he added thoughtfully, 'though it seems to me more than a simple cure.'

'The man was dead,' reiterated Maistre Pierre with emphasis.

'The more of a miracle, Father,' said Alys, her hand on his arm.

'Hmph,' said her father. 'Does he recall anything that might help us?'

'No,' said Gil. 'Nothing, he said.'

'He was hanging for half an hour at least,' said Maistre Pierre. 'There was no heartbeat, no pulse.'

Alys eyed him, and gave Gil a significant look. 'We have

found where the cart came on to the green,' she said, pointing. 'We found the mark of one wheel, yonder in the vennel.'

'From Rottenrow,' said Maistre Pierre, turning to look. 'Does that tell us anything?'

'It suggests,' said Gil slowly, 'it suggests the Deacon was not killed anywhere close to the bedehouse, because then the approach from Castle Street would have been nearer.'

'More likely he was killed nearer to St Andrew's,' said Alys, 'and someone knew of the cart, whether the murderer or his accomplice.'

'So do we come back to the idea that the man was waylaid in the street?' asked Maistre Pierre. 'And by more than one individual, as we thought at first?'

'Yes, I'd let that slip my mind,' confessed Gil. 'There were the two blades that stabbed him. I suppose we do come back to that, yes.'

'I don't know the chapel,' said Alys. 'May we go there now?'

They made their way back out on to Rottenrow, with Maistre Pierre still muttering at intervals, 'I would have sworn the man was dead. No heartbeat, no breath.'

'He had not begun to stiffen,' Gil observed.

'Hmph,' said Maistre Pierre again. He halted as they reached the Wyndhead, and with a visible effort pointed out the wooden walls of the Caichpele above the rooftops of the Drygate.

'There is where the man's mistress lives,' he said. Alys nodded, surveying the layout of the streets. They turned towards the cathedral, and made their way round the western towers, where the first of the senior men of law were just leaving. Here a rumbling of wheels on the cobbled way proclaimed Luke, with the handcart. Socrates pressed against Gil's knee, head down and hackles up, until Gil reassured him.

'Ah, good laddie,' said Maistre Pierre. 'He has persuaded the priest. But what has he got on the cart?' He peered into the dim light. 'Not another corpse, I hope.'

It was certainly a large, bulky bundle, loosely tied on to the cart. Luke saw them and halted, lifting his knitted bonnet and ducking in a general bow.

'Maister, mem, Maister Gil. I got the cart,' he said unnecessarily. 'The priest was wanting to go and say Vespers, so he just let me in the end.'

'But what is this?' His master prodded the bundle, which Socrates was now inspecting cautiously, his long nose raised to sniff at one overhanging portion. 'Matting? Rush matting?'

'I hope it's no hairm, maister,' said the young man anxiously. The dog growled quietly, and Gil snapped his fingers to call him away. 'The fellow that dwells by the chapel came out his house as I came away, and asked me to lift this for him out his hall. It's all wasted wi blood, I suppose it's where the man was killed the day morn, and he wanted me to take it and burn it on our fire at the yard. It'll no wash out, that's for certain.'

'Oh, for certain,' agreed Maistre Pierre. He turned to look at Gil. 'Well, what think you? Do we burn it?'

'No,' said Alys.

'No,' said Gil. 'Can Luke take it round to Rottenrow? Maggie can find an outhouse to stow it dry till daylight.'

Maistre Pierre nodded. 'Wise, I suppose. We will see more by daylight. Aye, take it to Canon Cunningham's house in Rottenrow, Luke. And perhaps the cart may lie there too.'

Luke laid hold of the handles of the cart again.

'It's no that bad on the level,' he said, 'like on the dirt roadway, but it's the deil to manage on these cobbles. So I've to say to Maggie in your kitchen, maister, that it's all to lie dry in an outhouse till you get a look at it?'

Gil concurred with this, and he trundled away. Alys pulled her plaid up further round her head.

'Where is the chapel?' she said.

They continued round on to the north flank of St Mungo's, into the little street, where lights were springing in many of the houses. Cooking smells floated in the damp chill twilight as servants made the supper ready before Vespers and Compline were sung at the cathedral. The chapel at the mouth of the street was lit, its door open, and a small gathering was listening to the same Office within, early and convenient for folk who had a hearth and a meal to see to.

'This time yesterday,' said Gil, 'I spoke with Hob, poor devil. They were singing the Office like this when I came away.'

'Shall we go in?' said Alys, and slipped in at the open door without waiting for an answer. Gil and her father followed, to stand among the congregation and their lanterns at the back of the box-like nave, while beyond a cast-iron grille in the narrow chancel arch, a priest and two acolytes dealt efficiently with the Vespers psalms.

Gil looked round, studying the little building. It seemed to be well supported, for all it stood in the shadow of St Mungo's. The floor was paved with slabs of stone, the narrow windows were glazed with what looked like coloured glass, and the walls were painted with scenes from the life of St Andrew. There was a particularly lively depiction of a fishing scene, lit by the lantern in the hand of the elderly woman nearest it. Marks on the west wall suggested the place where the handcart stood when it was at home. Overhead the painted beams were hung with votive gifts and funeral wreaths, and the thatch rustled faintly above them.

The clerks in the chancel had completed Vespers and moved on to Compline. Beside him Pierre and Alys both murmured the responses with the acolytes. Gil stepped away, peering in the gloom at the flagstones where the handcart would rest, and the black shadows overhead. Socrates came to help, but seemed to find nothing to interest him.

'*Liberavit me de laqueo venantium*,' recited the clerks. *He has delivered me from the net of the hunter . . . He shall cover you with his wings, you shall find refuge under his pinions.* Was that where Humphrey got his fixed idea about the birds? Gil wondered. And if the Deacon was a robin, who was the sparrow? And yet he said there was no sparrow. What else would kill a robin? Both Maister Veitch and his nephew he saw as kites, his own brother was the white eaglet. A white chick, an unfledged youngster, would hardly hunt for itself, but the parents might bring it a robin. The Agnew parents are dead, surely. I am not on the right trail here, he thought. I have lost the scent somewhere. I wonder if Humphrey has forgotten that as well as everything else? Sweet St Giles, deliver me from the net of the hunter.

At the end of the Office, the congregation drifted out into the street, sharing lights, passing flame from lantern to lantern, but showing no inclination to make their way home in the deepening twilight. The day's news was much more interesting; the bedehouse miracle was much discussed, but Gil caught several versions of the fight in Agnew's garden, and two people were as convinced as Tam had been that Hob had sat up and denounced his killer.

'What now?' said Maistre Pierre at his shoulder. 'It must be near supper-time. Should we attempt anything else, or call it the end of the day?'

'I should like to do more today,' Gil said. 'I've done little enough for John Veitch's case since Marion asked me to help. I need to find if he asked anyone for Agnew's house.'

'One of these neighbours might know,' said Alys softly.

'My thought,' he agreed, and moved forward to the nearest knot of people. One of the women in the group, raising her lantern to light his face, exclaimed,

'You were here the morn, maister! Are you no the man that gart the corp speak?'

'The corp never spoke, Isa,' said the man next her. 'I was

253

at the door and seen it all. He cried out when the man touched him, but he never spoke a clear word.'

'A terrible thing,' said Gil, recognizing the impossibility of correcting the facts. 'To be slain at his work like that.'

'Aye, terrible,' agreed the woman who had spoken first. 'And likely it could ha been any of us! The man you took for it must be stark wood, to go into a house and slay a stranger!'

'I had a word wi Hob just after Prime,' observed someone. 'He was out wi a lantern cutting old kale leaves to clean the matting like I tellt him. And next I heard he was deid.'

'I spoke wi the madman,' said a younger voice behind her. Several people turned their lanterns to reveal a young man in St Mungo's livery, who ducked his head shyly in the sudden glow of light. 'He was a great big fierce fellow, but he didny seem wood to me,' he added.

'When did you speak wi him?' asked the man next to Isa.

'They can be awfy cunning about hiding madness,' said someone else sagely. 'They can seem like you or me, till out comes the knife to slit your throat.'

'Hob's throat wasny slit,' objected another voice. 'He couldny ha spoke wi a slit throat.'

'When did you speak wi him, Eck Paton?' repeated the man beside Isa. 'Was it the day?'

'Oh, aye, Maister Pettigrew, it was,' said Eck earnestly. 'He asked me whereabout Maister Agnew dwelt, and I pointed him to the house there.' He nodded at the darkened dwelling. 'And he went in, and not the space of an *Ave* after it Maister Agnew came home and cried Murder.'

'And where were you the while?' asked Isa in suspicious tones.

'Cutting kale in my maister's front yard,' said Eck righteously, 'and I stopped to lift a hantle o weeds while I was about it.'

'In case you found out anything more about Maister

Agnew's caller,' suggested Pettigrew. Eck ducked his head again, but grinned.

'I did, an all,' he pointed out.

'What time was this?' Gil asked.

The boy shrugged. 'Well into the day. After Sext, maybe.'

'And you're certain the man wasny in the house long when Maister Agnew came home? Did you hear anything?'

'No a thing.' Eck looked round, and expanded visibly as he realized the entire group was hanging on his words. 'See, I went on lifting weeds, and the madman went to Maister Agnew's door, and tirled at the pin, but Hob never answered it. And then the man pushed at the door and it opened –'

'You mean it wasny latched?' Gil asked him.

Eck shrugged his shoulders. 'I never heard him unlatch it. Just he pushed and it opened, and it squeaked the way it aye does, and he called out and stepped within. And I never heard another sound till Maister Agnew came round the corner o the chapel here to his own gate.'

'And then what?' asked someone else.

'Why, he went in at his door and began to cry Murder.'

'As soon as he stepped in the house?' Gil asked.

'Oh, aye.'

'Tell the Serjeant,' suggested another voice. 'You're a witness, laddie.'

'No me!' said Eck in alarm. 'I never saw anything! I helped capture the madman, but I never even seen the mats that Maister Agnew took out his house,' he added regretfully, 'all wet wi Hob's blood. A fellow hurled them away on the St Andrew's handcart the now afore Vespers, and I never got a right look.'

Gil edged his way backward out of the group, and found Alys waiting at its margin, the dog at her side.

'Useful,' he said, and reached into his purse for his tablets to make a note of the young man's name. He checked in dismay as his fingers encountered, yet again, the brocade cover of Thomas Agnew's set instead of his own.

'What is it?' said Alys as his expression changed. He shook his head.

'Not here,' he said guiltily, and drew her away from the chapel. 'Where is Pierre?'

'He went to make sure the men had shut everything down. He said he would go home after.' She looked back over her shoulder. 'Does that fit, do you think? Is the boy a good witness?'

'He seemed very clear,' Gil agreed. 'I wish we had a light – I never meant to be out so long. Come back to the house and get a lantern, and I'll walk you down the hill.'

Maistre Pierre had not gone home, but was waiting for them in the house in Rottenrow, alone in the hall with a jug of spiced ale.

'I knew you would come this way,' he proclaimed, acknowledging Socrates' greeting. 'You would need to fetch a light. Your uncle is home,' he added more soberly. 'He is above just now, speaking with your sister.'

'And Dorothea?' Gil asked.

'Has returned to the castle meantime, though she said she would be here for supper.'

Gil nodded. 'I'm just as glad to see you here,' he admitted. 'Pierre, I'm still carrying Agnew's tablets about with me. What on earth can I do with them?'

'Agnew's tablets?' said Alys. 'What do you mean?'

Her father grinned. 'An object lesson in the perils of excess, *ma mie*. He purloined them last night from the man's chamber, on our way home.'

'*Mon Dieu!*' said Alys. 'No wonder your head ached today.'

'I haven't drunk so much since I left Paris,' Gil said, a little defensively, annoyed to feel his cheeks burning.

She smiled, but held her hand out. 'Give them to me, Gil. I can return them.'

'You?' he said involuntarily, but his hand went to the purse. 'How can you –?'

'I'll find a way. You have enough to worry you. Is there anything useful in them?'

'The notes for the new will Naismith was to make. The family copy of the disposition for Humphrey's support is in there too. I saw nothing more.'

She nodded, and tucked the brocade bag into her own purse.

'I'll contrive something. Now I must go down the road, or there will be no supper tonight. Are you coming now, Father, or later?'

'Now, I suppose.' Her father got to his feet and lifted a lantern from the hearth. 'Lucky I left this in the lodge the other day. We need not borrow one. What will you do next, Gilbert?'

Gil shrugged. 'Speak to the Sheriff after supper, likely. He should know what that laddie was saying.' He recounted the kale-cutter's tale, and Maistre Pierre nodded.

'Certainly Sir Thomas should hear of that. It puts another view of the matter entirely. I wish there had not been so many witnesses to the trial by blood. And what of the matting?'

'That,' said Gil firmly, 'can wait till daylight.'

Chapter Thirteen

Sir Thomas Stewart, extricated without visible reluctance from an evening's music in his own lodging, heard Gil's report of Eck Paton's evidence with a frown.

'I see what you mean,' he agreed at the end. 'If the laddie's that certain, our man had by far too little time to do his business afore Agnew came home. The corp was last seen alive just after Prime, you say? Did his maister say when he saw him last? Had he left by that hour?'

'You'll need to get that from him, sir,' suggested Gil. 'I ken I saw Maister Agnew at the bedehouse no long after Terce the day. I can ask Andro Millar what hour he got there.'

'Aye, do that. And the bedehouse. The bedehouse!' said Sir Thomas impatiently. Small, neat and balding, he tipped back his head and peered at Gil across his cluttered desk. 'What's this I hear about the second man that died? That was the bedesman, wasn't it no? The one that's mad? Only now he's rose up and cured of his madness?'

'So it seems,' agreed Gil with caution.

'Did the poor soul do away wi himself first,' Sir Thomas crossed himself at the thought, 'or did someone else do it for him? And if it was murder, was it this fellow Veitch? He's got kin in the bedehouse, hasn't he, he'd have the run of the place likely.'

'Humphrey doesny recall,' said Gil regretfully. 'He says the last he minds is going to his rest after dinner yesterday. There's some doubt in my mind whether he hanged himself or someone else did it for him, and if it was someone

258

else, then it's surely linked to the Deacon's death some way. As to the servant in Vicars' Alley, I need to find out more.'

'The Deacon!' said Sir Thomas. 'I ken you're looking into it, Maister Cunningham, but are you anywhere near bringing me a whole tale for the quest on Deacon Naismith?'

'I might be,' said Gil circumspectly.

'Are they all separate? Two deaths in the bedehouse is bad enough, another in Vicars' Alley as well is too much to swallow, maister. It wasny this man Veitch killed all three, then?' suggested Sir Thomas again, without much hope.

'Likely not all three,' said Gil. 'May I speak to him? I've a thing or two to ask him.'

'Aye, you might as well speak to him. He's not been questioned yet.' Sir Thomas rose. 'Is there anything else you need to tell me?'

'Not at the moment,' said Gil, considering the point. 'I've the matting that Agnew's servant lay on when he died. I'll get a look at that the morn's morn afore the two quests.'

'What good will that do?' demanded the Provost.

'It might tell us how he bled, which of the wounds was the most fatal.'

'I suppose so.' Sir Thomas contemplated the idea, and gathered his wine-coloured velvet gown about him. 'Sooner you than me, laddie. Come down now, and I'll bid Archie let you in to see the man Veitch. And then, I suppose, I'll have to get away back to hear these musicians my wife brought in. Howling like cats, they are, and all in French or some such tongue. What her ladyship's thinking o I've no idea.'

John Veitch's clothes were already showing the effects of half a day's imprisonment. The cell he lay in stank of damp and human waste, and the smell and the green mould clung to his hose and his brown plaid and short furred gown. His spirit did not appear to be daunted.

'Aye, Gil,' he said. 'I looked for you sooner. What's ado, then, can you tell me that?'

259

'No yet,' said Gil. He looked about him in the light of the candle Veitch had been allowed, and sat down cautiously on the end of the stone bench. 'Tell me what happened, John.'

'Tellt you that already,' Veitch pointed out, sitting down likewise. 'I found the door standing unlatched, so I pushed it open and went in, and found the poor fellow lying in his blood. Then while I was still trying to see if it was worth calling help to him, his maister came in and set up a cry of Murder.'

'As soon as he stepped in the door?' Gil asked. Veitch looked sharply at him, suddenly very like his kinsman in the bedehouse.

'As soon as he stepped in the door,' he confirmed. 'I heard the step on the doorsill, and turned my head, and he took one look and began to shout.'

'When you got to Vicars' Alley,' said Gil after a moment, 'did you speak to anyone?'

'Oh, aye. I asked the way a couple of times, never having been there. It's no easy to find, tucked away at the back of St Mungo's like that. A woman at the Wyndhead, a fellow by the Consistory wi a mason's apron. Then when I found it there was a lad cutting kale or something in one of the wee yards, and he pointed me at the door next to his, which was Agnew's.'

Gil nodded. 'I've spoken to the boy cutting kale,' he said. 'If we can get him to speak up the morn, he'll confirm that.'

'I'm glad to hear it.' Veitch grimaced. 'A man can meet his end at any time, I ken that, but I'd as soon no meet mine being hung for a killing I didny do.'

'And the man Naismith?'

'I didny do that neither,' said Veitch firmly. 'The last I saw him, he went out my sister's house in a strunt because she didny take it well that he was to wed and put her out from under that roof. I never set eyes on him again till he was laid out in the washhouse at St Serf's.'

'Would you swear to that?'

'I would.'

Gil felt in his sleeve and produced the stained linen scarf again. 'Have you seen this before?'

'Is that –?' Veitch took it and turned it round, holding the embroidery to the light. He felt the stitched initials between finger and thumb, and nodded. 'Aye, it's mine. Where's it been? How'd it get blood on it? It was clean the day I lost it.'

'When was that?'

'Same day I last saw Naismith.' Gil raised his eyebrows at this, and Veitch frowned. 'It's a long tale.'

'I've time to listen.'

It seemed to be only half the tale nevertheless. The previous Saturday Veitch had ridden in from Dumbarton where the *Rose of Irvine* was lying, and taken lodgings with the widow in St Catherine's Wynd. On Sunday he had traced his sister to the house by the Caichpele, and appeared on her doorstep with gifts to receive a warm welcome from Marion and later a chillier one from the Deacon when he arrived to eat his supper and deliver his unwelcome news.

'I judged she deserved better of him,' said Veitch, indignation still warming his tone, 'and tried to tell him so, but he wouldny listen to me, called me an ignorant mariner and accused me of wanting to live off my sister.' He laughed shortly. 'If he'd kent what the *Rose*'s last cargo was worth he'd ha sung another tune. So then he said he wouldny stay there to argue wi me, and he'd no look to find me there when he returned, and he went down the stair and collected up his cloak and hat and left. And I wondered if he'd lifted my neckie and all,' he admitted, 'for I couldny find it when I left the house myself, but searching for the thing by lantern-licht was a fruitless task. So where did you find it?'

'On the Stablegreen,' said Gil.

'The *Stablegreen*? St Nicholas' bones, man, how'd it get there?'

'I'm still trying to find out.' Gil reached out to take the

object back. 'What did you do after Naismith left the house?'

'Now I tellt you that already as well. Comforted Marion so far as I might, sang the wee one a song when she was in her cradle, the bonnie wee lass she is,' an involuntary smile spread across Veitch's face, 'and gaed down the hill to my lodging.'

'And that would be what time?'

Veitch shook his head. 'Two-three hour afore midnight, maybe. Time passes different on dry land, somehow.'

'Did you meet anyone on the way?'

'Oh, aye. No that it was busy, that time o night, but there was the usual traffic atween taverns, and the odd serving man or maid heading for home, and a pack o merchants' sons whooping by the Tolbooth, out for trouble. Oh, aye, and one bonnie lass walking up the High Street. I thought of her when I saw the young callants, but she'd been up by the Bell o' the Brae when I saw her, and she'd a man wi her, carrying her box on his shoulders, so I reckoned she'd be safe enough.'

Gil noted this, and set it aside to consider later. 'And then what did you do?'

'Went back to the Widow Napier's house and gaed to my bed.'

Gil tipped his chin back and gave Veitch a challenging stare in the candlelight.

'Did you so?' he said.

'Aye.'

'That's not what the Widow Napier said.'

'Is it not?'

There was a pause, in which the man on guard outside could be heard whistling dolefully. Then Gil said, 'It's not what I think either. I think you went to Dumbarton.' He patted the sleeve where he had stowed the embroidered linen. 'I showed this to Marion and she denied knowing what it was, let alone whose, but when your friend Rankin Elder came into the house he knew it at once for yours, and said you'd missed it already the night you fetched him from Dumbarton.' Veitch was silent under his gaze. 'Did you borrow one of the boats down by Glasgow Brig?'

After a moment the other man grinned, and nodded.

'If you've worked out that much,' he admitted, 'there's no point denying it. Aye, I borrowed one of the fisher-folk's boaties. Neat wee thing she was, got me down to Dumbarton afore midnight wi a sail someone had left in St Nicholas' chapel at the vennel-foot, and the tide was just on the turn by that so we took a couple pair of oars out the *Rose*'s tender and came back up with the flow.'

'And stowed the oars under the Widow Napier's bed,' Gil hazarded, suddenly recalling the bundle of timbers. Veitch nodded. 'And the reason it was so needful to bring Elder upriver afore the dawn?'

'You mean you've no worked that out yet?' said Veitch mockingly.

'To protect your sister, of course,' returned Gil, 'but what had you done to make it so urgent?'

Veitch grimaced. 'Nothing I'd done, Gil, I gie you my word on it. It was the state Marion was in at the thought o being homeless – threatening to do away wi herself at one point, crying out that she'd sooner be dead than back keeping house for our brother, which I can well under-stand, and then I put two and two thegither and realized Frankie was never Naismith's get. She's got Marion's een, but wi that hair and the age she is, she has to be Rankin's bairn. Now Rankin's a sight closer to me than my brother William, we've shared a cabin on and off for four year, and he's never mentioned a bairn. So I gaed down the water to have it out wi him, and as soon's he heard –'

'Ah!' said Gil. 'Nothing would do but he come up the river to speak to Marion?'

'That's it,' agreed Veitch. 'As soon as he could get into the house to see her in private, he did, and if we all come out of this wi our heads on, he'll wed her within the week. They'll no want a big occasion,' he said ironically, 'no like some.'

Ignoring this, Gil considered the big sailor carefully.

'Right,' he said. 'Anything else you want to tell me now?'

'No that I can think of,' said Veitch after a moment. He got to his feet as Gil did, and hesitated again. 'Gil, what's my chances?'

'Better than they were afore I came in here,' suggested Gil. 'Beyond that, John, I'm no sure. I'll do what I can. It depends on the assize.'

'Should it not go to Edinburgh?'

'You were found wi the corp. Sir Thomas would ha been within his rights to hang you this day.'

Veitch swallowed.

'Pray for me, Gil,' he said. 'And Gil – will you tell my uncle, if nobody's let him ken afore this?'

Canon Cunningham was seated in his hall, spectacles on his nose, working on a drift of papers by the light of a great branch of candles. Socrates was sprawled at his feet. They both looked up when Gil came in, and the dog leapt up to greet him. The Official marked his place with one long forefinger, and said, 'Aye, Gilbert. And where are you at now wi all this? Is that right what Maggie tells me about the bedehouse?'

'It depends what she told you, sir,' said Gil, replacing his hat and acknowledging his dog's welcome. He sat down, craning his neck to see the superscription on the documents, and Socrates leaned against his knee. 'Is this the Murray perjury case you were talking about?'

'It is. Maggie said one of the brethren was raised up in his shroud and going about doing miracles. Seems hard to credit in Glasgow.'

'I wouldny put it that strong, sir. It's the one who was mad. We certainly thought he was dead yesterday – Pierre said he could hear no heartbeat – and today he woke and is as clear-headed as any in the burgh.'

'Well, well.' His uncle removed his spectacles and polished the lenses on his sleeve. 'Both risen and cured? How did he die?'

'By hanging.' Gil grimaced. 'It was me that cut him down.'

'Ah.' Canon Cunningham closed his eyes and tipped his head back. 'There was a man in Edinburgh, in '79 I believe it was, hanged for stabbing his son's schoolmaster afore witnesses, but breathed again afore he could be buried. And another at Perth, in James First's time.' He opened his eyes and looked at Gil.

'That's what I thought,' Gil agreed.

'I'm glad to hear it. Now what of the other matter? You said little enough at supper but I think there's been another death?'

'Aye, and John Veitch taken for it.'

Gil recounted the events in Vicars' Alley. His uncle listened attentively but, somewhat to his disappointment, when he had finished only said, 'Clear enough. You'll present this at the quest, o course.'

'Aye, and so much depends on the assize,' said Gil.

'Tommy Stewart's no fool,' said Canon Cunningham. 'Now away up and deal wi your youngest sister.'

'Deal wi her?' repeated Gil. 'Surely it's for my mother to chastise her? I'd not wish to usurp that.'

Their eyes met. The Official's long mouth quirked, but he nodded solemnly.

'That's a true word, but you're the head of the family, Gilbert.'

'Not you, sir?'

'No me. She's expressed a bonnie contrition, though I doubt whether her confessor would be convinced by it, and she's had my forgiveness, but that's all I'll take to do wi the matter, Gilbert. Dorothea tells me you demanded money off James Douglas.'

'It was the first thing I could think of,' Gil confessed.

His uncle nodded. 'A good notion, for all that. Dorothea says it made him think.'

'It stopped him roaring.'

265

'I'm glad I wasny present,' said David Cunningham, then, while Gil was still taking in this admission, 'Away and speak to your sister. She asked me to say she wished a word wi you.'

'And I've a thing or two to ask her,' Gil admitted, getting to his feet. Socrates, sprawled by the brazier again, raised his head to watch him, but went back to sleep when he showed no sign of leaving the house.

Tib was seated by a small brazier in the bedchamber where their mother would sleep when she arrived, reading in a prayer book by the light of two candles. When Gil came into the room she put the book aside gratefully.

'I'm trying to be good,' she said, 'but it's no easy. My uncle was saying I should seek confession, but how can you be contrite about something you don't regret, Gil?'

'I don't know,' admitted Gil, drawing up another stool. 'Maybe recognizing you shouldny ha done it would be the first step.'

'I suppose so,' she said, and sighed. 'I never thought it would be such a –'

'Such a what?' he said after a moment.

'I thought it was just atween Michael and me,' she said, her face softening as she spoke her lover's name. 'It never came into my mind that the rest of the family would make such a tirravee about it.'

'That was foolish.'

'I suppose.' She shrugged. 'It still doesny seem right to me. Here's you and Kate both wed for love – why can I no follow my liking too? It's no fair, Gil.'

'Life isny fair.' He studied her face in the candlelight. Despite her brave tone, it was clear she had been crying. 'Tib, I'll do what I can for you, but I'll make no promises. Sir James is very angry, and he'll have to be talked round first afore anything else. As to what Mother will say when she gets here – and you'll have to make your peace wi Kate as well.'

She nodded, shivering.

'But no wi Alys,' she said. 'I'll tell you, Gil, I never took much to Alys till now. She's been as kind to me the day – sitting up here letting me talk, when she'd all to do at her own house.' She smiled briefly at Gil in a way that reminded him of Alys's elusive expression, and went on diffidently, 'And there was something she said that made me think a bit, Gil.'

'What was that?' he prompted when she paused.

'Well. She's got no mother, and no sisters, only that Catherine who's more like a nun than our Dorothea is. She's got no one to –'

'To what?'

'Well, I asked Margaret years ago what it was like to lie with your husband,' she said in a rush, 'and she and Kate both had Mother's wee lecture, which maybe I'll be spared now, and I'd wager Dawtie kens at least as much as I did afore I went to Michael's bed, but – but Alys – she doesny ken what to expect –'

'Are you saying she's afraid?' Gil demanded, enlightenment reaching him. Tib nodded. 'Of me?'

'No, not of you, of your – of bedding wi you.'

He was silent, staring at her. It would explain it, he thought, it would explain so much. The way she shied away from kissing, her reluctance to say what Dorothea had meant . . .

'Yes,' he said after a moment. 'Tib, my thanks for this. I should ha seen it for myself.'

'You're too close to see it,' she said.

'You'll be as fearsome as Mother when you're older,' he said.

'Spare me! I'd sooner be like our grandam.'

He sat staring at the brazier for a little longer, fitting the things which had worried him into this idea. It made sense. It might take longer to work out what he lacked himself, but that could be dealt with at another time. Just now he had a case to make out for John Veitch. He remembered the questions he had for his sister.

267

'We found a handcart,' he said abruptly. 'It's here in our washhouse the now. If you get a look at it in the daylight, could you tell me if you mind it?'

'I might mind it better by lamplight,' she said reasonably. 'Where was it?'

'St Andrew's chapel in Vicars' Alley. It's the one they use for gathering alms for the lepers. It was already at the gate to the bedehouse when you got there?'

'It was. And someone moving about on the green, too.'

He thought a moment further, fishing for a distant memory.

'Tib, did you say you'd seen John Veitch? When was that?'

'Aye, I did. He was coming down from the Wyndhead when Andy Paterson and I came up the High Street. He'd a lantern, but I got a good look at him as well by someone's torch on the end of the house-wall. I kent him well enough.'

'What time would that be?'

She shrugged. 'About nine o' the clock or a bit after, maybe?'

'And he was going down the hill,' said Gil slowly, 'and then when you got on to the Stablegreen, after you'd got rid of Andy,' Tib gave him a contrite smile, 'the handcart was there and there was someone in the trees. So John Veitch didny put the Deacon's body over the wall.'

'I never thought he did.'

'But this makes it certain.'

'I suppose it does,' agreed Tib, sounding surprised. 'Is that important?'

'It is.' Gil got to his feet. 'Thanks for that, Tib. And for the other.' He bent to kiss her, and she returned the salute.

'Have I been a help?'

'Oh, yes.' He paused. 'How did you get rid of Andy, anyway? Did Maggie not hear you in the yard?'

'She was out,' said Tib, 'at some of her friends', which was a bit of luck, and Matt was no to be seen either. There was only daft William in the kitchen. I never had to explain myself to anyone. Then I walked in in the morning as if Andy had just left me there.'

'Maggie was out,' repeated Gil. 'Tib, you are a great help. And if you'll look at that handcart the morn's morn that'll be a help too.'

He raised his hand to make the sign of the Cross, and recited their mother's evening blessing. She spoke the familiar words with him, and he went out and back down to the hall, where his uncle was still immersed in the Murray perjury papers.

He sat down on the stone bench in his uncle's oratory, staring at the gleam of candles on the Virgin's gold-leaf halo and piecing the sequence of events together. He was nearly there, he knew it. Two of the stories were beginning to make sense, though the third one was harder to fit into the picture. What must I still do? he asked himself. Put my hand on Naismith's cloak and hat, find the place where he was stabbed, identify the two weapons which stabbed him and hence name the guilty persons. Prove that John Veitch didn't kill the man Hob, though I probably can't prove who did kill him. And Humphrey – what about Humphrey? Does he truly not recall what happened, or is he simply not willing to tell it? And if he's unwilling, then for which of two possible reasons?

'Gilbert,' said his uncle's voice, rather sharply, and he realized the Official had spoken several times already. 'Either be quiet or speak loud enough for me to hear you. I canny be doing wi you muttering away over there.'

'I beg your pardon, sir.' He rose from his seat, blinking as he turned his eyes away from the gleaming halo. 'I was miles away.'

'I can tell that,' agreed his uncle. 'It's late, Gil. Bid Maggie set the ale on to warm if she's not done it already.'

Gil moved towards the kitchen stair, but before he reached it there was a loud knocking at the street door.

Socrates leapt up and barked once. Gil paused in surprise, and Maggie's voice floated up from the kitchen.

'Our Lady save us, who's that at this hour, and Matt out winching and me wi my stays unlaced?'

'I'll get it,' Gil called. He lifted a branch of candles and crossed to the other stair, wondering how many more times he would answer the door today. The dog followed him, paused in the doorway, then hurried down the stair, claws rattling on the stone steps, tail swinging in the candlelight.

'It's ower late,' said Canon Cunningham disapprovingly. 'Who would come calling at this time o night?'

'I think I know,' said Gil, his spirits lifting, as he heard voices, indistinct through the heavy oak door, one deep, one lighter, male and female.

'I had to show you this,' said Alys, under her father's apologies to Canon Cunningham. 'I'm certain it's significant.'

'She would come up the hill now, nothing would do but I bring her – I must apologize for disturbing you at this hour,' Maistre Pierre was saying.

'What is it?' Gil asked, taking her hand. She's afraid, he was thinking, afraid of – she's a gently reared girl with no sisters and no mother. How do I reassure her?

'No matter, no matter,' said the Official. 'Is it something important?'

'I think it is, sir,' said Alys. Her clasp on Gil's hand tightened briefly, then she let go and went forward to greet Canon Cunningham. He kissed her with obvious pleasure and seated her on the bench by the brazier. Socrates sat down beside her with his chin on her knee.

'It's aye a pleasure to see you, lassie. Fetch some refreshment, Gil.'

'No need for that,' said Maggie from the stair door. She came forward, wrapped in her plaid for decency, and set down the tray of spiced ale and little cakes. 'Good e'en to

270

ye, maister, lassie. I hope nothing's amiss down the road?'

'No, all's well,' Alys assured her. 'All goes ahead as we have planned. Only, I wished to show Gil what I have found in this document.'

'Document?' said Canon Cunningham, pricking up his ears. 'What document, lassie? No your contract, I hope.' He laughed drily at his own joke, and Alys's elusive smile flickered.

'No, sir. It relates to the death at the bedehouse.' She opened her purse and drew out Agnew's tablets in their brocade bag. Gil froze in dismay, but without glancing at him she went on, 'I'm not at liberty to say how I came by this, sir. It is a set of tablets belonging to Maister Agnew, and with them this.'

She extracted the parchment with its dangling seals. The Official took it from her and unfolded it.

'A disposition, ten year since,' he said. Gil paused in handing beakers of spiced ale to look over his uncle's shoulder. 'For the support of their son Humphrey, Thomas Agnew and Anna Paterson gifting a significant plot of land . . .' Canon Cunningham ran his eye down the crackling sheet. 'And after his death – yes, yes, very provident.'

'Provident?' Gil leaned closer. 'That wasny my opinion. What does it –?'

'No, no, it reverts to the donors or their heirs,' said his uncle, tilting the document to the light. 'It's perfectly clear. Quite well worded, indeed. *Thomas Agnew, younger, wrote this*. Aye, very neat work.'

'Exactly,' said Alys, meeting Gil's eye across the hearth. 'Do you have the bedehouse copy, Gil? You were going to bring it here for safe keeping.'

'If it's that poke of dusty papers you brought in the other day, Maister Gil, it's under your bed,' said Maggie from where she stood in the shadows.

'Why?' demanded her father. 'What is this? She has not explained it yet.'

'The bedehouse copy wording isny the same,' said Gil

cautiously. 'I'm sure I mind a quite different final disposition.' He handed over the beakers he carried, and made for the stair. 'I'll fetch it down the now.'

'Are you saying the two copies do not agree?' said his uncle as he left the hall. 'I would ha thought better of Thomas Agnew.'

Returning with the sack full of documents, Gil sat down beside Alys. She reached in to extract the nearest bundle and inspected it, oblivious to her father and Canon Cunningham who were still exploring the different ways in which the two copies might have come to differ. The bundle they wanted was, inevitably, the last; Gil shuffled the rest back into the sack, while Alys untied the tape and picked through the folded dockets.

'This is it,' she said, opening it out. 'And the map that was with it, as well. Yes, I was sure this was what I remembered, Gil.'

'Well?' demanded her father. 'What does it say? Was it worth dragging me up the hill at this hour in the rain?'

'Oh, it was,' said Gil. 'This version has the property revert to the bedehouse absolutely after Humphrey's death.'

'Ah!' said his uncle.

'And what happens now, maister?' asked Maggie from the shadows. 'The man's deid, right enough, but he's risen again. Does it stay wi the bedehouse, or go back to his family, or what? What's the law when someone rises up?'

'What's more to the point,' pronounced the Official, 'is, why are these documents no the same and which is the true one?' He straightened his spectacles and looked about him. 'We need a good table. Over yonder.'

With the two documents spread out side by side on the altar in the oratory, lit by all the candles they could squeeze into the space, all four of them peered at the lines of neat writing while Maggie waited hopefully by the hearth.

'Neither looks to have been altered,' said Gil after a

moment. 'The dates are the same, and it's all scribed in the one hand. Agnew tried to suggest to me,' he explained to his uncle, 'that Deacon Naismith might have altered some of the papers.'

'No,' said Canon Cunningham thoughtfully. 'The one man has writ all of both these, and the hand and the pen are the same in the text as in his signature and monogram. I'd no swear to it being the same batch of ink, but that happens to all of us. I wonder . . .' He ran careful ink-stained fingers over the surface of the parchment nearer him. 'Gilbert, what do you think to this?'

Gil did the same, then bent to view the document against the light of the candles. It took a little time as he found separate angles to view the several folds of the parchment, but eventually he shook his head.

'This one's a single draft,' he said firmly. 'There's been no erasure. No even a word scraped out, that I can detect.'

'Nor this one,' said Alys in puzzled tones. 'There's a correction here to the name of the bedehouse, but that is the only one.'

'The signatures,' said Maistre Pierre. 'Do they accord?'

'Whose marks are they?' Alys asked. 'The Deacon's is there – whatever is his name? Aller – Allerinshaw? *Diaconus sancti Servi*. And the sub-Deacon. Both these are the same on the two documents.'

'Here is Thomas Agnew of Kilsyth,' supplied Maistre Pierre, 'and his wife's mark below it, properly attested in both places. And also their son Thomas Agnew younger, who I suppose is the man we know. Is this what you mean by his monogram?' he asked, one large forefinger on the elaborate penwork below Agnew's signature. 'What does it depict? A mercat cross?'

'Aye, that's his monogram,' agreed Gil. 'And the wit-nesses – James Paton, William Scott. I wonder if either of them would recall the terms of the gift? No, I doubt it, they're both clerks in the tower, aren't they, sir? They'll witness a dozen such things in a week, and this was ten years ago.'

'They are.' David Cunningham was still running his fingers over the lines of script on the two documents. 'This is very odd, Gilbert. I canny think what he's been about here. The seals are undisturbed, all the signatures compare, the writing is original in both, and yet –'

'May I see that one, sir?' said Alys, nodding at the copy further from her. The Official handed it over, avoiding the candles, and stepped back.

'It's ower hot here wi all these lights,' he complained. 'I've seen as much as I want for the now, let's be more comfortable. Maggie, is there more o that spiced ale?'

'There could be if you're wanting it, maister,' said Maggie. 'Have you no found what's wrong wi the papers then?'

'I think I have,' said Alys. 'Look here.' She spread out the document she held in front of the Annunciation. 'All the signatures and the seals are here at the foot of the writing.'

'Where you would look for them, in effect,' said her father.

She flicked him a brief glance and went on, 'There's a crease right across between the signatures and the main text, but otherwise nothing to show any difference. Not even a change of colour. But if you look on the back of the skin –' She turned over one margin of the document. 'See here? See the join? It doesn't lie on the crease on this side, it is easier to see.'

'It is,' said Gil, feeling carefully. 'It is a join. He's scraped the skin down so well it barely shows, and the colour matches as you say, Alys.'

'Is that how you mend parchment, then?' said Maggie with interest from behind Gil's shoulder. 'You make the two edges thin and then stick it thegither? It's just like joining pastry.'

'Before or after the inscription was written, do you

274

think?' asked the Official, peering at the fold of parchment. 'Maggie, what about that spiced ale?'

'If I was using a mended piece like this,' said Gil deliberately, 'I'd turn it so that I wrote across the join, simply to avoid questions like that.'

His uncle nodded. 'Aye, you've a point there.'

'The signatures have been removed from the original,' said Alys, 'and attached to a different text.'

'*Mon Dieu!*' said the mason. Gil nodded.

'Well, well,' said Canon Cunningham. 'You've sharp eyes, lassie. I'll ha you to my clerk any time Richie's away. And which copy is this, then, that's been tampered wi?'

'The family copy,' said Alys. 'The copy which was with Maister Agnew's tablets.'

'So whose work is that?' demanded Maggie. 'Why would the man change one copy and no the other?'

'He had not yet succeeded in altering the bedehouse copy,' said Alys. 'Gil, did you not say he was looking for it?'

'He was,' agreed her father.

'It would not have been easy to convince other people his was the true version,' she went on thoughtfully, 'for the Deacon had clearly looked at his copy recently. See, Father.' She handed him the paper which had been folded inside the disposition. He gave her a quizzical look, but tilted it obediently to the light, and whistled.

'Indeed!' he said. 'Look at this, David. The man had most ambitious plans for the plot that was gifted.'

Alys stepped away from the window-embrasure and Gil followed her.

'I meant to tell you as well, Gil,' she remembered, 'that our man Thomas told me he met a stranger by the Consistory tower, today about Sext, who asked the way to Vicars' Alley. Could that have been John Veitch?'

Gil nodded absently, and looked about the hall. Maggie had gone to fetch the second batch of spiced ale, their elders were still discussing Naismith's building project, and they had a moment to themselves.

'Alys,' he said softly, taking her hand. She looked up at him, with that expression which always made his heart turn over. 'Sweetheart, I've worked it out, I think. What Dorothea meant.' And no need to admit my youngest sister had to help me, he thought. Alys had dropped her eyes, colouring up in the candlelight. 'We won't – we don't have to do anything we don't want to.'

'That's the trouble,' she whispered. 'I do want to. I just –'

He pulled her into his arms, and kissed the top of her head. Her hair was silky under his lips, and smelled of rosemary.

'All will be well,' he promised. 'We love one another. Nothing else matters.'

Chapter Fourteen

'I'd swear to it being the same cart,' said Tib, eyeing the heap of matting askance. 'The more so wi that great bundle of stuff on top of it. What is it, anyway?'

'More evidence,' said Gil. 'It's the flooring from Agnew's hall, that I want a look at. You're sure, then?'

'Aye.' She bent to trace the swirls of white paint on the dark end panel of the handcart. 'I mind thinking it was unusual, these curly bits instead o denticles or arcading or the like.'

'Thanks, Tib.' Gil took hold of a corner of the matting, and pulled. The bundle came off the cart, and he shook it so that the stiffened folds opened out across the flagged floor of the washhouse. Socrates loped in from the yard to look, but Tib stepped back, gathering her skirts together.

'What's the stains on it? Is that blood, Gil?'

'It is.' He was bending over the creases. 'This is where the man died yesterday.'

'The man John Veitch slew?' She crossed herself.

'The man John Veitch found dead,' he corrected. 'No, this tells me little enough. It must have lain –' He dragged another fold aside. 'Something like that, I suppose. The man lay on his belly about here, and these are the –'

'Ugh!' said Tib, crossing herself again. 'But what does it tell you? Can you say who killed the man, if it wasny John Veitch?'

'No,' said Gil thoughtfully. 'No yet. I wonder why he was lifting the matting?' He looked over his shoulder at the door of the outbuilding. 'Is it still dry out in the yard?

277

Aye, dry enough. Tib, go and see if one of the men's about, to give me a hand wi this.'

'I'll help,' she offered, a little reluctantly, and bent to lay hands on an unmarked section. 'Do you want it out in the daylight?'

They carried the bundle out between them, and spread Thomas Agnew's prized possession on the damp cobbles.

'Aye, it was this way up,' said Gil. Socrates stepped delicately on to the braided squares, his nose a nail's breadth from the rushes, his hackles standing up all down his narrow back. Gil pushed the dog away, arranging the folds again. 'And he lay there. But what's this?'

Tib came to look where he pointed, using her knee to keep the dog off.

'It's all just blood,' she said. 'You'd think the poor man had been cut like a stag.'

'Oh, he was.' Gil drew the overturned folds of the matting further. 'He bled to death. No that he could ha been saved, by what Pierre says, but he needn't a been left to die alone. Look at this, though, Tib. Would you say these two stains were the same age?'

'What would that mean if they were?' She bent closer. 'Anyway, they areny. That's nearly fresh, and this is going brown. Socrates, get off. Leave it!'

'That's what I thought. And it doesny go right through the matting the way the fresh one does. Are there more like the older one?' He shifted the folds again, and Tib pounced, just ahead of the dog.

'There! And there's another.'

'And here,' he said with satisfaction, 'is one where the fresh one crosses the older one.'

'So what does that tell you?' she asked, straightening up. Socrates, finally unimpeded, blew relentlessly across the stained squares.

'It tells me why Hob was killed.'

'Why?'

'For doing what he was paid to do,' said Gil grimly. He sat back on his heels, rubbing at his palm where the braided rushes had left their mark, then paused, staring at his hand. The impression on the skin was ridged and furrowed, like ploughland left to grazing, like a rope binding. 'And it tells me more than that,' he said after a moment. He pushed the dog away, drew the layers of matting on top of one another and lifted one end. 'Give me a hand to put this back under cover, Tib. I'll need to take it to the quest, but first I'll need to get a word wi the Sheriff.'

The interview with the Sheriff did not take long. Sir Thomas was distracted by a demand from his overlord the Archbishop for some information which he was sure had already been sent, and agreed to Gil's request without undue argument.

'Could it be in the press there, Walter? If your notion clarifies the business so the assize brings in the right verdict, maister, I suppose it's worth the time,' he said, flapping a hand at his clerk. 'Take a note o that, Walter. We'll take the two quests thegither and hear all the evidence, and the same assize will do for both.'

'It should save time, Sir Thomas,' commented the clerk, reaching for the tablets hung at his waist. 'It's all called for noon, the Serjeant says, and a sound assize assembled.'

'Aye, likely,' said Sir Thomas, rather muffled, his head in the wall-cupboard. 'Walter, I canny see that docket. I'll swear it went to my lord last month. You have a look, man.'

Gil removed himself. After a word with the journeyman Thomas in the masons' lodge in the building site by St Mungo's, he extracted Maistre Pierre from its snug shelter and led him round to the little chapel in Vicars' Alley.

'But what do we do here?' complained his prospective father-in-law. 'We were here last evening and there is no more to be seen in a place this size.'

'That's what you think.'

'Yes, it is.' Maistre Pierre eyed the space beyond the

chancel arch, where the clerks had finished Sext and dis-
robed, and were now engaged in their endless tidying
round the altar. Gil ignored him, cast along the western
wall of the nave until he found the marks he had noticed
before, and stepped back, peering up into the rafters past
the wreaths and votive objects.

'It should be about there, I think,' he said. 'Pierre, could
you give me a leg up here? Or make a back, or something,'
he added, recalling belatedly that his companion had been
injured barely three months earlier and was not fully
recovered.

'Eh? What have you found?' Maistre Pierre came forward to stare upwards beside him. 'I see nothing but
shadows up there.'

'I agree, but shadows can hide a lot.' Gil tried jumping
for the nearest of the painted crossbeams, but missed. 'I'm
a handspan short – make a back,' he requested again. The
mason bent obligingly and Gil scrambled on to his broad
back, and pulled himself up to perch on the beam above
him. It creaked in complaint, and the laths under the
thatch rustled and cracked.

'How old is this roof?' wondered Maistre Pierre,
straightening up to watch.

'Who knows? Not too old to support me, I hope.'

Each of the crossbeams was the base of a triangular
structure with two uprights in it, so that there were three
spaces, one large enough for a man to pass and two small
ones. Gil moved cautiously to the mid-space of the next
beam. Wads of dust fell, scattering on a withered wreath of
hawthorn leaves, and below him the mason stepped
smartly aside. The building looked quite different from
this perspective, and the smells of old incense, damp stone
and damp thatch were overwhelming. Next to him was the
beam nearest the wall-plate; directly below were the marks
the handcart had made on the wall and flagstones.

'What are you doing?' demanded a voice from the
chancel arch. 'Sir John, thieves! Thieves in the kirk!' Hasty
footsteps echoed.

'Fetching something,' Gil returned, reaching into the shadowy triangular space across from him. His hand met only bare wood. Incredulous, he groped the length of the space, and nearly overbalanced, saving himself by snatching at the upright beside him.

'There's nothing there.' A different voice. 'What are you looking for?'

'Something we left here,' improvised Maistre Pierre.

'A cloak and hat.' Gil pushed himself back into a stable position and looked down. The priest, a tubby balding man in a rusty black gown, was staring up at him, his two acolytes beyond at the chancel arch. 'A black cloak,' he expanded, 'with a lot of braid about it, and a velvet hat.'

'Oh, aye. I took it for a donation at first,' said the priest a little sadly. 'Then I kent the badge on the cloak. You wouldny care to purchase it back, maister? It'd go to the lepers,' he explained. 'I could buy them blankets. They're right cold at this time of year, the souls.'

'I will certainly do so,' said Maistre Pierre, patting his purse.

'And I,' said Gil. He dropped down from the roof and began brushing dust from his hose. 'Tell me, sir, you leave the chapel unlocked?'

'Aye, we do. The chancel gate has a good key.' Gil glanced beyond the man, but the cast-iron yett was not visible in the shadows. 'We leave that locked, so none can get in and steal the Host, but folk can aye come in here for a wee word if they wish it.'

'And these garments. When did you find them, sir?'

'Monday, it would be,' said one of the clerks, a skinny youth in an oversized jerkin. 'You saw them after Terce, Sir John.'

'Aye, that would be it,' agreed Sir John. 'As soon as it was light. You'd left yir bundle well enough hid,' he said, 'but for a corner hanging down, and it just catched the light coming in that window there.' He turned away. 'It's in the cope-kist. Come and I'll gie it you.'

'But Sir John,' said the other clerk, a smaller darker man still lurking within the chancel. The priest paused, looking at him. 'How do we ken it's theirs?' he objected. 'It hasny a name on it, only the badge.'

'Nobody else has come looking for it,' pointed out the priest, 'and this fellow gaed straight to the place it was hid. Why did you hide it there, anyway?'

Gil looked at him, hesitated, and admitted, 'It wasny me that hid it.' The tubby man eyed him expectantly. 'If you ken the badge, maister, you've maybe guessed who put it there.'

'What's he saying, Sir John?' demanded the second clerk. 'Will I call for the Serjeant? Is it thieved goods right enough?'

Several expressions crossed Sir John's plump face. Puzzlement, understanding, surprise followed one another, and finally a wary look descended.

'And what's it to do wi you? I've seen you round the Consistory tower. You're that nephew of David Cunningham's, aren't you no? What are you wanting wi the cloak, then?'

'It's wanted for the quest this noon,' said Maistre Pierre, breaking a long silence.

'What, about Hob next door?' said the first acolyte.

'Same as our handcart that the boy took away yestreen?' said his fellow.

'Aye, but Hob was slain yesterday by a madman,' objected the first one, 'the whole street kens that. That cloak was here on Monday after Terce.'

'Would you swear to that afore the Sheriff?' Gil asked. The three clerks looked at one another.

'Aye, I suppose we could,' agreed Sir John.

'Then would you bring the cloak and hat to the quest at noon,' said Gil, 'rather than gie them to me?'

'We could say Nones a bit early,' suggested the younger acolyte, looking interested.

'But what about the charity for the lepers?' asked the priest anxiously.

Maistre Pierre reached for his purse. 'This will warm the lepers,' he said, extending a generous handful of coins. 'Now will you bring the garments to the quest?'

'We've a fair bit to determine,' pronounced Sir Thomas, stepping on to the dais and sweeping the castle hall with his scowl, 'so we'll get on wi it. Who's for the assize? They'll need a strong stomach for it. We're deciding on Deacon Naismith as well as Hob Taylor, and he's been lying about a good wee while.'

The place was full. Genuine witnesses, others who thought they might be witnesses, and anyone who wanted to hear more about the deaths of Hob and the Deacon of St Serf's, were all crowded into the large space. John Veitch had been led in between two men-at-arms, his hands bound before him, to a volley of hissing and pointing. The corpses had been firmly excluded, and lay in state, sheltered from the rain under a striped awning in the castle courtyard, with two more men posted well upwind of the Deacon in his coffin.

Gil had found himself a place behind the table where the Sheriff's clerk sat with his pen-case and inkwell, several pieces of clean parchment before him. Beside him Maistre Pierre stood studying the people assembling in the body of the hall, and fidgeted through the long procedure of selecting fifteen householders of good repute. Gil, well used to it, thought that it went faster than usual today. Most of those present wanted to get to the interesting part.

Once the assize was selected, the names written down, the men sworn in by Walter the clerk holding a worn copy of the Gospels, they were led outside to inspect the two bodies, and returned looking a little green in places.

'Well, they were warned,' said Maistre Pierre. Gil nodded.

'Now,' said Sir Thomas with relish, 'we'll take Hob Taylor first. Who identifies him?'

'I do,' pronounced Maister Agnew, standing forward out

283

of the crowd. 'That's my servant Hob Taylor right enough, lying dead out there in his shroud, crying out for vengeance. And I accuse the man John Veitch yonder of his murder.' He raised his arm and pointed at John Veitch, who looked back at him without expression.

'He doesny look mad,' observed a woman near Gil. 'He's a good-looking chiel.'

'Och, you, Jennet Clark,' said her neighbour.

'Let's hear your reasons,' said Sir Thomas. Agnew launched into an account of returning to his house to find Veitch standing red-handed over Hob's bloody corpse, a scene which caused him to wipe his eyes when he described it.

'And what did you do then, maister?' asked Sir Thomas.

'I ran out into the street and shouted Murder,' declared Agnew. 'And all the neighbours came running and took the man captive, and we bound him wi stout ropes and brought him here to the castle.'

'That's no just how I heard it,' said Sir Thomas, looking round. 'Maister Cunningham, where are you? Step up here and tell the assize what you found.'

Gil came forward, bowed to Sir Thomas and to the assize, and then on a whim to the audience. They seemed to like it.

'I got there just as John Veitch was taken captive,' he said clearly, 'along wi my friend Maister Peter Mason, master mason in this burgh and kent to many of you. We had a look at the corp, and so did one or two others that were standing by.' He looked about him, and identified Maister Sim, standing near the dais with the other members of yesterday's impromptu assize. He described the scene in Agnew's hall, the blood-soaked matting, the pile of kale leaves, the way Hob lay face down in his blood, and Sim and the other three nodded as he spoke and gave their agreement at the end.

'What's these kale leaves to do wi it?'demanded Sir Thomas.

'I'll come to that, sir,' said Gil.

'The man was standing red-handed over my poor servant,' said Agnew loudly. 'Hae an end to this waste of your time, Sheriff, and take him out and hang him now, take a rope to him! *Repay him for his iniquity, wipe him out for his wickedness*,' he declaimed.

'No, no,' said Sir Thomas. 'No use of your Latin in my court, and this is a good tale. Go on, Maister Cunningham.'

'Maister Mason had a look at the corp,' said Gil.

Maistre Pierre stepped forward, to recount his conclusions about the length of time it would have taken for Hob to die.

'You're still saying this madman stood over him and watched while he bled to death!' expostulated Agnew.

'No,' said Maistre Pierre simply, 'for he had been dead some time when I saw him.'

'How d'you ken that?' asked a man in the assize, a blocky fellow in a shoemaker's apron. 'Had he set, maybe?'

'Aye, he had,' agreed the man called Willie, who was standing beside Habbie Sim. 'I noticed that mysel. Just his head and his neck, see, so it wasny that long, but longer than the madman had been in the house.'

'No telling how long he'd been there –' began Agnew.

'Oh, that's easy enough,' said Gil. 'I've questioned the sister of the accused man, and a working man who spoke to him on his way, and a witness who was in the next garden when he reached your house, maister, and they're all agreed on that.'

'Aye, where's this laddie that was in the next garden?' demanded Sir Thomas irritably. Eck Paton was dragged forward to the edge of the dais by several of his neighbours eager to see him make his contribution to the day's entertainment, and stood reluctantly to be questioned by the Sheriff. His story seemed to disappoint many of the audience, and some of the assize tried to suggest he was mistaken.

285

'No, no,' he assured them, 'for I wasny out that long, and I saw it all.'

'Eck Paton's story agrees wi the time the other witnesses gave us,' Gil said.

'Then the madman must have been there earlier,' objected Agnew, 'and slew Hob and went away.'

'I never left my sister's house till Sext,' declared John Veitch from where he stood by the wall. One of his guards elbowed him sharply in the ribs, and he flinched.

'You be quiet the now,' said Sir Thomas. 'You'll get your chance if it's needful.'

'All these witnesses is all very well,' said another of the assize from within their roped-off enclosure, 'but you canny get past one thing, Sheriff, and that's the way the corp himself sat up and accused the man that slew him. The whole town kens about it, and it canny be denied.'

'He never sat up!' declared Maister Sim. 'I was there and saw it all!'

'You willny deny he groaned,' said Agnew sharply, 'and we all saw the blood run from his mouth, enough for the villain to bathe his feet in!' He wiped at his eye again, and Maister Sim nodded reluctantly.

'Aye, that's true,' he admitted.

'That is wrong,' Maistre Pierre muttered. 'It is the right-eous who will wash their feet in blood. We are in the Psalms, I fancy.'

Gil glanced briefly at his friend, and stepped forward again.

'Maister Agnew,' he said. Agnew looked at him, slightly suspicious. 'I mind you took John Veitch's hand, to make certain he touched the corp.'

'Aye, I did.'

'Would you show the assize how you took hold of him?' Gil held his hand out. With some reluctance Agnew reached out and took hold of his wrist.

'No, that wasny it,' said Maister Sim from below the dais. 'I could see that much from where I was standing. Your grip was lower down. Aye, more like that,' he added as Gil shifted his hand within Agnew's grasp. 'You'd a good hold across the back o his hand, Tammas, and your fingers –' He stopped, and looked at the Sheriff. 'His fingers went right round under his hand,' he finished.

'That's what I recall,' said Gil mildly. He turned to look at the members of the assize, and held his hand up, Agnew's still clasping it. The other man snatched his away as he realized Gil's intention, but at least some of the assize had seen how two sets of fingers were turned towards them. 'Who touched Hob?' Gil said to the crowded faces. 'It looks to me as if they both did, so who did he accuse? Was it John Veitch, or was it his master?'

'I'm never accused of his death,' began Agnew.

'I'm saying,' said Gil, 'that on this evidence you'd as well be accused as John Veitch, and the other evidence, of finding him red-handed, doesny stand up.'

'So who slew the man?' demanded one of the assize, as Agnew gobbled like a blackcock at this assertion.

'Aye, well, that's what we're here to establish ,' said Sir Thomas crisply. 'Get on wi it, Maister Cunningham. What have ye to tell us now?'

'Can we turn to the other corp next, Sheriff?' Gil asked formally.

'We've no dealt wi this one yet,' objected someone.

'I hope we can wind up both matters at once,' said Gil. 'But maybe we should set John Veitch free, since it's clear he couldny ha slain Hob Taylor.'

'No yet,' said someone in the assize. 'I'm no convinced yet.' There were rumbles of agreement round the audience.

'No, no,' concurred Sir Thomas. 'We'll keep him under guard a while longer.'

'Is this a new heading?' demanded the clerk Walter. 'Or is it a whole new quest? Do I need a new bit parchment or no?'

'Aye, a fresh page, Walter,' said Sir Thomas, and the clerk muttered angrily and took out his penknife to scrape out a line he had written. Gil stared at him, and Sir Thomas went on, 'Now, if we're to look at the Deacon's death, best get on wi it, maister.' Distracted, Gil bowed, and made a handing-over gesture. 'Oh, aye. Who identifies the other corp? I hope ye all had a good look at him.'

'Aye, from upwind,' said the shoemaker from the assize enclosure, and there was general laughter.

'Did ye study the wounds?'

'Aye,' said another man doubtfully, 'but no very close. It looks like there's been more than one weapon at him, like it was a man wi dagger and whinger maybe.'

'Aye, two weapons,' agreed Sir Thomas. 'Who identifies him, then?'

Andrew Millar pushed his way to the foot of the dais and agreed that the second corpse was that of his superior, Deacon Robert Naismith of St Serf's bedehouse. The Sheriff dealt in short order with the finding of the body, the manner of death, and the probable time of death. Maistre Pierre, explaining this, made reference to the idea that the body had been moved, and the shoemaker spoke up again.

'Let's hear more about that, maister. How can you tell?'

'He had begun to stiffen while he lay in one place,' said Maistre Pierre, glancing at the Sheriff, 'somewhere he lay on braided matting which left a mark on his face which was still visible the next day. Then he was moved, and continued to set in the new position in the garden.'

'Could he no ha moved himself?' asked another of the assize.

'Don't be daft, Rab,' said his neighbour, 'the man was deid, that's why he'd begun to set. Who moved him, that's what I'd like to ken.'

'I hope we'll find out,' said Gil.

'I fear it's clear enough,' put in Agnew. 'My poor brother must ha stabbed the Deacon in his madness, and later bore the body out into the garden. He's got no recollection of it now, but it's the only explanation.'

'No quite,' said Gil. 'For one thing, there's no rush matting in the bedehouse.'

288

'That's his brother that's rose up again,' whispered someone behind him. 'They're saying he's cured of his madness and seeing visions.'

Ignoring this, Gil led the assize carefully through what was known of the Deacon's last movements, detailing the meal at the house by the Caichpele, the argument with Marion Veitch and her brother, at which several of the assize looked darkly at John Veitch where he stood under guard by the wall, and the departure to meet Thomas Agnew, who agreed that he had last seen Naismith an hour later. Andrew Millar came forward again to describe how he had heard footsteps in the Deacon's lodging after he came in that night.

'Aye, aye, hold up here,' said an assizer. 'This was at an hour or two afore midnight, did ye say?' Millar nodded. 'And we've just heard, wi the way the corp was set, it looked as if he was deid no long after supper.' Millar glanced at Gil, and nodded again. 'So who was it was walking about in his lodging, maister?'

'I'd like to hear the answer to that and all,' put in Sir Thomas.

'You'll have your answer,' Gil assured the man. 'Once we've all the facts, the answer will be clear enough.'

'So you say,' said Agnew, 'but I maintain it's obvious already. Can we no ha done wi this nonsense, Sheriff, and get about our business?'

'Let's hear your facts, Maister Cunningham,' said Sir Thomas, ignoring him.

Gil took a deep breath, and bowed to all his hearers again. This was extraordinary. He had expounded his solution to a death before, to much smaller groups; making it clear to fifteen householders whom he did not know, and a hall full of onlookers, was quite different, but he was enjoying it.

'The corp was found near the back wall of the bede-house garden,' he began. Carefully he explained where the body was lying, what made him think it had been put over the back wall, and how it had been taken round to the

289

Stablegreen. Without naming his sister, he told the assize about the handcart, with its burden, and the movements in the dark.

'Now the same person,' he said, 'had seen John Veitch going down the High Street not half an hour earlier. It wasny John Veitch put the Deacon's body over the wall.'

One or two of the assize nodded. A small flurry of movement and hissing whispers behind Maistre Pierre suggested Marion had tried to speak and been hushed.

'What I think happened,' Gil went on, watching the members of the assize, 'is this. Deacon Naismith ate supper in the house by the Caichpele, and announced that he was about to make a will. Then he left the house, and went to meet somebody else. Sometime that evening he was stabbed. He was left where he died, for an hour or two, and then moved on the handcart, put over the wall at the back of the bedehouse garden, and the handcart returned to its place. Then the person who stabbed him walked into the bedehouse wearing his cloak and hat, and slept the night in the Deacon's lodging. In the morning he joined the bedesmen for the first Office of the day, and then left the chapel and went back to his own house.'

'How was he no recognized in the chapel?' demanded the shoemaker.

'It's dark in the chapel, even by daylight, and this was well afore the dawn,' said Gil. 'He was seen in the shadows, and taken for the Deacon sitting out of his own seat.'

'And what happened to the garments?' asked Sir Thomas, regaining control of his enquiry. 'Since I take it he wasny seen in the street and taken for the Deacon, else you'd ha tellt us by now. Did he plank them in the wash-house, or something, afore he went out?'

'I think he took the risk of being seen,' said Gil, acknowledging the witticism with a grin. 'Since we've tracked them down.'

'What, wi that dog o yours?' said someone from the hall, and there was laughter. Gil shook his head, looking round for the three men of St Andrew's. He found them near the back, and pointed to them.

'Sir John and his clerks found them,' he said, 'and took them for a donation to the lepers. Come forward, Sir John, and tell the Sheriff about it.'

The tubby little priest made his way to the front, his acolytes behind him carrying the two garments. One or two bystanders attempted to snatch the hat from the small dark clerk, until Sir Thomas rose and snarled, 'We'll ha none o that now! Meddling wi the evidence is worth a fine, and I saw ye, Will Cowan, Jaikie Renton. Right, Sir John,' he turned to the witness in front of him, switching voices. 'Tell us about this cloak and hat then.'

Backed up by his subordinates, Sir John identified himself and his charge, described finding the garments tucked into the rafters of his church, and agreed that it had been on Monday after Terce and no later.

'And you didny see who put them there?' asked Sir Thomas. The three men looked at one another, shaking their heads. 'No, I see you didny. How did they get into the roof, Maister Cunningham? Are we looking for a man three ells high? He should be easy enough to discern in this burgh if that's so.'

'No, no,' said Sir John through the laughter, 'no need for a tall man, for they were stowed above where we keep the handcart. He'd but to climb onto it and stretch up, to put his hand on the roof-beams. That was how Mattha here got them down.'

'Aye, this handcart,' said Sir Thomas. 'We've heard a deal about it. When are we going to see it, then?'

'When you like, sir.' Gil nodded to Maistre Pierre, who nodded in turn to his man Thomas waiting by the nearest door. With some thumping and cursing, the little cart was handled through the door, into the hall and up on to the dais, through a growing murmur of exclamations.

'What's this? What's this?' demanded the Sheriff as the cart and its burden emerged from the crowd in front of him. 'What have you brought here, maister? This should be on a garden fire somewhere, no cluttering up my court session. What is it anyway?'

'It's the mats from my hall, stained wi my servant's blood,' said Thomas Agnew angrily. 'I gied them to a man to take and burn, yestreen! How did you no do as I bade you, fellow?' he demanded of Luke. 'Your hands are defiled with blood, and your fingers with iniquity!'

'My maister bade me itherwise,' said Luke simply.

'It's the mats that Hob Taylor was lying on when he bled to death,' Gil agreed, and gave Luke a hand to lift the bundle down onto the dais.

'Get them out of here!' exclaimed Agnew. 'This has nothing to do wi the matter! We're dealing wi the Deacon's end now, no Hob's, we don't want all this lying about. Take it away, clear it away out o here! Pluck it up from the land!'

'The Psalter again,' muttered Maistre Pierre. 'Gil, be wary of this man.'

'No, no,' said Sir Thomas. 'If that's what they are, maister, we'll let them alone the now and just get on wi the Deacon. So this is the handcart, is it, Maister Cunningham?'

'Yon's the St Andrew's cairtie,' said the man Willie, still watching with Maistre Sim at the corner of the dais, and his friend nodded agreement. 'I ken it by the pattern atwixt the shafts. It's no like any other in the Chanonry, wi they curlicues.'

Sir John, appealed to, confirmed this.

'It's been recognized by those same curlicues, as the cart that was by the bedehouse gate,' Gil said.

'So does that mean the man was stabbed in St Andrew's?' said one of the assize dubiously.

'Surely no!' exclaimed Sir John, crossing himself in dismay.

'No, no,' said Gil. 'I think he was stabbed elsewhere. Maister Agnew,' he said, turning to the other man of law. 'You've told us you saw Deacon Naismith in your chamber in the Consistory tower.' Agnew nodded. 'What were you discussing, maister?'

'Why – as I said afore,' said Agnew, a little impatiently, 'his new will.'

'Why did he need a new will?' demanded Sir Thomas. 'He wasny sick to death, was he? Nor like to be wed?'

'Well, as it happens, he was like to be wed,' said Agnew, 'to a kinswoman of mine.'

'Ah,' said the Sheriff, nodding, 'so he wanted to arrange his affairs. Very proper.'

'And then he left you,' said Gil. 'What time would that be?'

'Maybe an hour after he joined me,' suggested Agnew.

'And you went out after him?'

'I did.'

'Was St Andrew's dark as you passed?'

Agnew looked sharply at him. 'You don't pass St Andrew's leaving the Consistory tower,' he said. 'I went down the Drygate to a friend's house,' his smile to the assize conveyed what sort of friend he meant, 'so I was nowhere near St Andrew's till I went home in the morning.'

'What's it to do wi the man's death,' asked the shoemaker, 'where Maister Agnew was the rest of the nicht?'

'No a lot that I can see,' said Sir Thomas irritably. 'The light's going, Maister Cunningham. Let's get this over afore we have to bring in torches.'

'Very well, sir,' said Gil, bowing. 'We'll take a closer look at this matting, then.'

Under the Sheriff's scowl, he and Maistre Pierre arranged the rustling bundle as near as they could in the same stiffened folds he had displayed to Tib earlier. The assize were released from their pen and stood round it, with members of the audience complaining loudly that they could not see, while Gil pointed out the way Hob had lain, the way the blood had soaked into the folds of braided rushes, and where the pile of kale leaves had lain.

He called Maister Sim up to confirm what he said, but Sir Thomas cut across his agreement.

'Here's these kale leaves again. What have they to do wi the matter, maister?'

'Hob had cut them earlier,' Gil said. 'He cut them to use in cleaning this matting, which was stained. He and his maister separately told me Maister Agnew had turned it because it was marked.'

'Aye, wi a spilled drink,' agreed Agnew loudly. 'I spilled a glass of Malvoisie –'

'No,' said Gil. 'I think there was no spilled drink, though Hob had found a glass in a corner of your hall. What Hob found,' he bent to twitch a corner of the matting into a better position, 'when he turned back the piece you had already reversed, was this.' He pointed. Several members of the assize craned closer.

'That's blood and all,' said the shoemaker.

'It's more of Hob's blood, surely,' said his neighbour.

'No,' said another man. 'It's older. That's a different stain.'

Sir Thomas rose and shouldered his way between the assizers, to bend over the marks Gil pointed out to him. He studied them carefully, and stepped back, eyeing Gil.

'Go on, man,' he said. 'Where are ye taking this?'

Gil waited while the assizers were led back to their roped enclosure, then looked round the faces at the edge of the dais. Alys, his sister, Marion Veitch at one corner; Andrew Millar, Habbie Sim, the plump priest of St Andrew's, all looked back him. Alys smiled as his eye met hers, and he turned back to the Sheriff, spirits rising.

'It's blood,' he agreed, 'a day or two older than the stains from Hob's blood. How did it get there?'

'A good question,' agreed Sir Thomas. 'How did it get there, Maister Agnew?'

'Nonsense,' said Agnew, with icy calm. 'We've all heard enough of these dunderheidit blethers. I've a friend who'll swear to where I was that whole night, and it wasny wandering the Upper Town wi a corp on a handcart.'

Aha! thought Gil.

'Aye, Ellen Dodd,' said a voice from the hall. There was some laughter, and a few comments, until another voice rose over the rest.

'Is that Ellen Dodd that dwells off the Drygate?' it said. Gil turned to look, and found attention centred on a plump woman in a crisp white headdress, a grey plaid round her shoulders. She coloured up as people stared at her. So Maggie found you, mistress, thought Gil gratefully. 'Well, is it?' she persisted.

'That's who I spoke to,' Gil agreed. 'She said Maister Agnew had been with her from the middle of the evening.'

'Is that right, maister?' Sir Thomas asked Agnew.

'Aye,' he said reluctantly.

'She's leein,' said the woman bluntly. *Some can flater and some can lie*, thought Gil. So I was right. Agnew reddened, and made his gobbling gamecock noise again. 'I'm Jennet Clark, sir,' Mistress Clark curtsied to the Sheriff, 'and Ellen Dodd was in my house the whole of that evening till near midnight, we were telling tales and casting futures and she was at the crack wi the best of us. There's four or five o my freens will swear to it, sir, and see if I ever let her across my door again, I'll be coffined first.'

'You've mistaken the day, woman,' said Agnew fiercely. 'She – my friend will support me –'

'Aye, maybe,' said the Sheriff. 'Maister Cunningham, I see where this is going now, but you canny get past one thing. There was two weapons slew Deacon Naismith, we've heard that already. Who was the other man?'

'What other man?' demanded Agnew, alarm in his voice for the first time. 'Sheriff, what are you saying?'

'There was no other,' said Gil. 'Naismith was talking to his man of law. They were working on his will when they quarrelled. A scribe works wi his pen in one hand and his penknife in the other.'

295

'His penknife,' repeated Sir Thomas. 'You're saying, Maister Cunningham?'

'I'm saying, sir, that Thomas Agnew stabbed Naismith left-handed wi his penknife, and then drew his dagger and completed the task.'

'No!' shrieked Agnew as the noise increased in the hall. 'No, I –'

'Hold him!' Sir Thomas rose, pointing. 'Hold and bind him, Archie!'

'Why should the way of the guilty prosper? Why do all who are treacherous thrive? I did not –'

'In his own hall, maister? Aye, there's the blood to show it, I suppose.'

'And the marks of the matting on Naismith's face,' Gil added, 'where he lay on it as he began to set.'

'No, no!' shouted Agnew. 'Not the ropes, not the ropes!'

'And what about the servant?'

'Thomas Agnew came home yesterday after Terce,' Gil said over the uproar, stepping back from the rush as two of the men-at-arms dragged Agnew struggling to the wall beside John Veitch, 'and found Hob turning over the matting to clean off the stains he had talked about. Maybe Hob saw they were bloodstains and accused him of killing the Deacon, maybe he asked him for money to keep quiet. Agnew stabbed him, and went away leaving him to die. He returned later, found John Veitch with the body, and set up a cry of Murder.'

'So it wasny the madman at all?' said one of the assize.

'He's just proved it wasny,' said another. 'Listen to what's said, man.'

'But why should Maister Agnew ha stabbed the Deacon?'

'Aye, a good question,' said Sir Thomas, and turned to Agnew, just as one of his guards struck the man a great buffet on the side of the head. 'Why did you kill the Deacon, man? What profited ye?'

'No profit,' shouted Agnew, spitting blood, 'but vengeance, the vengeance of the fatherless and the orphan! Loose these ropes from me, for I am justified!'

'I suppose it was the question of his brother's support,' said David Cunningham. He had demanded a dissection of the whole affair as soon as he came home from the Consistory tower; Maggie was listening avidly, and it seemed likely the dinner would be late.

'That's it, sir,' agreed Gil, and sat down beside Alys. She put her hand in his; he rubbed its back with his thumb, and they smiled at one another.

'Has he admitted it?' asked Tib.

'Not yet,' said Maistre Pierre.

'He may not,' said Gil reluctantly. 'I suspect he has inherited Humphrey's madness. The way he was spouting vengeance and bloodshed from the Psalter at the quest, I don't see him being fit to plead.'

'I think the Sheriff will put him to the question none the less,' said Maistre Pierre.

'So how do you know it's about his brother?' Tib persisted.

'Was it him that hanged his brother, anyway?' Maggie demanded across the hearth.

'No way to tell,' said Maistre Pierre. 'Humphrey insists that he recalls nothing.'

'It's not about his brother,' Gil corrected Tib, 'but about the land which was given to support Humphrey. Naismith was appropriating it to his own use, and Humphrey's dole was getting less and less. Bad enough the land going to the bedehouse, but if it was to end up in Naismith's hands, I think Agnew couldny stand it.'

'But is that reason enough to kill someone?' Tib asked.

'It's a valuable parcel of land,' Gil said, 'but I think it was maybe the way Naismith planned to use it that angered Agnew. His notes for the new will end at

297

that property, though the Deacon had plenty more to dispose of.'

'So he enticed Naismith round to his own house, you think,' said Canon Cunningham, 'to drink a toast to the marriage, and then stabbed him.'

'I think so,' Gil agreed.

'Why not in the Consistory tower?' Alys asked.

'Too public. There was always the chance of meeting someone on the stair. Not to mention the problem of getting a corpse as big as himself down that stair,' Gil added. 'If he got him back to Vicars' Alley he could leave him in his house while he worked out how to get rid of the body. Then I suppose it occurred to him to try to put the blame on Humphrey by putting the corpse in the garden.'

'And after that he went round into the bedehouse and pretended to be the Deacon.' Dorothea leaned back against the settle. 'It's been a right fankle, Gil, and you've unravelled it well. I see now how Robert Blacader thinks you're worth a benefice.'

'Of course he is,' said Alys indignantly.

'There is a strange thing,' said Maistre Pierre, with an indulgent smile at his daughter. 'Since Humphrey's resurrection, or whatever one calls it, there have been some remarkable happenings at the bedehouse.'

'Remarkable?' said Dorothea.

The mason shrugged. 'Maister Barty has his hearing back. The one with the trembling-ill is by far steadier, the one we could not understand has recalled his Latin and also speaks Scots like a Christian, the very old man – Father Anselm, is it? – is clearer in his head than he was – all small things, but each in its way a grace.'

'Mistress Mudie is silent,' contributed Alys, 'as if she has obtained peace.'

'Millar has lost his stammer,' said Gil, 'and seems by far more confident.' And Alys and I have got past whatever was troubling us, he thought, and smiled at her again.

'And yet Humphrey's own brother has received nothing,' went on Maistre Pierre, 'is taken up for murder and will be tortured for his confession.'

'He has Humphrey's forgiveness,' said Alys. 'That must count.'

'If he was the instrument of Humphrey's martyrdom, *maistre*,' said Dorothea, 'he will obtain a special judgement. Nevertheless, if he murdered his servant and the Deacon, he must pay the price the law requires.'

The final fragment of the picture only dropped into place a week later.

On the morning after the wedding, Gil woke in the late November dawn, warm and comfortable, and fully aware of where he was and why. Alys was curled relaxed against him, her hair silky on his cheek, and the steady sound of her breathing was intensely pleasant in his ear.

Al nicht by the rose ich lay. He spent some time dwelling with satisfaction on the events of the last twelve hours, the verse going round in his head. And before that – before they had avoided the wild jokes of the bedding-party and the rough music in the courtyard, before the dancing in the drawing-loft and the feast in the hall, there had been the moment when he and Alys stood in front of his uncle in a side-chapel of the cathedral and exchanged promises and rings. She had smiled up into his face, confident and confiding. All would be well.

The whole day had gone well, though he suspected Alys had moved through it in a daze. All the guests had enjoyed themselves, only a few had become unpleasantly drunk, and he had noticed his mother talking intensely to his godfather at one point, her gestures emphatic. Her glance had flicked to Tib in her scarlet gown, Michael in dull green velvet, in opposite corners of the room, and the fiery Sir James had nodded meekly and offered her his hand. It seemed likely that some sort of future awaited the miscreants.

He turned his head on the pillow and drew the red

woollen curtain aside to look out into the chamber, where the early light was growing. The blue milk-paint had dried to a pleasant misty shade, though now it looked colourless. The four Cardinal Virtues showed up well on the wall by the hearth behind his head, and opposite them, facing the foot of the bed, Maister Sproat had depicted his own choice of saints: the Visitation, with the Virgin and St Elizabeth dressed like Scots women and crowned with jaunty rose-bordered halos; and in plain halos, St Giles and his pet doe standing stiffly by St Mungo. One could tell it was St Mungo; he had a mitre as well as a halo, and held a green branch in one hand and a robin the size of a goshawk on the other, its red breast showing bright already as the light strengthened.

Like any son of the grammar school or the University, Gil knew the story, how Mungo's fellow pupils had killed the bird to get him into trouble with their teacher St Serf, whose pet it was, and how Mungo had brought it back to life. He lay in the dawn looking at the image, wondering if he could bear seeing it every morning in life, and suddenly recalled Humphrey. *He was a shrike, but now he's a robin, because he's deid.*

'Of course he was a robin!' he said aloud. 'He was left in the garden to get someone else into trouble.'

'Mmf?' said Alys. He turned to her, getting up on one elbow. She opened her eyes and smiled up at him. Now this on the other hand, he thought, I really could bear to see every morning when I wake.

'Naismith,' he said. 'You remember Humphrey said he was a robin.' She made a faint noise of assent. 'I was looking for a sparrow, but I had the wrong robin. Agnew tried again and again to get Humphrey into trouble – to get him accused of killing the Deacon. Of course Humphrey said Naismith was a robin. St Mungo's robin, who was killed to get him into trouble.'

'Of course,' said Alys, blinking sleepily at him.

He leaned down and kissed her, and she put her arms round his neck and kissed him back.

300

'Gil, are we really married?' she said after a moment. 'I didn't dream it all?'

'We're really married,' he agreed. 'And no prospect of an annulment, if I mind matters aright. *Darf ich naught the rose stele, And yet ich bar the flour away.*'

'I don't know why I was afraid,' she admitted.

'I hope you'll never fear me again,' he said seriously.

'It wasn't you I feared.' She curled closer to him. 'Gil, listen. When my father bought this house, there was a ceremony with the two men of law, when they handed him a padlock and some earth –'

'Sasine,' he agreed. 'He would have to take sasine of the property, and those represent the building and the land it's on.'

'Yes. And I thought, yesterday, that the rings we gave.' He felt the hand at the back of his neck stir as if she was rubbing her ring with her thumb, the fine gold circle with the little hearts and the Latin word *SEMPER*. 'That was as if we exchanged sasine, wasn't it?'

'Sasine of one another,' he amplified, and tightened his clasp on her, charmed by this idea. 'So you're mine, and I'm yours, sasine given and taken, without limit of term.'

'For always,' she agreed, and drew the covers further up round them both. 'Just as it says on my ring. Always.'

301